THE MODERN KNIGHT

PALADIN

Raleigh Minard

KITSAP PUBLISHING

Paladin

First edition, published 2018

Cover Artwork by GermanCreative

Copyright © 2018, MINARD RALEIGH

Paperback ISBN-13: 978-1-942661-97-9

Published by Kitsap Publishing

P.O. Box 572

Poulsbo, WA 98370

www.KitsapPublishing.com

Printed in the United States of America

150-10 9 8 7 6 5 4 3 2 1

*Thank you Leo for buying my book.
I'm honored, I hope you enjoy it.
See you at Carving*

Raleigh Menor

I want to acknowledge my Lord with
all the help he has provided. I want to
thank Donna Lee Anderson for being
my mentor and Gwynn Rogers for the
editing of my manuscript.

I learned a lot from you all.
Thank You!

What if you made an earth-shuddering discovery that could destroy the world's economy?

What if nothing would be safe anymore because anyone could teleport anywhere in the world?

Chapter 1

I'm setting down my story for my family. Over the years my children keep asking how I gained my ability to move around the world as I do. Little did I know that my life was not my own. In my later years I found many threads to my life, and my family's that I was clueless existed. Not everything is as it seems. I'm rambling on so let's get back to the story. My name was Steve Storm, and I graduated from MIT and Stanford Universities. I majored in Physics, Biology, and Computer Sciences. My plan is to build a Living Artificially Intelligent Computer. To keep fit I work out in a gymnastics gym, primarily swinging from the rings. I'm pretty good at it, but not good enough for the school team. I dabbled in the school theater arts where I learned how to use makeup. I even developed a latex process which I patented, and then sold to pay off my tuition. When I graduated I didn't owe any money for school?

This allowed me to go my own way without any strings, other wise I did not have to sign up on any contract with any scientific group that came along, I could pick and choose who I would work for as I saw fit. Or so I thought. I found a scientific think tank in California who was looking for perspective people like myself. There I learned that I could work on my own projects, but I also had to work on a few of theirs. I did not mind helping out so I joined them. They liked my idea for my computer, so I was able to spend as much time on my project as I wanted. I failed many times at making the computer, I could not discover a way to connect living tissue to inorganic materials. After one of my failures, I decided to go home for the day to maybe get a fresh perspective on my Computer project.

On my way home, I was driving on interstate five heading home to Oxnard. At that hour of the day when it was "more like a parking lot than a freeway," I see an old beat up '55 Chevy pulled off the road just ahead of me, steam pouring out from under the hood of the car. I was going to ignore the car until this pretty woman gets out of the car with a disgusted look on her face. Then she kicked it. I couldn't resist a 'hot Chick' so I pulled out of the line up on the freeway to see if I could offer her some assistance. She looks at me "do you know anything about fixing cars?"

"Well not really."

"Then what possible help could you be to me?"

"I thought that I might offer to take you to your destination."

"Where are you going?"

"I live in Oxnard."

She looks at her car and then makes a call on her cell phone to the towing company to pick up her car.

"OK, if you want to help I need to get to Van Nays, to the theater, there can you do that?"

"Sure" I said, I'd be glad to."

She walks over to my car and stands by the door, then light dawned --- I realized she wants me to open it for her. So I rushed over and opened the car door for her as she sat down and swung her long, gorgeous legs in. On the way to the theatre in Van Nuys, I was hoping to have some conversation with her, but all she did was chat on her cell phone. I did notice that she was very pretty, with long raven black hair, green eyes, and clear white skin. When we arrived, she directs me to a parking spot and invites me to come in with her. The stage hand tells Pam she is late and to get to wardrobe and make up. Pam points at me and tells the stage hand to get me a seat in the auditorium. I was then lead out and down in to the seating area, where I promptly take a seat.

It was an excellent play that I would have even paid money to watch. It was a play on King Author and the Knights of the Round Table. Pam played a lady in waiting to the queen. Where Pam's part was not a large part, she brought the character to life. After the play ended, I managed to catch Pam to see if she would be willing to eat dinner with me. She looks at me for a few minutes trying to see if I'm some pervert or something and asks. "Is it alright if I bring a friend along?"

"Sure" I stammer.

"OK, then just wait out front and I'll be along in ten minutes with my friend."

I wait, and after fifteen minutes passed I'm ready to leave thinking I have been stood up, when she walks up with her friend. It is the woman who played the queen. We introduced each other, so I finally get to meet Pam & Tammy that night.

"So, you were the Paladin (Knight) that saved Pam and the show tonight." Said Tammy.

"I just happened along at the right time. Is all! And I just wanted to help out."

The night moves along with small talk. We exchanged our likes and dislikes, hobbies, and I tell them about my job as an inventor. I mentioned one of the items I invented, that they use in the theater, like the latex for the masks, and make up. They appeared to be impressed. In our conversation Pam mentions she likes to go hiking. I said I like to do that too. Before I realized it, we have a date for next Saturday to go on a hike. Now what do I do? I have never been on a hike before. Well at the end of the dinner, Tammy and Pam are leaving, but before they walk out the door, Pam turns to me and asked for my phone number and home address. When I asked her for her address, Pam responded.

"Not now, maybe after we get to know each other better."

"Ok", I stammer. Such a pretty girl, she makes me confused.

As I drive home my mind is racing what will I do? I have never been on a hike, what will I do?

At work the next day I remember Ted hikes with his family a lot, So, I get with Ted at the water cooler, and tell him what happened as he laughs at me.

"Trying to impress the new girl, now are we? Well I can help you out. Come over to my house for dinner tonight. I'll walk you through the gear you will need and how to use a map, and compass. You also need to be aware of some safety precautions so you will look like you know what you are doing."

I get to Ted's that night and meet his family. Ted's wife cooks a pot roast with all the trimmings. After dinner Ted takes me out to the garage where we sort through several back packs, when Ted remembers his old one. Here you go Steve, this will make her think you are an old hand at hiking. Ted equips me with all the necessary equipment before he hands me an old map of the desert with great hiking trails. Ted gives me a list of items to go buy at the store, he including what clothes to wear. I thank Ted for all his help and leave for home.

Saturday arrives and Pam is to be at my place by 4:00 AM so we can get an early start. 5:30 AM. Arrives and I get the feeling that I'm being stood up. I start to put the gear away, when a knock sounds at my door. There is Pam with her gear, "Well are you ready to go?"

"I thought you stood me up and I was putting my stuff away, but yes I'm ready to go."

"I thought about standing you up, but you did rescue me and since you like to hike, and so do I, why not take another chance?"

Elated to have a date (which has been since the High School prom) I grab my equipment. Head out the door, and we set out for the California Mountains. It takes a good three hours to reach Big Pine Pam talks nonstop the entire way about her life. I'm entranced as I feel like I may want to get to know her. At just before sunrise we pull to the side of the road next to a blooming Century plant to start our hike.

We both take out our compasses to take a position of where we are so we can return to the car. I cheat a little as I use the GPS on my phone. What I did not know was that Pam using her phones GPS too. We set off toward the north. At first, we are quiet, listening to the chirp of the birds, with not much by way of conversation passing between us. We stopped at a large rock to take a break and have a sip of water. Suddenly the whole sky lights up as bright as midday, as a meteor streaks across the sky over head. Shortly, there is an explosion as the meteor impacts the earth. Now Pam gets to see the real me. After the explosion subsides, I want to go see what has happened, so I hurried us along to where it fell. Two hours later we arrived at the small crater of the impact.

I realized I would not be able to get at the meteor for several hours, so I take out my Cell phone to mark the place on my GPS. "What are you doing Steve?"

"I want to return here to dig up the meteor."

"Why do that?" Pam asks.

"Why not, it fell from space, why would you not want to dig it up." Questions Steve.

"Let's go back to the car, I want to return to the nearest town to get some shovels and anything else we may need to dig up the meteor before someone else does."

Pam complains the whole way back to the car. Then on the drive into the nearest town she still complained about missing the hike, and that her day is messed up, and it was my fault! I stop at a hardware store and buy a pick and shovel. I drove through town, and I found a place where we can rent a dune buggy. In an hour we were on our way back to the GPS coordinates of the crater.

Two hours later we pulled up to the crater. I get out to check the place over, it appears no one else has been here. So I get started digging as Pam watches and fuming the whole time. Three hours later I find the meteor. It is still warm, but it is about the size of a large marble.

"Is that it? Asks Pam Just that small rock? Can we go now, it's getting late and I want to get home."

I fill in the hole, and head back to town to return the dune buggy and pick up my car. Hours later we arrive at my house. Pam is acting strange. She is mad, that she had missed her friend for her ride home. She will either have to stay with me or have me take her home. I'm busy with my meteor, and it is not what I expected, as it is too light in weight. Meteoric iron should be heavier.

"Hey! I have not eaten all day, I'm dirty and tired." Pam complains.

"Oh, I'm sorry, the kitchen is through that door, and the bathroom is down the hall, and the washer and dryer are in the utility room next to the bath room. Please make yourself at home."

Pam gets very angry and goes into the kitchen, and makes herself some dinner. I'm too busy studying my meteor to be hungry, as all my thoughts were on getting to work tomorrow to start running tests on the meteor. Pam calms down after eating, and then she takes a long shower. She finds my robe and puts it on, then washes her cloths. Fed and cleaned up Pam is more like herself. I looked up at her and asked, "Do you want me to take you home?"

Again, she looks at me trying to apprise me in some fashion. What I did not know at the time is, that she had a problem with one of her past boyfriends, and he kept dogging her at her home, and she did not want another one.

"No, I'll get a ride in the morning, where can I sleep?"

I looked up at her and said "let me get my things out of the closet and you can have the bed room, I'll sleep out here."

Pam thought about that for a minute and said "Ok."

So, I get my clothes out and go back to studying the meteor. Pam is very mad and goes to the utility room to check on her clothes. Pam moves her cloths to the dryer, then comes back into the living room. After watching me for a few minutes, she throws her hands up and goes to my book shelf, only to get upset again.

"Don't you read anything but science books?"

I looked up at her and said "well no, not really, I never gave it a thought."

"Do you have a TV I can watch?"

"It is in the bedroom, on the dresser."

Pam looks at me "I never! This is the first date I have ever had where I did not have to fight off a guy who was making a pass at me." And slams the bedroom door.

I'm confused, she made it clear that I should not try to take advantage of her and now she is mad that I didn't. It did not matter, this would be the last time I would see Pam; and for some reason, I did not care. Pam retrieves her clothes an hour later and goes to bed. I stay up late that night looking up information on Meteoric iron. I finely went to sleep anxious for the morning to arrive. The next morning, I'm up early, and get dressed. I waited for Pam, and she finely comes out dressed.

"My ride will be here in thirty minutes."

Thirty minutes later right on cue her friend Tammy honks her car horn and Pam is out the door as if she were in a race. "Good bye" I called.

But she does not answer me. That was the last time I saw Pam.

Chapter 2

Now I'm off to the lab to begin doing tests on the meteor. I run many tests on the meteor, X-ray, weight tests, radiation, anything I can think of. And still the meteor does not return any of the expected data. It is too light in weight; yet the X-ray does not penetrate the shell. So, I decide to cut the meteor in two. I dissected the meteor and managed to split it open. The structure is crystalline. It is not like any other crystal here on earth, so there is nothing to compare it to. After subjecting the crystal to many more tests something happens. I was applying a one-and-a-half-volt electrical charge to the crystal when it disappears, a moment later I hear something fall to the floor behind me. I turn to see that the crystal has reappeared only a few feet away.

I repeat the test and the same thing happens. This is unexpected. I make several entries in my computer journal. Little did I know my entries were being read by someone else. I continued to perform more tests and discover something I had been looking for. The crystal has properties of both organic and inorganic materials. This may be what I need to carry on with building my artificial intelligent computer. To test the idea of the organic materials I barrowed one of the test mice. At first, I decide not to name him. I implanted a chip fragment in the back of the mouse's neck to see what will happen. At first the mouse is very sick and I'm afraid I may have killed him. I leave him over night in his own cage and will return in the morning to see how he is doing.

The next morning the mouse is up and about just like nothing had happened. I figured I would leave the chip in the mouse for several weeks then open him up to see what may have happened with the crystal in his body. On the same day I put the chip in the mouse I put a camera on him to have a twenty-four-hour surveillance, other than seeing that the mouse recovered quickly from the implant. Nothing else happened, A very good sign. That means the crystal would be safe to use. I hope it will prove to be what I need to build my A.I. (Artificial intelligent) computer.

As it turns out one of the other scientists is doing an experiment on a female mouse and she places her cage on a table across the room. That night the male mouse (Romeo) as I came to call him had disappeared from his cage. One moment he is there and the next he is gone. I came in the following morning and saw the empty cage. I could not figure how he had gotten out. So, I started looking around for him. Then Sandy the scientist who is using the female mouse, asked me if I had put my male mouse in her cage?

"What?" I said

I wander over to look, and sure enough there is Romeo the mouse. I put him back in his cage again and recover my recording from that night to see who moved Romeo to the female mouse's cage. To my astonishment as I watch Romeo disappears from his cage. Finally I recall what happened with the crystal when I applied a one-and-half-volt battery to the crystal.

That night I moved Romeo's food and water to another cage and put a camera on all three cages to see what happens. The next morning Romeo is back with the female. What did I just discover? That the crystal can cause movement from one place to another, and also that the crystal can connect to organic tissue. I made all kinds of notes about the possibilities of the crystal and its properties, what a find. Someone else is also watching and is not very happy with what I may have discovered. I was running one more test on Romeo, when someone moved the female's cage and turned it around, so the wheel was in the same place Romeo would port to.

The next morning when I came in I did not expect to find what I had found. Romeo is dead, when he ported in to the female's cage he ported into the wheel. He died instantly, his poor body was part of the wheel and the wires passed through his vital organs killing him. I got another cage, to move the female into and took Romeo to another lab and cut him off the wheel, I dissected him and found what the chip attached itself to his nervous system. So, Romeo was able to control the chip. I learned or would remember that line of sight teleporting would keep me from the same death that Romeo experienced. I put this into my personal log, and this would be the death of me.

I realized that I may have made a different discovery, so I prepared another crystal for implantation, this time it was for me. I took a small crystal shard and went to the lab doctor and told him what I wanted to do with the crystal. I explained that it would allow me to better connect with the computer I was building. At first, he was not going to do it, but I managed to convince him that it would be safe to do.

Chapter 3

That afternoon I had an appointment with the doctor. He had me lay down on my stomach then the doctor gave me a local anesthetic. And made a small incision at the base of my neck to implant the crystal. Like the mouse I got real sick and the doctor was going to remove the chip, but I told him to leave it in as my illness would pass in a few hours.

"OK, but in two hours I will remove it if it you do not get better."

I agreed and he left me on the cot to recover. In the two-hour period, I wanted to die. I experience fever, the chills, and a head ache; the head ache was the worst I have ever had. Then it all stopped, I felt like my old self. I got up on to my feet and then the doctor was right there to check me over.

"Well Steve you appear fine, but I want to keep tabs on you. Come see me tonight before you leave for home, and tomorrow I'm doing a full check up on you."

I agree and go to my desk to record in my computer journal about the crystal's affects.

I wrote about the impact of inserting the crystal into me, and I speculated on the possibilities of what I had just discovered. The possibility of growing more of the new crystal. Could result in generating a new type of transportation, computers, and maybe other things yet to be discovered, I made copies of my report to put into my personal safe at work. Also, I wanted to lock away the crystal. Its value is beyond all expectation. I used my key then dialed in my pin code, I opened the door, and placed my reports into the safe. I was just reaching for the crystal in my pocket when the safe explodes. At first it is like watching things in slow motion. I see and feel the blast then I'm in a field surrounded by fire, laying in a large pond of water, just before I pass out.

I wake up in a hospital room, my hands and face are covered in bandages, I start to panic. A soft voice, tells me I'm going to be OK, please relax and all will be explained to you. Since I'm being restrained. I do what she tells me to do.

"I can't see, where am I?"

"I'm nurse Addy, and you are in a hospital for the mentally ill."

"Why?"

"The police found you at an arson scene, and since you have been in a coma for a while, they placed you here until they can determine if you are a danger to yourself and others."

"I did not start any fires."

"That may be true, but the evidence is against you. Do you know your name?"

"Why yes, its, its, I don't remember."

"That is not surprising." Speaks Addy. "you have had quite a trauma to your head, and the doctor said you might have some memory loss. So, the police want you to stay confined here until you remember."

"I guess so." I said.

"When will I get the bandages off?"

"The doctor will be here tomorrow to look at you. You were burned pretty badly. We did not expect you to live."

"So how long has it been since my accident?"

"Almost six months, the doctor feels that the coma is what saved your life, as it kept you from feeling the pain which allowed you to heal."

"Wow! I not only lost my memory, but months of my life."

"I'm sorry." Addy said.

"Addy if I may ask, where is here exactly?"

"You are in Washing State, at the sanitarium in Spokane. Now that you are awake, the police will also be coming tomorrow to question you."

"I understand; who will be my first visitor tomorrow?"

"The doctor will be here early in the morning to see to your bandages, followed by the police, I'm very sorry, you seem to be a nice person."

"I thank you for that, were you my nurse the whole time?"

"Yes, I have watched over you the whole time."

"Are you married Addy?"

"No, I have not found the right man yet."

"I smiled, but she cannot see my smile due to the bandages (also I find I do not have any lips to smile with). Addy gives me my drugs, and soon I fall asleep. The next morning the doctor wakes me up.

"Well young man, let's see how your burns are doing."

He carefully removes the bandages, and from the look on Addy's face, I can tell I must be badly scarred. Even my hands are so burned that they no longer have any prints. They are nothing but scars.

"May I have a mirror, so I can see my face?"

The doctor asks, "Are you sure you want to see?"

"I believe I do."

"Ok, be prepared, you were badly burned."

I slowly raise the mirror to look at my face and head. I'm, in shock I have no hair, and my head and face are as unrecognizable as my hands.

"Whoa, that is one ugly kisser."

The doctor asks, "Do you remember anything?"

"No, where was I found?"

"Outside Missoula Montana, between Missoula and French Town, some place called Primrose station, does this mean anything to you?"

"No, it does not ring any bells."

"I was afraid of that, as you had a bad concussion. There is one thing in your favor."

"What is that Doc.?"

"The clothes you were wearing helped to protect you from the fire, only your hands and head were burned, it could have been much worse, if more of your body had been burned you would have died for certain."

"Did I have anything on me, identification, anything?"

"No, the only thing you had was this crystal in your hand, it took us a while to pry it out, if you still want it, here it is."

The doctor hands the crystal to me as he continues to watch me waiting for me to react. Nothing! I did not have any reaction to seeing or touching the crystal.

"It looks like a crystal, nice color of blue and purple."

"Right now, the police want to have a talk with you are you up to it?"

"I guess so, I don't know what they will learn from me, I still do not remember anything."

"OK, Addy let the detective in, I told them he may not remember anything."

The detective enters the room, he seems to be pleasant, he asked me many questions, but I cannot give him any real answers. He watches my every move trying to detect if I'm lying to him. He finally leaves, and he said I will stay here until he gets his answers.

For the next few days, I talk to Addy to find out more about her, she is not married. No real family, just an aunt living in California in a nursing home. No boyfriend, and she just lives down the road. She has a cat that is named Thomas. Over time she seems to become enamored with me, and I did not want that to happen. She is feeling sorry for me and my predicament, to the point where she is falling in love with me. I did not want to hurt her so I put off showing her anything but friendship. A month later I'm looking out my window wishing I could be outside, when it happens. I found myself standing just past the bushes. "WHAT!" I exclaimed I'm free, and I can leave. I decided to return to my room, more to see if I can. Sure, enough I concentrate and I'm back in my room. Something else happens to me, my memory returns.

I sit down to think through what just happened, I remembered the safe, then a blinding flash of light and heat, and a lot of force. It must have been an explosion, but why? Steve is lost in thought when Addy enters his room.

"How are you doing today?" Addy queries me.

"I feel fit but caged up, will it be possible to ask the warden if I can go for a walk on the grounds, I promise not to do anything like run away."

"I'll go ask him after I check your vitals."

"You appear to be different today, did you remember anything?"

"I had a quick flash back of someone, it was a woman with long black hair and green eyes, and she was wearing a medieval dress."

"Someone you know then?"

"I do not know" I lied.

"It may be a start of your memory returning, I'll let the doctor know."

Addy finishes what she is doing and then leaves to get permission to let me go out back to walk around. Addy returns, and says the doctor cannot give you permission without the Police department's permission.

"That's ok." Maybe tomorrow.

That evening when Addy goes home, I port to the lab in California to see what I might learn. They started rebuilding the Lab, so I sneak in to see if any of my stuff is still there. My desk and the area where I was before, I disappeared is gone. It is just a hole in the floor, which is in process of being filled in. I move to the basement and find a box with my name on it in storage. So, I open it up, and find some of my cloths which I take. Rummaging around I find my note book where I'm planning out my computer. I take that as well. I returned to my old apartment and find it has been rented out to someone else. I had to find my stuff in police storage. I find my bank card and port to my bank ATM to use the cash machine to withdraw most of my money. Running around in my pajamas will soon draw some unwanted attention, so I port back to the hospital, where I stashed my clothes and money. The next day, I start planning out what I'm going to do. Steve Storm is dead to the world, and somehow, I feel that it might be the best thing to do, is to stay dead.

With my plans made I write a note to Addy saying good-bye and that I have my memory back. That evening I watch her leave for home. As she is crossing the street an out of control car is headed right for her! She will be killed, so I port up behind her lock my arms around her and port to the nearest bushes out of the way. Where I release her and port back to my room. I watch her as she brushes herself off and looks around for the person who saved her life. Several people run up to her checking to see if she is alright. For some reason she turns to face my window from across the way, and I can see the question in her eyes. I change my clothes to street clothes, collect my things, and I port to one of the many places where I have lived as a child. I wound up in Dalles, Oregon. It is a small town on the Columbia River. I get a room for the night. At first the owner is not sure he wants to rent me a room because I'm wearing a ski mask.

Chapter 4

When I pulled off my mask, he relents, and I pay for my room for the next two days in advance. The next day I managed to get to the Court House to start the process of getting a new Identity. I'm able to convince the court that I have lost my memory after I showed them my face and hands. Due my traumatic injuries I do not know who I'm. So instead of being called John Doe, I took my first name and my mother's maiden name, so I'm now to be called Steve Ball. I leave the court house, I know I will soon run out of money, so when I returned to my room, I try to figure out ways to earn money. I hit on an idea while watching TV about drug dealers and their money dealings. I can take their money, and they cannot consider that blood money as being stolen. And besides who will they tell?

The first thing I need to do, is make a disguise. I know how to make a latex mask to cover my burns so I will not be easily identified. So, I return to the new lab and locate all the materials I will need to make my mask; when I come into some money I will repay them for the supplies I have taken. The next place to go is to the theater to see if I can find a wig, Eye brows and a mustache. I put all that I pick up in the back pack I purchased earlier. I return back to my room knowing I will have to leave tomorrow. I will need to get enough money to put down on a house so I'll have an address. Otherwise I will not get my new identity. I see in the newspaper they are looking for me back in Spokane; it is a good thing that I could not have traveled from Spokane to The Dalles in a few hours by conventional means. This will give me leeway time, before I have to go somewhere else.

I pack up my stuff and port to Chicago's out skirts. I have been there before; my car broke down there once while I was traveling back in my college days. This time I traveled by porting by line of sight and hitch hiking until I reached the inner city, where I managed to find a greasy spoon café. I go in to ask for a job. The old man takes one look at me and is ready to send me away, until I tell him that I was burned, and I'm not going to hold him up. I tell him I will work for room and board, nothing more. He gives in. Where else would he get someone to wash dishes, for just a meal and a place to sleep? He sets me up in the basement with a cot and a blanket, then he puts me to work. I spent the rest of the day cleaning not only the dishes, but all the tables and chairs. I'm just about to start on the walls, when he tells me to stop and eat my dinner. He sits with me as I eat; I tell him a story about the accident that took away my memory and caused my burns. He thanks me for all the work I'm doing, the last guy, just barely got the dishes done. And here I'm cleaning the whole place.

"Thank you" I said.

He pats me on the shoulder and tells me to go to bed, as the rest of the work can wait until the morning.

Well I spend a few hours cleaning up my sleeping area. I swept the floors, dusted all the shelves, and ledges. Now to be honest, I was not trying to be a clean person, but when I start to make my mask I will need the environment to be clean as possible. I'm very tired so I decided to get some sleep. The next morning my boss is shaking me awake.

"Oh, I'm sorry I over slept"

He looks around at the basement.

"Well I see you cleaned up down here last night, so I guess I can overlook it. You did a nice job. Now come up stairs and have breakfast. From what I see you have more than earned it."

"Thank you!" I said.

So, I go upstairs to have breakfast.

"Do you have a place nearby where I might get a bath?"

"Well now there is a YMCA just a few blocks from here, will that do?"

"That will be fine." I said.

At the end of the day, the boss, tells me that I can have the night off, and tomorrow too.

"Is everything Ok?"

"Oh yes, I just take Sundays off."

"Fair enough"

So that night I manage to finish early. When I make my mask it will take twenty-four-hours to cure the mold, and another, twenty-four-hours to cure the mask. So, after I make the mold, I go to the YMCA to get a much need shower. I attracted a lot of attention and scare a few kids due to my scars and lack of lips, so I leave and get out into the street where I cover my face with my ski mask. Then I see a drug deal happening, so I walk by, then move off into the shadows so I can watch the dealer. In a couple of hours, I see a car drive up and a couple of goons get out of the car to brace the dealer for his money. Then they get back into their car and drive off down the street. So, I follow. I port down the road behind them just keeping them in sight. They stop several times, to collect money from other dealers.

Chapter 5

Eventually they pull up to a downtown building with an underground garage. I walk up to look in when a large security guard put his hand on to his gun, and his four-legged friend is growling at me. I turn away to walk down the street. Well I'm off tomorrow, so I'll see if I can get into the building. I port back to my room and decide to get some sleep. When morning arrives, I go upstairs and have a donut and milk for breakfast. Then I port to the alley near the building. I walk up to the door and try to go inside. I run into another security guard, and he turns me back out into the street. That is Ok, when I return in the night, I'll be able to port into the building without being seen.

I get back to my room to find my mold is cured so I can make my mask. I pour the latex into the mold and spread it over the mold; it will have to sit for twenty-four-hours, then I can paint it and add the eye brows and mustache. So back to work for the next few days while I get my mask ready. As it turns out my boss gives me some money for the work I have done. So, I purchase some black spandex pants and a top, I have enough left over to buy a pair of biker gloves without the fingers. I'll be able to use my fingers if I need to. That night I put on my latex mask, the wig, and over that I put on the ski mask. I port to the inside of the building in the front lobby. No one is there. It's night so I have the run of the lobby area. I set out to explore the area especially the stairs leading to the parking garage. I soon find the door to the garage, and fortunately for me the door has a small window so I can see the inside of the garage, so I port into the garage and find a place to hide where I can wait. After midnight the two goons drive in to the area where I can see them. But they stay in their car. A short time later another car shows up, and two people from that car get out. The other goons step out of their car and wait for the other two men to reach them.

"Where's the money?"

The two goons from the first car open up the car trunk and take out a case that is full of money. Wow! I think. The goons hand it over and get back into the car and drive off, leaving the second two standing there to watch them drive off. After the other two leave, it makes the odds a little better. As the two goons stand there they are talking, I realize something else is about to take place, and I decide to get while the getting is still good. I port next to the case of money and grab it, one of the guys says.

"Hey you, what are you doing?"

he pulls out his gun, so I port back to my room with the cash.

"What a rush!"

I stash the case under the cot, break up my mold, and put away my mask and new cloths. I decide it is time to go back to Dalles, Oregon. I leave a note thanking my boss for the place to stay, and I also leave him a thousand dollars for his troubles.

Chapter 6

I get back to Oregon and rent another room, wearing my new mask. The following day I contact a land agent to search for a house where I can work from without being noticed. So, I tell the man what I want and he shows me several pictures on his computer, none of the locations are what I'm looking for.

Then as he thinks, he says "There may be one place that might meet your needs. It is located fourteen miles from here, in the town called Duffer. I don't have any pictures, but it is a short drive from here would you like to see it?"

"Let's go." I said.

So, he drives us out to the house. It is a very small two bedroom house, farmhouse with a barn, a shop for repairing cars, and a bunk house. Most of all it is secluded. There are no other neighbors within a mile. Now as to the shop and barn, well I can convert them in to what I need. Then I see some construction on the back side of the house.

"Do you know what was being built?"

"I think he was adding another room."

I inspected all the property walking all around it.

"What is the price?"

"The asking price is two hundred thousand dollars"

"If I put down cash, let's say one hundred thousand dollars now and the balance at signing can we reduce the price to one hundred seventy thousand?"

"I'll contact the seller, and see what they say, where can I reach you Mr. Ball?"

"I'm staying at the hotel room 2B."

The agent returns me to my room and says he will have an answer for me tomorrow morning.

"Ok" I said.

The next day the agent shows up at my door and says "the seller will accept your terms."

"Good, when can I purchase the place."

"It will take several days in escrow to have all the paperwork ready to be signed; so how about two weeks from today?"

"When do you need the one hundred thousand dollars?"

"Today if you can."

"When will your office be open?"

"In an hour, will you need transportation?"

"No, I'll be there as soon as I make some calls and have lunch" I said to the agent.

"I'll see you there Mr. Ball."

I take the case of money to the bank and make a deposit of five hundred thousand dollars in to a new account, and then I ask for a cashier's check for one hundred thousand dollars.

I walk to the agent's office just down the street to start the transaction of buying a house.

"Here is the one hundred thousand dollars I said I would provide you, now you can process the paperwork. The rest of the money is in the bank down the street, and I will have a cashier's check made out the morning I will be signing."

"Thank you, Mr. Ball, I'll get right on it, you'll have the paperwork in two weeks, I'll let you know if it changes."

"You know where I am, you should be able to reach me at the Hotel."

I go shopping and pick up some new clothes, a laptop computer, and a cell phone that will allow me to have WI-FI for my computer connection. I get my new identity from the courthouse after giving them my new address. So I'm now a member of a small community, the money in the bank and the pending purchase of a home went a long way toward convincing the judge to decide my favor. I'm now Steve Ball.

Now I need another base of operations, some place so secluded and out of the way as to be difficult for anyone to get there. With the laptop computer, I do some searching and find a mountain lodge in the Rockies, the only way to get there is by helicopter. I decide to go take a look. I send an E-mail to the agent who did the posting, to see if it is still For Sale. If it is when can I view it? The next morning, I received an e-mail saying it is still available, and if I can arrive on Friday morning, she will get transportation to take us to the lodge. I replied that I will be at her office on Friday morning.

Chapter 7

I call the first agent to let him know that I will be gone for a few days. Then I port to Kalispell, Montana. I had been there before as a kid, my father had a worker's picnic there and, I got to swim in Flathead Lake. It was a lot of fun, a long time ago. I port to a city park and walk to the agent office to go see the lodge. I knock on the door and she opens it immediately.

"So, Mr. Ball are you ready to fly in to see the lodge?"

I said "Sure, as matter of fact I have my sleeping bag and backpack. I thought I might spend the night there."

"Are you sure you want to do that; the cost of the helicopter is like one thousand dollars per trip?"

"I'll be glad to pay for it; I want to make sure that I want to buy the place after I look it over."

"You can talk to Rudy, about your arrangements when we get to the airport."

"That will be just fine."

We arrive at the airstrip an hour later and the pilot is just finishing up his preflight. The agent makes the introductions, and we set off for the lodge. During the two hours to get there, I talk to Rudy about making another flight out to the lodge in a day or two, he agrees.

When we get there the pilot flies around the mountain top to give me a bird's eye view of the place. There are no out buildings, but the lodge appears to be a large place.

"So, what can you tell me about this place, like who built it and why he wants to sell it."

The agent says "We never got much out of him, he was quite a loner. He never left here once he moved in."

"Then how did he get supplies?"

"Rudy would fly in supplies once a month."

"He must have been wealthy."

"No one around here knows who he was; all we know is that he paid his bills."

"You sound as if he died."

"He did, Rudy found him on his last supply run a few months ago. He appeared to have fallen from his balcony and broke his neck."

"So, who is selling the property now?"

"Basically, the state, I was the only nearby agent who would handle the sale. So far you are the only person who has made any kind of request to see it. When others find out how remote it is, well you can guess."

"Ok, show me around."

Rudy lands the chopper not too far from the house and shuts down the engine. We all get out and the tour begins. It has two stories, a large kitchen, wash room several bedrooms some with bathrooms. There also is a large dining room with living room, and a library.

"I assume since we have not turned on the lights it is because we do not have any power?"

"That is right Mr. Ball, the power company will turn on the power after you contact them."

"Ok, when do you need to leave Rudy, I assume you will need to leave soon."

Rudy looks at his watch and says, "Wow I did not know it was this late, we need to get going. So, I will be back in two days, is that OK with you?"

"That will be great."

I walk out to the chopper with the agent and Rudy and I wave to them as they fly off.

The house is furnished, so I take one of the beds upstairs and put my sleeping bag on it. Then I take out my flash light to do more exploring. I'm glad Rudy did a fly over so I was able to get an idea as to how big the house is, for some reason the outside does not match the inside. With flash light in hand I go poking around. The west wall is thicker than any of the other walls, almost by four feet. So, I tap on the wall and find nothing, maybe it is just a mistake. The next day I hiked around the lake that is there. No fish in there as it is manmade, and I suspect it freezes solid in the winter. It is more like a pool than a lake. It has a lot of trees, and a few paths. The only animal life I can see are the big horn mountain sheep and birds, not much more than that. I'm still disturbed by the four-foot-thick wall in the house.

I still have several hours before Rudy will be returning, so I set about checking the discrepancy. I find nothing until I hear the chopper. Then quite by accident, I find that the fire place contains a loose rock which is a switch that opens a wooden panel. I depressed the rock again and the panel closes. I'll have to come back on my own and do some more exploring. I have decided to buy the place, now to find out the damage. Rudy lands and I stand ready to board with my pack and sleeping bag. On the return trip I'm talking to Rudy about the possibility of setting up the same or similar deal as the former owner had with him. He agrees, then he asks me if I have seen the big horned sheep. And I smile.

"Yes, I saw them when I went on a hike around the property, I was thinking I may have to brush up on my bow hunting."

"Why not shoot them with a rifle?" asks Rudy.

"That would keep them away after a while, and I may want to depend on them as a food source, a bow is quiet, they won't get scared off so easily. Why do you ask?"

"Well I would like to get permission if you buy the place to hunt here."

"I suggest you get a bow, and we'll both do some hunting together."

"Steve you got a deal."

Back at Kalispell the agent meets me at the door again.

"Well she asked, what do you think?"

"I would like to buy the place, if the price is right."

"The bank wants two Million for the place."

"If I pay for seventy five percent in cash what would the price be?"

"I do not know Mr. Ball; I'll check with the bank."

"Well I have to be returning to where I currently live, here is my current cell phone number, call me when you find out anything."

"Ok Mr. Ball I will."

I leave her office and when I enter the nearby alley I port back to the lodge. I want to see what is behind the sliding panel. Once inside the lodge I go to the switch in the fire place and press it. It opens the panel and I take a flash light out of my pack. I flash the light into the opening, and find some stairs, so down I go. In what looks like a basement, but it turns out to be a lab. The previous owner was a drug designer. I find bags of drugs, and one that looks like it burst open. It makes me wonder if the owner really fell from the upper floor or was pushed. I will need a way to get rid of this stuff and clean up the drugs that are all over the floor. Otherwise this huge basement will meet my needs. I'll be able to build my inventions and stay out of the lime light at the same time.

I port back to my current place in the Dalles in a nearby alley and walk into my hotel room to wait for word on both houses. A few days later I sign the paperwork on the house in Duffer and make my last payment. I decide to purchase a used truck, so I can be seen driving around. It would draw too much attention if I'm seen in the Dalles; then a short time later be seen in Duffer, especially if I do not have regular transportation. I take stock of my money and realize I will need more. So, I can pay for the lodge, and to purchase the equipment I will need for my computer. I decide to go to New York for the next job. I had gone there once a few years ago, on assignment for the lab that I worked for, and I also visited certain areas when I attended MIT and Stanford. I port to Central Park to a secluded part of the park where I would not likely not be seen and if I were no one would believe whoever did see me.

Chapter 8

For four nights I hunt for a pusher, or someone looking for a fix. What I'm looking for is probably all around me, but since I'm new at this, it takes me a while to find someone. As it turns out I see this woman approach a man dressed in a suit, and she asks him to spot her some drugs, she even offered to give him sex. He brushes her away; and leaves her in the throes of withdrawals. She is in pretty bad shape. The suit turns and walks away. I move up to the woman, and she thinks I'm going to kill her. I reached down and port her to a hospital in an out of the way town where drugs will be hard to come by. I leave a note for the nurse that I would make payments for her recovery and leave them with one hundred thousand dollars to begin her treatment. I port back to the park and soon locate the dealer.

I stalk him for several days and then I locate his supplier. I now follow the supplier as he drives down the street, two hours later I find the place where he buys his stuff. More money changed hands. I figure I'll stalk this supplier to determine the best way to relieve him of his ill-gotten gains. They meet at a warehouse in a deserted area. I follow this supplier for several nights and check out the meeting place to be sure of all the hiding places. Then on the next night I decide to take their money. A much larger deal must have been planned by the mob. I wait up on the catwalk until the players all show up, and it is like everybody is coming out of the wood work. It is a small army that shows up and four cars pull in and more men with guns show up. I had to port to a different location before I was discovered. I continue to watch the drama unfold. Two guys from each car get out, each one carrying a large case and they go to a table and open up two cases which have money, the other two cases contain drugs, a deal is going down.

I need a distraction, so I call in a 911 to the police and give them details of the drug exchange. I even send pictures on my cell. A few minutes later the police sirens are closing in on their location. Everyone turns to that sound, so I port down to the table, and touch the cases with the money in them. When someone shouts at me, I grab the cases, and port away. Each side thinks the other side is trying to pull a fast take, and they start shooting at each other. By the time the police arrive, they have several wounded, and all the drugs they need to bust everyone there. What no one can explain is where the money went. All anyone saw was a man in black appear then disappear with the money.

I port back to my hotel room and receive a message to come down do the agent's office the next morning to sign and make my final payment on the house in Duffer. I port the money to the Duffer house and return to the hotel. I pick up my truck and load up my belongings. I'm at the bank as it opens and get the cashier's check for the balance of the money that I owe on the Duffer home. All the paperwork is signed off, and I now have a home. I drive home and, on the way, I purchase a card table and a folding chair. I have the power turned on and I set about purchasing furniture for this home, and Computer components for my AI computer that I plan on building. After I make the purchase of the components I realize what a fool I am. Not too many people will be purchasing these kinds of components and it will make me stand out like a sore thumb.

Chapter 9

I decided that having a fake company someplace else, will be the best thing to do, but where? I set that question aside for now and count the money I have taken. There is nearly ten million dollars. Well that should take care of my demands for a while. I put two hundred thousand dollars in the Dallas' bank, to pay for the furniture, and anything else I may need. Where to put the rest of the money? For now, I store it in the hidden room at the Lodge in Montana. It will be safe there for the time being. If the deal falls through I'll remove it. I decide to take a trip to the hospital where I dropped off the young woman to see how she is doing. I port just outside the building and was going to enter when I remembered that I'm without my mask, I do not wish to stir up any problems so I return home and put on my latex mask, and I pocket a few thousand dollars, to make a payment for the woman's recovery. I make it to the hospital and ask the desk nurse where I might find the girl, I get her room number and walk to her room.

She is in better shape than what she was, but I can tell she needs more recovery time. I do not enter her room, as I turn to go.

"Who are you, my benefactor?" she asks.

"No, I just found you out side and brought you into the emergency room."

"Are you also paying my bill here, and if so what do you want of me?"

"Me I want nothing."

"So, I guess you are the Good Samaritan?"

"I guess in a sense I am."

"Oh Lord, just what I need a bleeding heart, you would have been better off leaving me alone."

"Why?"

"My life is a mess, I'll just go back when they let me go. You wasted your time."

"I don't think so, let me show you a messed-up life."

I remove my mask, and the woman almost cringes in fear. I put my mask back on and she is looking at me wide eyed.

"What happened to you?"

"I was caught in a fire." I took off my gloves, and she sees my hands.

"I know why you saved me. You want me to be your girlfriend."

"Not really. You needed help and so I helped you, after today you will never see me again."

I leave her room and go to the business window and ask how much to pay for the woman's care and about how much more she may need. I give the money to the clerk and leave the building, never to return. I return to my new house and look up where and how to decontaminate meth drugs. I will need a Hazmat suit, oxygen mask, and special equipment to clean the floors and the air of the dust particles. I down load the procedures so I can return and rid the lodge of its' poison. A week later I have all that I need, I also whipped up a gadget to test the air and surfaces to determine how dangerous this substance is. If the gadget works well, I will sell this on the market, for the police to use. It may save a few lives.

Chapter 10

I spend a week cleaning the hidden room, then I go through the lodge upstairs and test all the rooms and do more cleaning. I dispose of the drugs at a safe place where the fire department puts all their hazmat materials. I am finely done with my cleaning. Two days later The Agent from Montana calls. "Mr. Ball the bank's counter proposal is that if you pay in cash, they would reduce it to $1.7 million"

I did not want to seem too eager to buy.

"Is it ok if I mull it over for a few days? Also, will a cashier's check be acceptable, and I can wait until it clears the bank before I sign the paperwork?"

"Call me when you are ready to decide."

"I will, I'll call you at this time in two days with my answer."

The next day I return to Kalispell to open a bank account, at a different bank, a more local one. I deposit ten million dollars, this will be used to retain Rudy the chopper pilot and pay for my supplies.

On the second day I call the agent as promised and accept the terms. The bank also accepts the terms of getting a cashier's check. I tell the agent to get the paperwork in order and I'll bring the check tomorrow. I'll be over in your area anyway. I'll give you the check so the bank can clear it, and I can then sign the paperwork. I would also like to talk to Rudy. I hang up the phone and the next day I port over to the Missoula airport at the same time as a commercial plane lands, then I go rent a car for the day. I port the car and myself to a school parking lot in Kalispell, and then drive over to the agent's office, where I drop off the check. She tells me that as soon as the check fully clears she will have the paperwork ready to be signed. I thank her and ask where I can find Rudy. I drive out to the local airport and I soon locate Rudy, working on his aircraft.

"Hi Rudy, do you have a moment to talk about an arrangement for transportation, and supply deliveries to the lodge?"

"Sure Mr. Ball."

"Please, call me Steve."

"Sure, thing Steve."

"So Rudy, what was your arrangement with the previous owner?"

"Well I would receive his mail, and the store would drop off his supplies off at my office and depending upon the time I would either fly out that day or the next to make a delivery. He would then pay me one thousand dollars and I would leave after I unloaded his supplies."

"That sounds reasonable."

"As fortune will have it the price of gas, and repairs have gone up some; the cost will have to be higher."

"Ok, how much?"

"It will be fifteen hundred dollars a trip"

"I can do that. So it is settled then when I own the lodge, you can bring in my supplies, there may also be some other items for my inventions that may need to be delivered. Now is there any time during the year that you may not be available?"

"During hunting season. I'm either hunting or taking hunters out to remote areas, and during Summer I might get involved in a search and rescue, or forest fires."

"Seems like I may need to get a Radio setup so I can call you to make sure you are available"

"That was something I tried to get the other guy to do but he did not want to."

"Who knows, maybe you and I can go Bow Hunting for the big horn sheep" I said.

"I'll hold you to that Steve."

We shook hands to seal the deal, and I left to go back to Missoula. Then I port back to Duffer to wait for the Bank to clear my check.

Now I will need a small warehouse in another state, I decided on a Southwestern state, Nevada will do. I have not been there before, so I'll have to use more conventional transport, like a car. I put on my latex mask and port to Oxnard, where I can get a rental car to drive to Fallon Nevada. It is large enough town so I won't be noticed, and yet small enough not to be a big city. I check with the Land Agents and soon locate a warehouse that will suit my needs. I manage to purchase it at a cost of seventy-five thousand dollars. This will be great, as with a new address and this location I can have the parts shipped here where I can port them back to my Lab in Montana. In time I may need this place to ship my inventions out. All in all, not a bad buy at that. I return to Duffer to start ordering my computer parts to be shipped to my Fallon warehouse for delivery.

The next day the agent in Montana contacts me to come and sign the papers for the Lodge. After I have signed the papers, I contact Rudy to give me a ride to the lodge. I have a special two-way radio to install at his office, with a hands-free unit for his chopper. Rudy agrees to take me in the morning of the next day. I drive by to drop off the radios at Rudy's office and to set it up for him, and that is when I meet his wife. She runs the office while Rudy takes care of the flying and the chopper maintenance. She meets me and realizes I'm the person who just bought the lodge. She appears to be grateful for the money and the more permanent job I have given her husband. I thank her and tell her if she would like to fly in with her husband I will be glad to show her around. She accepts and by the way she says, "My name is Margret," and I know your name is Steve.

"Well Margret, we'll be on the radio from time to time, so it is nice to have a face with the voice."

"I have the Radio installed and here is a hand-held unit that Rudy will be able to use when he is out flying.

"Margret, I'll be back tomorrow for my ride, and next week Rudy can start bringing my supplies. I have it set up with the store to deliver the food I'll be requesting, and they will drop it off here. They are instructed to coordinate with you, so that you can deliver them to me that day. I have it set up with the bank to handle my account, so when a delivery is made, the bank will pay the invoices.

"Every six months, I'll return here to settle accounts and see that money is maintained in my account."

"I like that." said Margret.

"I brought a radio set for me to set up at the lodge, and a weeks' worth of canned food I contacted the Power folks and paid for the power to be turned on. I'm now all set to use the lodge. I'll have Rudy fly me to my new place, and that he will be back in a week with my supplies. I indicated to him that with winter coming on that I will be ordering more food than I can use in a month so I can stock up, in case you can't fly in for a delivery."

Margret said "That would be a good idea."

"I'll be back in the morning."

The next day Rudy flies me out to the lodge and on the way, we chat about hunting. Then Rudy spots another helicopter.

"I wonder what he is doing out here?"

Neither one of us pay it much attention we just continue on our way to the lodge.

I watch Rudy depart as he leaves me at the lodge alone. Now I can start to work on my computer system. I took my research from the lab when I last made my visit there. I hoped no one will realize it is gone. I get on my personal computer to hook up to the internet and realize I do not have a signal. Ok, I go to

Duffer and make my internet connection so I can place my orders to be sent to Fallon. I ordered some minor equipment which will be sent to Rudy to be flown in to me at the lodge. I remember that I told him I was building a computer system. He'll be less suspicious of me if he has to fly in a few components for me. In a months' time my components will have arrived at the warehouse and are dropped off. After the driver leaves I port all the equipment back to my lab where I start work on my computer. All the mechanical parts go together fairly quickly; it is the organic part that concerns me. And then during my work I finally see what I need to do.

CAT is Built

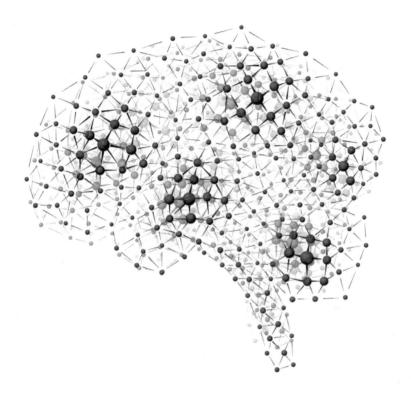

Chapter 11

I take out the crystal from its hiding place, and I decide to clone my own brain using the crystal, with some of my DNA; and the knowledge that I learned at Stanford, I'm able to grow a small brain the size of my fist that has a crystal appearance and is nothing like a normal human brain. I encased it in a steel casement. With my crystal brain I'm able to attach it to the computer hardware. I have to admit I'm afraid of turning it on. So, before I do, I set up fail safes to make sure I can destroy my computer if in case it does not take my programing. I programed it to use 'Asimov's, three principals' and I also add some ethics programs of my own creation. I fire up the program and CAT is now on line. It takes a while before we can converse, it is like teaching a very fast baby to talk, MAMA, DADA and it progresses from there. Within a week CAT has a vocabulary like a teenager, another week and CAT is at a college level. At the time I did not realize that CAT had taped into my laptop and discovers the internet, and off he goes exploring the world.

I had to rein CAT in, but like any child he did not stop what he was doing, so I had to disconnect my laptop all together. For the time being I need to keep CAT contained until I teach him not to go blundering into the world and become known. Several weeks later I'm able to convince him of what I need for him to be doing. I'm spending money like it was everlasting and soon find myself needing more. I set CAT a task to learn the geography of the planet, and I give him his own network connection, before I know it CAT has infiltrated several Government agencies, and finds locations not otherwise known.

"CAT we need to do some experimentation; I would like to port to Florida can you give me any coordinates like on an isolated beach?"

"Sure Steve."

CAT feeds the coordinates in to my crystal and before I know it I'm standing on the beach, or almost on the beach. CAT put me one foot above ground, so when I get there I have a shock from my fall and fall flat on my face. I pick myself up and dust off the sand.

"I guess I'll have to work on that." I say to myself.

I port back to the lodge.

"Now I need to go earn some money."

"How do you do that Steve?"

"In a sense like Robin Hood CAT."

"I could divert the money from their accounts will that not work?"

"In a way CAT it would work except, when you do that kind of stunt the transaction can be traced back to here and I do not want you found so I must demand of you not to do it without my authorization, is that understood?"

"Yes Steve, I understand. I will do as you say."

"Thank you, CAT. Now I can use your help, can you locate any drug deals going down in the next few days?"

"I'll scan the communication systems and see what I can find Steve."

In the mean time I port to Duffer to make an appearance. I mow the lawn, clean around the house, drive into town to buy some groceries, mostly to be seen. One of the things I need to invent is a way to communicate to CAT from anywhere in the world. I spend the night in Duffer and then the next morning I port back to the lodge in Montana.

"Well CAT have you found anything?"

"Actually, Steve I have found several drug deals, all within the next week, two of them are looking for you to show up, and three of the others just normal business."

"Which of the three has the largest amount of money to pick up?"

"There are three that are dealing in a million dollars or so from what I can make out from their communications, but if you were to hit them all, you could collect about five million dollars. Would that do?"

"That would pay the bills for a while CAT, I have a couple of new tasks for you."

"What are they Steve?"

"One I need a way to communicate with you, where ever I am, and I need some kind of suit that will protect me from small caliber bullets. Now to change the subject when are these drug deals going to take place?"

"The first one is in California not too far from the Mexican Border, the second one in Texas on the coast not far from Corpus Christy and the third one is going down in Argentina also on a deserted coast."

"What is the time table CAT?"

"They are going to happen within an hour of each other."

"Which one will be first?"

"Argentina, Texas, then California" says CAT

"CAT put me down a hundred yards from the one in Argentina, I'll play it by ear, and then come back for the next set of coordinates."

CAT provides the coordinates to the beach in Argentina. Great plan I think, I do not know where the Drug dealers will be from where I have landed. To make matters worse I do not speak Spanish, I'll have to have CAT learn all the languages so he can translate for me in the future. Soon a couple of cars with lights show up down the coast from where I am, so I port closer to see what I can see. Four men get out of their cars and the four goons, pull out their guns and flash lights to check out the area. I have to port to several secluded places to avoid detection. Satisfied that no one is watching they each pull out a couple of large cases from their car trunks and open them up. The first case contains and I assume cocaine. I watch how they test a couple of bags, and then the other guys open the case with the money. I continue to watch and the first set of guys close the cases and then turn to shake hands. I port up to the car where I can place my hand on the money case. As the goons turn they see me, and start to pull their guns from their holsters so I quickly port back to the lodge with the cash.

"I'm ready for Texas. CAT"

CAT puts me a hundred yards away from where the action is to happen. Again, I move around looking for my prey. I see some cars with their lights on, but this time several people are patrolling the area. I port from one spot to another trying to keep out of sight. Finally, they settle down and each group goes through the process of showing each other their goods and money. I spot the money case and the drug case as they are beside each other, but with the goons moving around so much I'm not sure which is which so, I decide to take both. For some reason the large well-dressed men or gangsters do not seem to like each other and they are busy posturing. So, I pick my moment and port next to the cases, grab them and port away. It is a good thing I did not hesitate as before I knew it bullets were flying. I returned to the lodge.

"CAT I'm ready for California."

So, CAT places me at the warehouse near the border just as the drug deal is going down, this time it only has two people involved.

The building is empty, so it will be hard to move around in there as they will see me. Now I'm dressed all in black with my ski mask so I can hide in the shadows. I also have my latex mask on, just in case. I did not want to advertise my real face. Anyway I watch from a door way hidden in the shadows. I see the cases and both are open. They are testing the quality of the drugs. I decide to make my move so I port in next to the cases when this big gangster's hand which was twice the size of my hand reaches out and grabs me. It is like he has a vice for a hand. He lands a punch to my stomach causing me to double over, and he lets me go. I'm trying to catch my breath, and my wits when the other gangster grabs me from behind.

"Look Bennie, this must be the Magician that the people in Chicago are talking about, and here he is in our lap."

The big guy is now in front of me winding up to deliver a haymaker to my jaw. I gathered my wits long enough to slam the back of my head in to the face of the guy holding me. He relaxed his grip long enough for me to port to one side and watch the big guy's fist plow into the face of the goon who was holding me. (That looked like that hurt, I'm glad he did not hit me!)

Again, I was stupid. The big guy recovers and grabs the front of my shirt. I did not want to port with him attached to me. He stops for some reason and decides to pull off my ski mask. Well, he grabbed my mask so hard, that he also got my latex mask as well. Pulling the mask off, and gets a shock he was not expecting---my burned face. He freaks out and let's go of me. I port to the cases and port away.

"Hi CAT I just learned that tonight I need some form of weapon, or I need to learn how to fight, If that giant gangster had not pulled off my masks, I might not have gotten back in one piece."

"Steve what kind of weapon did you have in mind?"

"I'm not sure CAT, something I can use to disable a guy without killing them."

Chapter 12

"CAT have you come up with anything for a protective suit and a way to communicate with me in the field?"

"Yes, Steve I have. I contacted various companies to have the parts shipped to your Fallon warehouse. The parts should be there in a week. As to your weapon, what did you have in mind? I would recommend something that would render them unconscious or paralyzed."

"CAT what can I get that would do that and be nearly soundless?"

"Steve, a CO_2 dart gun would meet your need, but you would have to be a very good shot."

"So, CAT what would be the drug to use to put them down?"

"Never mind, I'm the biologist, what would be the best concoction to use, something that would not kill, but merely put them to sleep. I know of something from my lab days that one of the other scientists was working on as a drug for surgery, and it works pretty fast. I'll port there tomorrow night and get the formula. I'll also pick up a couple of CO_2 guns with darts as well."

So, I turn in to get some sleep. In the morning I start working on my weapons, I get a couple of dart guns that run on CO_2, so I buy a bunch of CO_2 cartridges. Then several packages of darts and a two-holster set up to wear. In the back of my mind I keep thinking is there a better weapon that I can use, or would it be better to learn how to fight? I decide to port to my old lab after it shuts down for the night and locate the formula. I arrive and just miss being seen by a guard, so I port to a different location and wait for the guard to return to my current location, it takes a little while and I port back to my friend's desk and look through her files. I soon find what I'm looking for and I take pictures of her formula. And then port back to the lodge.

"Steve, question?"

"Yes CAT"

"Did you just steal that formula from that lab?"

"Yes, CAT I did and I did not, you see I worked on this formula as well, but I did not perfect it, so half the formula is my property."

"Steve what about the part that is not your work, is that not stealing."

"You got me there, CAT, yes that would be stealing, so if I expect you to do right I guess I should too." So, I tear up the formula.

"I can buy a drug that would do the same thing. CAT locate a firm where I can buy that compound based on the formula you were fed, then I won't be stealing it."

"I'll have it shipped to Fallon Steve."

"I'm going to test my dart guns and see how bad of a shot I am."

I walk outside to do some target shooting. After firing a few shots, I realize I couldn't hit the side of a barn from ten feet away. If I put a laser on the gun that would improve my ability to hit the target, but it would possibly give me away to my enemy, so I continue to practice. After several days I can at least hit a human sized target, but I need to get it down to the area the size of a six-inch target, like the neck, where the drug will have the best effect. I return to the lab, and CAT informs me, my shipment is at the warehouse. I port there to pick up the equipment. The next thing I know is that I'm being surrounded by police and I'm told to put my hands up. I do not know why but instead of doing what they say, I fall on my equipment and port away back to the lodge.

"CAT, find out why the police in Fallon were looking for me."

"Ok, Steve."

Thirty minutes later CAT tells me they are looking for a killer in that area.

"CAT did they catch him yet?"

"No, Steve."

"What is the story on this killer CAT?"

"It appears that he killed his family and several others. He has been hiding out in that district, when they tried to contact you for questioning, they could not reach you. So, they decided to stake out the area, then they saw a truck make a delivery. So, they watched the area. When you appeared, they assumed you were there all along, and decided to arrest you. Then you vanished! Now they really want to talk to you. They have a statewide APB out for you."

"I guess I cannot use that place anymore. Well I have what was there. Now I need to set up a communication link with you that will reach around the world so to speak, what have you come up with?"

"Here is a schematic drawing that I formulated for your suit and communication devise."

I look over CAT's schematic.

"This is great CAT, what is it doing generating a field of force?"

"Yes, Steve, but you will need to be careful, the suit will deflect the bullet, but you will still feel the force it passes on to you. So, you can be hurt, but not killed. You will feel the pain at the impact site."

"Is there any way that we can stop that?"

"Not at this time Steve, one cannot change the laws of physics."

"What about the helmet?"

"It is a new type of ceramic that also has a Nano-Carbon-poly fiber. It is opaque from the outside, but on the inside, it is clear. You will be able to see all around you, I have also had the company that makes it set it up to be like a computer screen. When it is attached to your suit it will make an air tight seal, so you will carry an on-board oxygen generator the battery life is about ten to twelve hours depending upon your excretion. It also contains your communication device.

47

However, in that small box I have provided a hearing aid that you can wear, which will allow me to communicate to you when you are not wearing your suit. There is a pair of glasses that will act like the helmet's inner screen, in that you will have a computer screen using the lenses it can also project a keyboard onto any surface."

"Great I should try this stuff out and do a good field test."

Paladin meets Grandmother

Chapter 13

"CAT I'm going to go to New York Central Park to do some of my testing, I think I will go there at ten o clock pm their time. But in the meantime, I'm going to do some physical test on the suit."

I go outside and do some jogging, exercise, and I go to the jungle gym I have set up to see how the suit moves with me. After falling a few times, I realize I'll have to get use to the suits limitations.

"CAT is there some way you can improve the flexibility of the suit, and make the helmet smaller, make it conform more to my head, I feel like one of the gray aliens, with the big head like a fish bowl."

"If I do that you will lose the ability to seal the suit, and the helmet will have to be in two pieces. I will send for another suit, and helmet, may I send them to your Duffer home?"

"Yes, when can you get it there?"

"I will have a new design for the suit and the helmet by tomorrow, and it will take a month for it to be made, and about a week in shipment, I do not want to raise any flags Steve."

"Sounds good CAT in the meantime I'll play with this one."

"Speaking of Duffer, I'll be spending the day there tomorrow, for appearance sake, I'll be able to test your communication device, and the eye glasses. I'm off to New York now, to test this suit."

I port to Central Park in a hidden place, thanks to CAT I'm able to look into the area, before I port, I really do not want to wind up like poor Romeo, Embedded in someone or something. The Communication with CAT is perfect, I see through the helmet as if it were day light. I see if I move my eyes about, I can change to infrared scanning, I can amplify the sound around me.

"CAT this is just great, I love this helmet, can I speak through it?"

"Yes, Steve you can at several levels of sound, it will also mask your voice, and you can eavesdrop on all conversation even cell phones with in a fifty-foot area."

I switch to infrared and see several people all around me, and in one place I see what appears to be a gang. In another area four other guys hide in the shadows, like they are waiting for someone. I amplify the sound to see if I can catch a conversation.

Then I hear, "She'll be along any time now, keep your eyes open. She needs to pay for what she has done to all the others."

"Be quiet or she'll know we are here."

Twenty minutes later I see a lone girl coming their way, I get ready rescue her and take her away, when something in my mind says to wait. I decide to watch instead. The goons wait until the girl is right next to them when they spring from cover. They surround her and a few have knives and one has a gun, and the last one a chain. I decide I'm going to port in, but my mind says wait, so I hesitate. What I see makes me believe, this girl does not need me in the least. In mere moments, three of the goons are on the ground. They look like they suffered some broken bones. The gang member with the gun is lying on the ground, and the girl is concentrating on the last goon with the chain so she does not see that she is about to be shot. I port next to him and use my dart gun to put him to sleep. Next, I hear.

"Drop your gun, and why are you here?"

I see she is an oriental girl, and very pretty, with Deep Green eyes and raven colored hair. I put my gun away, and tell her she was about to be shot, when I came up and put him to sleep.

"Why would you help me stranger?"

"Well truth be known, I was out testing my new toys."

"You are lucky I did not associate you with them and put you down as well."

"Thank you for not doing that, however, you are not done yet."

She turns to face me and goes into a stance, I assume of defense.

"What do you mean stranger?"

"Whoa, I'm not a threat to you, there are several more of these goons just up ahead. I assume they are waiting for you, and one of them has an automatic weapon."

"How do you know this?"

I tap my helmet and said, "I can see them. It looks like they now have twelve people, and another one also has an automatic weapon."

"I can handle several people in a fair fight, but not that many" she said.

"If you'll trust me, I can get you past them without any trouble."

"With your face covered how do you expect me to trust you?"

"A fair question, I can assure you that I do not have the skill to take you on, and my intentions, are honorable."

Here take my hand, she takes my hand, and I port us to the far side of the park.

"What did you just do?"

"It is a bit difficult to explain, but if I wanted to; I could take you anywhere you want to go, it is like opening a window here then stepping through it to another place, without moving our feet."

"If you can tell me where you live, we can be there in mere moments."

She is reluctant to tell me, but what I did not know is that she and her grandmother are being forced to move. Otherwise she would not have given me her address. I port us to the front door, and she hurries us in so no one will see us. Soon we enter the house, and before I know it, I'm lying on the floor and this spry old lady is on top of me with a sword to my throat and in Japanese is asking me what I want, and what am I doing here. I hold up my hands, and in Japanese (Thanks to CAT) I tell her I'm not her enemy. She lets me up and asks her granddaughter what is going on? She explains that I brought her home safely and may have saved her life.

Chapter 14

Grandmother lets me get up on to my feet. I see all the boxes around the apartment.

"Are you moving?"

"We are being forced out, so they can tear down the building."

"Are you going to be close by here, I may have a proposition to make you."

"We do not know where we are going to move to, not much is open in our price range."

"May I make a suggestion?"

Grandmother asks, "What is your suggestion?"

"It is like this, I need to learn to fight, you need a place to live, I have a couple of places you may live in for as long as you like. You may pick which one, I'll see to all the bills, and food, all I want in return" "Here it comes." said the girl. "Now we'll see what he wants."

"All I want is to learn how to fight like her, nothing more. Tomorrow if you like I'll take you to both of my houses and you can choose which one you would like to live in. no strings attached."

"And you want me to believe that too I bet" the young girl said.

"Will you be here tomorrow?"

"And where else would we be; since we do not have any place else to go."

"Very good, I'll return at 9:00 AM, to pick you up."

I port away to the lodge. After I leave, Samantha and her grandmother go into a dialog.

"Grandmother I don't trust him."

"Why, what has he done to deserve your anger and distrust?"

"Nothing, but I have been burned by other men, all they want is what they can take."

"I do not think he is like that daughter, what did he do for you this evening?"

"He may have saved my life, and now he wants to give us a place to live, for no reason."

"He has a reason granddaughter."

"Well grandmother what is his reason?"

"He wants to learn, that is his reason."

"You will be here tomorrow daughter, and we will go with him, I think you will see that not all men are takers, as you believe."

The next morning, I put on my latex mask, and a nice suit of clothes, when I'm finished sprucing up CAT tells me it is time to be in New York, so I port outside their door, and I knock.

"Come in"

I heard their response, so I open the door and enter.

"Good Morning Grandmother."

As I bow to her. I also bow to the girl.

"I see you do have manners and you do show respect. May I know your name stranger?"

"I am Steve Ball" I said.

Grandmother said "You may call me Grandmother, and this daughter is called Samantha."

"Thank You." I said. "Are you ready to go for a trip?"

"Yes" said Grandmother.

"I hold out my hand to Grandmother, and my other hand to Samantha, then I port to the lodge. It catches Grandmother off guard.

"Where are we?"

"We are in Montana in a very remote place. You can only get here by helicopter and by me. Please look around, if you like it here you may stay here, otherwise I have a small farm house in Duffer, Oregon, which is closer to a couple of towns. We can go there after you look around here."

"This place is very cold; I would like to see the other place now."

"Ok give me your hands."

I port us to Duffer and show them around.

"This is very nice. It is also remote, but I like It." says Grandma.

"Samantha says when can we move in?"

"Now if you like, I can go get your stuff, and be back shortly. Please pick any of the rooms you want. Grandma you may have the master bedroom. I can live at the lodge and come back from time to time to keep up appearances here in town. With you living here, the place will be better off. There is a truck in the barn that you can use. I'll set up an account for you to draw from, for whatever you need."

"Yea, and what will it cost us?" said Samantha. "A life of servitude?"

"The only thing I want from you."

Samantha interrupts, "See Grandma here it comes."

"Quiet daughter, let him speak, and hold your speech, until I ask for it."

"Yes, grandmother."

Grandmother glares at Samantha and Samantha lowers her head.

"Pay no attention to this unworthy daughter, what were you going to say?"

"All I want from you is to learn how to fight. I saw your daughter fight in the park, and thought that should be what I should learn, so I can deal with drug dealers and thugs without killing them."

Chapter 15

"Are you the magician they have been talking about?"

"I do not know, what is this about?"

"Well there has been talk of a man who appears then disappears taking the money and drugs from the dealers, are you this person?"

"I am."

"Then I will teach you, but answer me this question, why are you doing this?"

"I was blown up in an explosion that was supposed to kill me. But I survived, not well, so to remain hidden, I wear a mask. It looks like my real face, but it covers many scars."

I remove my latex mask. The look of disgust on Samantha's face, hurt me to the quick, but Grandma did not bat an eye. She asked the same question.

"I cannot go get another job, without calling attention to my attacker, and I need to make money so I decided this is the best way to use my gift. I now have the funds I need to wage a war on the bad guys, and I'm able to pursue some of my other dreams."

"Steve, I will teach you to fight, but you must agree to my terms, what do you say?"

"What are your terms?"

"You will be here every day and do what I say. I will be very hard on you, also I will teach you to be able to kill your opponent. So, you will not be so helpless. Only your ethics will dictate its use. I expect total compliance, when I'm teaching you."

"I place myself into your hands Grandmother." And I bow to her.

"Now son, go get our stuff, so we may live here."

A few moments later I return with all their stuff and I place it into the house in the back bedroom.

"Grandmother, I need for you and Samantha to pack a bag, I will port you to a bus station where you can catch a bus back here. Then I will pick you up with the truck and bring you back here. Or it will draw suspicion."

"You are very wise. Yes we will do as you ask."

"I'll find out when the next out of town bus will be here and where it is coming from. So, I port them to that town and get them bus fare. They board the bus and will be at the Dallas bus stop in a couple of hours. I return home to get the truck, and drive to the bus stop in the Dallas to wait for them to arrive.

As I wait, the sheriff approaches me, "Are you waiting for someone?"

"Yes, I am, I met a friend of mine, and they need a place to stay for a while they were living in New York. They had lost their home. So, I offered them mine. I'll be moving to the bunk house, but that works for me, I'll get my meals made up for me, and they get a place to live."

"Now there you go." Said the sheriff. "Have a good day, and I'll see you around."

"Thanks sheriff."

A few minutes later the bus arrives. I get out to help with their bags, and get them into the truck. At the farm, I take the bags in and move my stuff out to the bunk house. Then before I return to the lodge, I say good bye to Grandmother. As I get ready to leave, Grandmother stops me with a word.

"We will start tomorrow, be here at 6:00 AM for the start of your training."

I bow to grandmother and tell her I'll be here.

"Grandmother, I will not teach him!"

"No daughter you will not teach him, but you will work with him and you will do as I say."

"I will not like it; I can barely stand to be near him."

"I cannot direct your heart child, but I can make you obey, what you will feel for him is your own choice. You must make that decision on your own. I will tell you this, this man has honor, and does not lie as others have. Daughter I also tell you this, you are not worthy of this man, despite what he looks like." "We'll see grandmother what kind of a man he is. Starting tomorrow, and I tell you this. I will not hold back, just because he is learning."

"Good! I have a feeling he would resent it if you held back."

The next morning, I arrive at 6:00 AM dressed in regular street clothes ready to start my training. Grandmother is waiting outside and Samantha is beside her. Grandmother walks up to me and pokes and prods me with her cane, then exclaims.

"You are fat and weak. You move like an ape. I need to start from scratch here. Ok, you will start by running ten miles a day, so get started and I want you to keep up with Samantha. Now go."

I chase Samantha for ten miles, and I was never so tired, I collapsed at grandmother's feet when we returned.

"Get up Steve, you are just getting started."

I was thinking the Marine Corps had nothing on Grandmother. I get up feeling tired, but I asked for this. The next thing is to do more stretching and exercises, I'm aching by the end of the day, Grandmother decides I need a different menu for all my meals, so I'm obligated to eat with them, I'm given one day off, to be by myself at the lodge. I decide I will need to have some kind of communication with Grandmother and Samantha, so I get CAT to order a special communications device I can leave at the house in Duffer.

A week later I'm running, and exercising much better when Grandmother changes it up. She has Samantha and me on a mat in the work shop. Grandma would tell Samantha what to show me, and I would try it. Samantha does not pull any punches. After the first days of working out, I'm so sore from top to bottom, and bruised in places where Samantha has hit me. After dinner, I port home, to the lodge, and find my way to a very hot bath.

"CAT has my communication device arrived yet?"

"Yes Steve, it is at Rudy's."

"Ok, I'll call him tomorrow and have him deliver it to the lodge."

I finish my soak in the tub. And tomorrow, I'll call Rudy to come and deliver the device, and some supplies.

"CAT, contact the store in Kalispell for the usual supplies, and make the payment to them.

I finish my hot soaking in the tub, and go to bed, to just crash. I do not get up all night, and in the morning CAT has to rouse me out of bed. I think I'll shut CAT off for waking me up with the Marine Corp anthem.

"CAT, I'm going to turn you off for this." I growl.

"Steve you did want me to wake you up."

"It is bad enough that grandmother and Samantha, beat me from head to toe, like I was in the military and now you, with your wakeup call."

"Steve, you need to call Rudy."

"You're right."

I go to the radio, to call Rudy. Are you up for a delivery today? There is a part I need, that should have been delivered to your door yesterday."

"I can do that; will the supplies be here as well?"

"Yes, I contacted them and they should have my supplies delivered to you this morning."

"I will be there this afternoon."

"I'll see you when you get here Rudy."

Well the afternoon arrives and Rudy does not show up.

"CAT locate Rudy for me."

"Steve, he has crashed, his wreck is located at the base of the mountain, from the satellite picture, he is not moving and he may be hurt."

"I'd better go see if he is Ok."

I port to his location thanks to CAT. I move to the damaged helicopter.

"Rudy, are you Ok?"

I hear nothing, I manage to get the door open, and he is unconscious.

"CAT he is badly injured and will not survive the night. I will have to take him to the hospital."

"Steve, you should return here and put on your suit, so you will not be known."

"Ok, CAT."

I port back to the lodge, suit up, and then port back to Rudy. I take his hand and port us to the hospital in Kalispell. I scare off a few of the orderlies, then a doctor approaches.

"What happened?"

"He was in an accident, and I brought him here, do you know who he is?"

"My good Lord, that is Rudy, does his wife know about this?"

"I doubt it, his helicopter is at the bottom of a mountain, or at least that is where I found him."

"Nurse Get him admitted, and I need all the tests run NOW!"

The nurse takes Rudy on the gurney into a room and removes his clothes for doing the usual procedures. I port away right in front of the doctor.

Chapter 16

Back at the lodge.

"CAT monitor Rudy at the hospital, as I want to know when he is out of danger, I'm going to call his wife."

I placed the call, and Rudy's wife answered the radio.

"Steve, my husband is in the hospital. I received a call just moments ago. I'm on my way to the hospital now. I do not know how we are going to pay for all this?"

"Tell you what you let me worry about it, you just go take care of your husband, I'll be fine."

"But all the supplies, and the special part Rudy was bringing you. How will we ever…."

"Not to worry, I can order another part, and the supplies; well they can be replaced."

"Thank you, Steve." And she turns off the radio.

"Steve you caused quite a stir about your saving Rudy, and you're leaving the hospital."

"CAT can you guess what it would have been like if I was without my suit and had done that?"

"Steve it appears that the Doctor, may be a friend."

"How is that CAT, he told the Police, and the reporters that you walked in and walked out. All you said was take care of this man. He might be worth paying him a visit."

"Thanks CAT I may just do that."

"Well now I have to go face the music with Grandmother. I missed today's breakfast, and lunch, she is going to want to know why. You know something CAT, I'm beginning to love that old bird. Well off to my scolding."

I port to Duffer, knock on the door, and it is opened by grandmother.

"Where were you Steve?"

"I will not offer an excuse; I will however give you a fact. A friend of mine crashed his helicopter in to a mountain, and I saved his life. He is in the hospital fighting for his life, and I hope you can find it in your heart to forgive me. Also, if you could give me a day off tomorrow I need to see to his bills. I'll see if I can get him a new helicopter as well."

"Steve you have both, you are a good man, and I will never doubt you're not showing up again. Now go eat and take your day off. But you will still do your exercises, do you understand?"

"Yes Grandmother, I do not wish to be a flabby man."

I lean down and kiss her on the cheek, and she looks deep into my eyes.

"Go on, get to the table, you kept me waiting long enough!"

And she whacks me on the bottom as I pass her on my way to the dinner table.

The next day, I do my exercises, put my battle suit back on, and port to the hospital in the back so as not to be seen. CAT has provided me a layout of the good Doctor's office. I port into his office to inquire about Rudy's condition, but the doctor is not there as he is out and about looking in on his patients. I wait there in his office until he returns. After he recovers from seeing me he asks me what I want there. I tell him I'm here to see about the pilot I brought in. I find out that he has a concussion, broken leg, and he would have bled to death if I had not brought him there. A knock at the door, and the doctor springs up to get it so the nurse will not have to enter.

"Thanks nurse, and please see that I'm not disturbed for the next half hour." He closes the door and turns to me.

"Who are you?"

"That I cannot tell you, not that I don't want to, but it is necessary. I would be putting you and this hospital into danger if I did."

"How did you find Rudy?"

"Let's just say, I have a special communication system and I was informed where to look. I was glad to find him."

"Stranger, if I were to need you, how would I contact you?"

"For now, contact Rudy's business by phone, and have them call a man named Steve, Rudy does not know it but I have a tap on his radio, and I'll respond in kind. Do not tell anyone about this, or you may become a target. You may call on me in great need, I'll do what I can."

"Thank you, stranger."

"Please call me Paladin."

"I can think of no better name, and I will keep this secret."

I shake the doctor's hand and tell him that I will be back to check on Rudy.

"Well to ease your mind friend, Paladin, Rudy will recover. It will just take some time is all."

"Thanks, Doctor."

"Call me Donald."

"Sure, thing Donald. I may see you around, but you may not know me."

"Good, now get out of here."

I port back to the lodge.

"That went well Steve."

"Thanks CAT, I may want to give the good doctor, a more direct link to reach us. CAT see to it that Rudy's bills are paid, and that his wife, gets enough money for her needs as well, until Rudy can take care of himself."

"Yes Steve, Rudy's only source of income is the helicopter, and the insurance will only cover part of it." "CAT check his records and see what Rudy is rated for as far as a chopper goes. Maybe we can get him a better one, like military grade, something larger, and faster."

"Steve I will do some searching and I'll have some options for you tomorrow."

I port back to the farm, to have dinner and let Grandmother know I'll be there for lessons tomorrow morning.

"Here Grandmother, I have a communications device to give you, so you can reach me anytime you want."

She reaches out to me and I put it into her hand, and she gives it to Samantha.

"You take care of it."

Samantha, just gives me a look that could kill. I think, I'm going to feel that tomorrow during my lesson. I'm not wrong, the next morning after the exercises Samantha teaches me what to do as far as the lesson, but she beats the tar out of me during the sparring. I return to the lodge to recover by soaking in the hot tub.

"Steve, you are being called."

"By who CAT?"

"It is the Doctor."

"Can you put him through to me?"

"Here Steve."

"Paladin, are you there?"

"Yes, Donald, what do you need?"

"Someone was here, asking about you, he claims he is a reporter, but I know a government man when I see one."

"Thanks, Don, I'll keep a low profile.

"CAT, check into that and see what you can find out. Also, did you look into the items I asked for yesterday?"

"Yes Steve, Rudy was an Army pilot, and earned a purple heart during the last war, so he can fly a military grade chopper."

"Did you locate a new one for me?"

"Yes Steve, a new chopper will be ready for delivery, at the end of the month. Already painted, I took the liberty to add the radio to the chopper. With Two external carriers for Search and Rescue needs, I also added a winch that is rated up to a thousand pounds."

"So, after the damage, how much money do we have to operate with?"

"After I paid for the Helicopter, and Rudy's bills, we have a million left."

"Is there anything brewing in the drug or weapons running industry that I may interfere with?"

"Several Steve, some of them are expecting you and have planted bombs in the case with the money, and some with homing devices."

"I guess I had to figure on that, which one will be the least problematic?"

"The deals without problems, don't have much money involved, you could do like you did last time, hit multiple times. I have the time schedules, and you can do four of them this time and they are widely scattered."

"When do we start CAT?"

"Tomorrow night Steve."

"What is the time table?"

"We will start, in New York at midnight, then Orlando Florida, Huston Texas, and the last one in Las Vegas. We will need to be timed down to the second Steve, will you permit me to trigger your teleporting?"

"Between each place no problem CAT, but at the location, I may need to make that decision." "As you say, Steve."

I suit up and take my pistols, extra Darts, and CO_2 cartridges with me. I also decide to check the new helmet. "

"CAT send me to the first place, I want to look around, then to the next, and so on. A little looking around might make all the difference."

CAT ports me to each of the different locations so I get a chance to get the lay of the land. I return to the lodge to make a simple plan to port to a nearby place at each of the meeting locations, then I'll port into their midst and take both of the cases the drugs, and the money. The drugs to be disposed of at a volcano in Hawaii.

"Let's start the show CAT, it is almost midnight in New York."

CAT ports me to an out of the way spot near where the scheduled drop at the first location near a warehouse, is to take place. I watch from the shadows next the the warehouse as the cars pull up.

"CAT something is wrong here."

"How so Steve?"

"I cannot explain it, but this is not what it seems. I'm just going to watch; can you pick up on their conversation?"

"No Steve, can you get closer?"

"I'll try."

I port closer to one of the groups of people standing about ignoring the two cases.

"CAT it is like they want me to take the cases, I suspect it is a trap."

"Steve is it possible to port up and take the cases and go somewhere else to drop them off."

"I can, and I know the place, but after I get them will you be able to scan them?"

"I should be able to Steve."

I port up to the cases, and thanks to my new battle suit, the bullet is deflected, but I'm sure going to be bruised in the morning. I port away with the cases, both of them are rigged, one to explode, and the other has a tracking system in it, I put both of them into the lava pit and watched them burn. It seems that the gangs are working together to kill me, or at least find me so they can assonate me.

"Let's go get the other targets CAT."

The last three went off pretty much as they have in the past. I get the cases with the drugs and the money. The drugs go into the Lava pit, and the money goes to various banks to be shuffled around by CAT. CAT puts the money into two accounts, the one in Kalispell and the bank in the Dallas, this way the money trail leads to dead ends, and cannot be traced.

Now to go to Duffer to get my next lesson, I try not to show that I'm bruised by a bullet otherwise Samantha will exploit it, and I know it will hurt worse for days. As we spar I see that I'm holding my own with Samantha. Yes, I'm still getting beaten up, but not so badly. I'm actually getting in a few licks of my own. Grandmother is also impressed, and I even catch Samantha by surprise. I finished my session and returned to clean up back at the lodge. Oh a well-deserved nights rest, here I come! I get up early the next morning, and decide I need to start wearing my battle suit to the practices, so I can get use to fighting in it. When I was sparring with Samantha this time I find out that my suit is absorbing her hits, and the force field within the suit gives me more strength. For the first time I'm able to best Samantha. This angers Samantha to no end. If she ever finds out about the force fields, she will come for my blood.

Tracked by the CIA

CIA

Chapter 18

At the end of the session, I return to the lodge.

"Steve, I have traced, those people you wanted."

"Who are they CAT?"

"The CIA, according to their records you must be caught, or eliminated as soon as possible. You are considered a threat to national security since they do not control your actions, they fear you may turn against the countries best interest."

"I see; do you have the top person's name?"

"His name is Franklin Dudy."

"Does he have a family?"

"He has a wife and a small girl."

"Get me pictures of them, I think I will impress upon Franklin how dangerous I can be."

The next morning, I take my leave of Grandmother to go have a visit with Franklin. I port into his office just before he arrives. I'm sitting in his chair as he comes in, he automatically reaches for his gun. I hold up mine which I have pointed at him.

"Mr. Franklin, please sit in the chair."

He holds up his hands and sits in the chair that I indicated.

"Now what is your problem, to date I have done nothing that warrants any attention from you or your organization."

Franklin says, "You are a security risk, and you need to be brought under control, this country cannot have a loose cannon that can go anywhere and do what he pleases, as you can."

I hold up his family picture.

"Nice family, how hard do you think it would be for me to remove them to some place less hospitable than where they are?"

"You wouldn't."

"Normally you would be right. However, when you threaten my friends, neighbors or loved ones, I might reconsider what I would normally do. I would recommend that you drop your investigation and leave me to my own devices. I will assure you that I will in no way harm this country. I will defend it with my life."

"How do we know that?" said Franklin.

"I guess you will have to do that which goes against the grain, you will just have to believe me. Let me demonstrate my power."

Before Franklin can move I port to his side, and then port to the Lava Pit that I use. Franklin stands there in shock.

"What did you just do?"

"That is my power, I could have dropped you into that pit you saw, or into a worse place like a third world country prison. To date I have not killed anyone, but so far I have had two people try to kill me. One, I do not know yet, and the other is you."

Franklin says "You will have to admit that I was just doing my job."

"My self-perseveration would be to kill you. But I won't. I'm going to return you to your office, with a warning. Let it go."

I reach down and pick up a lava rock the size of my hand, and I port Franklin back to his office. I leave the rock on his desk.

"I brought you something to remind you just how dangerous I can be."

Then I port away leaving Franklin pretty shaken up.

"CAT I left a bug in his office so you can monitor him, and to let me know if he decided that I'm, a threat, or not." "Steve if he does not let it go what will you do? As you are not a killer."

"I'm not sure CAT, and you are right, I will not kill him. I might isolate him for a time, but I would not kill him."

"I heard that you threaten his family as well Steve."

"And that is all it was, a threat or better yet a bluff, I might displace him, but not his family."

"Would that not also hurt his family Steve?"

"It could, but again, my intent is to make him believe I would kill anyone.

"I'm glad to hear that Steve, after all that would be against my ethics program that you gave me."

"CAT, I will not give you one standard to follow and then I follow another, since that would be wrong, I'm not going to take life, not unless I do not have a choice in the matter."

"Thank you, Steve, I was becoming concerned."

"I have to go see Rudy, at the hospital, and then his wife. When is the new chopper being delivered?"

"It will be at Rudy's hanger this time next week."

"Thanks CAT, now I'm going to make a business deal with Rudy and his wife."

I go change my cloths and put on my latex mask, before I port to the airport, and walk up to the office.

I enter the office, to talk to Rudy's wife.

"Hi Margret!"

She is perplexed, "Steve how did you get here? The last I talked to you were still at the lodge. I have been frantic, that I could not get any supplies up to you."

"I'm fine, I used the radio to call at another airport at Helena to find another pilot who could bring me here. He'll be back in a day or two to take me back."

"I'm so glad." She said.

"Now we need to talk some, and I would like to go see Rudy, is that OK?"

"Sure, what do you want to talk about?"

"Well I took it on myself to help you both out. In a week or so a new helicopter will be arriving for Rudy.

I would like to go into business with you as a silent partner. I can cover all the bills until you get back on your feet."

Margret, throws her arms around my neck and plants a kiss on my cheek, and starts crying.

"I'm sorry if I hurt your feelings Margret."

"You didn't" she said as she wiped away her eyes.

"You just lifted a big weight from my shoulder. Let's go see Rudy, he'll be so glad, that we are not going to lose our business."

We get to the hospital, and we are entering the hallway where Rudy's room is located, I see a man there that does not seem to fit, I put on my glasses, and whisper to CAT.

"Can you identify that man?"

"Yes Steve, he is from the CIA"

I go with Margret to Rudy's Room.

"Hi Rudy, when are you going to get out of bed and go hunting with me?"

"Steve, you're here! How did you here when you can't fly, and you don't have an aircraft?"

"I have a connection or two, just in case I need them. In this case, I called in one of my favors and he brought me here. Now I have a proposal to make. And it will be profitable for everyone. I want to buy into your business, at forty nine percent. I have replaced your chopper with a military grade chopper. And it will be here next week. Another favor that I called in."

"I'm not sure Steve, I like you well enough, but I do not want to lose my business."

"You won't, I will have some deliveries to be made, and you will be able to buy me out if you decide to. However, in the meantime, you and your wife will be taken care of. Then when you are up to it, and you start flying again you can buy back my forty nine percent."

"I don't know Steve."

"Tell you what Rudy, you still own fifty one percent, you still make all the decisions, the business is still yours; all I want to do is help you out. So, you will help me out by being my taxi from time to time and dropping off my supplies. In time you may even consider hiring another pilot, and a mechanic, to help with the operation."

"That sounds good and all, but I do not want to be beholding to anyone, I want to stand on my own two feet."

"I can understand that Rudy, but sometimes, you can stand better with a friend. Besides, you'll be my boss, on top of all that I have my inventions to be shipped out to various places, and I almost have one of them ready to be sent for testing. So, quit being so bullheaded, and accept my deal. I'll bet in a year's time, you'll own the entire company."

"Ok, you are my partner."

Margret was on pins and needles during the whole discussion, hoping her husband would take my offer. She is so happy that she hugs me and gives me another kiss.

"Hey you two, I'm still here in bed you know."

And Rudy let out a loud belly laugh and shakes my hand.

"Ok, I need to go find a room in town until I can get a pilot to take me back to the lodge. By the way, I have not heard. How did they find you and get you here so fast?"

Out of the corner of my eye, I see the stranger move up to the door.

"I was unconscious when I was brought in here, I never saw or heard anything. All the doctor said was a man in a black suit and helmet dropped me off, and then left."

"That's odd, that is what I heard too, any way you get better."

"Steve, you are being recorded, and your picture taken."

"Can you mess up the picture CAT?"

"Already done, Steve."

"Margret, I'll see you at the hanger tomorrow. I have some things to take care of around town."

"Steve, you can stay at our home in the guest room."

"That is alright Margret, I'd rather have my privacy, and I'll be able to work on my inventions in the quiet."

"Ok Steve, but as soon as I get Rudy home you must come over for dinner, I make the best fried chicken you'll ever eat."

"That's no tall story either Steve, she sure does."

"I'll look forward to dinner with you two then. See you both later."

I leave the hospital, and I have a tail.

"CAT I may have to play a game here for a while, to throw this CIA person off the scent."

"Should I tell Grandmother?"

"That may be a good idea CAT, in the meantime, I'm going to play John Q plain citizen."

"For how long Steve?"

"Maybe a week, if I can lose the tail I may make a stop by Duffer to visit Grandmother."

"Well here goes, let's play cat and mouse."

I head off down the street just like I do not know I'm being followed. I get a taxi, and ride to a hotel. I register and go to my room. I quickly port to the lodge, and pick up my suit case, and return to my hotel room, a moment later

I hear a knock at the door. I open it up and the CIA man is standing in the door way. He flashes a badge at me and announces that he is from the CIA.

I ask, "What may I do for you?"

"I'm investigating the crash that involved your friend Rudy."

"What about it?"

"We are not sure, but we think that this magician guy is responsible."

"What are you talking about? What magician guy?"

"The guy who brought Rudy here. We want to know where Rudy was before he went down. We think, he shot down the Rudy's copter."

"Well if you think so, what can I do to help?"

"If I can get a chopper could you take me to your lodge, so I can look around"

"I guess so, but I thought they found the copter at the base of a mountain, not on top."

"Very true, but Rudy was shot down. He did not crash. We found evidence to support his being shot down, and we want to cover all the bases."

"When do you want to leave?" I ask.

"I can get a copter here in two days." He said.

Chapter 19

"See you in two days." I said.

He walks off, and this time I followed him.

"CAT, can you track this person? He seems to be kind of strange acting, like he wants more than he is saying."

"I'll do some checking on him Steve and will get back to you."

I port to Duffer to check in with Grandmother, and then I port back to my hotel.

"Steve, the CIA man is not what he appears to be. He was in the CIA, but got into trouble, about some missing money; like about ten million dollars."

"I wonder if he knew the previous owner of the lodge. This will bear watching. I'll be home in Two days CAT."

"Be careful Steve, he has killed several people, he may try killing you."

"I think you may be right CAT, check into the ATF and see if they indicate that the chopper was shot down."

Two days later, the CIA man shows up to my hotel, and asks if I'm ready to take a trip. We go to the airport. Where I stop in to see Margret and let her know I will be gone for a couple of days.

I get into the chopper and we take off for the lodge. It is quite most of the way there. Suddenly when we come in sight of the lodge the CIA man pulls his gun, and pushes it into my ribs, "This is where you get out."

"But we are not there yet."

"Too bad he laughs, now jump!"

I acted scared then I jump. Once I fall below the copper I port to the pond at the lodge, and it hurt hitting the water I came up spluttering and coughing.

"CAT where is the chopper now?"

"It is landing on the landing pad."

I port to the lab and put on my suit and helmet.

"I'll wager he may even know about the hidden switch for the lab. CAT I want you to shut down as much as possible without going totally off-line."

"Done Steve."

I wait in the shadows, and I do not have long to wait, sure enough both men (The CIA guy and the pilot) come down the stairs, and turn on the lights. I crouch down behind some boxes to see what they are up to.

"You killed Steve too soon, the lab is gone, the drugs, and the money."

The CIA man said, "Simmer down! He walks over to a wall, and feels along it (looking for a loose molding), then stops, here it is."

I hear a click and a panel slides open reveling a bail of money.

"See I told you we would be rich."

Then the pilot turns to the CIA man and shoots him.

"You mean I'll be rich. He laughs."

I decide to take action, I draw my gun and aim for the pilot's neck and pull the trigger. The dart hits him, and as he raises his hand to the dart, he passes out.

"CAT, come back on line." CAT powers up.

"What are you going to do with the pilot Steve?"

"He deserves death for killing his partner, attempted murder on me, and he knows of this place."

"So, are you going to kill him?"

"No CAT, but I will place him some place where he will wish he were dead."

"Where will you put him Steve?"

"I'm not sure, is there a record on the pilot?"

"Yes, Steve, he was in the military, served overseas, in the Middle East, does he know any Spanish?"

"It is not noted in his records."

"Good, I know where I will place him, get me the coordinates for a prison in Mexico."

"Steve there is a prison on a small island off the cost of Mexico, will that do?"

"Thanks CAT."

I walk over to the pilot and remove his ID, his weapons, and put the CIA credentials in his pocket. "This should, keep him out of trouble for a time."

"Steve will this not mean they will kill him?"

"That is more or less the luck of the draw, you see. If he demands to be let go, the CIA will have him. Same, as being, left in the Mexican prison. Or the Mexicans may want some satisfaction, and he will be kept. He could die either way, but it won't be by my hand."

"But Steve, by your actions you are killing him."

"No CAT, by my actions, I'm giving him a chance to live, which is more than he gave me or his partner." "I see Steve; it is his choice?"

"And the choice of his captors."

I see that the pilot is starting to come around, so I'll port him to his new home in prison."

It is very dark when we get there, and I hold him down.

"I say to him, I would not cause a ruckus if I were you the people who live here, are not partial to Americans, and especially the CIA."

"But I'm not CIA."

"Good luck convincing them of that."

I port away leaving the pilot behind. I return to the lodge. When I look into the hidden panel, I find almost twenty million in cash.

"Well CAT, I should be able to work on my other inventions with this money and help some other folks as well."

"Steve, are you not afraid that the pilot might tell someone about this place, and that you can be found here?"

"Not really CAT, when I finish my upgrades to your system, I will make this place invisible to everyone." "What about Rudy, Steve?"

"I have a thought about that too, what if an avalanche took out this mountain top, and Steve died." "How will you do that."

"I'm thinking of a holographic projection, one to simulate the slide, and the other to make it look like everything is gone, lodge and all."

"So, what happens over the years?"

"By that time CAT, no one will be interested in coming here, friend or foe."

"When will this happen?"

"Within a year, I will need to study with your help, to see if we can fake an earth quake then set the holograph in place, we will have to time it so Rudy will see it."

"In the meantime, find what you can about holographs and projectors, also if it could be possible to emit some kind of light, or sound that would keep people away from this mountain."

"When do you want the results Steve?"

"In a week, I still have some other stuff to take care of, like how do I convince the police that the dead man over there was shot and killed by the pilot."

I decide to port the body to a morgue in New York, and let them try to explain it. Now the chopper is going to be something else. Next I port the chopper back to the airport at night when no one is around. With the helicopter back at the landing pad, and my return, everyone assumes the pilot abandoned it due to cost. Anyway, Rudy could have a second chopper to move stuff about.

The Death of
Steve

Chapter 20

I spend my time about town, during the day, and at night I port back to Duffer for a quick dinner then on to the lodge to do some work. I just invented a hand-held device I call a sniffer to detect Meth. It won't replace a dog, but it could save people from being harmed by careless chemists who make Meth. I'll get a patent on it and produce several to distribute to a few police stations to see how they like it. A few days later CAT informs me there is a company that makes really good projectors, but the cost in money and energy, is prohibitive.

"CAT how effective is one projector?"

"For what you want, it will not be sufficient."

"Could we enhance it any, and how many do you calculate we would need in projector units?"

"Steve, I can order one for you to see, and we can decide from there"

"Good idea CAT, when can I pick it up?"

"I will place the order now and pay for it. You should be able to pick it up tomorrow."

"I told Grandmother, I'll not be there tonight, that I'm having dinner at Rudy's house, to celebrate his home coming."

"Steve when will you be returning by chopper to the lodge?"

"Not for at least two weeks maybe more, why?"

"We could stage your death as he leaves."

"CAT that is a very good idea, get the specs on the projector and determine what we can do to enhance them."

CAT goes to work on my request for the project, while I port to Kalispell to meet Margret and Rudy for dinner, I rent a taxi from my hotel room and am dropped off at Rudy's and Margret's home. We have a great time, and I have to admit, Margret does make the best fried chicken I have ever tasted. I talk with Rudy and Margret, about when Rudy will be able to fly, and the doctor said in three weeks.

"Good, I have some traveling to do, and some legal paperwork to finish, and then I'll be ready to get back to my lodge. I have a few inventions, that I need to finish up."

"If you are in a hurry, I can get another pilot to take you back, if you want."

"Don't worry about me Rudy, as this time here will let me take care of personal business. Besides, I'll expect another delicious dinner like this one, before I go."

Margret came over to me and planted a kiss on my cheek.

"Now that is a compliment, a woman likes to hear, are you taking notes Rudy?"

Rudy laughs, "You know, Honey that you make the best dinner of anyone."

"Now that is a compliment dear."

And we all laugh. I spend some more time with my new friends, and soon I leave for the hotel, I can use some sleep.

The next morning CAT contacts me.

"Steve, the holographic projectors are ready for pick up."

"Where are they? I will go pick them up?"

"Go to an electronics shop in Oakland, California and they will have the boxes ready for you. You will need a truck to pick them up though."

"Ok, I'll port to a U-Haul place and rent a truck, then return it later."

So, CAT locates a U-Haul place where I port close to it, and walk into the shop. Soon I have a truck to drive to the electronics store, and pick up my stuff. I return the truck to the U-Haul place, and port to the lodge with all the equipment.

"Well you have had time to go through the specs CAT? What have you figured out?"

"If we replace some of the components, with the components form a Japanese company I located, we should be able to upgrade the holographic projectors."

"Have you ordered the components from that store?"

"Yes, Steve, they will be ready for pick up tomorrow evening our time."

"Ok, I'll port to the Japanese store, walk in and then carry out the package, I will be able to carry it won't I CAT?" "Not really Steve."

"Ok, I'll take a chance and port away when they are not looking."

It takes several long nights, and between CAT's instructions and my sweat, I manage to put the system together. We do a test run in the lab and the holographic projector seems to work out just fine.

"CAT what would be the best placement of the Holographic projectors?"

CAT gives me a map with the placement instructions. After a good night's sleep, I place the Holographic projectors about the mountain and around the lodge. Then I do another test run using the holographic projectors to simulate an avalanche. The test is successful when it is run it looks like the whole mountain above the lodge has collapsed and slides down to cover the whole top of my lodge.

"CAT, we will need to access the seismologist's instruments to simulate an earthquake, can you do that?" "I can Steve, we should start simulating the earthquake now so the seismologist think nothing new is happening when we do our show."

"I agree CAT, make it happen."

The day comes when Rudy is up and about. He is anxious to try out the new helicopter. "Let's go for a spin Rudy, and in a few days, you can take me back home."

Like a kid with a new toy, Rudy checks out the copter, and fires it up. Soon we are flying around the Air field. Doing check outs, landings, and putting the copter through its paces.

"Steve with this new chopper I'll be able to fly you home in less time than before, and I can carry more weight than I could before. Thank You man!"

"The look on your face, is all I need for a thank you. You can then take me home day after tomorrow." "You got it partner."

I go to a lawyer that afternoon and have my will made up giving Rudy and his wife the whole business if anything should happen to me. The morning of the day we are to return me to the lodge. Margret fixes me breakfast. After a few hugs and a promise to return, Rudy and I take off toward the lodge.

Chapter 21

That morning I contact CAT with instructions to have the holographic projectors and the simulation ready to go into action after Rudy takes off. I set up a charge of C-4 explosive on the mountain CAT will trigger the explosion after Rudy lifts off, and then CAT will run the holographic projectors to simulate that the avalanche has decimated the lodge and the surrounding area. Rudy lands us at the lodge's landing site, so I offered to make a lunch for him.

He said "No offence, but I do have a delivery to make, so I'll say bye until next month."

I close the door after I get my bags, and step back out of the way of the chopper to watch Rudy takeoff. When Rudy is a hundred feet in the air CAT sets off the C-4 and an avalanche starts down the hill toward the lodge. CAT kicks in the holographic projections and from Rudy's perspective the whole area is devastated. He watches me and the lodge disappear in a covering of rocks. The damage does not really cover the area, but Rudy would not know that.

Rudy hovers over the area, trying to see if he can land, but the holo-projectors indicate there is no place for him to land. Rudy has lost a friend, devastated Rudy flies home to tell the police what happened. Thanks to CAT the seismic equipment showed that an earthquake triggered the land slide. The next day Rudy flies the Sheriff out to the site but they have no place to land. Officially Steve Ball of Montana died. Rudy and Margaret, get the business free and clear.

Because I care, I go see them as someone else, just to see how they are doing. I plant a listening device in their office so I can keep tabs on them for their safety.

"Well CAT we should be more secure here now that we are officially gone now, I sure hated to deceive Rudy and his wife that way, but it was necessary to secure this location. It seems too many people know of its existence."

Space Shuttle

Incident

Chapter 22

Something is about to happen that no one could have foreseen. A space shuttle was launched a few days earlier to repair a satellite that is in orbit, and with the repairs complete the astronauts prepare to return to earth.

"Ground control this is Commander Will Jakes, we are completing our final orbit, we are closing the bay doors and will be dropping out of orbit in T minus ten minutes. Just as the bay doors start to close a meteor about the size of a baseball impacts the shuttle at an angle taking out the flight controls and engines. Then it sends the space shuttle into a flat spin in orbit.

"Ground Control we have a problem! We have been hit by something according to the computers we do not have any propulsion systems, or flight controls. We are in a flat spin. Lt. Samuel is checking the condition in the cargo bay area."

Samuel looks through the window port which looks in on the cargo bay area, to sees that Captain Barry is dead. He sees a rather large hole through the back of the bay.

"Commander, we have severe damage, and Captain Barry is dead."

"That is not all" says Samuel, the meteor has put us into a flat spin. Control have you got that?" "This is Control, we hear you."

"So, Control, what are our options?"

"We'll get back to you Commander."

"Samuel, take stock of our systems. The way I see it, we will not be going home any time soon."

"Yes Commander."

An hour later.

"We have enough life support for twelve hours. If we turn off all non-essential systems we may extend the life support another three hours."

Commander Will turns off all communications.

"Samuel, they will not be able to rescue us, even if they send up a ship, which they do not have. We can't leave our ship, as we do not have an EVA (Extra Vehicular Activity) suit to travel with; Barry had it when he was hit. Also, with the EAV the flat spin of our craft will cause problems for us in attempting to leave the ship, or for anyone to come to our ship. We need to do all we can, but we are not going home."

"I understand Will."

Will turns on the communication system.

"Control, here is what we have, we can sustain our life support for a little over twelve hours, so what is the plan?"

"Commander we are still working on it, we are going to turn over every rock we can find to bring you home safely, don't give up hope."

"We hear you Control."

"You heard them Samuel."

"Yes Commander."

The reporters at Control, leave the room to broad cast the news about the space mission and the trouble the astronauts are in. CAT has been monitoring the space mission since it left earth and knows that the Astronauts are doom to a cold death in space.

"Steve, there is a problem that only you may help solve."

"What is the problem CAT?"

"Have you seen the news Steve?"

"No, I have been exercising and sparring with Samantha, I'm sore from all the hits, and I'll be back at the Lodge as soon as I take my leave of Grandmother."

I go see Grandmother and give her my thanks and respect then I port to the Lodge.

"CAT what is so important?"

CAT tells me of the situation of the space mission.

"Steve, the space mission flew in to space a week ago to fix and upgrade a satellite. They were hit by a meteor which killed; one of the crewmen of the shuttle. There is no back up ship to bring them down. Even if there were, the space craft is in a flat spin, spinning in a yaw direction, and they do not have an EVA to leave the ship."

"Steve you are the only possible hope they have."

"How do you mean, I'm their only hope? I have no way to port on to that ship. If I did I would be splattered all over the inside of the ship. Because of the difference in speed of the earth as compared to the ship, so tell me how I would save them?"

"I can cause you to port next to the ship. Where you could use a harpoon to attach yourself to the ship, then you can reel yourself into the cargo bay. The next part will be tricky, as you will have to blow the nose off the shuttle and bring the nose section down into the ocean, to absorb the impact of the different velocities of the ship and the earth. Steve you may not survive that teleport."

"Will it save the two people on the ship CAT?"

"Yes, Steve the odds are they will survive."

"CAT do I have a chance to survive?"

"Steve that is an unknown. I cannot predict your chances, if you'll survive, you will be in their hands."

"Will you be able to port me out?"

"Only if you are conscious."

"Contact the space agency and outline the situation to them. One thing I will need is to have an explosives expert to show me how to set the explosives to separate the nose from the rest of the shuttle so I don't kill us all up there."

"Steve, I have contacted the Space agency, they seem to think I'm a crackpot."

"Well let's show them I'm not, can you port me into the control room?"

"Any time you want to go Steve."

"I'll get suited up and then let's go impress the folks."

CAT ports me into the control room.

"Who is in charge here?" Steve asks.

The people around the room look up in shock.

"I'm in charge here, what are you doing here? We are in a situation, and don't need a buffoon getting in the way."

"Buffoon am I."

I port over to the head man place a hand on his shoulder and port him to the lodge, in the lab room. "We have a proposal to save your men, and you call me a Buffoon."

"Where am I?"

"In my lab, CAT show him what you have."

CAT shows and explains the scenario of how to bring down the men. He does not reveal what can happen to Steve.

"OK, Paladin or whoever you are, I'll do whatever it takes to help you."

I port the head man back to the control room.

"I'll be back in an hour you know what I need."

"All right people this is how it is going to go down. Contact the shuttle and let them in on what we are going to do. CAT, show us what is going to go on here. Let's make this plan work people."

I return to the space agency in an hour and get fitted with a space suit. I receive some instruction on how the suit works. My Harpoon arrives, and the special cord that I requested is supplied. The cord will stretch three hundred percent of its length. This will help me to reach the shuttles velocity. Then a Marine sergeant soon shows up to show me what to do for setting the charges, and how to set them off, in order to blow off the space shuttles nose. To make this work I have to port to a place on earth where the shuttle will pass directly above me then teleport up into the space shuttles orbit.

"Well CAT, I'm all most ready. I just need to put on the space suit and collect all the gear. When I'm ready to go, the astronauts will only have about four hours of life support left."

"CAT how much more time?"

"Steve, I will port you in 3, 2, 1."

CAT ports me to the location in Africa then up into space.

"Wow! This is so cool. Ok CAT where am I in relation to the shuttle."

"Steve they should be coming from the East of your position."

"I see them; they are moving pretty fast"

"Steve don't miss the shot."

I take aim but the ship is out of range, so I port closer to the shuttle then take aim and fire the harpoon. The force of it pushes me in the opposite direction. Yet the spear penetrates the tail of the shuttle. Then the cord stretches until I reach the end of its limit allowing me to reach the velocity of the shuttle. What I did not expect was that the tail of the shuttle in its flat spin to wind me up to the shuttle much faster than intended. I have to time this strategy just right as I'm pulled over the open cargo bay. I port inside and bounce around the cargo bay area of the shuttle. Then I catch a pad eye for tying down cargo and manage to stop myself. I carefully approach the window, and knock on the door. Crewman Samuel sees me and starts to shout for joy.

I hold up a sign telling them I'm going to set the explosives and then enter the cabin. It takes thirty minutes to place the charges around the shuttle bay area so between the bulkheads of the shuttle command so it will separate the nose from the rest of the shuttle when CAT sets off the charges. I insert the electronic detonation caps. Then I make a final check to make sure that I did it the way the Sargent had told me to. I want to separate the nose from the shuttle not blow us up. Satisfied with the placement of the charges and how they are set up, I move back to the window. By this time both crew members are at the window. I wave them back away from the area and I port inside the cabin. The commander and Samuel help me out of my space suit. I explain what is about to take place, and ask them to turn off all communication. I have another request to ask of them. When they agree to my request and then communicate down to Control to let them know we are almost ready to come down.

"CAT when do we start the fireworks?"

"Who are you communicating to?" asks Will.

"You would not believe me if I told you, but suffice it to say, CAT is my personal friend, who got me here."

"I sure hope he knows what he is doing then."

"Rest assured, he does. Now everyone strap in as the ride is about to get real rough and remember my request when we get down." (The Request was to protect him from being taken by the FBI or CIA if possible).

"Steve you are going to be in position in 5, 4, 3, 2, 1 and now."

CAT sets off the explosives that separates the nose from the shuttle.

"Steve wait, as once the nose is slowing down, and I detect the proper moment, Steve port down now."

I port the shuttle nose to the position not far from the rescue ship as discussed, we drop into the water and sink like a rock, Will and Samuel come around and note we are underwater.

"Samuel check our rescuer and see how he is."

"Will, he is alive, but unconscious. He said this may happen."

"Then we will protect him as we said we would."

Within the hour, the nose of the shuttle is brought aboard the ship. After another hour the door is cut open to let the crew out of the nose. Paladin is still out of it. The Captain of the ship tells them to take them all down to sickbay for a checkup.

Paladin and the shuttle crew are taken to Sickbay, Paladin is placed in a bed, and two armed marine guards are placed outside the door to their room. Will also notices a couple of men in black if you will, Government men that is.

"We need to wake Steve up! Samuel block the door and we'll hold out as long as we can."

Samuel closes the door and bars it with a chair.

"Paladin, wake up! You have to come around. Please, we do not have much more time."

They shake him roughly, Paladin comes around for just a few moments, and then CAT ports him to Duffer into the living room of the house.

Will and Samuel, are arrested and put into the brig per the men in black, they want to know where Paladin went. The charge is for letting Paladin escape.

"Well sir we cannot tell you, what we do not know."

"Well Commander and Lt, you will both be broken down to privates."

"Well sir, we're Navy men, we would be taken down to Seaman, not privates."

"So be it, you will be broken down to Seaman. Do you not know what you have done? You have let a man who can invade any country, or any place in the country and take state secrets, and sell them? We wanted him so we could contain him and keep him from doing this kind of damage. Commander you and the LT. will pay dearly for this."

The Government men leave. Will starts to laugh.

"What is so funny Commander?"

"In all honesty, they cannot do anything to us. When we appear on TV, we can tell the whole world about a man who was willing to save us and bring us home, at the expense of his own life."

Several days later the shuttle crew is brought to the White House for a press conference.

The press, and the President call on the Commander and the LT to commend them on a job well done. When Will steps up to talk to the press he talks about a man called Paladin and how he saved their lives. He is the one who deserves all the credit. Otherwise, the whole crew would have died in space. There was not a dry eye in the whole place. Then the outcry started; who is Paladin, why does he not come forward? Will explains that he was hurt, and for now he may not even be alive; I hope he is. And they end the press conference. The next day it is in all the papers that Paladin is a hero.

Chapter 23

I lay on my back on the floor of the living room in Duffer, Grandmother finds me first.

"Son, what are you doing here?"

After a few minutes' grandmother realizes I'm hurt.

"Samantha, get out here, Steve is here and injured, I need to get him in bed and out of his clothes." "Grandmother where do we put him?"

"We'll put him in your bed."

"My bed!"

"Yes, your bed."

They drag me to Samantha's bed room and somehow, they get me out of my suit and helmet, then wrestle me into Samantha bed.

"Grandmother where will I be sleeping?"

"Until I know more about what is wrong with Steve you need to stay close to him, so you can wake me if necessary."

"I'm not sleeping in bed with him."

"No Daughter you will sleep on a cot over there."

"Yes Grandmother."

On her way back to her room Grandmother picks up the helmet, and while she is looking inside of it CAT speaks to her.

"Grandmother, Steve has lost a lot of vital energy, and it will need to be replaced, he will need a lot of rest."

"Who are you strange one?"

"Steve calls me CAT."

"Who are you cat?"

"For now, Grandmother I'm a friend and I need Steve to get well. I will try to do all I can to help him that is why I ported him to you. Now put the helmet next to Steve and I can help keep an eye on him. If you need to talk to me just touch the helmet and talk to me, I'll hear you anytime you might want to talk to me. Also, if necessary, I can wake you if Steve needs you."

"Very good one named Cat."

Grandmother puts the helmet next to Steve.

"What do we do one named Cat?"

"Grandmother let him sleep for today, we'll try to wake him tomorrow. It takes a week before I came to. "Hey I called out, where am I?"

Grandmother came quickly into the room.

"Steve, my son you are awake."

"How did I get here?"

"The one named Cat brought you here."

"Well, help me up. Please"

"No, you have to rest"

"Grandmother help me up!"

"No son, you are too weak to sit up yet."

"Ok, I'll just have to do that myself."

As hard as I try I cannot even move an arm.

"What is wrong with me, CAT what is wrong with me?"

"Steve, your vital energy was drained so low it almost killed you, but you are healing."

"How long will it take before I'll be fit again?"

"Steve it will take some time, as much as a couple of months."

"Months, but my muscles will start to atrophy."

"That is why I brought you to Grandmother. They will take care of you."

"Ok, I will put myself in her hands, and I'm sure I'll be sore before this is all over. CAT you did good. Did I save the astronauts?"

"Yes Steve, you did, and you have become a national hero."

"I'm not much of a hero, I just did what I can, nothing more."

Grandmother is standing there and hears the whole story but said nothing. She smiles down at me and places a hand on mine.

"I love you my son, you have done well. You are the best man I have had the pleasure to know."

I fall back asleep that little bit of talking exhausted me. The next day, Grandmother and Samantha, started exercising my arms, legs, and neck. I find muscles in my body that I did not know that I had. I was so sore when they finished working with me. I spend most of my days resting, and the two women in my life take care of me. They feed me, clean me and look over me. I realize that I love them both. I love grandmother as a mother, and Samantha as a sister. I would have liked Samantha to be more than a sister, but I will settle for that as a relationship.

It takes many months to recover, when I can walk. I move out to the bunk house and give Samantha back her room. In another month I'm jogging, and soon after that I'm back to running my ten miles, and back to sparring with Samantha. My speed is still slow, but over time I make a full recovery. I have yet to try teleporting, CAT advises me against doing it for the time being.

"Steve, I have ordered another communications device for Grandmother."

"Not a bad idea CAT, when will it be here?"

"Tomorrow, Steve."

I run off, to get in my evening run.

"Well daughter what do you think of Steve now?"

"I do not understand what you mean grandmother?"

"Do you still distrust and hate this man?"

"Yes, grandmother I do."

"Do you not know what he has done?"

"No grandmother, what has he done to deserve, such praise from you?"

"Well my foolish daughter, listen to what I have to say. Steve is more than you will ever know. As you know he has been in war with the Drug Lords taking their money and drugs to prevent them from being peddled to people. Then he just risked his life to save those men trapped in space."

"What are you talking about, he took the money from the drug lords to further his own agenda, and what about the men from space, I have not heard."

"You are still so stubborn, have you learned, nothing? Steve was lying in our house dying, until we helped him. He had just saved those men from dying in space. If you do not believe me go look it up at the library."

"I don't believe you."

"Then don't believe me, go check it out for yourself."

"I will."

Samantha takes a trip to the library to do research and discovers that all her grandmother has said is true. Speaking to herself Samantha decides to prove grandmother to be wrong about men. That night after Steve goes to his room in the bunk house, Samantha dresses up in a revealing outfit, and goes to Steve's room. I hear a knock at my door and when I open it Samantha is standing there all dolled up. "What do you want Samantha?"

"I found out that you are a hero and I wanted to reward you for saving those men from dying."

"What do you mean reward me?"

"Do you want me Steve?"

"I'm sorry, what do you mean want you?"

The Domestic life

Chapter 24

"I'm going to make love to you Steve."

"No, you won't."

"Why not? You are a man; all men want to have a woman."

"Samantha, not all men take advantage of women. When I make love to a woman, she will be my wife, not a stray cat."

"But..."

I port to the lodge leaving Samantha alone.

"Steve, what is wrong?"

"I just ran away form a very pretty woman, and one I cared about, before my accident. I would have loved to marry her, and she just threw herself at me."

"And you did nothing Steve?"

"That's right CAT."

After I left Samantha, she falls to her knees, sobbing.

"What have I done?"

Samantha lays there crying. Sometime later grandmother shows up and walks in, not knowing what to expect. Samantha is lying there by herself crying, and when grandmother kneels down beside her. "Daughter what happened?"

Between sobs "I threw myself at him. He turned me down and left, what have I done. I'm so stupid about men."

"Daughter, I have tried to help you understand, but in the end, you still have to learn it on your own." Samantha looks up at grandmother.

"What will I do? As scared as he is, I have fallen in love with him, now he hates me."

Grandmother tilts up Samantha's face.

"Daughter, listen to me, Steve has been in love with you ever sense he brought us here, he will forgive you."

Wiping her eyes "Do you really think he will forgive me?"

"Apologize to him and explain why you did what you did. He may not like it, but he will realize you really care for him."

"But he is not coming back."

"He will daughter, he needs more training, and he left his helmet here."

"Then I have a chance."

Samantha runs back to the house to get Steve's helmet. She finds it where he left it on the counter. Holding it close to her, she whispers "Steve, please come back, I'm so sorry."

In mere moments Steve returns.

"Samantha?" Samantha looks up, drops the helmet and rushes in to Steve's arms.

"Please forgive me."

"Sure, I'll forgive you."

Samantha lifts up her face to look into his eyes.

"I need to talk to you."

"Ok, Samantha."

First, she said, "Call me Sam."

"Sure, Sam I'll be glad to, anything else?"

"Yes, let me explain my actions."

"Shall we go for a walk Sam, I know it is night time, but we can walk to the edge of town and back."

"Ok, I have a lot to tell you."

"I promise I will listen."

Grandmother enters and is wearing a smile like the cat who got into the cream.

"Now you children scoot and do not stay out too late."

And both of us say "yes grandmother."

During our walk Samantha tells me of her past boyfriend and how she became pregnant with his child, I was expecting him to marry me, but he ran off with another woman leaving me to fend for myself and a baby to come. Then I had a miscarriage and lost the child. I became very bitter. Every man I encountered until you, has always wanted and never give in return. When I came to you tonight it was to prove you were no different than any other man, wanting and not giving. But instead of taking what I offered, you told me no, and left. I realized that I had fallen in love with you and may have just lost you.

"Steve, I do not deserve you, but if you will have me as a wife, I will honor you as my husband for the rest of my life."

Steve says "don't take this wrong, but I need to think about this, before I answer you. This is a bit sudden for me, I'll give you my answer tomorrow."

I port us back to the house, and then I port to the lodge. What I wanted has been handed to me, but why am I not excited about it? is what happened to her bothering me? Besides, would another woman have me?

"Steve."

"Yes CAT?"

"I know what is bothering you."

"Oh, what is that CAT?"

"You wanted a partner, now you have one."

"So why am I bothered CAT?"

"Because you do not believe it yet Steve."

"Thanks CAT, I do love her, I do need her and I do want her. CAT where can I get a nice wedding ring set tonight."

"Steve as late as it is, France will be the best place to go."

"I'll be back in a bit." I go up to my costume room and put on a latex mask, and some clothes more fitting for my trip to France. I put on my communication devise and my glasses.

"CAT I will need you to translate for me and help me communicate to the shop owner."

I port to France, and CAT locates a jewelry store for me, I soon have a ring and I port back to the lodge. "CAT do you know if Sam is awake right now?"

"She is awake Steve."

"I'll be right back CAT."

I port to the living room and clear my voice.

"Samantha are you awake?"

Samantha rushes out of her room.

"I'm here Steve."

I get down on one knee and hold up the ring box.

"Samantha, will you marry me?"

She burst into tears and kneels down beside me and peels off my mask, and kisses my face, then she starts crying and laughing.

"OH, yes Steve I will be your wife!"

I slip the engagement ring on to her left hand and hug her.

"Samantha you have made me very happy."

Chapter 25

Grandmother is standing in her door way, all smiles.

"Hey you two, keep it down out here, I'm trying to get my beauty sleep."

And she rushes over to be included in the hug.

"Now off to bed both of you, tomorrow we will have a lot of work to do."

"I'll see you in the morning Grandmother, Samantha."

I return back to the lodge. I sleep in that morning quite pleased with what has happened, I'm going to be married. I arrive at midmorning in Duffer, I knock on the door. It gets flung open and Samantha literally jumps into my arms after a great show of affection, she drags me into the house.

"Grandmother and I have been making plans for a simple wedding, do you want to hear what we have been planning?"

"I would love to."

They both outline what they would like to do for the wedding. What it all boiled down to is the wedding would be Japanese style. Then I was asked if I would take them to Grandmother's old village. So, after agreeing to their demands I ask the most critical question.

"When will we get married?"

They turned to one another, then back to me and said "April 14th. All the spring flowers, and the blossom trees will be blooming."

"I laugh, and say, Ladies of my life, your wish is my command."

They both turn to each other and start jumping up and down and hugging each other.

I think to myself, what have I gotten myself into.

"Well Ladies, I'm going to go do some other things, so you can make your plans, Samantha, come here for a moment."

I pull the ear jack from my pocket and give it to her.

"With this you can reach me, almost anytime."

I walk over to pick up my helmet.

"I'll be back this evening." Said Steve

"Bye Honey, we'll have dinner ready for you."

I port to the lodge and go to put on my battle suit.

"CAT locate Commander Will; I would like to pay him a visit to thank him."

"Steve here are the coordinates"

"Very good, CAT."

I port to Florida to a very nice back yard. Off to my right I see a man in a hat planting flowers.

"Hello, where can I find Commander Will?"

The man stands up and tilted his hat back.

"That would be me stranger, what are you doing here?"

"We did not get a chance to know each other at the time, but my name is Paladin, I saved your life, and you protected mine. I just stopped by to say thank you for that."

Will sticks his hand out for a hand shake.

"I want to thank you Paladin, you saved our lives, and now I'm retired. I enjoy what I'm doing. If Samuel were here he would also thank you too. I would offer you a drink or coffee, but you would have to remove your helmet, so I understand."

I take my leave of Commander Will, and return to the lodge, where I change my clothes to go meet the ladies. I port to the front porch, and knock. Samantha opens the door and pulls me into the house. Samantha is excited and shows me all her plans. I tell her that they are wonderful, and I ask what's my part in the ceremony is, and do I need to have anything? I'm given a list of things to do, and by the time the women finish telling me what they have planned I ask. "What's for dinner?"

"Dinner?" Samantha says.

"Yes, you know the last meal of the day."

"We totally forgot about dinner."

"Well I sort of figured you would do that so let's go out."

"Steve it is very late, there is nothing open here at this time of the day."

"I think I can find a place, so if you ladies would each take an arm, we can get going."

I port us to Japan. Tokyo to be precise, and we soon find a restaurant. Armed with my glasses and ear phone I'm not left to wonder what I have ordered. Grandmother watches me the whole time to see what I would do, but she then realized I'm talking to CAT. What I find amusing is that Samantha, cannot read or speak Japanese either. So, I lent Samantha my glasses, and the ear phone.

"These glasses are a marvelous invention Steve."

"Thank you." I said.

When we have finished our dinner, we go for a walk, and Grandmother is our tour guide.

"Steve, where do you want to go for our honeymoon?"

"Right now, I do not know. I would like to go someplace special though."

"If you were to choose?" pressured Samantha."

"Well, how does Paris sound?"

"You're kidding right?"

"Samantha, you forget, I can take us to anyplace on the planet."

"That's right, you can, I would love to go to Paris, under one condition."

"Setting terms my beloved?"

"Not really Steve, I want a pair of glasses like yours, and the ear phone too."

"Well that was to be a wedding gift for you is that ok?"

Samantha grabs me in a hug and buries her face into my chest, then looks up at me.

"This wedding, is the greatest gift I could ask for."

"Well I hope there will be other gifts just as good."

I reach out and move her raven colored hair to one side.

"Samantha, you are the greatest gift I could ever hope for."

Grandmother just stands there and watches for a few moments, for her this is also a great gift; Steve and Samantha together. Maybe I'll yet see a great grandchild before I pass on. She thinks.

I return us to Duffer and head off to bed. In the morning I remember in amongst all the things I need to do, is come up with two friends who will stand with me. I contact CAT.

"CAT is Dr. Donald busy and can I catch him at his office?"

"He is there Steve, but he has been bugged by the FBI, I do not know if he knows it."

"I see."

I go to my makeup room and make a new mask, and put on a hospital maintenance uniform, and port to a closet at the hospital in Kalispell. I take out one of my calling cards a knight (Knight in full armor, not a chess piece) with the word Paladin on it. On the back of the card, I write, change your clothes and meet me in the parking lot. After I give the card to the doctor, I put the cart away and port to the parking lot to wait. Soon I see the doctor come out and head for his car, and I intercept him before he can get there.

"Doctor Donald."

"I'm sorry sir, but I have to meet someone can you not talk to me later?"

I restrain the good doctor and tell him.

"I'm Paladin, thanks for coming, please come with me we are being watched."

I lead the doctor around the corner and port us to the lodge.

"Where are we?" asks Donald.

"This is my place, and you can talk freely here, none of the bugs that you are wearing will work."

"What do you need of me my friend?"

"I need someone to give away my bride. Her parents are dead and I was hoping you would be willing to do that for me."

"You get me out of the hospital for something like this, when I'm needed in surgery, in a few minutes."

"I'm sorry about the timing Donald, but my time is running out too, if you do not wish to help me, I'll find someone else."

"Well after you saved the Space crew, how could I turn you down, when and where?"

I tell him the date and then the place. "Japan!"

"Yes."

"I don't have the time or the money to get there."

"Not to worry, I'll take care of the transportation. I can pick you up and return you all in the same day."

"Ok, I'll do it, now take me back, I have an important operation to do."

I port the doctor to his office and leave him there.

"I'll contact you Donald for the where and when to meet."

Then I port away. My next destination is Florida, I port into Will's garden, to find him working away.

"Steve, watch what you say, this place is covered in electronic bugs."

"Thanks CAT."

I take a card out and write, how would you like to take a short trip from here? Will looks up at me, and nods yes. I put my hand on him and port us to the lodge.

"Where are we?" Will asks.

"it's best not to tell you, CAT are we clear, can we talk here?"

"Yes Steve, all the bugs are disabled here."

Will asks "What do you want of me?"

"To be my best man at my wedding."

"WHAT!"

"If you don't want to I'll understand."

"You came to my house knowing I'm being watched, to ask me to be your best man?"

"Yes."

Will looks at the floor, then starts laughing.

"You know, I would be honored to be your best man, and can you imagine what this will do to the men in black? When and where?"

"It will be in Japan and I give him the date and time."

"I see knowing you is going to be amazing. Where do you want me to be so you can pick me up?"

"I will drop a letter at the spot where you were digging, about the particulars."

"You got yourself a Best Man, and a mighty proud one too."

With that settled, I return Will back to his home, and then leave.

I return to the women to let them know that I have a man to give Samantha away, and another one for my best man. Samantha plants a kiss on my check, (when I don't have my latex mask on I don't have any lips, as they were burned off).

"That sounds great Steve, and I have someone to be a bride's maid for me, but we'll need to go see her." "We can do that now if you like?"

"Would you?"

"All I need is where she lives and we can go."

Samantha provides me the address for her friend.

"CAT, give me the coordinates to the nearby alley, be sure no one see us."

We port to the alley outside of the building where Samantha's friend lives. Samantha can hardly contain herself. We go up to the door and announce ourselves. The reunion is rather tearful, and the two women put their heads together. There is a lot of talking, and giggling going on in the girl's bedroom. Soon I hear what sounds like squealing and the then words Yes! Many times.

Soon Samantha returns, and I can see from her face that she is going to ask a favor of me. "Steve, can you leave me here for tonight, and pick me up in the morning?"

"What time would you like me to be here?"

"9:00 in the morning?"

"Ok I'll see you tomorrow then."

I port back to Duffer, and grandmother is waiting there.

"Son, would you take me to my village, I have much to do there, and I can catchup with old friends." "Yes, grandmother, I'm beginning to feel like a taxi driver."

"What was that my son?"

"Nothing grandmother, nothing at all."

"Good, now son let's get moving."

I drop grandmother off, at her village, and warn her not to mention how she got there. I return to the lodge to get some rest; it has been a busy day.

"Steve, Steve."

"What is it CAT?"

"Time to get up, you just have time to get dressed and go pick up Samantha."

"Oh my, that's right."

I rush around and put on my latex mask, then my clothes. I port to the alley in New York and enter Samantha's friend's home through the front door.

Samantha is ready to go when I get there, her friend Tammy is there to give her a hug and say good bye. Before we leave, I talk to Tammy with Samantha there. I caution her about telling anyone about what she has seen. If you tell

113

people you will draw the interest of the Government, and some of the criminal interest. You would be putting your life at risk. Tammy says she understands, Samantha told her the same thing.

"I'll be back for you when the time comes, I recommend you go apply for a passport, and get your shots up to date."

"I will." says Tammy.

I port Samantha home to Duffer.

"Grandmother?"

"Oh, I took her to the village yesterday, at her request."

"She mentioned that she might do that."

"What I told Tammy will go for you as well. You need to go apply for a passport and get your overseas shots, and I should do the same thing."

"Are you going anywhere today Steve."

"I had not thought about it; why do you need me to be here?"

"No, I don't need you, but I want you to spend the day with me."

"Now that sounds, like the best offer I've had all day, I know this will not be all fun, but let's go take care of getting our passports and our shots."

"That's not exactly what I had in mind, but at least I'll be with you."

So, we spent the rest of the morning in line to get a passport, then our shots. After it is all over.

I said "I'm hungry. How about we pick up some chicken, and a salad and go for a picnic, I know the perfect spot, and we'll be the only ones there."

"Sounds like a good idea."

We pick up what we need at a deli, once we get outside away from people, I port us to the lake at the lodge.

"This is perfect Steve, where are we?"

"My mountain top hideaway, if you walk in that direction for a mile, you will see the lodge"

"After we finish eating, will you show me around again?"

114

"I would be glad too."

We spend an hour having our lunch asking questions of one another, so we can get to know each other better. When we finish it is getting to be well into the afternoon. We pick up our stuff, and I port us to the lodge. I show Samantha all around the lodge.

"Steve, who is the cat person you talk about, is he someone I should get to know?"

"Funny you should ask, come with me."

I walk over to the fire place and push on the hidden switch, the door next to it opens. I lead Samantha down into the lab below the house.

"CAT, introduce yourself to Samantha."

"Samantha, it is nice to meet you."

"Where are you cat?"

"Samantha, I'm the computer just in front of you."

"That is right Samantha, CAT is my computer. Without him I could not teleport around as I do."

"But, you can go anywhere, I have seen it."

"When I first developed a way to teleport, I could only go places I have been. When I amassed sufficient funds, I was able to develop CAT and he can connect me to anyplace on the earth as well as space. Without CAT I could not have saved those men on the shuttle."

Samantha is speechless.

"Come with me Samantha. I take Samantha outside; do you see the haze at the edge of the mountain?" "Yes."

That is a holograph projection, if anyone flies over this mountain all they will see is where a land slide covered the whole mountain top, with no place to land. I have to keep this place safe and protected." "You are far more than I thought you were."

"I hope so, and I hope I never let you down."

Samantha puts her arms around my waste puts her head against my chest, and just stands there. After a few minutes she looks up into my eyes.

"My heart is so full at this moment."

I pet her hair, "as is mine."

We walk back into the lodge, and I take Samantha to a room.

"You can spend the night here in this room. My room is just down the hall if you need anything."

"Steve, I have nothing to sleep in."

"Just a minute."

I go to my room and return with one of my tee shirts, will this do?"

"Yes, it will. Steve what will we do tomorrow?"

"I don't know yet."

We go off to bed, but I toss and turn, then I get up and put on a robe and go down stairs. I sit at the table and drink a cold glass of milk.

"Steve, is that you?"

"Yes, Samantha, I'm at the table."

Samantha walks over and puts her arms around me.

"I can't sleep, I keep thinking this is a dream, and I'm going to wake up."

"It is not dream, I have a small set of gym clothes. We could spar for a while."

"You're on." she said. And be sure, just because I'm your girlfriend that I'm not going to go easy on you."

"I would not dream of it, but likewise I'm going to do my best to beat you."

They change clothes, and Steve takes them down the stairs into the gym. Samantha wastes no time in sparing with me. She almost kicks the stuffing out of me, but toward the end, I start holding my own. Samantha is realizing, I'm starting to be her equal. The harder I try to beat her the harder she fights in the end it's a stalemate.

"Good fight Steve, you will no longer need me to teach you."

"It's about time! I was getting tired of my bruises."

Samantha smiles, I think I could use a bath, and then some sleep. I show her to the large bath room where she can clean up and I go get her a clean tee shirt. Soon we are in our own beds, and it does not take long to fall asleep.

In the morning I go down to the lab to talk to CAT.

"CAT what have you figured out about the crystal, can we grow others?"

"Steve, I have not discovered any way to make more of the crystal. The small piece you have can be split into six pieces and they would work, any smaller and they would be too small to do anything."

"Ok, I want to put one of the crystals in Samantha and teach her how to use it. One question, Could I put a crystal in a car, and get the same result of teleportation?"

"I suppose you could, but I'm not sure you should."

"Why not?"

"If you can port a car anywhere, why waste the crystal."

"In case I need to get away and I'm not able to."

"I'll work on it Steve."

"Steve, Samantha is up and she is looking for you."

I port upstairs to the living room.

"Good morning Samantha."

Samantha lets out a scream.

"What's wrong?" I ask. "

You scared a years' worth of life out of me." "I'm sorry. I guess from now on I should get used to walking around the house, instead of porting."

Paladin's Car

Chapter 26

The wedding came and went without a hitch, to me it was just a blur, transporting people and packages, and then returning everyone home. Finally we are off to France for the honeymoon. I remember the fun times, the passion, and a lot of silly other things that came about. We returned to our home in Duffer, and we argued with grandmother about her staying. So, to settle the whole thing; I proposed we build another house next door, and we would move in there. That was acceptable to all parties. Within the year we had another house being built where Sam and I would make our home.

I had to divide my time up now so I can spend time working on my inventions, and waging war on drugs. I make a raid at least once a week, throughout the country. What was once a river of drugs has now dwindled down to a small trickle? The price of drugs is so expensive almost no one can buy them anymore. Now to look for other pursuits.

"CAT, I want you to find me a good car engineer and set up a private place to meet him. I have decided that having a mobile unit in the field would be a great idea."

"Steve, I will do as you request."

A couple of days' pass, and Samantha and I still exercise together, and spar here at the lodge, while the house is being built. Being domestic, is also a chore, I enjoy cleaning up the house, dishes, laundry and so on. As long as Samantha is helping it goes faster. I think she likes telling me what to do. All in all, I find that I love it. I have a family now something I missed after my parents died.

Every night at dinner time we port into Grandmother's house as she wants to hear all that we did that day. When I go places I take Samantha with me, and on occasion she has me take her to this friend or that one to spend the night. On one of these trips of hers, CAT has setup a meeting with Samuel Travon, a car engineer who is out of work. As it turns out CAT purchases a building that has no large doors, but the work space inside is 30 by 30 feet and 20 feet high. Soon Samuel enters the building.

"Are you Steve Ball?"

"Yes, I am, and you must be Samuel?"

Samuel is a Harvard graduate with a Masters in mechanical and electrical engineering, and he has worked for both Ford and GM at one time.

"Samuel, with your credentials, why are you not working?"

"That is a fair question, as you can see I'm Black, and because I'm black no one wants to listen to my ideas. When I pointed out some of problems with the new cars, they decided to fire me."

"I can see that, so how would you like to design, and build a one of a kind, car for me?"

"Depends upon the money."

"Tell you what, I own this building, I'll bring in all the equipment you will need, and if this building is not big enough, I'll get you another one. As far as the budget goes I'll give you two million to design and build my car, your salary will be two hundred thousand a year."

"That sounds interesting, will it be illegal?"

"Yes and no, I need a car and I need it to be kept quiet, and no one is to know about it."

"When I finish your car what then; do I get laid off?"

"Would you be opposed to maintaining the car for me? You can keep all or any designs that you come up with except the one you make for me. Then if you like you can begin to turn out your own brand of cars."

"Steve you have a deal, but I would like to know why it has to be a secret."

"Ok, I'll show you."

I reach over and take Samuel's hand and port us to the lab at the lodge.

"You're HIM!"

"I guess? Who do you mean?"

"You're the magician, the man who saved the people on the space shuttle?"

"Since you put it that way I guess I am. Will this be a problem?"

"No, I mean, yes, I understand, and I would help you without the money. You saved a cousin of mine, by stopping the drugs. I want to shake your hand and do anything I can do to help you, I mean it!"

"Well Samuel will you take the job?"

"Yes!" I take Samuel's hand and return us to the building.

"I would like to meet with you tomorrow, and we can talk about the car, and what I would like to have it be able to do."

"You got it Boss!"

"No, Boss Ok. Just call me Steve. I want your friendship and your opinions, I don't need an employee." "Ok, Steve."

"Bring a lunch. I intend to make a day of It." said Steve.

I port away back to Duffer.

"I walk up to the door and knock, and Samantha opens the door springs into my arms and covers my face in kisses.

"I missed you, husband of mine."

"I missed you too Samantha, I really do. That was a nice reception I may have to be away more often."

"The carpenters, are doing a nice job on our home Steve. It won't be long and I'll be able to get the furniture, and décor."

"Samantha darling, whatever makes you happy."

She kisses me and says "right now I couldn't be any happier, I have you with me."

I walk into the house with Samantha and greet grandmother.

"Samantha, I will be gone all day tomorrow, and for several days following, I'm working on a new project, with someone."

"Who is it that you are working with?"

" His, name is Samuel Trevon. He is an Engineer who designs cars. I'm having a special one made up for me."

"Will I be able to drive it?"

"Do you know how?"

"Now Steve just because I don't have a car does not mean I don't know how to drive. Who do you think drives your old truck when you're not here?"

"Good point, yes you'll be able to drive the car."

"CAT will also be a part of it as well."

We spend the night at Grandmother's house. The next day, before I make a trip to meet Samuel, Samantha interrupts my thinking.

"What are you going to be doing today Steve?"

"I'm going to meet Samuel and give him some of the specs I want the car to be able to do, and then leave him to his work. I have had CAT order up a computer with CAD capabilities, so CAT and Samuel can talk. CAT will also handle all the administrative stuff for Samuel."

"Can I come along with you?"

"If you want." I said.

I port us to the lodge, Samantha dresses in a simple dress, and I put on a mask, and a business suit.

"Are you ready to go Samantha?"

"I'm ready whenever you are."

I catch her in a hug, and port us to the building. As we stand there in an embrace, I hear someone clear their throat. Embarrassed I pull away from Samantha. She laughs and gives me a seductive smile. "AAH Samantha, this is Samuel."

Samantha takes Samuel's hand and gives him a big smile.

"Steve has told me a lot about you Samuel, I wanted to meet you."

"Well he never mentioned you to me at all, especially as to how beautiful you are."

"Steve, are you taking notes?"

I blush under my mask, and I can feel the heat from it.

"Aaa sure Samantha."

She laughs again and hugs my arm. Soon Samuel and I are at a table that CAT had delivered, and I set up the computer, to show Samuel how to access CAT. I tell Samuel that I would like the car to be able to vanish in plain sight. He is puzzled, "How?"

Chapter 27

"There are a couple of possibilities, the first one is using holographic projectors, and the other is a screen that uses cameras to reflect onto a screen. So for instance I park the car next to a brick building, the camera on the building side would project it to the screen on the opposite side, and in essence make the car blend in and or disappear. Also, if programed properly, I can select different colors, and make its shape appear to change as well.

"That's some car, how will I get this technology."

"CAT will provide it for you. CAT can also assist you in your design."

"Wait a minute, who or what is CAT?"

"CAT is a very special computer. He has been instructed to help you, but you are in charge. CAT will make recommendations. Also CAT will and can procure either information or components that you may need."

"So, when I start construction, how will you get the equipment in here that I need?"

"Really Samuel."

"Never mind, I forget who I'm talking to. Now both of you scoot, I have a lot of work to do, and I need to get to know CAT. Oh, before you go, would it be Ok to get an advance on my pay? Being off work for a couple of months, I need to pay some bills."

"CAT you heard the man, pay his bills, and give him some extra for essentials."

Samuel takes my hand, "Thanks Steve, I owe you."

"Friends, do not owe friends anything, they help each other out, and if you build my car, it will be payment enough. I'll return in a month or tell CAT and he will inform me of any meetings, bye for now." I take Samantha by the hand and we port to a big mall.

"Now how did you know I wanted to go here?"

"When you have been married as long as I have you just know these things."

Samantha punches me in the shoulder.

"We have only been married for a little over a year."

"Really, it seems longer than that." Samantha slugs him again, and I laugh, and hug her in the mall.

In the next month I drop in on Samuel to see how the design is coming along for the car.

"Hi Steve, CAT said you would be dropping by this morning, what is this no Samantha today?"

"No, she is at home doing domestic things."

"Well Steve, I hope you don't mind, but I brought some one along to meet you?"

"Ok, who is it?"

Samuel calls out his ten-year-old son, Fredrick.

"Frederick, this is Paladin, the man who saved the astronauts."

At first, Fredrick does not believe his father.

"You can't be him, your pulling my leg."

"Well Fredrick what would it take to convince you?"

"I don't know."

"Hum, how did they say I got into space?"

"They were a bit sketchy about that."

"I teleported there, if you like I can teleport you some place, where would you like to go?"

"I don't know?"

"Have you ever seen the Pacific Ocean?"

"No."

"Good, I take his hand and his dads, and I port us to California, to Laguna Beach. Frederick's eyes light up, and his father is laughing.

"You really are him, aren't you?"

"Yes, I am, now that you know. I'm sorry about this, but you can never tell anyone about this. This has to stay a secret, or it could get your dad or your family killed."

Frederick looked at me for a moment.

"My dad told me the same thing. I promise, that I won't tell anyone not even my best friend."

I take us back to the building.

"Now Samuel, how is the design coming along?"

"With the use of CAT, and some of the materials he can procure this design is amazing. CAT runs the simulation for the car."

CAT puts the concept up on the screen and Samuel does the explaining.

"Wow, this looks like a beefed-up corvette."

"It is, with a lot of modifications. CAT is purchasing this model of Corvette, and it will be here in a week. I will have to modify the engine to add more horse power to power some of your systems. I will modify the car to only work to a few people's DNA signature. Mine of course, yours and whoever else you want to add. Your TV panels are being shaped to the car panels, and CAT has ordered the cameras, projectors, and the power supply to operate your system. Nice thing about the panels they can act as solar panels to help run most of your electrical systems without the engine running. Which means I will have to beef up the frame and drive train."

"That is wonderful Samuel, I like it. So, when do you estimate you will have it ready for a test run?" "About two months."

"CAT will contact me when the car arrives and I'll port it in."

I shake Samuel's hand and then Fredrick's, before I port back to Duffer.

The Amoeba

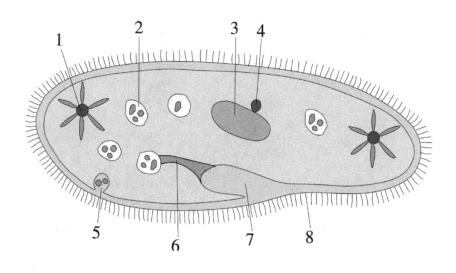

Chapter 28

Doctor Pine PHD, is a brilliant Biologist, he is studying gene splicing. Over time he discovers he can make changes to single celled animal to change its makeup and how it reacts to its environment. The government becomes interested in Pine's work, thinking it may be weaponized. So they fund his work, through different shadow corporations. Pine is not into making weapons, but he is hoping he can make man better by curing disease, and making man's immune system stronger. Doctor Pine is an idealist, working with single celled animals will not bring out cries of animal cruelty, and he still can prove his point.

Doctor Pine is not progressing fast enough for the military, so they send one of their men to confront Pine.

"Doctor Pine, how has your experiment progressed?"

"Actually, not bad, I have managed to improve on the amoeba, by changing some of its DNA. It can now live outside of water, whereas before it could not."

"Is that all Doctor? My people are wondering when you are going to deliver some usable results."

"I'm sorry, that you feel that way, but this type of work is slow and painstaking. It cannot be rushed as the consequences can be devastating. We can prevent a catastrophic blunder that may endanger people only by going slow."

"Sorry doc, you're fired, you have two days to pack up and leave."

Having one's ego crushed, doesn't help. In his mind, Doctor Pine formulates a plan. He packs up all his equipment and notes then puts them into his van. He drives out to his dead aunt's farm in upper New York where Pine sets up his lab in the old house.

"I'll show them, Pine thinks.

At first Pine returns to the Amoeba to see if he can do more with it. While he is at it he captures one of his chickens and begins to experiment on it. Over time it is like he becomes a freak maker, crossing chickens with other animals, and then other animals. All his creations are hideous and some of them dangerous. He keeps everything locked away in cages. But his prize is the amoeba. A single celled animal, you normally need a microscope to see. You can now hold in your hand if you dare. He keeps it in a large 10-gallon aquarium. The amoeba is as hungry as a shark, it eats anything put into the tank. At first it is insects, then mice, and now the occasional rat.

With each feeding the amoeba grows, it now fills the bottom of the tank. Measuring it, it is about two centimeters thick. Pine kept extensive notes on his creations, especially the amoeba. Pine was watching the amoeba and saw that it pushed pseudopods up the sides of the aquarium. Pine decided he needs to put a tight seal cover on the tank before the amoeba gets out. If the Amoeba escaped, it would eat who ever touched it. Pine would cut sections from the amoeba to experiment on. Pine subjected the animal parts to fire, cold, and different environments but only the cold affected it, and nothing could kill it. Pine contacts one of his colleges at the lab and tells her about the Amoeba, and some of his other less pleasing experiments.

She makes an appointment to come and visit Pine at his home, so he can show her what he has done. A week later she appears at the house, and Pine lets her in.

"Are you OK?" she asks.

"I'm fine. Come here with me Pam, and I'll show you my menagerie."

He leads her to the back of the house and starts showing her the freaks he has created.

"This is just wrong Pine, it is all wrong, you should not change the nature of animals. You do not know when one of the changes may endanger everyone."

"Not to worry Pam. I'm keeping a tight rein on my creations. After I'm done may be pigs can fly."

Pam says "Tell me you didn't do that."

"No, I haven't done that, now over here in the fish tank is where I have the amoeba."

Doctor Pine takes Pam over to the tank, except for a slight blur in the bottom of the tank the amoeba is difficult to see, even more so as the amoeba pushes its way up on all sides of the tank in a search of food.

"It is still here Pam, let me show you."

Doctor Pine goes to a cage of a live rat, catches it, and then walks over to the fish tank to drop it in. In this case he reaches in part way in an attempt to get a pseudo pod to stick up to grab the rat, instead the amoeba collapses from around the side of the tank on to Doctor Pine's hand and starts eating the rat and the doctor. It oozes up Pine's arm to his shoulder. Pine is in great pain as the amoeba eats his arm. Pam tries to help, and becomes entangled with the amoeba, soon the doctor and Pam are engulfed by the fast-growing amoeba. If there had been a spectator present they would have watched in horror as the flesh is melted off both people as the amoeba consumes them.

Once the amoeba finishes its grizzly meal, it goes in search of more food, soon all the animals in Pine's house are eaten. The amoeba then finds a one-inch hole and oozes through it to the outside. If you followed the animal, everywhere it oozed, all life in its wake is consumed. It made its way onto the dirt road; the very road Arthur Perkins is traveling on with his bike to go to his friend Ryan's house so they can go goof off. Art was riding at top speed when he saw what looked like a mud puddle. It had not rained for a month or more why is there a puddle? Well as boys will do he charges full speed into the puddle, expecting to make a big splash. Half way through the puddle, the bike screeches to a halt, and Art is thrown clear of the puddle. But what he sees scares him out of a year's growth.

Art's bike is totally engulfed in goo. At this point Art runs to his friend's house a mile away. He tells Ryan what happened and Ryan does not believe him. Ryan insisted to the point that Art take him back to the place where it happened. The boys go to the place where Art left his bike. It lay in the puddle, and Art cautions Ryan not to get too close. Art is scared. Ryan takes a stick goes over to the goo, and started prodding it. Soon the goo engulfs the end of the stick and a pseudo pod reached up the stick in search for food. What Ryan fails to see is the amoeba has oozed around him. Arthur screams at Ryan to get away, but it is too late. Ryan is engulfed and being eaten in front of Arthur. Arthur tries to run away to get to some place safe. The amoeba follows Arthur, not fast but the movement is steady. Arthur spies a tree and climbs up into it. He is too tired and scared to think clearly.

Arthur sits high up in the old oak tree, crying. When he gets a hold of himself he sees that the creature has surrounded the tree, there is no way for Art to get down. Fortunately, the creature does not seem to be able to climb that far up into the tree. For hours Arthur sits up in the tree, it looks like the creature may have moved on, but fear keeps Author where he is. At dusk the sheriff's car stopes on the road not far from the tree. The sheriff gets out and calls up to Arthur.

"You have several people out looking for you, what are you doing up in the tree?"

"Get away sheriff or the creature will get you, like it got Ryan."

"Where is Ryan Art?"

"He is over there dead."

The sheriff walks over to where Art is pointing and sees Ryan's bones stripped clean.

"Ok, Art where is Ryan?"

"That's him that creature ate him."

"The joke is over, now come down out of that tree."

Reluctantly Arthur climbs down to where the sheriff can take him down.

"Come on, I'll take you home."

Just as Arthur is in the sheriff's hands, the amoeba encircles his legs and starts feeding. The sheriff almost drops Arthur and realizes what is happening and throws Author clear of the creature, and through the pain the sheriff tells Author to get into the car and call for help. In horror Arthur watches the sheriff die like his friend. Arthur enters the car and closes all the windows and the door. Arthur turns on the radio contacts the Deputy.

"Ross this is Authur, we need help. The sheriff is dead, and so is Ryan."

"Where are you Art?"

Arthur gives his location. What Author did not realize is that the creature has pooled beneath the sheriff's car, and it has found a hole in the floor board of the car. It starts oozing into the car. Standing on the seat Arthur does not see any way out and calls the deputy back.

"Ross it has me, hurry."

Then the deputy hears Arthur's screams, and realizes that this is not a prank, and races to the scene.

The creature oozes out of the car and moves on in search of more food. The deputy arrives, to find a grizzly mess. He looks into the car and sees Authur's bones and starts to heave up his dinner. When he has finished he looks around the tree and finds the sheriff's bones. This is more than what I can handle and he calls the State Police. The next day the state police show up and tape off the area to investigate what has happened. One police officer sees a strange trail, leading off into the field, and decides to follow it in one direction. It leads him to an old farm house. The officer knocks on the door and gets no answer. So, he calls out then opens the door, what he finds makes him sick to his stomach.

He finds skeletons of all kinds of animals, and two humans. This seems to be the place where it started. Looking around he finds the journal Doctor Pine kept. On the skeletons he finds identification of each of the two remains. He returns to the command area with the journal and reports what he has found. Soon a team of people are at the house, and the State Police call in a Biologist to go over Pines journal to see what they might be facing. As it turns out a couple of reporters sneak into the area to take pictures, but none of them are looking at the ground in front of them. To them all they see is a puddle until one of them steps in it. The amoeba reacts and soon engulfs the reporter. Who is screaming for help? One of the other reporters tries to pull his friend from the puddle but is soon entangled as well. It is not long and both men are incased in the amoeba. The third reporter, runs to the command station to tell them what he saw.

The reporter appears to be unhinged and wild eyed. The man in charge is not sure what to believe. He sends one of the officers with the reporter which is reluctant to go. As they approach the area there are two more skeletons laying on the ground with their clothes and cameras.

"Now where is this creature?"

The reporter looks around and spots the puddle.

"That's it right there."

Pointing to the puddle.

"Are you sure?"

"Look I just watched two of my friends get eaten by that thing, worse of all that puddle is bigger than it was."

"Let's go back and tell the commander what we found."

They return to the command center, and the officer confirms what the reporter told them. The officer takes several men with him to go follow the creature. They soon find it, and it seems to sense them as well and starts oozing toward them.

"Look at that, it's like it knows we are here."

"Keep away from it or you will end up like the others."

One of the officers' empty's his rifle clip into the creature, and nothing happens.

"Two of you follow the creature, the rest will return with me to the command center. Do not bother the creature, stay away from it. Just keep tabs on it."

The officer in charge returns with the rest of the team.

"Sir, we found that creature, and one of the men fired on it; it is like shooting at water, there is nothing we can do to stop or contain this creature. The worst part is, it is growing."

"I left two men to keep track of it, but I don't think that will be necessary as it is now following us here. I expect to see it sometime tomorrow."

"Good says the commander, it will give us time to set up some explosive and blow it up."

That evening the biologist shows up with Doctor Pine's journal.

"Do you know what you have on your hands commander?"

"Not really."

"What Pine did was take an amoeba and enhance it."

"Now wait a minute Doctor, don't amoebas live in water?"

"Yes, that is correct, but Doctor Pine spliced its genes and it now can live out of water as well as in water. It can withstand heat, or anything else you throw at it. It is quite possibly is indestructible. The only thing that will affect it is extreme cold and all that will do is slow it down."

"Well we are about to run our own experiment Doctor, as we are going to blow it up. There is enough C-4 out in that field that it can reduce a tank to particles."

"No, you mustn't do that! Do you know what will happen if you attempt to blow it up, it will spread that monster all around, and instead of having one creature, you could have thousands."

"Are you sure?"

"Yes, you would make the situation worse."

The commander gets on the radio.

"Stand down, do not set off the explosives. Now tell me what we can do to destroy this thing." "According to Pine's journal, the only thing that will affect the creature is cold. It will not kill it, but it would stop it until it thaws. I would suggest getting a couple of trucks of liquid nitrogen, then we might collect it, and put it into a container to seal it up. Eventually it would eat itself to death."

"Ok doctor let's do it your way."

Test Drive

Chapter 29

At the same time. I port to Chicago to see what Samuel has done with the car. I port in and I see this silver-gray car, which no longer looks like a Corvette. I catch Samuel off guard.

"Yikes! He exclaims, I'm never going to get use to your simply appearing out of nowhere."

"So how is the car coming along Samuel?"

"Great, it took some doing, but I have all that you requested incorporated into the car. I had to beef up the suspension, change the lines of the car, and add some horse power to the engine. This car should out run any set of wheels out there. Now let me demonstrate the features."

Samuel gets into the car, and it suddenly disappears, then it reappears.

"See just like you wanted. Now watch, Color RED", and the car turns Red. "This has a color changing feature, and you can mimic any color of any car. The license plates are holographic as well and can change at will."

"Wow, I'm going to like this."

Samuel gets out of the car, and Steve gets in. Samuel shows Steve the console, the weapons, and so on. This car would make James Bond green with envy.

"Samuel let's take this for a spin."

"I thought you would never ask."

Steve gets into the passenger seat. Samuel stops and looks at him.

"What are you doing Steve?"

"I'm not going to drive this car first. I want the person who designed it to do that; just in case it needs to be adjusted. Besides, you deserve the first test drive, you built it."

Samuel does not argue, he gets into the driver seat and starts the car. Steve ports them out on to the street. Samuel hits the gas and squeals the tires as the car flies down the road.

"What a rush, Samuel this is great! OH, OH we picked up a flashing blue light behind us."

Samuel turns a corner and pulls to a stop where he turns on the holo projector. The car vanishes in front of the police car. To the policeman the car is invisible. Samuel turns up into a turn out area to get out of the way of the speeding police car.

Samuel that is great, CAT, monitor all police calls in the area, I want to see how much of a stir we caused.

"Steve there are four police cars driving in the area looking for a silver car and he lists the license plate. "What else will this do Samuel?"

"Watch, Samuel says Mini Van."

And the holographic projector projects an image around the car and it now looks like a minivan, make it white, says Samuel. The projector makes the Van white, change plates." Then Samuel drives past a couple of police car doing the speed limit, and the police totally ignore them.

"Ready to go back to the barn?"

"Yes Steve, I see that there are a few adjustments I need to make and this car, is ready."

Steve ports them back into the building.

"I have one other thing I want you to add to the computer." Said Steve.

I hand Samuel a chip and said. "Contact CAT. He will tell you where and how to place the chip."

"Why Steve?"

"It will allow me to contact CAT from the car."

"OK, Steve. Now I will need you and your wife back here in a couple of weeks, as I'm putting in a DNA detector and lock, so if someone breaks in to the car, they will not be able to drive it or operate all the gadgets in it."

"Very good Samuel, we'll be here. Besides Samantha will want to drive it."

"Good bye, Steve."

"See you in a couple of weeks Samuel. You did a great job on the car! It is worth every penny and so are you!"

I port back home.

In a week Samantha and I return to the building where Samuel is working. CAT announces our coming so that Samuel won't lose a year's worth of living when we appear.

"Thank you for the warning. That helps a lot."

Samantha exclaims "This is the car? Oh, Steve can I drive it?"

"Well I don't know, but that is the reason why I brought you along, Samuel is it ready to take it for a spin?"

"Almost, I need some DNA from both of you first."

Samuel takes the samples and puts them into the mechanism he designed.

"Now all you have to do is talk into the microphone, and we'll all be set."

So, we both talk into the microphone reciting Mary had a Little Lamb, and Samuel does some adjustments. Then the car is ready.

"Samuel what was that all about?"

"With your DNA and voice print, no one can operate the car. Right now, only the four of us can operate the car."

"Which four?" asks Steve.

"You, Samantha, CAT and myself."

"So, CAT can control the car? Said Steve "Let's give it a test then."

"CAT, trigger the crystal to teleport the car."

"Yes Steve."

"Samuel, Samantha get into the car. CAT take us to the salt flats in California."

CAT ports both the car and Steve to the salt flats.

"What did you just do Steve?" asks Samuel.

Do you remember the crystal I gave you and I asked you to attach to the computer of the car?"

"Yes, I thought it odd, but CAT told me how to do it, but not why."

"The why is so that he can control the car and move it from one place to another, when the need arises."

"You mean that is how you teleport about?"

"Not quite, but in essence yes, it is a rather long and complicated story and process. Now let's see what she will do. Explain to Samantha and me all the weapons; offensive and defensive."

Samuel demonstrates the weapons, guns, missiles, cannon, before he shows us the chameleon changes for color, invisibility, and finally how well it drives and performs. The computer screens through the options and functions. After explanations, Samantha has to drive the car. With Samuel in Tow, she speeds off down the empty salt flats. Samantha speeds up to over two hundred miles per hour, and almost loses control of the car.

CAT corrects the car and keeps it from wrecking. While they speed off, I port back home and bring in a tent and chairs, then I go back and get some drinks and food for a picnic. I suspect that Samantha will be driving for a while. Eventually they return and see that I have made myself comfortable. Samantha stops the car next to the tent and shuts it down. When Sam gets out of the car, "Steve, Honey when are you going to get you a car like this so we can race?"

"What do you mean get me a car?"

"Well I sort of decided I want this car. Besides with you able to port around at will, why do you need this car?"

"Yea, Steve why did you want this car anyway?" asks Samuel.

"Actually, for two reasons, the first one being I may need a mobile command station, and the second is, it is for Samantha to use on some of my adventures."

"You mean this is my car?" exclaims Samantha.

"It's our car, and you may have use of it. I suspect I will not have as much need for it as you will." Samantha, acts like a teenage girl who just wheedled the credit card from her tight wad father.

"Samuel, how did the car handle?"

"The car handled great thanks to the intervention of CAT saving us from any potential damage that may have happened." "So is it ready for any field testing."

"I believe that would be a good idea, just return the car and me back to the building and I can check it over to make sure it is in tip top shape."

"Sure, just as soon as we all have lunch."

With lunch over, I have CAT transport the car and Samuel back to the building, then I port Samantha home.

"Steve how will I get the car if I'm here and it is in Chicago?"

"Very easy dear." I hand Samantha an ear piece, and a pair of glasses just like mine.

"When you want the car, contact CAT. He can transport the car to where you are. But before you call for it make sure Samuel is not working on it. It would be rude to take him on a trip he is not ready for." "Thank you, Steve,"

Samantha throws her arms around Steve's neck and covers his face in kisses.

"I'm going to have to remember this for the future."

"Steve, you need to come to the lodge, something is going on that may need your attention." "Ok, CAT, I'll be right there. Samantha, would you like to go with me to the lodge?"

"I can't honey; I have a doctor's appointment in a couple of hours."

"Ok, I'll see you when I return. Are you feeling alright?"

"I feel fine silly, now get a move on so I can clean up."

I give Samantha a kiss and port away.

"What is up CAT, why could you not tell me what is going on then?"

"Steve, I did not want Samantha to overhear, the situation."

"What is going on CAT?"

"It appears someone has created a super amoeba and it is growing out of control. Nothing can stop it, the best they can do is slow it down by freezing it."

"So, what can I do CAT?"

"You can open a space window and send it in to space, I would suggest a trajectory into the sun." (Paladin has to be careful about opening a window into space, the vacuum could pull him in as well. The windows allow Paladin to not only look into places, but reach out and touch through the window. And he has found that it can be used as a weapon.)

"Then I guess I had better get going."

Chapter 30

CAT provides the coordinates for a safe landing and I show up to offer the police my help. The situation has been taken over by the National Guard. So, I ask to be taken to the command post to talk to the man in charge. I'm escorted by two armed men to the Commander who is running the show. "Who is this man, I thought I told you no one gets in here!"

"Well sir, they could not have kept me out even if they thought to."

"Put him in Irons, until I can decide what to do with him."

"Ok, you leave me no choice Commander."

I port over to him and then port away to a remote location.

"Now Commander, are you going to listen?"

Looking around the Commander says, "What choice do I have?"

"None really, let's quit playing I'm in charge here and help each other out. From my dog and pony show that I just conducted, you now know who I am."

"Yes, you are the one called Paladin."

"Good, now the only way to get rid of your current problem is to send it into space, and I can do that, but not without your help."

"What do you need?"

"I need a three-quarter inch steel plate four feet by eight feet, and on it I need three fully charged nitrogen cylinders welded on and aligned to each other. Then place three small C-4 charges on the valves so we can set them off at the same time. I'll set off the charges when I get it into space this will take the creature away from the earth. If the calculations are correct it will send it in to the sun."

"Ok son take me back and I'll do it. Tell me how do you plan to get the creature onto the steel plate?"

"Bait, I will have to use a live animal to get the amoeba onto the plate. Next you will need to hose down the creature with liquid Nitrogen, to slow it down long enough for me to get it into space."

"Let's do this." said the Commander.

Three hours later the plate is ready, and I show up with a goat for bait, I'm also in a special suit I had taken from NASA to prevent the creature from eating me. The suit sealed from space and has its own oxygen supply. I step onto the plate with the goat and port everything to the creature, the nitrogen trucks are not far away. I open the face mask on my suit to conserve my oxygen for the trip into space. Slowly the amoeba senses me and the goat on the plate, and oozes in our direction. In fifteen minutes, it has mostly oozed on to the plate and has engulfed the poor goat, now it is oozing up my body. I port us into space.

"CAT I'll have to leave the suit behind so open my window over the lake, and make sure I have ten feet to fall in to and set off the charges too."

CAT opens the window for just me and I fall into the lake at the lodge, leaving the suit behind.

"Steve the canisters have been discharged, and the cold of space has frozen the creature. It is now on its way to the sun.

"I'd best get some clothes on and go home, to see how Samantha is doing, she has been acting strange lately."

I port to Duffer, and Samantha comes out the door, and slaps my face.

"What was that for?"

"I saw you on TV risking your life. You can't do that! I can't take it, you have to stop."

Samantha breaks down in tears.

"Honey what is wrong?"

"I am going to have a baby, and I need you to be with me. Not running off to some corner of the world putting your life in danger."

"Did you just say you were going to have a baby?"

Samantha looks up into my eyes and puts her arms around my neck.

"Yes, I'm going to have a baby, I'm three months along, and so far, it is healthy."

I was shocked and amazed, and when the realization hits me; I started laughing and crying all at the same time.

"That is wonderful!" I shouted.

Grandmother then appears, and she is almost ready to jump in for the kill.

"What is all the fuss about?"

"Grandmother, I'm having a baby."

You could have knocked grandmother over with a feather. She cracks the biggest smile I have ever seen. "It's about time you two. That means I'll have another grandchild to help raise."

If I did not know better grandmother almost did a jig right on the spot.

"I'll leave you two alone for now."

I keep near Samantha, to make sure she is Ok, until she tells me.

"Go play with CAT, you have to get out of here."

"What's wrong honey?"

"You keep watching me. I'm beginning to feel like a lab animal. Now scoot! Let me have some space."

"Ok, I have a few things I can do at the lodge. See you later." I port to the lodge.

"CAT anything going on?"

"Several Steve, but nothing that can't be dealt with by someone else."

CAT reels off several things that have happened that the news media doesn't know about yet. I decide to help a Senator's son who has been kidnapped in a

146

Middle Eastern country, while trying to help war victims. If his father does not come forward and denounce the US government, he will be beheaded.

"CAT have you pinpointed his location?"

"Not exactly Steve. I know which country he is in, but not an exact location."

I head upstairs to my makeup room and select a mask that will clearly define me as a white American.

"That should get me picked up. What time is it there, CAT?"

"Steve it is later on that side of the world."

"Great, I'll port in and get myself picked up."

Dressed in blue jeans, tennis shoes, and a cowboy shirt. I port to the little village where the Senator's son was taken. I walk into town and go to what looks like an inn and I go inside, armed with my glasses and ear piece, so CAT can translate the language for me.

Senator's Son

Chapter 31

As I enter everyone stops what they are doing to look at the stupid American, I pick a table and sit down. No one approaches me. After a while a dancing girl approaches me, and in broken English. "You must leave; they are planning to kill you."

"I'm looking for the American they captured here a few days ago, can you tell me where he is?"

"I do not know. Please, you must leave."

"Ok, I'll go."

I get up from the table and go outside, in the dark I see the heat of several men as they have me surrounded. Some with guns, and others with knives or swords, as they have me surrounded. They do not intend to kill me as much as capture me, so I let them. With my training, I could have taken them all out, but then I would not know where the Senator's son is, so I get captured.

After I get hauled into a truck we drive off away from the village at the break of dawn, we arrive in the mountains, and there I meet the Senator's son who is in a cage next to mine. We exchange pleasantries and then I ask him if he would like to get out of here.

"Sure, did you bring the Marines with you?"

"Well in a matter of speaking."

"You are just a bit late, on that regard, I'm to die this morning."

"Ok, can I shake your hand?"

He extends his hand and I grasp it and port us away from the site to a friendly country.

"Stay here, I'll be back for you, I need to do something else before I can return you to your father." "Whatever you say friend."

I port back to my cage, and then there is a big stir, the intended victim is gone.

I get pulled out of my cage a bit roughly and I'm taken to the man in charge.

"What have you done with my prisoner?"

"I don't know what you are talking about."

One of the men there punches me in the stomach so that I double over in pain.

"Now let's try this again, where is my prisoner?"

"Ok, I'll Tell you."

I create a small window and cut my bonds like a knife. Then I take out everyone in the room, the six men did not have a chance. Thanks to Grandmothers training, and the one who punched me, I broke his nose and his arm. I grab the man in charge and port him to where I left the Senator's son.

"What are you going to do with that terrorist?"

My answer "Something unexpected."

I port to the lower levels of the CIA and leave the terrorist in a broom closet.

"What are you doing asks the Senator's son?"

"I'm leaving an enemy here as a present."

I port to the Senator's house and leave my charge there, and then back to the lodge.

"CAT contact the CIA operative, and let him know he has an unexpected guest in the closet on the top secret level of his building."

"Steve it appears they already know."

"Get me a secure line to his office CAT."

I call the CIA commander, who was in pursuit of me some time ago, and informed him that it is Christmas. I delivered the Senator's son back home and I left a present for you."

I hang up the connection.

The terrorist breaks out of the closet that I left him in only to find himself in a room full of secret documents. In his blundering around, the terrorist sets off several alarms. In mere moments he is confronted by many agents, all of them asking him to get down on the ground, and put his hands behind his back. Soon he finds himself in a room with men asking the questions as to how did you get there, and who is he? Someone looks up his picture, and finds that he is the terrorist who was going to cut off the Senator's son's head. The terrorist denies that he is the man in the picture.

"I see Paladin was right, we have been looking for this person for some time."

"This is the man who has beheaded several people on camera, I believe we will question him extensively and when we are done with him, maybe we do to him what he has done with others."

"CAT, how is Samantha doing?"

"What do you mean Steve?"

"What is she doing at this minute."

"From her heart rate, and breathing she is doing exercises."

"Ok, I'll go work on one of my other projects."

"Steve, what is going on with Samantha."

"CAT look up the biology of women, reference pregnancy, Samantha is having a baby."

"I see Steve, but why the change in her emotions."

"That's a tough one to explain, and the problem is I can only go from a man's point of view."

"Please explain Steve."

"I'll give it my best CAT, the baby causes change in her body and mind; the research should tell you at least that much."

"It does Steve."

"Then you are now more up to date than most men, I had a professor who explained it this way to us. Men's minds are a lot like small boxes within boxes, we have a tendency to compartmentalize problems in to these boxes, and no box shall ever cross over another box. When we are ready, we take a problem out of a box and deal with it, then the next problem until the immediate or critical items have been dealt with.

"That makes sense Steve."

"Well CAT you need to be careful about that, because a man, me built you, not a woman. So you are likely to lean toward a male influence."

"I see, you were my father, and I'm your son so I have a tendency to be male in my programing." "Close enough CAT, now to continue, my professor indicates that women's minds are interconnected, everything touches everything else. And all of that is powered by emotions."

"That seems to be inefficient."

"Again CAT, you were designed and build by a male not a female, but I have to agree with you. But don't take me at my word. After all I'm a man and to date there is not a man alive who can figure out a woman's mind. Now let's leave it at that before I get myself into trouble."

"I will do more research on this difference, maybe I can figure it out."

"Good luck with that CAT, but you let me know when you do, the answer you come up with will be interesting just the same."

I go down into my lab and work on one of my inventions. I'm trying to figure a way to grow more of that crystal.

Micro Sun

Chapter 32

Doctor Ernie Cord, is into New Energy Technology he has theorized a way to create a micro sun, using a small collider to bring together the components to actually make a sun so small as to be nearly microscopic, yet it will be powerful enough to provide power to the whole planet. His main problem is to contain the micro sun. A magnetic bottle could do it once the sun is generated, by using the micro sun's own power it would sustain the power needed to contain it suspended in a magnetic bottle. The cost is very high to build a collider (collider would be used to create the micro sun by using hydrogen molecules to smash into each other to create fusion at a microscopic level. In essences it would be like our own Sun.), for just a one-shot use. However, with this power being broadcast, there would be no need for fossil fuels, or atomic power, the micro sun could sustain the whole planet for a million years.

Doctor Cord is being watched. This watcher has plans to do whatever it takes to keep this micro sun technology from ever happening. Doctor Cord approaches the American government with his findings and is turned down. Dr. Cord is scorned. He tries Russia, France, all the major powers, except China. That is because of the US sanctions against China at that time. After being turned down time and again, Dr. Cord decides to put all his research in to a locked safe, to be sent off for storage possibly for the future. There is a knock at the door of his house, Cord opens it to find someone who looked Asian standing on his porch.

"Good day Dr. Cord."

"Who are you?"

"My name is not important, but why I have come is."

"Ok, why have you come?"

"Your proposal of a micro sun has intrigued my employers, and they would like to fund your project."

Dr. Cord invites the man into his house, and offers him a refreshment.

"Now tell me, did you say your employer wants to pay for my Micro Sun?"

"Yes, we would like to fund all the work, but you would have to agree that the Micro sun would belong to my employers."

"Only if I'm left in charge of it." says Dr. Cord.

"We can work out some arrangement along those lines. I must leave now, but I will return tomorrow with their answer."

Dr. Cord is beside himself. He realized he never questioned who was buying his work and his soul. The next day just before dawn Dr. Cord is awaken by a pounding on his bedroom window.

"What is going on?"

He calls out as he opens his window.

"You must hurry Dr. Cord, your life is in danger, I must get you and your research out of here!"

Dr. Cord pulls on his pants and his shoes and goes to his back door to open it. He finds the same Asian that had visited him yesterday, and he has a couple of men with him.

The Asian asked if the research material is handy, Dr. Cord points to the two large boxes, and the men pick them up and start for the back door. Dr. Cord is also rushed out, then hurried across the back yard and down the alley.

"What is going on?"

"Be quiet Doctor, and watch."

In the next moment Dr. Cord's house explodes. Stunned Dr. Cord is lead down the alley to a waiting car. "What is going on."

"Sorry Doctor, you will have to wait until we are safely away from here, then all your questions will be answered."

It is not a clean get away. Despite being rushed into the waiting cars, and speeding off down the road. From behind, another car is speeding up to catch them. Gun fire breaks the back window of the trailing car. It is a fire fight all the way to the airport, and the trailing car breaks off the attack when the police show up to investigate.

The two cars stop and the Asian man gets out of the car presenting his diplomatic passport. The police have to let them go. The two cars drive around the airport to a hanger on the far side, where a plane stands ready to take off. Everyone is ushered out of the cars and Dr. Cord's research is put on the plane.

"Where are we going?" asks Dr. Cord.

"For now we are going to a place of safety. Who wants to kill you?"

"I have no idea, nothing like this has ever happened to me before."

"Well whoever it is seems to be determined, see the car lights over there?"

"Yes, that is the car that was following us and shooting at us."

The Asian leaves the Doctor to go to the cockpit.

"Get us off the ground now, or we may not get out of here at all."

Soon the plane is in the air and climbing to thirty thousand feet. The Asian man tells the Doctor that they will be nearly twenty hours in flight and that he might want to get some sleep.

"I'm so wound up that I can't sleep" says the Doctor. The Asian waves at one of his men and they give the Doctor a glass of orange juice. The Doctor drinks it and down it in one gulp. Soon he is Fast asleep. "Now that the good Doctor is fast asleep, we will not have to answer so many questions. Call the Boss and let him know we have the package."

"You, I want to know who that was that blew up the house, and who was shooting at us. Check the feed from the car's camera maybe we can get a face or a license plate we can look up. I have to admit that they did help us to get the Doctor without any fuss."

The security man goes off to do his task. The rest of you get some sleep, but I want someone watching the good Doctor until we turn him over to our people."

By the time they land, the security man has a report.

"According to my contacts, the family that owned the car are all dead, the police were taking the bodies from their home when our man got there. The face I got from the camera does not match any thing we have on file. So, I approached another operative at the US Pentagon to see what she can find. This man is too professional to be a nobody. I hope to have more information on him before long."

"We need to find out who we are dealing with, they could disrupt everything. So, find them."

"Yes Sir"

The security man returns to his computer.

The Asian goes to the cockpit.

"Call ahead and after we land I want you to taxi straight into the hanger. The people we are dealing with may have help here in China, and we do not want to lose our prize."

Soon after landing, they taxi into an open hanger and the doors are closed. Then everyone is hurried into armored cars, all that is except the Doctor, and his research. The Doctor and his research is put into a non-descript car and left inside the hanger. The armored cars set off down the road toward the city, and an hour later the non-descript car drives around the airport then heads toward town on a different road. As it turns out, it was a good maneuver, as the armored cars are attacked, and the people in them killed. The Asian and the Doctor make it to their destination safely.

They drive inside the building and seal it off. The Doctor wakes from his drug induced sleep. "Where are we?"

"You are now in China."

"What? I'm not suppose too be here, according to my government, I'll be branded a traitor to my country."

"It is a bit too late for that now Doctor. Your country tried to kill you, and they have not given up attempts, as it would seem. You see I sent two decoys of armored cars to reach this destination. Both cars were destroyed. All my people were killed."

"Then how did I get here?"

"I had my own car at the airport and I took you with that car in a roundabout way. As you can see it worked, we are both here and now for the moment we are safe."

"I must return to my country" says Dr. Cord.

"I will not stop you from returning, but your research materials will stay here."

"You can't keep it, it's mine, I put a lot of effort and research into it."

"So true, but saving your life, has a price. Then again when you are returned, your research won't do you any good any way. You see, who ever tried to kill you, still wants you dead."

"So, if I return to my country, I will either be locked up, or killed. Neither one sounds appealing. I would like to make my micro sun, and publish it, will that be acceptable?"

"Yes, Doctor Cord, we would allow that."

"Alright then, I'll build my energy sun for your country."

"Thank you, Doctor, now I must talk to my superiors."

The Asian Leaves Dr. Cord.

"Well Len (The Asian), what do you have?"

"Sir, I have just collected Dr. Cord and his research on the micro sun. Did you perchance send someone to kill him, or induce him to come along?"

"No Len we did not."

"Then what the good Doctor has to offer is very valuable."

"Does he know anything yet Len?"

"No Sir, I think if he did he would not help us."

"Ah, I see, then keep him in the dark."

"We will soon be ready to strike Len. I have others of our scientists working on a weapon and it will soon be ready, then we are going to need that power source."

"You have not told me of your plan sir. What are we trying to accomplish?"

"Think about this Len. What if something happened to the world as a whole? Let's say everyone lost all their power. We have a micro sun to put in place, and the world has to buy their power from us."

"That would mean in essence that we would own the world Sir."

"Quite so Len. I want you to help our new quest with whatever he needs. I need to know how long it will take to build the micro sun; timing will be everything."

"Yes, Sir"

Len (The Asian) returns to the doctor to get the Micro sun project started.

After listening to Doctor Cord, Len decides that they need to be put in to a hidden place where he can control security. Also building the micro sun will attract attention if built in China, so it will need to be done outside of China. Len starts looking for an island in and around the South China Seas. "Doctor, what is the smallest land mass that we can use to build the collider and still have it work?" "The one in France is what we need to scale to."

"So, we need a couple of miles or more. After searching, I have found a nearly deserted island in the South China Seas that should meet our needs. We will leave for the island in the morning."

"Ok, Len, I will get my instruments ready for traveling" says Dr. Cord.

The next morning, they take a jet to the southernmost city in China, Zhanjiang. From there they are put on a destroyer to make the rest of the trip to a South Seas Island. A few days later the ship moors off an island where they are to build the collider. Dr. Cord surveys the area and determines that it will be possible to build the collider right here on the island.

Before they leave Len requests all the supplies and materials to build the collider, scientist, engineers, and construction personal will follow in a month if Dr. Cord gives the say so to build on the island. Everything is set in motion. It takes several months to build the collider and support structures. During the construction. The man who tried to kill Dr. Cord manages to sneak on to the island. He is there to kill Dr. Cord. He was not sent by the U.S. Government. He was hired by a private concern to stop Dr. Cord from building his micro sun. Over time the other scientists become familiar with Dr. Cords research and work, just in case something happens to Dr. Cord. Len had orders to remove Dr. Cord at the proper time after the Micro Sun is up and running. The stranger waits for many days watching the routine of Dr. Cord, and one-day Dr. Cord came out of the compound to take a walk along the beach. He finds the walk helps clear his mind. He is always followed by his two body guards. The Doctor does not pay attention to his surroundings as he is walking. One guard goes down with a bullet to the head, and by the time the second guard realizes what is happening, he is also killed. Finally the Doctor is also assassinated.

Later Len goes looking for the good doctor and finds out that he went for a walk. Len sends out security to find Dr. Cord and his body guards. An hour later they find the bodies. Len has the island shut down, but it is too late. The killer swims away. Len has aircraft out checking the waters to see if any craft are out there. If any craft are found they are to be destroyed. The killer is on a junk trying to get away. The MIG shoots at the junk killing the crew. The killer is injured, but not dead. In time a Chinese ship shows up and captures the killer taking him to Len for questioning. Len holds a meeting with the scientist and they believe they can still build the micro sun, using Dr. Cord's research. They do not know how to make the magnetic bottle yet so that the micro sun will power its own containment. Without that containment the micro sun will not stay micro, it will eventually consume the Earth, moon and possibly other planets. Len pushes the project ahead, to keep in time of the EMP (Electro Magnetic Pulse) cannon which needs to go off just after the micro sun comes into existence, then they will own the world's only power supply.

Chapter 33

Len turns his attention to the assassin.

"Why did you kill Dr. Cord?"

"I was payed to kill him."

"By whom?"

"I do not know, it was all done on the internet, I never saw him nor got a name."

"How unfortunate for you my friend."

Len turned to the guards.

"This man is no longer of any value, take him out and kill him, and make it slow."

The guards drag the assassin out of Len's office, and all the while the prisoner is screaming that.

"You can't do this."

As they are going through the door, Len tells him.

"On this island I can do whatever I please."

Len finds this perplexing; is the U.S. involved, or someone else? Len calls his security chief to have a discussion. The Security Chief is fearful of Len when he enters. He is not sure if he will be alive at the end of the meeting.

"Chief, I want you to cut this island off from everything, and I want all our people rechecked, if there is a questionable person here on this island I want him here in front of me."

"Yes sir, Mr. Len."

"Chief if another incident occurs I will hold you personally responsible."

With fear clear in his eyes.

"Yes Sir, Mr. Len"

The Security Chief puts more guards around the island, and then starts his security checks into all the people on the island. Several days later one of the security officers reports to the Security Chief that at the North end of the island they found natives living on the island. The Security Chief, goes to Len to give him his daily report, and one of the items is the natives.

"After all this time Chief you did not know of the natives? I have known of them before we landed on the island. I keep wondering why I keep you in your position."

"What do you want me to do with them Sir?"

"Nothing, they are no threat to us."

"But Sir they could have let the assassin on the island."

"We will go see your natives Chief, follow me."

Len and the Chief with a couple of guards walk to the north end of the island where they stop at the edge of the village. Len gives the Chief a machine gun.

"Go in Chief and kill your threat."

The chief sets off into the village and soon realizes he is alone. He calls out to the guards to follow him. Len restrains them.

"No Chief you do this alone."

The chief walks into the village. It seems deserted, so he fires his gun into the sounding huts and brush to kill the natives. When he is finished he turns to leave, but is captured by natives. He screams for help but the natives kill him.

"That's one chore done, let's return. The fool did not read the reports on these people. We tried to get rid of them and it cost us a lot of people already."

Len and his guards return to the compound. The micro sun project continues. If all goes well they will be ready at the same time the EMP weapon is ready.

Chapter 34

"Steve, I have detected something that is going on in China, you may need to know about it." "What is it CAT?"

"Steve, in the communications I have found a couple of projects that they are doing."

"Alright CAT tell me about them."

"The first project is called EMP it is located in a remote area of China; it has to do with using the satellites to broadcast a pulse all over the world."

"CAT did you say EMP?"

"Yes Steve." "Electro Magnetic Pulse."

"CAT we have to stop it. Can you stop it from reaching the satellites?"

"No Steve I may not have time, but I could redirect the pulse out into space, then it will only affect the immediate or local area."

"CAT do that, if that pulse goes off it will in effect kill you, I have not figured a way to protect you from such an attack as yet."

"Steve I will have them set up in two hours to send the pulse into space, but what is to keep them from doing it again?"

"Do you have the coordinates to the installation?"

"Yes Steve."

Steve opens a window to see the installation and uses the window to peer into any place to see what is going on at the EMP site.

"CAT if I were to shift the important stuff into Deep space, will they be able to rebuild it very soon?"

"No Steve, most of the metals in the EMP generator will be difficult in the extreme to replace, and it will be noticeable if they try to rebuild it."

"CAT can you cause the people to evacuate the complex, so I can destroy it?"

"I believe I can Steve."

"CAT, get me some C-4 explosives so I can destroy that complex."

"Steve, the only place you can get the explosives is from the military."

"Then I guess I will have to take it from them, where do I need to go CAT?"

"According to the inventory you can get what you need at Fort Lewis in Washington."

I put on the battle suit and port to the Armory in Fort Lewis. It is night time so only a guard is watching the armory. I put him to sleep with my dart gun, and I leave my calling card on him with a list of the C-4 I took and what I'm using it for. I take the explosive and port back to the Lodge.

I open windows and place shaped explosives throughout the structure and control areas. Then I have CAT cause an evacuation of the complex convincing everyone of a radiation leak. Once I'm satisfied that the area is clear, I have CAT help me open a window into the EMP cannon and I drop it into deep space. Then I drop the nuclear device which would power the EMP cannon into deep space as well. Last of all I set off the explosives which destroys the whole complex so it falls into rubble. The Chinese Government claims a large earth quake in the area had caused minimal destruction and no life was lost. The Chinese government did not want to own up to what it was they were up to. They realize only one person could have done this kind of work, and not killed any people, Paladin. And since no one can catch him, not even his own country, they drop the whole incident.

"CAT will we be able to do the same thing to the Micro sun complex on that island that you found?"

"No Steve we will not be able to do that from here; you will need to actually be there so I can help you open a window close to the Sun in order to pull the micro sun through the window."

"I did not think they had built it yet."

"Steve as of moments ago, they hadn't, but they just started the process and in minutes from now the micro sun will be in suspension."

"How long will the magnetic bottle hold, not more than an hour Steve."

"Then I guess I had better get going then."

"Steve, you realize that, you will die in the process."

"No, I did not."

"You will be burned from the radiation, but as long as you are close to the micro sun I can still use your crystal to, push the micro sun into our Sun, Steve."

"Do I have time to go home and say good bye."

"Only if you hurry, Steve."

I port home and take a moment to tell my wife good bye, at any time now she could deliver our baby girl. I explain I have to go to an Island and set a problem right that could affect the world.

She smiles at me and asks if I'll be back in time for delivery of our child. I tell her I hope so. I take Grandmother outside to tell her what is going to happen and what will happen if I do not do this. She looks long into my eyes.

"Have you told Samantha?"

"Some of it."

"I understand my son; I'll take care of her."

"CAT will send the car so you both can get to the hospital when you need to and he will also make sure you have all the finances you and Sam will need."

"You are a good son; I will miss you."

"I love you all very much."

Grandmother kisses my cheek, with tears in her eyes.

"We all love you my son."

I port to the island, there are explosions going off all over the place and everyone is primarily running to the ships at dock.

"CAT what is going on here?"

"Steve the micro sun is loose and the magnetic bottle has been shattered by the micro sun, it is now like a hungry animal consuming everything. You have to reach it now, before, we cannot get rid of it."

I port to the micro sun chamber and I see for the moment all the people in the room burnt to ashes.

Chapter 35

"CAT, hurry, make it happen, I'm dying."

CAT opens the window and the gravity of our Sun pulls the micro sun into it and CAT closes the window. I lie dying and my last thoughts are of my family and how I will never see my daughter. The pain is so great, my mind sinks into darkness. The Islanders, make sure the people on the island leave, and a few of them find Steve. He still has a very small spark of life left. The islanders are not what they seem, they are more like insects than people. Similar to ants or bees than anything on this earth.

"Is he alive?" the Queen asks.

"Yes, says one of the workers but not for long."

"You will be his life support hook on."

"But the pain!"

"I know, but he has to be saved, now do it."

The creature sticks a couple of stingers into my burnt flesh, and soon my pain subsides. The creature however is suffering. It is taking on my pain and pumping life into me.

The day comes when Samantha is to deliver the child. CAT has the car there to transport Samantha and grandmother to the hospital. CAT transported them to the edge of town, and then drives the car to the emergency area of the hospital. Samantha is rushed in and sent to the maternity ward. grandmother also follows her granddaughter. So, CAT drives the car off and parks it. Samantha spends the rest of the day in labor, and then is taken in for the delivery. Soon a baby girl is born. Samantha is very tired but is so happy to meet her new daughter. She has a lot of her mother's features, and her father's eyes. She is very happy, but sad too. Her husband is not there as he promised, and she is beginning to resent that he is not there to not only see his child but support her through the labor.

Samantha is beginning to return to the bitterness she had before she married Steve. Grandmother seeing this decides it is time to tell her daughter what happened.

"I was going to wait until you were stronger to tell you about my Adopted Son, but you leave me no choice. You're a silly girl."

"What right do you have to defend him? He promised me he would be here."

"If your husband was here we would not be. He went off to save you and his daughter, knowing it would be his life."

Grandmother puts the headset on Samantha so CAT can explain what Steve just accomplished.

"No!" Screams Samantha and she breaks down crying. The nurse comes in and sees her in hysterics and gives her a shot to put her to sleep.

Back on the island I keep falling in and out of conciseness I seem to see strange things, one moment I see natives that might belong to the island, and the next I see insect like creatures the size of men. I'm not able to move, and it appears I'm covered in some sort of gel only my face is not covered, or at least my eyes and mouth. One day the head native comes in to see how I am doing. I cannot hear him; the gel is covering my ears.

"My Queen the human known as Steve is healing, it is a slow process."

"We need to do what we can. We still have time, but he will need to be fully recovered with in three of the next full moons on our world. He must be returned to his wife by then. When will we be able to open the casing and let him out?"

"In half of a moon cycle, my Queen."

"That will have to do."

A couple of days later, CAT transports every one back to the home in Duffer and then parks the car in in the garage. Samantha has regained her composure, and realizes her husband had no choice in what he did. She forgives him. Now she lavishes all her love on her daughter, and she tells her of her father. Of course, the baby will not understand for some time but Samantha will make sure her daughter knows how great her father was. One-day CAT is experiencing some minor problems, and he contacts Samantha to ask for help.

"Samantha, I need you to help me, would you get in the car so I may bring you to the lodge?"

"What do you need CAT?"

"I need for you to replace one of my relays before I have a major failure, can you help?"

"I can try, but no promises."

"Thank you, Samantha."

Samantha gets into the car and CAT brings her to the lodge. Samantha goes into the lodge and then to the secret room where CAT is.

"I'm here what do I do?"

"Open the first panel on the right Samantha"

Samantha opens the panel.

"Now do you see a relay that looks damaged?"

"I see this little box with a burn spot."

"That is the very one Samantha. The tool kit is over on the bench across the room."

Samantha walks over to the bench and brings back the tool kit.

"Take out the Philips screw driver and loosen the four screws."

Samantha uses the screw driver and removes the screws and pulls the relay out.

"Now what CAT?"

"See the wires the Red and the White, Samantha?"

"Yes."

"Now use the screw driver and remove the screws that hold them on the relay."

With that accomplished.

"CAT do you have another one?"

"There should be another relay in the drawer on the bench where you picked up the tool kit Samantha." Samantha goes over and opens and closes several drawers until she finds what she is looking for. She returns back to CAT and reinstalls the relay.

"Thank you, Samantha, I'm running much better now."

"If you are ready I can send you home now Samantha."

"Ok, CAT."

Samantha and the car are returned to Duffer.

Steve's recovery is very slow, or it seems to be to him. One morning one of the natives comes in with an ax to break open the casing, but at first Steve is thinking he is going to kill me now. I let out a scream and the person in charge comes in to see what is wrong. Realizing that I was in a panic he knocks me out.

"Continue, to break him out."

Soon the casing is broken away and I lay on the ground under the sun. A little while later I wake up and then sit up. I look at myself, my arms, my legs, torso, my hands, they are all smooth and healed. There is something about my hands; I try to remember. My hands should look different and my face feels different too, much like it did before the accident. Now what accident? Then it dawns on me, my scars are all gone. The scars I got on my hand when I fell out of the tree when I was a kid are gone. What is happening to me?

Reborn

Chapter 36

I try to stand up but it's like being a baby all over again. I'm very unsteady on my feet and I fall. I try a few more times, but I'm too exhausted. Soon I fall asleep. The Queen comes into my hut to check on me. From out of the corner of the hut one of the insect creatures materializes.

"How is he progressing?"

"Slowly my Queen."

"What does he know?"

"He knows that he is healed, and vaguely recalls his past."

"That must be suppressed for the time being, where is the medic?"

"ZXC is out for a walk and will be returning soon."

"Tell ZXC I want to see him now!"

"Yes, my Queen."

The watcher leaves to go bring back ZXC. The Queen stands there looking at Steve.

"you will endure much our savior in the time to come. According to our histories you will fight the great beast and save my people. Rest for now and gather your strength."

In the Queens hut ZXC shows up.

"You requested my presence my Queen?"

"Yes, you need to work with the one called Steve, he needs to be ready to leave our world and return to his soon I want him better than he was before he came to this island."

"Yes, my Queen it will be done."

The next day a native comes to me and helps me to stand. Soon I'm able to walk, and after that my so-called drill sergeant is running me into the ground with exercise. Then I am sparring and using all manner of weapons. For the longest time my teacher beats me brutally. Then over time it goes the other way, and when I bested my native teacher, I'm brought to the head man's hut (Actually the Queen's).

"With them controlling my mind all I can see are men, no women, no children and I definitely did not see their true form.

The head man motions for me to come closer to him, so I walk over to him. Then he motions me to sit in front of him. I sit down and feel a sting in my shoulder, as I drop off to sleep. They return me to a different island back on earth. When I wake up I remember who I am, and what I can do. I seem to remember everything except what happened over the last several months. I port back to the lodge; I did not want to port back home with no clothes on.

"CAT."

Then alarms are going off.

"Intruder alert, identify yourself, or I will terminate this place."

"CAT it's me Steve, read my chip."

"You are dead you died months ago in the south China seas taking care of the micro sun."

"You did take care of the micro sun CAT, and I think I did die or was close to it. I know, let me look into the retinal scanner and you will see that it is me."

I look into the scanner, and CAT confirms it is me.

"Steve should I inform Samantha and Grandmother; you are back?"

"No CAT, I would like to do it."

I go upstairs to my bedroom to look for some clothes then I pass a mirror for the first time. I'm shocked as to what I see. I'm all healed except for my shoulder, as it has a round scar about the size of a dime on it. My face is also healed, and it is not much different than my old self before the explosion. I hope Samantha will approve of the change. I finish changing into some clothes just before I port to Duffer. "Steve, I should let them both know you are coming."

"No, CAT I would like to surprise them."

I port to Duffer. I should have listened to CAT. As it turns out, I wound up fighting for my life. I shout from the front porch.

"Samantha, Grandmother, I'm home."

Before I know it, I'm fighting both Grandmother and Samantha trying to convince them; of who I am. Then I break free of them and sit down. I did not make a single move to defend myself. This stopped them in mid stride.

"Who are you?" asks Grandmother.

"I'm Steve your adopted son."

"Stranger that is not possible. You are not scared, my son was scared from burns, why you are smooth and un-scared. Now answer me who are you?"

"Where is my husband stranger?"

"Please, listen, I am your Steve. Check with CAT he can confirm it. Samantha enters the house to contact CAT and he does confirm that I'm Steve.

Samantha comes back and starts asking me questions that only I can answer, after an hour they both let up on me, and invite me into their house. So, I tell them of what happened on the island, and that I was badly burned. I should have died; but that some natives saved me, and I do not know how. But they healed me. Then they taught me how to walk and to fight, when I was healed they disappeared leaving me on a deserted island. Matter of fact that was today. Somehow, they played tricks on my mind. I did not remember anything until I was returned to the island.

"Did I say that?"

"Anyway, I'm not sure of what went on."

"Do you believe me Samantha?"

"I'm not sure." She said.

I walk over to Samantha and take her hand. I port us to where we were married then on to where we had our honeymoon.

"Do you know anyone else who can do that?"

Samantha looks deep into my eyes.

"No, I don't. So, this really is you my husband?"

"I am."

She throws her arms around his neck and gives and gets the first kiss sense we've met. With my burnt face I did not have any lips. But now that I'm healed, and I no longer have the scars and my lips are there. Steve and Samantha stand there in Paris near the Effie Tower and they both enjoy that very first kiss.

After that Samantha says, "Take me home, the baby."

So, I port us back to Duffer and Samantha runs into the house, and into the bedroom. I follow her. The baby is standing up holding on the rail of the crib and bouncing up and down crying. Samantha picks her up and coos to her, then asks me if I want to hold her. With trembling hands, I take the small baby into my arms. I am besides myself to see my little girl for the first time, like any father I feel fierce Pride and protectiveness toward this baby girl. Then I realize why she is crying, she is wet and needs a change.

I try to hand her back to her mom, when mom says, "You have been off partying all this time, and it is about time for you to learn how to change a diaper."

"But I have never done this before."

"Then it is time to learn."

So, I submit to my wife and when the ordeal is done I realize it is not such a bad thing after all. The worst part is the washing out the diaper. I decide to take the next month off so I can be with my family. It gets to be a bit trying.

Everywhere I go Samantha is right there. I guess I can understand; she went from losing a husband to having him back only better. I go to the Dallas court and ask to get new pictures for my driver license Passport and such. To explain my new face, I had to say I went to a Specialist in Europe a plastic surgeon that used some special new techniques to fix my face and hands. Now Steve Ball has a new look.

My last suit was burned up due to the micro sun, so I had CAT order me the stuff to make a new one, then I decide to make one for Samantha as well. They look much like the first one except between CAT and I we can employ two sets of force fields, one which will deflect projectiles and the other to become like an exoskeleton, which would make us stronger and a bit faster in our movements. As hoped, I checked on my experiment of growing the crystal and I find That they had grown (What I did not know at the time was the Insect creatures put a new crystal in the dish) I can now give Samantha a crystal of her own. I port back home to ask Samantha if she would like to be like me. Once the baby was fed and put to bed and we were alone I popped the question.

"How would you like to be able to do what I can do and port from place to place on your own?"

She looked at me and smiled.

"That would be nice dear, but you told me that you did not have enough crystal and that it would not be possible."

"Let's say an experiment I was working on allowed me to grow more crystal, would that interest you?" "Do you really mean it?"

"Actually yes."

"When can I get it?"

"Well we would need a baby sitter and a couple of days together, so you have time to recover from the insertion of the crystal. Then you will need to learn to be able to use it, especially the do's and don'ts. Those rules I learned the hard way, and so did Romeo."

"Who is Romeo?"

So, I tell Samantha how I found the crystal, and tested it on the mouse, and how the mouse died, I related the story on getting the crystal, the explosion, and so on. Samantha looks at me for a few minutes and said "You really meant what you just said?"

"Yes, if you are not careful you could port into a solid object, and like Romeo you would die. Fortunately, CAT can keep you from doing that until you learn better on how to use the crystal."

Chapter 37

"OK, so when do I get the crystal?"

"Tomorrow if you like."

"Good, I'll get Grandmother to watch baby Kim."

"Tomorrow it is"

"This is going to be like a date weekend." Said Samantha.

I port us to the lodge the next morning.

"You won't think so when I insert the crystal, you will be sick and weak for several hours as your body and the crystal knit together with your nerves."

That day, Grandmother takes charge of her tiny granddaughter.

"I have everything ready for you, so we can begin when you are ready."

"I'm ready Steve."

I have her lie down on the bed, face down, then I make a very small incision at the base of her neck and insert the small crystal. As I had experienced Samantha grew very tired and sick as her body dealt with the crystal. I give her an injection to put her to sleep. Hours later I wake her up to check on her progress.

"Does it always feel this way?" Samantha asks.

"As far as I can tell, yes. Romeo felt that way too when I put in the crystal."

"When will I feel better?"

I look at my watch, in about two more hours, you should start to feel OK."

Samantha drops off to sleep. Two hours later Samantha gets up.

"I do feel better but knowing what I know now I would not want to do that again."

"The worst of it is over now. In a little while when you recover more, we'll test it out."

"Will I be able to do what you do?"

"I honestly do not know, as it took me a while to be able to do some of the things I can do now. I noticed the more I do the teleportation the easer it gets. It's the same with moving objects. It took a while to for me to move larger objects. Each time I moved something, it was easier, and I'm now able to move larger and larger objects. Like the space shuttle nose, I can now move an object that size. It would tax me, but I would not pass out like I did before."

"So, let's start now to see what I can do."

"No, we will do it tomorrow, there is much I need to tell you, and you will operate better tomorrow after a good night's sleep, and breakfast."

So, I lead Samantha up the stairs to the living room, to have a conversation.

"Let me tell you some of the rules about this ability we both have. I told you of Romeo and how he died. One other thing is you can usually teleport to any place you have been, just make sure you consult with CAT before you go, as you do not want to teleport into something or someone."

"I could do that?"

"Yes, things change, people are always moving about, when I was first doing this I picked places that were seldom used, and mostly I choose line of sight teleporting. One time before I had CAT, I took a bus and walked about to broaden my teleporting options."

"Will I have to do that?"

"I do not know, for the most part CAT can place you safely close to where you want to go."

The next morning with CAT to help, I was able to get Samantha started in being able to teleport from one place to another here at the lodge. With both of us being able to teleport, we would have to be careful. We would not want to teleport to the same exact spot and be merged together. So, we decided to let one or the other do the porting or have CAT do it.

"Now I'll be able to go with you more on these little adventures you have Steve, and I can watch out for myself."

"Ok, having brought up the subject, I have a gift for you."

"I needed a new suit, so I took the liberty to make one for you as well."

"You made a suit for me?"

I walk over to the lockers and open it up to pull out and display a battle suit just like mine only smaller. "Here try it on so I can see how it fits."

Samantha puts on her suit. It is a bit tight in a few places, and loose in others.

"Well this is the first time I have ever made clothes for a woman. I need to make some adjustments. Samantha go stand over by that screen and take your clothes off."

"CAT, scan her to get the proper measurements."

CAT scans Samantha to get her sizes, so Steve can make changes to Samantha's suit. With the scan complete. Samantha walks over to Steve.

"Now if you wanted me to undress, would it not be better if we were upstairs?"

Samantha ports them to the bedroom.

"Now stop that, I have work to do. We can do this later."

Samantha laughs a sultry laugh.

"Maybe I'll get a headache later."

"I'll take my chances."

I port back to the lab to begin work on her suit. Minutes later Samantha appears and decides to help with the alterations. By the end of the day she puts on her suit and it fits just right.

"Let's return home and see how well you do with porting."

I take her hand and she ports us back to Duffer out in the front yard. I turn to Samantha.

"You are quite the wonder at this."

Samantha blushes and runs off into the house to check on Kim and grandmother.

Over the next couple of years, between Samantha and me we manage to strangle the illegal drug trade. Whenever possible CAT just calls the drug task force people and leaves an anonymous communication telling where and when the deals are going down. Other times Samantha and I stepped in and take care of the situation ourselves. Sometimes we port in and render the bad guys in unconscious heaps for the police to pick up. Others times I would open a window around the bottom of the drugs and drop them into a lava pit. I had to stop doing that as one time I dropped the drugs into the lava pit one of the thugs tried to save the case of drugs and fell into the lava pit with the drugs and died. So, I went back to the snatch and garb routine I was doing in the beginning. The nice thing about doing that is, it gives Samantha and me a chance to get a real work out. In a way, it has become fun, as with our suits on no one can really hurt us, unless they have a 50-callaber weapon to shoot us with, but we can usually port out of the way just in the nick of time.

Chinaman

Chapter 38

But all in all, we stopped the drug dealing down to barely a trickle. Somehow one of our old enemy's, learned where my family lived. (Later I was to find out that the insect people gave him that information, because it had something to do with their histories). One day while I was with Samuel going over some changes for the car. The Chinaman and his men showed up at our isolated home and captured our three-year-old daughter. Grandmother put up a fight but is shot in the chest. Samantha starts to get into the fight when she is told to do so would see her daughter shot in the head. Samantha does not move a muscle. She Watches helplessly as they attach a collar around her daughter's neck, then hers.

"Now my darlings if either one of you does something I do not like, I will press this button and kill both of you, do you understand?"

"Yes."

"I see in your eyes that you would like to kill me, is this not so?"

Through clenched teeth Samantha says "Yes!"

"Something you should know, you both will be my guests for the remainder of your lives, and your husband will do what I say."

"I would not count on that if I were you. My husband will free us and then he will hand out justice."

"Get us to the plane and let's get off the ground before Paladin returns."

"If I were you, I would run too, but realize there is nowhere you can go where he cannot follow. I would not want to be in your shoes when he catches up with you."

"He will catch up with us, but it will be on my terms. You see, you are his heart, and to protect you he will do whatever I want him to."

Samantha looks at her daughter and tried to reassure her that all will be ok when daddy gets here.

They get on the plane and it take off. As Steve finishes up with Samuel, CAT contacts him. "Steve, you need to go home now"

"Just a moment CAT."

"Steve Grandmother has been shot and is dying"

I port that moment to Duffer and find grandmother in the house. There is blood all over the porch into the house. I pick up grandmother and she touches my face.

"I tried to stop them my son, too many of them. It was the Chinaman, he took them both."

"It's OK, I'll get them back, it's you I need to get to the hospital."

Grandmother dies in my arms. A great rage fills my soul.

"CAT, where is Samantha?!"

"Steve, she is on a plane heading to Portland, where and when will it land?"

"Steve it should be in Portland in an hour. As to which run way it will land on, I do not know yet, probably the north one. It is used mainly by private aircraft."

Steve suits up and adds his pistols and darts, and a few explosives, then ports to the Portland airport to wait. Twenty minutes later their plane arrives. I pick a spot to watch to see if I can act or not without causing harm to my daughter or my wife. What I'm wondering is why Samantha has not ported away with our daughter. The reason becomes clear, they both have collars on and I detect the explosives in them. Then I see the Chinaman. In his hand he holds up the push button device, and I see it is depressed. If I do something and it is released it

185

will kill both my wife and my daughter. It does not take long, and they move to a hanger and board another plane this one a Lear jet, before they can board, I port on to the plane to set up several cameras, then I port off before they know I'm there. When the time comes I will need to know where Samantha and Kim are on the plane.

I watch them take off, and I have CAT track them, it will be about twenty-four hours before they reach Hong Kong. My plan at this point is to rescue them as they land at the airport.

"CAT, to prevent this in the future, I need to install a communication device, in both Samantha and myself. This not being able to talk to her, I see as a weak point in staying alive. I'm returning to the lodge, have the police been summoned to Duffer yet?"

"Steve it is done. The Sheriff wants to question you."

"Tell them I'll be there in a few minutes, I'll need the car, be sure it is ready, and bring it to the lodge."

I port back to the lodge, and change my clothes, then get into the car and port to The Dalles outside of town I then drive back to my house in Duffer. I see a flurry of police activity, and I park my car and get out. At this point I put on a show of what happened and where is my family.

The police tell me they found Grandmother dead. They have not yet found my wife or child, thanks to CAT, I was able to prove I was not in the area but had just returned from Walla Walla where I was conducting business. So, I was dropped off the suspect list. I gave them free reign to check my whole property over; they found nothing. However, they did find that a strange group of people had been in town looking for my house. The person who gave the directions to my house thought it strange that Asians were interested in my inventions, and so gave them directions. So, the search is on for the car. After several hours, and answered questions, the police leave my property. I take the time to clean up the blood and set the house in order. I go to bed to get some sleep, but sleep does not come. Somehow, I did manage to doze off. The next morning, CAT wakes me up.

"Steve, they have passed Guam after refueling. Now they are on their way toward Hong Kong."

"Great CAT, I'm going to suit up, what little sleep I did get gave me an idea of how to save my wife and daughter. CAT how much range does the explosive device that the Chinaman held have?"

"I believe if I send the device to the other side of the world the signal will not reach the explosives around their necks."

"Steve that should work, but they do have guns. Can they not shoot Kim and Samantha anyway?"

"Only if I give them time to do so, I do not intend to give them any time to do much of anything."

I suit up and add my guns, explosives, tool kit and a few assorted other tools. I'm thinking to myself, all I need now is a bat symbol, and a cape and I can play Bat Man. I port to the Hong Kong airport to await their Lear Jet. I still have several hours before they arrive, so I scout out the best place to ambush them when they land.

Thanks to CAT I locate the hanger that the Chinaman uses. I also have CAT give me the lay out of the Chinaman's plane, so I can figure out where everybody will be. The arrival of the jet is announced to me by CAT so I watch as the plane lands, and I just wait for the Jet to taxi up to the hanger. Once it stops, I open a window to look into the planes interior, and I find Kim, my daughter, and Samantha. It looks like they slapped Samantha around a lot, and my daughter is showing a few bruises as well. Seeing this makes my blood boil. I have discovered I can open a window within a window, so I open a window so I can see the Chinaman, then I open and the close a window over the Chinaman's arm with the device, cutting his arm off and sending it to China. I quickly do the same to the men with guns. At that point Samantha takes over, and she kills

187

three of the men. I keep watching, and a man comes up behind my wife with a knife, I decapitate the man with one of my windows and he falls to the floor.

My wife grabs our daughter and ports home, I enter the plane and the Chinaman is still alive trying to stop the blood. I reach down and grab him by his suit jacket, and I pull him up onto his feet. I point to the man on the floor without a head. I hold up the man and tell him, If I ever see you or hear your name again, what I did to his head, I will do to your whole body."

As it turns out one of his men was reaching for a gun and managed to get it. Before he can open fire I opened and closed so many windows through the man's body, he looks like pulled pork. The Chinaman turns totally white with fear.

I asked him "How did you know where to find my family?"

"I received an anonymous tip, so I checked it out, and it turned out to be true."

"Pass the word along that if anyone touches my family, I will turn them into hamburger, just like that man over there."

I port home to check on my wife and daughter.

I port into the house in Duffer, and find my wife and child sitting on the couch crying, I take off my helmet and sit next to them, as I wrap my arms around them. I hold them for quite some time, and both my wife and daughter fall asleep in my arms. I remove the explosive devices and get rid of them. I pick up Samantha and Kim to carry them into their bedroom to put them in their beds and cover them up. I change out of my suit and decide to teach Samantha how to use the port windows, not only to survey things, but as a weapon. I contacted the sheriff and informed him that I have my family back. The sheriff drives out to my house, as he wants to see them and question them. He asked me how I managed to get them I told him they wanted one of my inventions, so I traded it to them. He seemed a bit skeptical about it but could not deny they were there, safe and sound. The sheriff was satisfied and left.

Late in the day, Samantha and Kim came out of their bedrooms, both look better. Samantha starts to apologize about being taken so easily. I assured her that I could not have done it any better than she did. Protecting our daughter is important. I suggest we sell this place and move to the lodge.

"No Steve, we have to give our daughter a normal life, living on a mountain isolated from everyone is not a good thing, she needs to be around people in order to grow up properly."

"Fair enough. Then it is time to accelerate your training on the crystal's functions. I'm also going to have to do something to both of us so we can communicate with each other more easily. I have CAT working on that project as we speak. With the chip, I was able to track you, and when I teach you about the windows you could have dealt with them as I did, using the windows to stop them."

"Steve can you put something around the house to warn us of people on the property?"

"I think I can do that; I'll have CAT order that in as well."

It takes several weeks for Samantha and Kim to recover from their ordeal, and during that time I teach Samantha how to use the window. She can use it to look into places, and learns how to use it as a weapon. I take the time to set up a surveillance system around the edge of the property, and in and around the buildings. The last thing is I get the miniature radio that can be implanted in both Samantha and myself, so we will be able to communicate when we are not together. And for good measure I get an implant for Kim so we can keep tabs on her. CAT orders the items and they are ready for pick up. So, I port to the warehouse where they are delivered, and take them home.

Guardian of the

world

Chapter 39

"CAT, is this a mistake, these have to be surgically implanted."

"Steve that is correct, this way you can never lose them or misplace them."

"You got that right, but won't that also make it bad for private conversations?"

"Steve, I do not understand; would you not want to be in constant contact with your wife?"

"CAT, there are some conversations, that need to be private between husband and wife, and that would be very difficult to explain to you, or for you to understand."

"Steve, let me do some more research, maybe we can modify these units to serve that purpose."

There are some house fixes I need to do around the house too, so I start doing some of the minor repairs. Then I get a communication from CAT. Thinking it is about the communication devices. "Steve someone is trying to reach you, using your old name, Steve Storm."

"Does he have a message?"

"Steve, he wants to meet with you."

"Where and when?"

"Steve, he says he is the owner of Annex Oil Company, and he knows who tried to kill you with explosives at the lab."

"Did he say anything else CAT?"

"Steve, he gave me a location where to meet him."

"Maybe I should take him up on his invitation."

I go to suit up and tell Samantha, that I'm going to go see this person.

"The surveillance is on, and I also have the car here, I want to go see this man to find out why I was being targeted to be killed. This still may be the case, and I wish to head off the killer before you or Kim become targets again."

CAT gives me the coordinates to the place, and I port there. It places me at the front door of a rather large building. I look around and do not see any one. I get ready to return when over a PA system I hear.

"Please enter, the door is open."

I open the door and step in. I'm met by a jolly looking fellow.

"You must be Paladin?"

"I am."

"Please do not be alarmed, I'm the person who called you, and I made sure that we would not be bothered. Please follow me."

I follow the man down the hall, and into a room. It sounds like I'm in a bank vault, when the door closes behind me. The jolly old man turns to me and leads me to a chair.

"Here sit down so we can have a discussion."

I sit in the chair to see what will transpire. He then offers me something to drink.

"No thank you, I will not take off the helmet. Now do you suppose you can tell me why I'm here?" "Where to start? Well in a way I'm a guardian of sorts. As such I try to prevent inventions that will destroy our world. Your invention is just such an invention."

I jump to my feet.

"It was you who tried to kill me?"

"True, but let me explain before you do anything, you see your invention, would cause worldwide devastation. It will destroy world industry as we know it today. Just think, Oil would no longer be necessary, no need for cars, planes, or any transportation. All the connected industries would collapse. Then the safety of the world will be at odds. There would be no way to stop people from going anywhere and doing anything."

"Your invention let out to the world, would destroy this world, nothing or no one would be safe. Because of the destruction you would cause I must destroy you, like I tried years ago."

"How would you do that, knowing I can leave when I choose."

"Well while you were in here, I have moved this room far underground, you do not know where you are, so from my research you should not be able to leave here."

"OK, so how are you going to kill me then."

"In mere moments a bomb will be going off in this room which will kill us both."

"I see. I hope you do not mind that I try to leave."

"Go ahead."

I port to the old man and then port us out of the room to a remote Island.

"No, you can't do this!"

"Now that we won't be disturbed, I have some other questions for you."

"According to my research, you must be responsible for other deaths as well, like the man who came up with the Micro sun, and other transporter devices."

"Yes!" Screamed the old man."

"Unlike you I do not kill people, so I'm going to leave you here. There are enough resources here for you to live out your life."

"You can't do that I'm the most powerful man in the world."

"Not anymore."

I port off the island and I never see the old man again. With the room blowing up, no one knows that the old man is still alive.

Well I'm going to end this session of writing, there are many more adventures to come I hope you will enjoy them.

Chapter 40

Benison Static is a scientist in Molecular Mechanics and Energy scientist, and his partner Andy Johansson is an Electronics and Metallurgy scientist. Both men are working on a way to build a transporter. As they work on their idea they realized they need another partner who specializes in computers and programing. Andy suggests that they bring on an old friend from college Candy Lake. She is a wiz at computing software, she was the best in her class Candy agrees to become part of the team. But not before she gets even with Andy for dumping her for another girl, leaving Andy red in the face with embarrassment. After many months of trials, they manage to build a transmitter which looks like a round cylinder over six feet tall and ten feet in diameter and a receiver for their transporter is of the same shape and size. It is very clunky. Especially with all the wires and cables from transmitter chamber being routed to the computer console and then from the computer to the receiver, but they feel if they can get this system to work; they can begin to make refinements and stream line their invention at a later date. The theory of the device is that the transmitter will breakdown the item to be transported and transform it into data. Then transmit that data to the receiver, which will reconstruct that data back to its original form. The transmitter in essence destroys the object one molecule at a time and translates it into a data stream that the computer can read, then transfer the data to the receiver and it will take the data stream and rebuild the object to its original self.

They build two pods, and place one at each end of the warehouse that they are using. One end has the transmitter, and the other end the receiver. Both units are controlled by Candy's computers and programs. In this test they use an old block of wood, which they sent through the transmitter to the receiver or at least that is the plan. They place the wood block into the transmitter, and run the first part of the program. The wooden block is destroyed as it should have been and the computer stores the data stream. The next part of the program runs. And transfers the data stream to the receiver part of the transporter, where it rebuilds the wooden block from the stored data. What they get back is a pulverized block of wood.

"At least it was not burnt like last time! I have recorded the Computer record settings so we can keep track of the changes in the programming" said Candy.

"So how many runs so far?" asks Ben.

"To date twenty runs and all have failed, but this one is our best one yet, at least we got wood back and not charcoal. Let me run some analysis on this sample and I'll let you know if it is better." Says Andy.

Andy takes the sample to his work area to run some test on it. When he looks at it under the microscope, he sees what looks like some kid playing pick-up Styx and dropped all the wood fibers on to the floor in a pile. Andy reports to the other two his findings.

"Well from what I can see the transmitter takes it apart and that seems to be fine. However, the receiver does not put the pieces back together the way it was taken apart or better yet in reverse order." said Andy.

"Let me work with the program and see what I can do to correct that problem" says Candy. Candy takes a few days and rewrites, and tweaks her program. Then it is time to perform another test. Candy puts a block of wood into the transmitter. Then fires up the computer program, and then launches the sequence. You can hear the transmitter as it destroys the block of wood it sounds much like an old dot matrix printer as it chatters back and forth. Then moments later the receiver is re-integrating the data stream back into the block of wood. Candy opens the receiver and takes out a solid block of wood back.

"Andy, Ben get in here now! It seems to be working."

Both of them appear and Candy shows them the block.

Andy turns to Candy saying "Let's re-run another test. And use a new block of wood, then I can have two of them to test."

Candy puts in the new block then fires up the computer program. In mere moments it cycles through the sequence and the receiver gets another block of wood. Andy grabs both of them up and rushes to his lab to test the wood. Andy returns in an hour.

"The wood tests out alright. Now the thing is, is the wood we sent through the same as it was after reassembly."

"I see what you mean" said Ben, "let's try something else, I know I have this wooden bowl that a friend carved for me it has designs on it, this should tell us if it is being assembled correctly."

Ben puts the bowl into the transmitter, and Candy runs the computer program, and moments later they pull the bowl out of the receiver and it is perfectly intact.

"I think this calls for a party and a day off tomorrow." Says Ben.

"Then on Thursday we can re-run it again to be sure."

Andy and Candy agree. So they all go out to dinner to celebrate the day's success. On Thursday they all return to work and re-run the test on the bowl several times and each time it is successful.

Ben turns to Andy and Candy "Now we know we can put one object through the transporter, let's try two objects."

Andy brings in a block of wood and a glass ash tray and puts them into the transmitter. They get cycled through the transporter, and what they get is a wood ceramic.

"Wow look at that, it sure looks pretty but that is not what it should be" said Andy.

"Hey, wait a minute, I want to try something else."

Andy goes to a storage cabinet and brings a block of Steel and a block of Titanium and puts them into the transmitter, and has Candy cycle the transporter. Andy takes the new material out of the receiver. "Look at this! This is Fantastic! These metals will not combine under our current technology. I need to run some tests and I will get back to you both later."

"What is it Andy?" asks Ben.

Chapter 41

"If this tests out the way I hope it will, we can make millions creating new materials, this will give us the funds to continue our work on the transporter."

Andy takes the material to his lab and runs his tests. The next day Andy is all but dancing around.

"This is great stuff, I'm going to approach some of the metal making companies and let them have a sample of this material to see what they would be willing pay to have it made in quantity. I may want to duplicate our current set up on the third floor so I can keep making new and different materials and generate some money for us, so let me go see what the market will bear."

Andy contacts a few companies and provides them with his new material, in a week's time they want more material and the process used to make it. Andy decides to move his operation in to another warehouse down the road so there is an easier access to the inside of the building for trucks. Then Andy builds a bigger transmitter / receiver set up. He makes a deal to make the materials but will not give up the process on how to make it. The companies who want the new materials must supply the materials according to Andy's specifications. Andy will then process them into the new material for a fee.

Andy begins to make all kinds of new materials and their bank account is approaching the billion-dollar mark. Andy could have set them all up for life, but their goal is still make a transporter. Andy is making a new kind of material from steel and copper, when an unseen rat enters the transmitter chamber while the door is open. Andy closes the door without a second look then cycles the transporter and gets a strange shock when he opens the receiving chamber door. There in the middle of the chamber is a rat shaped metal composite the size of a small dog. The thing is heavy. Just what I need a statue shaped like a rat. Thinks Andy.

Andy puts the rat on the shelf, and closes for the day. That night in a meeting with Ben and Candy. Andy tells what happened today at his lab, and he tells them about the Rat shaped statue.

"What is this" asked Candy "you say a rat shaped statue came out?"

Andy responds "Why yes, does this mean anything?"

"Has this happened at any other time?"

"No, now that you mentioned it has not."

"Andy we need to go see this statue, and right now." Said Ben.

They leave the Cafe and go to Andy's lab there on the shelf where the steel and copper rat was placed it had moved and changed its position, from walking on all fours to sitting upright.

Andy was beside himself as he saw the rat statue. "This can't be! Said Andy. "I placed the statue in the middle of the shelf and it was on all fours, now look at it."

"Andy you must have had a rat in the chamber when you cycled it and it became part of the new material you were working on." mused Ben.

"I gathered that much now" said Andy, "but it is moving, it's alive, how can that be?"

Ben hazards a guess, the theory that rocks may be alive in their own way may be what's in play here. It takes the rat a while to make a move, much like watching the hour hand on a clock. We know it moves, but it is so slow that we do not see it move, if we leave the room and come back later we can see that it has moved. There is a theory that rocks might be alive, but they move so slowly they cannot be seen to move. Not that I believe in living rock. But the rat over there does suggest a lot of possibilities along that line. Right now the rat is not anything to be concerned with, so let's get back to our project."

Over the next few days the rat is totally forgotten, and it manages to escape, by falling out an open window. Then bounces into the gutter with a large storm drain opening, the rat manages to fall into the sewer system, and is never seen again. Andy has by this time amassed a fortune in his new metal process, and he shares it with Ben and Candy after all they all came up with the machine. Now they can proceed with the real project of building a transporter.

Chapter 42

Candy figures out how to send items through the transporter and get them back as they were transmitted. At this time all they sent are blocks of materials (Wood, metal, glass and plastics) now they tried to send shaped blocks, or blocks that have holes, or have an irregular shape. At first all they get are square blocks of material from the irregular shaped blocks. Candy tweaks her programs, and Ben tries to adjust the power settings to help make the system run more efficiently. They ran another test on a roller bearing and they get a roller bearing back. Ben gives the bearing to Andy so he can run tests on the metal to see if it is the same way as it was before the transport. Andy came back the next day and said it is a success.

"Ok it is time to see if we can get some backers or prospective buyers for our transporter" said Ben.

Ben contacts six transport or trucking companies with their idea only two of them show up. After seeing the demonstration, the company men want to know when and if they can get the transporter for their own use. Also they want exclusive rights to it. Then one asks how much cargo they can ship at a time. How about transporting cargo the size of a cargo shipping container full of product. At this point Candy speaks up.

"At this time that is not possible, you would need a super computer capable of handling and storing all of the data stream. With our current technology that is just not possible. Right now I'm using a six terabit computer just to do this demonstration."

Ben speaks up, "the process for the transporter is that the item in the transmitter is destroyed molecule by molecule and converted into data storage in the buffer of the computer, the program cycles the data to the receiver and is re-integrated back into its original form. That requires a lot of computer memory. Our team realizes that we will need to develop new technology such as a super computer in order to accomplish what you ask.

"Tell me doctors, will this be able to transport people?" asked one of the buyers.

Candy speaks to this, "In theory yes, but as we mentioned it will require a super computer to hold all the data, a person is more complex than a block of wood or metal. We have not tried to send a living thing through the process yet. But we intend to as soon as we figure out how to build a supercomputer." One of the buyers turns and as he is leaving said "when you have it all figured out, call me."

The other buyer stands there as if in thought "I did some research on you people, and have found that you do not need money. You each are fairly rich using this machine to fabricate exotic materials. I assume you are using this money to build your machine? Once perfected you could control the industry. Why contact me for support?"

"Candy answers "we will need to bring in more people to help develop this computer technology and it may well cost more than we are currently making. We are leaders in our field and we are not business leaders. We see that in the future we will need your experience, so why wait until the last minute to find that support."

"That makes sense, and I may have the person you need, his name is Randy Thompson, my son." (In the back of his mind, at last I may get my son to build a better crystal computer, that I can take from them and get control of the world's finances.)

Andy is perplexed, "Your son? Your last name is Byron."

"It's his mother's maiden name, Randy took it after she died, and he and I do not get along. But he is very talented with computers. This would give him something to do besides frittering away his life playing video games."

"Ok, send him to us and we will see what he is capable of, and does this mean you will support us?"

"I'll consider it for now. I'll have Randy here in the morning."

The next morning Randy shows up at the lab.

Chapter 43

"Are you the people who needs a computer geek?" asks Randy.

"Hi Randy we have been expecting you." As Candy introduces herself.

"This is Ben our power expert, and this is Andy who really makes us our money by developing new materials."

They incline their heads toward Randy.

"So why am I here?" Questions Randy.

"Your father suggested you may be able to help us."

"Don't say that, don't call him my father. He killed my mother, and I hate him for it!"

"No disrespect to you, and we will not mention it again" said Ben.

"Candy will give you a tour, then we will demonstrate our process, and maybe you can see how the transporter works."

"You're kidding right? A transporter like in Star Trek?"

"May be in the future we can make it like the one in Star Trek, but for now think of it more like a telephone call Transmitter and a receiver. We'll let Candy fill you in, she is our programmer and probably talks your language or at least close to it."

"Hey I'm not some dumb kid, I made my own computer using a crystal quartz and it is the fastest computer ever made, but Mister Byron hushed it up and has it locked away for safe keeping so he says."

Ben looks Randy in the eye. "Randy, at this lab if you choose to help us and work with us. You will be treated as an equal, not as a child. You will share equally in all that there is, even the money that we are making. Also we will share some of our dream projects, in time we hope we can place raw materials in Andy's machine break them down and then integrate into a finished product, for instance a car."

"When do I start?" asks Randy not confident in what they have said, he will reserve his judgment for the time being."

"Randy follow me, and we'll take a tour and I'll show you what we have done thus far" said Candy.

So for the rest of the day Candy and Randy tour the labs. Ben's energy lab, is where he has come up with different ways to use the current technology to generate power for their project. Then they move on to Andy's lab where Andy has on display several new materials that have been made, and lastly Candy's lab where the computers and programs are made.

"I'm impressed." Said Randy, "where do I get to set up a lab?"

"We hoped you would be willing to work with us so we made some space over there in that corner. There should be enough space for you there. Now for any equipment you may need just ask me and I'll see that you get it."

"You really mean that don't you?"

"Like Ben said if you want. You will be part of our team. We will expect a lot from you, and if you don't deliver, then you will be asked to leave."

Randy looks into Candy's eyes and says "I'll deliver, and I want to thank you guys for giving me a chance. And not treating me like the Boss's son."

"Your father does not own us, and so we can hire and fire as we choose, we only contacted a few companies. We are not business people, and we can use an expert to guide us."

"Then a word of advice from me. Do not trust Mister Byron; he will steal your inventions and leave you in the gutter. I have watched his tactics so many times. You would be better off hiring a person out of college than Mister Byron."

"Ok, Randy thanks for that piece of advice, I'll be sure to tell the others. Actually no you can tell them at our meeting at lunch time."

Chapter 44

Randy looks into the computers that they are using, and made some notes, he made some hardware changes to help make the computers run faster and be more reliable. He also put a proposal together for using a crystalline type of computer system using fiber optics and lasers. Lunch time comes around, and Candy takes Randy to meet with Ben and Andy. In the meeting each person takes his turn to tell where they are in the project. Ben tells of a new possible power source, Andy tells of the cash flow from the new materials he has been creating, Candy tells of the tweaks in her programs to better collect and transmit the data stream. Randy get his chance. He warns the team about Mister Byron's business tactics, and not to trust him. Then he goes on to tell about some of the hardware upgrades that would make the computers they have better. Last of all he puts his proposal on the table to change the Computer system over to using a crystalline and fiber optics system using lasers, by the time he finishes Ben, Andy and Candy are very impressed.

"That would solve a lot of our problems, the power, and storage would be unbelievable, and the speed of the system, Wow!" Says Ben.

The rest of the team looks at Randy.

Candy comments, "Randy scrap the idea of upgrading the current computers and let's build the crystal system computers. Give Andy a material list of what you need, and Andy will get it for you."

"Really"! exclaims Randy.

The team looks at him and in unison says "Really."

"This is the first time I've ever been a part of something where I have been taken seriously, Thank You guys!"

"Randy if this computer system you proposed works half as well as you say man! Wow, it will be worth whatever we spend on it. Get me your equipment list." Said Andy.

Andy pats Randy on the back, "if you were a little older I'd take you out for a brew, so would you settle for a soda for now? And if we were to ask Ben and Candy they would accompany us. You are a god send Randy."

That day Randy makes some new friends. The next morning Randy gives Andy a shopping list of materials. Andy looks over the list.

" You have asked for diamonds and rubies is there a size we need, you do realize that we can get these manufactured, but before I buy them which one would be better, the manufactured or natural gems, and which gem the rubies or diamonds?"

"That's a tough one each one has properties that would be better if they were packaged into a new material, like you do with the metals."

"So what are the properties?"

"The diamond makes great storage, while the ruby is less crystalline and will pass a light like a laser more easily than a diamond."

"Laser huh, that means the speed of the computer will be at the speed of light."

"That's why I suggested it, also you could use this computer with nothing more than lithium batteries, but I would have them special made so they do not explode."

"Randy you are full of surprises. That will mean Ben will have to concentrate the power on the transporter and not the computers. Randy this is great. I'll order all the items today, and everything should be here in a couple of weeks."

"Thanks Andy, I'll draw up the schematics for the computers today. Andy on that list I'll need fiber optics cable to make this work, be sure to get the best grade you can."

"You got it Randy." Two weeks pass, and all the materials ordered have come in.

"Andy I thought you were going to get manufactured Diamonds and Rubies already put to gather?"

"No, I said I would get them, and we'll put them together using my process."

Randy hits himself with the flat of his hand. "You are right Andy you can do that. When will we combine them?"

"In an hour, right now I'm processing more special metals, and when that is done we'll get your crystals combined, I'm rather anxious to see the new computer work myself."

Andy puts the diamonds and rubies in a pile in the transmitter in equal weight then turns to the transmitter and cycles it to transfer the crystals into the buffer. Then he goes to his second computer for the receiver and makes a few adjustments so when he gets the crystal composite it won't be in a strange shape, it will come out as a bar. Then Andy cycles the receiver, and there in the middle of the chamber is the crystal composite. The composite is clear shot through with the red of the ruby color. Andy calls Randy and tells him the crystal is ready and Randy rushes over to collect it.

"Randy I'm going to make another crystal so you can upgrade my computer too, I should have the components here in a few days, so when you get Candy's up and running you can come and do mine."

"That sounds great Andy, I'll be glad to do it."

Little does anyone know Randy's father has a spy watching and listening to their every conversation so he can know when to raid the facility to steal the crystal computers.

Randy gets all his components for the crystal computers and goes to his lab area to assemble the computer. Randy first puts Candy's new computer in place. Then Randy tears up the floor and hides all the components in the floor then sets up control through the old console. Then tells Candy to leave the old computer in place. So if someone brakes in to steal the computers they will take this one and not the crystal computers. When Randy finishes with Candy's computer (which took Randy a few days to build and set up). Then Randy turns to Andy's computer. After running the same steps on Andy's computer by putting the crystal computer under the floor, Randy tells Andy to leave the old computers in place. The next meeting all four meet for lunch and Randy asks "How's the new computer doing?"

Chapter 45

"The transporter works far better than it ever has and much faster as well" said Candy.

Andy chimes in and says much the same. Point in fact Candy wants to send a live animal through the transporter as she feels confident that the new computer can handle the data stream now.

That afternoon Candy gets one of the white rats and puts it into the transmitter, and cycles it through to the integrator and as she opens the door she throws up, the rat is not only dead, but inside out. Needless to say she went home for the day. Randy takes a moment to clean up the mess so Candy won't have to. Randy looks over Candy's program and tweaks it some more. He then runs another test, the rat seems to be in one piece and alive. The next morning Randy shows Candy what he did with her program, and Candy rejoiced that the rat he had sent through was alive. Randy suggests that they put the new rats through a maze before they send it through the transporter, then have the rat run the maze after transporting it to see if there are any changes to the rat. So Randy takes charge of the critters. he runs a rat many times through the maze until he is getting the same result each time, then Candy and Randy send the rat through the transporter and then re-run the rat through the maze again. Everything appears to be just fine. Now Randy wants to run a larger animal through the transporter, so he buys a spider monkey. Then he and Candy do similar tests before the monkey is transported. After the transport session with the monkey, they repeat the same tests. With no seeable problems or differences. Randy then decides to take the monkey to a Vet to get X-rays done and again nothing is abnormal. The monkey is given a clean bill of health by the Vet.

Chapter 46

Ben receives a call from Randy's father Byron asking if Ben would have dinner that night at the club, Ben accepts. That night over dinner Randy's father keeps asking about Randy and his new computer system and if it was working yet? This appears to be a father's pride talking, but then something that Randy had said when he joined the team, reminded Ben that they should not trust his father. Byron kept pressing about the crystal computer, which alerted Ben to play it down.

So Ben said "that Randy is still working on the computer, and it is showing signs of being promising." At the end of dinner Byron realizes, they have built the crystal computers. This is what Byron was waiting for. With Randy's crystal computers he can Take control of all the businesses in the world, even the military's; as Randy's computer runs stronger and faster than conventional computers. Byron will be able to use the crystal computer to control all other computers. And he will be the only one in the world to possess it. Byron leaves Ben and returns to his office. When Byron arrives at his downtown pent house and presses a button on his communication device to his security force. Then Byron commands. "Get in here!" moments later one of his security men enters Byron's office.

"Yes Sir." Byron tells him to sit down, and the security man sits as he is told.

"I want you to connect with the spy that I have watching these people, as Byron hands over pictures of the scientists and his son, they are at this warehouse and Byron gives him the address. "I want a report in a week of their habits. Now get out of here."

"Yes Sir."

The next day Randy goes to Andy's shop and loads up a CAD (Used for making drawings in three dimensions) system to Andy's computer and places a simple piece of steel into the mixer. They quit calling Andy's transporter a transporter as it has no real name, Randy calls it a Mixer since it combines materials. He then fires up the CAD system and programs the computer to make the block of steel into a bowel, he cycles it through the process and gets a steel bowel in return.

"Randy that's a great idea, how complex a part can we make?"

"I do not know yet, maybe something with only a few different materials in it. It will depend on how well we program the machine."

"This is going to be fun to play with." says Andy with a big smile.

The Security man has been watching the warehouse he has planted bugs and surveillance cameras throughout the warehouses so that he can record what happens as they work. Over time he discovers what his boss wants. The crystal computers are working.

Andy calls the other two members of their team Ben and Candy, and tells them Randy has gone back to work. The three of them have decided to throw a party for Randy, for all the good work he has done for their project. They have a cake and soda. They decorate the shop and then they get ready to call Randy when two men in ski masks barge in with guns.

"Now no one will be hurt if you do what we tell you." Said the first guy.

"Where are the crystal computers located?" said the second guy.

"What crystal computers?" questions Ben.

The first guy hits Ben upside the head with his gun knocking him unconscious. Then he turns to Candy and slaps her across the mouth.

"Where are the crystal computers?" Candy points to the computers over on the desk.

"Right there you, idiot." She then gets a punch in the stomach doubling her up.

"Well smart guy", as they turn to Andy "now you tell me where the crystal computers are."

Andy refuses to talk, so the men grab Ben, and they make Andy carry Candy to the transmitter and they put them into it and lock it down.

"Now wise guy tells us where the crystal computer is or we are going to put you in there with them."

Andy says nothing, and they force him into the chamber and close the door. The first guy walks up to the computer console, and turns on the transmitter.

"Hey this works just like the boss said it would."

Then he causes the transporter to cycle, and what they get at the receiver end is enough to make a sane man sick to his stomach. All three of them are melded together, and they are turned inside out, what was in the receiver does not live very long and all three people are dead. The two men look around trying to find the crystal computers, but Randy has hidden them so well they do not find them.

Randy returns to his work area and sees that Candy is gone. He decides to run an experiment. Randy puts his spider monkey and a ferret into the machine and cycles it through the process hoping that both animals will appear at the receiver unharmed. What Randy gets at the integrator puzzles him. All he gets back is the monkey where is the ferret? Randy puts the monkey in his cage and goes to inspect the transporter and the integrator. Randy checks from one end to the other and does not find the ferret or any problems with the machine. Randy muses about the problem of the missing ferret and takes a walk to think things over.

After returning Randy goes to check on the monkey and finds the ferret and the monkey is gone.

"What is going on?" asks Randy to himself.

Randy decides to put a camera on the cage to see what is happening, in the next hour Randy plays back the tape, he is amazed at what he finds, the monkey changes in to the ferret, and the ferret changes back. The camera shows this happening several times and what appears to have happened is the new creature which can melt and shift from one animal to another.

On one of the changes the ferret has the arms and hands of the monkey but keeps the ferret's body. Randy decides for now to keep this quite. Then it is time for closing down for the day so Randy considers shutting down the computer system and turning off the lights. When Randy sees that the other three left a call for Randy to come to Andy's lab area at the end of the shift today. What Randy does not know is that they were going to throw a surprise party for him. Randy is about to run a last experiment using a snake to transport through the transporter so he can make a report to the others on his findings.

Then Randy gets grabbed from behind, by two men wearing black ski masks.

"Where is the crystal computer" says first the men.

"They are over there said Randy." Pointing at the computer console.

One of them checks out Candy's station and sees just the run of the mill computer.

"These are not the ones we want kid, where are they? Where are the crystal Computers?"

"That's all the computers we have right there."

"No, they are not the computers I'm looking for." Said the first man.

Then Randy gets dragged to the transmission chamber and thrown in with the rattle snake being pitched in after him, Randy tries to avoid the snake to keep from being bit. Randy starts beating on the door, and screaming "Let me out."

The man that locked him in is laughing at Randy. The other man finds the controls to the machine and starts the transmission cycle of the machine and walks off talking about the other scientists. Randy hears them before he is transported with the snake.

"The others look like they were turned inside out and glued to gather. It sure is a mess in that other machine" said the men as they left laughing.

"The bosses' son will look much the same. Then we will have all the time we need to locate the crystal computers that Mr. Bryon wants"

The men walk off believing that Randy will meet the same fate as his friends.

Chapter 47

The machine cycles with Randy and the snake, but only Randy appears at the receiver end. He manages to cycle open the door and step out.

Randy looks down at his hands and sees scales, then he touches his face and feels more scales, he sees the open bathroom door and walks into it to look into the mirror. Randy sees his reflection part man part snake complete with fangs, he feels much stronger than he did before and his hands move at a blur.

"Father you are going to regret this and I'm going to make sure you do!"

Randy quickly runs to Andy's lab and finds what's left of his friends in the integrator. He drops down to his knees and pounds his fist on the floor crying out in anguish.

"Why father, why did you do this?"

It takes a while for Randy to get a hold of his grief and he forms a plan at the back of his mind of what he should do. Randy manages to get the remains of his friends into a truck unseen and drives them to his family's cemetery. Randy opens up the family crypt and inside he finds an open grave box and puts his friends in side and buries them in his family's crypt.

"You guys deserve better than this, and I'm going to make my father pay for what he did to you and my mother. Right now I cannot draw attention to myself. I loved you all, you treated me as an equal friend, and not like some kid, thank you and good bye."

Randy drives to his father's office building. On the back of the building there is a small vent about eight inches' square, he rips the cover off the vent and changes into a rattle snake that slithers into the vent. Randy follows the duct down into the basement, and into a larger duct. Randy comes to the vent cover inside and peers through to see if anyone is in there. It appears empty so Randy changes back into his human self and forces the vent cover open and drops to the floor. Slowly Randy walks over to the stairs making sure he is not seen or that anyone may have heard him as he kicked off the vent cover. Randy climbs up two flights of stairs and at the landing he stops to listens at the door. Randy hears the two men that killed his friends, bragging about what they did to them. Randy quietly opens the door and steps in side then changes back into the rattle snake, he slithers along the wall. Then under the locker room bench, and he waits coiled up being careful not to shake his tail.

Soon as the men walk past him. He strikes the nearest one in the leg, and the man falls down and is face to face with the snake. Randy strikes again and bites the man in the neck. The other man grabs his friend and tries to help him. Randy now bites him on his hand. He drops his friend and tries to get away, but Randy changes into a reptile like man and stands up. The man is frozen with fear and cannot move. Randy walks over to the man and bites the man in the neck, then changes back into himself. The second man asks "What are you?"

Randy knees down beside him and says.

"You should make sure a person is dead before you leave him alone", and both men die right there. Randy as himself walks out in to the lobby and takes an elevator up to the top floor. Before the doors open Randy changes back into a snake. When the door to the elevator opens Randy slithers out into the room.

"Who's there? Come on out! I have a gun, and I will shoot you if you do not obey."

Randy makes his way to the couch and slithers under the couch to locate his father on the far side. Byron walks over to the elevator and sees that it is empty and he mumbles to himself about having building maintenance look at it in the morning. Byron returns to his desk and off to the right of the room a door opens and a young girl enters the room.

"What is wrong? I heard you talking"

Byron looks up and smiles. "It was nothing. Go back to the bed room, and I will be in shortly."

Byron's new playmate leaves the room. Randy slithers up to his father's desk and transforms back to himself and stands up.

"Hello father, miss me?"

"What are you doing here Randy?"

"Why father didn't you expect to see me anymore? I can assure you the talk of my death is a bit premature."

"Ahh, yes how are you doing" as he reaches for his gun.

"Don't do that father, leave the gun there, or you'll be dead in mere moments."

Byron stops reaching for his gun and stands up. He does not see Randy holding a gun and figures he can still grab his gun and kill him. So Byron wants to see why Randy is here so he asks.

"What do you want?"

"You had my friends killed just so you can have my crystal computer. You killed them for nothing, and now I want your life."

Byron grabs for his gun, but before he can get his hand on the gun Randy changes into the man snake and with lightning speed Randy strikes (bites) his father in the neck. Byron looks on in horror at this son, and stammers out "What are you?"

"The men you sent to kill me; sent me through the wrong transporter, you see father I was working on a different project and I discovered quite by accident that the transporter set up causes transformations in my subjects, but I was interrupted and instead of the lizard I was going to put in, your men put me in with a rattle snake and cycled the transporter thinking it would do the

221

same to me as it did my friends. Now I'm changed, I can be a snake or a human or something in between, as you just discovered. Oh I see your dead, too bad."

Randy in his human snake form starts for the elevator when the young girl reenters the room and sees this alien creature standing in the room. In a blink of an eye Randy is standing next to her ready to bite her, when she breaks down in hysteria losing her mind.

Randy decides not to kill her. Going over to his father's desk he locates a little Red book that has all the passwords to all his father's accounts. Then Randy walks back over to the girl and just stairs at her. All she can do is scream. Randy turns and leaves the room to uses the stairs to leave the building. The next morning the guards find Byron and a crazy girlfriend in the penthouse, and the two security guards in the locker room. The coroner says they were bitten by a rattle snake, but can't account for the different sized fang marks in the victim's legs and neck. The crazy girl keeps mentioning a human sized alien looking reptile that bit Byron, but did not do anything to her. She is so distraught that they have to put her into an institution. The next day Randy reads the newspaper and smiles. Using the crystal computer in Candy's lab, Randy commences to drain all his father's funds into various fake corporations, banks and so on. By the time Randy is finished the money trail is so lost it will take a normal person years to find any of the money.

Randy also hacks his way into his friend's accounts and does the same thing. In this case Randy is truly sorry, but he will need the money to do what he has in mind next. Randy decides to run some tests on himself to see how he is, so he goes to a doctor as himself and gets a physical, then he makes an appointment with a specialist for a mental evaluation. Randy's test out normal. Randy's snake side of himself will become a problem in the future, but as it turns out that it is not a factor for now. (At least not yet). Randy decides to create a new world on a remote island. We will be known as the Chimerains. Who should I pick, what type of people do I choose to be this new race?

Chapter 48

After some consideration Randy decides that it might be prudent to test this out how the machine works on someone else before making others like himself. Randy sets out to find another person to transform into a Chimerian. At first Randy decides to get his people from the homeless this way no one would pay too much attention if they go missing. Randy leaves to go look for his first subject. So out walking through the alleys he comes across his first subject, an old Indian who looks like he could use the help.

"Hi sir may I help you?" asks Randy.

"Why would you help me? Besides I'm dying so go and leave me in peace."

"For the moment let's just say I'm a mad scientist and I'm looking for a subject to test my machine on, and if you are dying. Then if it fails it won't matter, what do you say?"

"Can I have a last meal before we do this?"

"Sure, what would you like and I'll get it for you."

"How about an extra-large peperoni pizza? I rather like them."

"Ok, here let me help you up and we can go to my lab."

Randy helps the old man to his parked truck just down the street.

At the lab Randy assures the old man that the machine will not kill him and if he wants proof Randy would prove it to him. Randy explains that the machine was used on himself, and he shows the Indian his snake side. The Indian's eyes open very wide and in amazement.

"Will I become like you, a snake too?"

So Randy calls in and orders the pizza then turns to the Indian to answer him.

"You will become whatever animal you want to be. What is your name?"

"In my tribe I was called Iron Eagle."

"What tribe did you belong to?"

"Black Foot Indians, of Flat Head Lake Montana, we are the southernmost clan, our totem is the Eagle."

"Very interesting, Iron Eagle, you can sleep over there on the couch to night. I'll get you a blanket."

"What is your name?" queries Iron Eagle.

Before Randy answers Iron Eagle, the Pizza arrives and Randy collects it and pays for it. Then gives it to Iron Eagle, Iron Eagle has been without food for so long, that he slowly devours the pizza savoring every bite.

"I'm called Randy. I have to leave you here for a time; I need to pick up something and I'll be right back, please don't touch any equipment. The bath room is over through that door, and a kitchen is through there. You may have whatever you want."

"Thank you Randy."

Randy leaves the room and later that night he brings back a Bald Eagle. Randy had gone to the zoo and located the bird. As luck would have it, it too is old and was to be exterminated so he bought it from the Zoo keeper at a modest price.

"Randy what are you doing? You might hurt that bird."

"He will be fine, now come over here."

Iron Eagle does what he is asked and gets into the machine.

"Here take the eagle in with you." As Randy Hands Iron Eagle the Bald Eagle.

"What is going to happen to us?"

"You will now become like me, but instead of being a snake you will be an Eagle."

So, Iron Eagle and the bird enter in to the chamber: Iron Eagle looks out the window.

Randy then cycles the machine and Iron Eagle and the Bald Eagle are transmitted to the integration chamber. Randy opens the door to the integrator chamber and out steps Iron Eagle, he looks like a young man compared to when he went in. Iron Eagle looks at his hands then into a mirror.

"What magic is this?"

"Not magic, science" says Randy. "Now watch me"; Randy goes through the change again from a man to a snake then back again. Now you try it, you should be able to transform into an eagle."

Iron Eagle transforms into an eagle and takes off and flies around the warehouse, then he transforms back into a man.

"Such Magic, and I see that I'm much younger, what have you done?"

"I can't explain it, but the people who built this machine were killed and the people who killed them; tried to kill me. Instead of killing me they changed me as I have changed you. I call us the Chimerians, and I wish to make more of them, will you help me?"

"Yes Randy. It would benefit whoever we allow into the machine. Look at me, I'm younger and stronger than I ever was, and I have my youth back."

"That appears to be the benefit of the transformation process." Randy muses.

For several days Randy and Iron Eagle search out other homeless people young and old and take them in to the warehouse to feed and clothe them and see to their needs. Randy sets out to find a place where he can move his new subjects to so they will be able to have a new life. Randy, in his search, finds at the edge of the Bermuda Triangle an island that his father had purchased from the Navy some years ago. It was abandoned after World War II and all the naval equipment was removed that was easy to remove or destroyed. It had been a Navy station set up to observe enemy ship movements at the time. Randy leaves Iron Eagle in charge and takes a trip to the island to see if it can be adapted for his use. After a few hours of travel by plane and then by boat Randy arrives at the island. As he surveys the island he sees that the bunkers from World War II are intact and will serve his purpose. Randy returns back to the warehouse in a couple of days. Randy then decides to pack up the warehouse and ship everything and everyone to the island. Randy only takes the one transporter system and one crystal computer as he hires a cargo ship to ship the equipment, people and animals. On the trip the people help feed and keep the animals in good health. Randy and his people land on the island a few weeks later. He gets the people who came with him to help bring in the animals and the equipment on to the island from the ship. Randy soon finds out that the island is nothing more than some huge rock sticking up out of the ocean. So with his dad's connections in the construction market Randy locates a willing excavation and construction company.

Randy has an excavation crew brought in and they build a small underground facility, complete with solar power, and a huge dome of concrete to house every one. Just after the construction is complete the construction crew leaves the island. Randy brings the rest of his subjects to the Island. On the first day after they arrive the weather changes and a large hurricane forms and passing over the island. Everyone inside the dome braces for the storms impact and then when it is over, they realize they weathered the first hurricane with no problem. Now Randy starts to purchase and import more animals. He tries to buy animals that were pets at one time, some are very old. He had over a hundred people on the island from runaway teens to old men and women and some in between. Everyone was looking for a new life.

Chapter 49

Randy went out of his way to make sure he did not pick up anyone that had a criminal record. He did not want to give criminals the kind of power and the ability to change their shape and form. A month after all the construction was completed Randy set up the Conversion machine and the crystal computer that operated it. Then he announced to the people what was going to happen when they entered into the transformation chamber. Many of the people are in disbelief until Randy and Iron Eagle display what could happen. The next day everyone showed up to get converted. Some of the people are scared out of their minds, while others are excited! At the very least they wanted to watch to see what happens. The old people are first to enter the chamber with their chosen animal. Some of the animals are their own pets, dogs, cats and even a parrot. When they come out of the chamber they are young again. The transformation is a sight to behold as they watch an old person enter into the disintegrator chamber and emerge from the integrator chamber a young person, but where is the animal? Randy cycles twenty-five people through the machine. Afterward, he stops so he can show them how to do the transformation. Randy with Iron Eagle shows them how to transform themselves. One lady who merged with a raven, changes in to a harpy. Others changed in to half men and half animal. The other people who had watched cannot wait to get into the transformation machine with their chosen animal. There are a few who are not sure if they want to get transformed, so they stay away, with a promise that they can be returned home, if they choose not to go through the machine.

After everyone who wants to be transformed has been through the change and likes what has happened to them; they now have something in common with each other as they are Chimerians. Amazingly they seem to get along with each other unlike how they got along before. With all the arguments, and fighting mostly because they came from different walks of life. There does not seem to be any of the social barriers that they saw back home everyone is a Chimeraian no black person, or white or any other race. Randy looks around at his subjects suddenly realizes he is the only reptile of all the Chimerians, there are mammals, and birds, but no other reptiles. So he decides he wants a few more similar to himself so he goes in search of others to become reptiles. In Brazil he finds several new prospects, and he brings them to the Island. Among them is an old Mayan Indian. He brings with him an old condor and a python. He wants to merge with these two animals. Randy is interested to see if it will work so he allows it to happen. After transforming the new people into various reptile people like iguanas, lizards and some snakes, none of which have any venom. Randy turns to the Mayan Indian to make sure he still wants to transform using the condor and the python. The Mayan is very sure and he goes through the transformation process. Once transformed the Mayan Indian steps out of the machine then finds he can change into a large Condor or a python, but when he wants he can become a feathered serpent much like the god that his people worship. Randy goes about setting up rules and regulations to help govern his new people. They use the same laws that they knew in America, and rules are established as to when they can or cannot transform. Like when a stranger lands on the island everyone has to transform into people, and stay that way until the intruders leave. Randy not versed in governing looks for Chimerians who are leaders or have even run businesses, to help set up a way to govern his new people in a fair way.

Chapter 50

As time moves on, the island Chimerians break into factions: reptiles in one group, birds in another group, and mammals in another. The next faction is the Indian Iron Eagle and the Mayan as they separated from the rest of the other Chimerians on the island. Both begin to see new problems. Iron Eagle and the Mayan know how to cope with their new animal nature. Yet some of the Chimerians keep reverting back to their wild natures. After one of the frequent hurricanes a python man goes for a walk along the beach, it is not long before he discovers a sail boat that has been beached. His human side is curious so he climbs aboard to search it. He finds a small child that is still alive, and when the child sees the creature (a reptile man) the child goes into hysterics. The snake's nature takes over the man's mind and he changes into a snake then it wraps itself around the child and squeezed it to death. The python then swallows the child whole. Now that the python has eaten it leaves the sail boat and crawls to the far side of the island to hide and digest its grizzly meal. A week later two others Chimerians go in search of the python man. They find the empty sail boat, and think nothing of it and move on down the beach in their search for the missing member.

Both creatures run on to the python man as he vomits the bones from his feast.

Tiger man says "what have you done?"

The python man changes into his semi human form.

"Nothing, it was already dead and I was hungry."

"You know that Randy will be furious"! says the leopard woman.

"Who cares, I can do what I want, besides who is going to tell him?"

"If it was already dead no harm is done." Speaks the leopard woman.

"Let's get back to the compound, we were sent out here to find you" growls the Tiger man.

They return to the compound in silence, little did they know they were being watched from the sky. Iron Eagle goes to Randy to observe him, and it soon becomes apparent to both Iron Eagle and the Mayan that everyone is changing not their appearance but their nature. It appears that the animal nature of their makeup is starting to assert itself, even Randy is affected. On one occasion Randy is feeding one of the many reptiles in his lab when one of them bites his hand in an effort to escape, but Randy in his rage changes into a rattle snake and bites the creature and watches it as it thrashes about until it dies from the venom he inflected on it. It is because Randy is the only Chimeraian who has venom that keeps all the other Chimerians in check.

Iron Eagle tries to get Randy to understand the effects of the animal nature on the human side of the people, and they are becoming more dangerous. Iron Eagle feels that something more serious is going to happen.

Randy asks Iron Eagle "won't this affect you too?"

Iron Eagle explains that since he has lived with the animals most of his life that it is easier for him and the Mayan Indian to accept the animal's nature and be able to guide it not be affected by it.

"The difference for us is we know we do not control the animal, but it does not control us either, we just understand it better."

"Then help me understand." begs Randy.

"I'm not sure I can, the Mayan and myself have lived with and studied all animals that we have ever lived with, especially the animals that can kill us, and the ones we admire. It is a lifetime of knowledge that I cannot impart to the others."

After that Randy seems driven to make more reptile people, all the birds and other animals are let go, and the lizards, snakes and toads and the like are kept. Randy has brought in more homeless people to the island. Randy wants to have more reptile people and an amphibian people over the mammals and birds that are already here. Randy's mind is being over shadowed by his rattlesnake mind. Randy's mind and the snake's mind are melding together and the predator is over riding the human side of Randy. Randy keeps making more and more people and soon the island is not able to support every one that lives there. The supply ships have quit coming; they are afraid due to the monsters they have seen from the ship. On a couple of occasions one of the Chimerians could be seen as they changed back to human form. The people from the neighboring islands are very superstitious at best, and the strange creatures they have seen scares them to the point they quit bringing supplies to the island as well. The island has become an evil place and none of the natives will venture there.

Chapter 60

Randy is not the only one affected, as all the Chimerians are exhibiting the same tendencies of being more animal than human. The factions are getting bigger as well, Reptiles in one group, cats in another and so on. Then one day when one of the cats is taking some water from the rations and it is caught by some of the other Chimerians. This starts the beginning of the war. The amphibian or toad man is bathing in pool of water, when a fight breaks out. How dare he use precious water so wastefully? When the fight is over the amphibian man is dead. Randy becomes angry and he bites the cat-person that killed the toad man, and that cat person dies. This incident sets off the war. At first it is like watching children having a war with snowballs only with claws and teeth. It was more like they would rush in at each other, then slash, bite, hit and make other attempts to fight. No one seemed to have any strategy of how to go about assailing each other. The only person on the island that has been at war is the Minotaur man, he has been in the army as a sergeant, and has some military experience, but he has distanced himself from all the other combatants by staying in the bunkers below the dome.

To the Minotaur the underground is his maze much like the story of ancient times and so he protects his domain. Everyone is afraid of him; even Randy has a healthy respect of the Minotaur. As long as no one enters the Minotaur's domain he leaves the other Chimerians alone.

The Minotaur man has gone underground into the tunnels. There are places there he can defend, and nothing can come up on him from behind. So he is able to face his adversary. This coupled with his strength will allow him to defend his position. The tiger man has no military experience, but is good at the games of strategy, he makes friends with some of the bird people especially the smaller ones. He is able to use them to get Intel on the other factions. The island is full of small birds and so they will not be easy to detect. The bird women get close to another faction and listened in on their conversations to see what they are up to, and then they would report back to tiger man, and from this he is able to counter what the others are planning to do to one another.

Iron Eagle and the Mayan Indian know things are only going to get worse. The fresh water is controlled by the reptiles, and the food is controlled by the cats. The birds have nothing, but they are able to subsist on the insects and seeds they find on the island. So they have no real concerns other than staying alive and out of the fighting. On one of the encounters a python man captures a leopard woman and crushes her to death, then drags her into the reptile camp where they shared her body out to all the other reptiles. Iron Eagle decides to go to the radio room and send out a distress call for help. So Iron Eagle flies off to one of the hatches that leads down into the next level, and he changes back into a man to makes his way to the radio room. Iron Eagle sneaks into the tunnels where at one place he is able to fly, so he changes back into an eagle and soars down the stair well to the lower level where the radio is kept. Iron Eagle manages to just get pass the Minotaur and makes it in to the radio room.

Chapter 61

"Mayday, Mayday, we are at latitude and longitude here at the edge of the Bermuda Triangle and we need help, we are at war, please hurry. Mayda...."

The Minotaur man destroys the radio with a single blow of his fist.

"No you don't, you invaded my territory and you are now going to die." Grunts Minotaur.

With the barest of luck Iron Eagle manages to get out of the room in his eagle form and flies down the hall, the Minotaur is right on his tail. As Iron Eagle reaches the door way the Mayan Indian is lying on the floor in his snake form and he manages to trip the Minotaur which allows Iron Eagle to escape. Then the Mayan changes from a snake into a condor and follows Iron Eagle into the levels above. In an attempt to get away from the fighting Iron Eagle and the Mayan manage to leave the dome through one of the doors.

"Did you send the message?" asks the Mayan.

"I hope so, I think I managed to get off a plea for help and this location, before the Minotaur destroyed the radio."

Just as the conversation ended two harpies dropped in on both the Mayan and Iron Eagle.

An aerial battle ensues, the harpies' talons are tipped in poison and will kill either one of them. It is fortunate that both Iron Eagle and the Mayan's bird form is much faster than the harpies, and the harpies are not able to catch them. In the aerial fight each harpy tries to take on the Eagle or the Condor. So the Mayan and Iron Eagle lead away one of the harpies, then they turn toward each other and fly as if they are playing chicken with each other. At the last instant the eagle drops toward the ground, and the condor heads for the sky. The harpies were so intent on their prey that they do not realize until the last moment what is happening to them until they collide with each other, sending them crashing on to the island.

Chapter 62

"Steve, you need to come to the lodge."

"Why CAT, I'm enjoying the day with my family?"

"Steve maybe you should go to CAT, he never bothers you unless it is important" said Samantha.

"Ok, but remember, this is your idea. CAT I'll be there shortly."

Steve kisses his wife and daughter Kim and walks into the house and ports to the lodge.

"Ok CAT what is the problem that you had to pull me away from my family?"

"There is a small island that the Navy once held in the South Atlantic, there is a war going on there."

"Well, let the Navy handle it, it is their island."

"Steve looked at the screen and saw who or rather what is fighting."

CAT shows Steve a satellite picture of the island.

"Is that camera messed up, that looks like animals that have a form of people. Are you sure this is not some movie like the Island of Doctor Moreau?"

"It is very real Steve, I have been watching since I received a call for help, this is real. And the next problem is the Navy is sending in a couple of ships and the Marines to investigate. This means a lot of people are going to get killed."

(What Steve does not know, is that CAT is off line and the Insect people are controlling CAT).

"Ok, I'll go see what is going on, and see if I can do something about it."

Thirty minutes later Paladin appears on the island, he is in total shock at the scene he sees before his eyes. Before he can make a move a harpy drops in on him knocking him to the ground and just as she is about to rake Paladin with her claws, a condor and an eagle pounce on her. Paladin rolls to his feet and shoots the harpy with his dart gun, but it takes a couple of darts to put her out.

Then Paladin turns to face the Condor and the eagle with his gun pointing at them, Iron Eagle changes back to a man then the Mayan Indian does the same, holding up their hands palms open.

Iron Eagle says, "You got my message?"

"In a manner of speaking, what is going on here?"

Suddenly out of the blue the other harpy attacks them, so to avoid her Paladin Ports Iron Eagle and the Mayan to another Island.

"Now what is going on?" Iron Eagle tells Paladin the whole story of the machine and how it combines the humans and animals, and then Iron Eagle and the Mayan demonstrate the changes.

Chapter 63

"Wow, you realize that the Navy is on its way to level this island?"

"No! Most of the people are good people, but it is the animal instinct that is driving them to fight. The lack of food and water causes them to fight as well. We must save them" implores the Mayan.

"I'm open to suggestion." said Paladin.

"The Navy will provide a common enemy; we just need to figure a way to exploit it." Said Iron Eagle.

"True but we do not want to hurt the Navy either, they are just doing a job." states Paladin.

Paladin ports the other two back to the island's furthest northern location. Who are the factions and their leaders?"

While the Mayan tells what he knows Paladin doubles the sleep potion in his darts.

"The first thing to do is take out the leaders, then the deadliest of the creatures, with this done we may get enough attention to get them to understand that I can take them somewhere else where they can live free and get away from here."

"As I recall you told me about a machine that can transform people and animals. We had better destroy that before someone else uses it for the wrong reason. Mayan how hard would it be for you to get to it?"

"Not so hard, except the Minotaur roaming the underground tunnels."

"Would you be willing to try? Iron Eagle and I need to put the leaders to sleep and see if we can get everyone's attention."

Paladin reaches through a window and provides the Mayan with a charge of C-4 (Explosive) to destroy the machine, and he shows him how to set the timer.

"All you have to do is plant this device and flip this switch and get out of there. You'll have ten minutes before it goes off, so that should be enough time for you to escape."

"It will be done." Promises the Mayan."

Paladin puts his hand on Iron Eagle and the Mayan and ports to the front entrance of the dome. Only to be surprised by the Minotaur coming out of the building looking for Iron Eagle. Paladin gets knocked to the side as the Minotaur tries to get at Iron Eagle. Paladin lies there trying to get his breath. "What was that?"

"That is the Minotaur, so now I will be able to reach the machine and plant your bomb."

Getting to his feet Paladin draws his dart guns and shoots the Minotaur several times before the Minotaur collapses in a heap on the ground.

Chapter 64

"Thank you said Iron Eagle, let's get to our part of the task."

"Wait a minute, I need to reload my dart gun, as it took almost all of the darts just to put him out."

"Steve, the Navy will be nearing the island in one hour, and from their communications they are going to give a brief warning then shell the island."

"Ok CAT, have they launched a drone yet?"

"They will in a few minutes, they want to see what they are dealing with."

"Great, with these animal people all over the place, they will shell first then ask questions later."

"Who are you talking to Paladin?" asks Iron Eagle.

"For lack of a better term he is a friend. The Navy is launching a drone, to see what is going on here. There are too many of your people out here in their animal forms we need to get them back inside the dome and into their human forms. Otherwise when the Navy sees them they will shoot first and ask questions later. If I were in their place, I would not blame them either. Iron Eagle if we are going to save the day here we need to get moving."

So Paladin and Iron eagle work their way into the dome, right off Iron Eagle is embroiled in a fight and tries to fly away. Suddenly Paladin stops Iron Eagle's antagonist with a couple of darts then pulls him aside.

"Here take this radio, and fly above all this and give me direction-- first the leaders, then the fireworks."

Iron Eagle takes to the air, the first leader is the one leading the cats, Iron Eagle gives Paladin the location and then Paladin ports up behind the first leader and instead of trying to talk to him, it seems the cat man is enraged and into his blood lust. Paladin shoots him from behind and puts him to sleep. The next target is Randy, Iron Eagle cautions Paladin to be careful. Randy is a rattle snake with venom. Paladin acknowledges Iron Eagle, and ports behind Randy, but before he can shoot him Randy turns in a blur of motion to face him.

Chapter 65

"Who are you?"

"I'm someone trying to save you and your people from destruction. The Navy is coming and will be here in an hour. Also a Drone is flying over the area. There are enough of your people out there to make things very bad for you."

"How so stranger?"

"The Navy will shoot first and ask questions later. Your people will scare the hell out of them and you know what humans will do when they do not understand and fear something or someone."

"So how can you help, you are just one man."

"Let's just say I can take you to a better place."

"Where would that be?"

"At the moment, I have a friend working on that, but right now we need to restore order, and get everyone together so I can be ready to move you all to a different Island."

"I was going to kill you, but now, I'll help you. What is your plan?" asks Randy.

"I have had to put a couple of your people to sleep already, the leader of the cats will be asleep for a while, so that faction has stopped. Trying to protect him. Can you call off your people and we may yet restore some order."

"Yes, Randy tells his troops (for a lack of a better term) to stop and pull back."

The python man says "why, we are winning."

"Either you pull back or you will feel my bite."

So, the reptile people pull back to their defensive positions.

With enough of the combatants stopped, Paladin pulls some fireworks out of the air and sets them off, this gets everyone's attention. Then Randy steps up to speak.

"We all will be under attack by the US Navy. They will shell the Island soon as we broke our rules by appearing outside in or in our alternate forms. At this moment a drone will be or has already flown over the Island. Since we are now different we will be their target. This stranger has come to help us, we need to follow him. I will back him up."

Just after the speech a missile hits the dome and part of the roof falls in. Paladin steps up.

"We need to get everyone back into the dome and into the lower levels. It will give us some protection so I can set up a portal to take us to a different Island. When I can find a better place for you to live. So you will not be bothered by anyone else."

Chapter 66

Several of the stronger animal people are given directions. They head for the doors to pick up and bring back anyone that is outside of the doors not able to move on their own. Paladin had to go out and port the Minotaur back into the building, because he is too big and heavy for anyone to carry.

"CAT I need the coordinates to move these people to an island, and I need it now."

At that moment the Navy starts shelling the island and the dome is taking a beating, one thing it did was to cover the explosive that the Mayan Indian put in place to destroy the transforming machine. Everyone (That is the Chimerians and Randy) just thought that the Navy did it with the shelling.

"CAT where are those coordinates?"

"Steve open the portal you now have the coordinates." (Again CAT is being directed by the insect people). Paladin opens the portal and ushers the people through, it is slow at first, then the pace picks up when the dome is breached at the far end, it is almost a panic rush to get through the gate. The last ones to leave the dome are Randy, and Paladin.

"Where are we? This is not earth." says Randy.

"I do not know, CAT what is going on?" From the brush behind them a loan figure steps out to confront Paladin and Randy.

"You have arrived on a world with no name, no one lives here anymore, but you and your people may make your homes here, everything you need is all around us." Said the insect creature.

"Who are you?" asks Paladin. "It seems that I should know you."

"We met before on an Island where you almost died, we saved your life."

"But why do I not know you?" asks Paladin.

Chapter 67

"At the time we cleared your mind of us, and implanted a memory that the Island natives saved you."

Before Paladin can ask more questions the creature stabs Paladin with a stinger so fast that only Randy saw it. Paladin falls to the ground. Randy is getting ready to strike, when the creature promises that Paladin is going to be OK. "That he is just sleeping, and when he wakes up, he will not remember what has happened here. Other than he took you all to safety to an island, one he will never be able to find."

The creature turns to Iron Eagle and the Mayan Indian.

"You will take Paladin back to his world, and both of you will stay there because you will help him in the future, and you will save many people from dying, Paladin as well. I will not take this memory from you as I have done to him. According to our histories, Paladin and his wife will save our world, so you both will need to make sure they stay safe."

The creature turns to Randy, "You are the leader?"

"Yes."

"Do not worry your people will settle down now and be as they were before your war, as I have said, you have all the materials here on this world to make good lives for your selves. I have been to your future, and you will thrive. This world is like many new worlds it will be a struggle at first, then you will build a new and wonderful life."

Turning to Iron Eagle.

"Pick up Paladin and I will send you back to his secret place."

Then to the Mayan "I will return you to your land, Paladin will not remember either you or Iron Eagle."

The portal is opened again. Iron Eagle carries Paladin through to his mountain Top lodge, he leaves Paladin on the front porch and changes to his Eagle form and flies off. The Mayan Indian is sent to his old village in Central America, and he walks off into the jungle and changes into the feathered serpent. He flies off into the jungle to confront the drug lords who are burning the forest, so he can put a stop to them. Iron Eagle flies off and flies around Paladin's mountain and sees the hologram and knows that this place has protection on top, so he decides to patrol around the base of the mountain.

The happiest part is that Iron Eagle is near his ancestral home in Montana, he can fly there from time to time to see what his people are up to. A year later while patrolling the mountain he runs onto some mountain climbers who were going to conquer the nameless (Paladin's) mountain. Having no desire to cause harm to any one Iron Eagle resorts to ghost stories. He flies a mile away and comes walking up to the people's camp at just about sundown. He strikes up a conversation. He tells a story of a shaman who cursed this mountain, and he points out that a helicopter crashed halfway around the base of the mountain. And that any white man or stranger will meet an untimely death. The campers, give him something to eat and drink. As they sit there eating and in conversation, they scoffed at the superstition of the Indian when in their midst he changes into his eagle form and flies off. The campers, sat there staring at each other, then gathered up their stuff and leave in a hurry. Iron Eagle watches them leave and from time to time as he follows them. They can hear him chanting, which speeds them along even more.

Chapter 68

Back on the new world which resides in the same place as earth just in a different dimension, the Chimerians take on the new world. It does not take long for Randy to discover who should be leading the people. Randy turns to the Minotaur and has him organize the people into teams to explore a place to set up their camp. One team finds a large lake with fresh water, and it has schools of some kind of fish, others bring in wood for a fire, and soon they have a camp.

"Now what do we need?" asked Randy to the Minotaur.

"We need shelter, food and water. We have solved the water and possibly the food problem, as we can live off the fish, and some of the other animals that live here. We need tools, and weapons to hunt with and to build with."

"Sounds good what do you want us to do?"

"For tonight we'll set out sentries, in four-hour shifts. Tomorrow we will continue to explore to see if we cannot find a better place to stay."

In the morning, they all meet at the campfire.

"Here is what I want to do, all the bird people split up and each group fly around the lake, this group will go to the left and the other group to the right, meet back here when the sun is right above us. The rest of us will explore this area. I want to find anything that would make weapons, tools, and food sources. Like the bird people, everyone meet back here when the sun is directly above us. Randy and a few others will stay here to guard the camp. Now let's move out."

They do this over the next few days, when one of the bird people locates a cave, a small distance from the other side of the lake. Minotaur and a few of the cat people take a hike to check out the cave. When they get there, the Cats ruffle their backs.

"What is it that you sense?" asked Minotaur.

"We do not know."

"Then let's be cautious." Said the Minotaur

Chapter 69

Minotaur enters first, the cave is large and will hold most of the Chimerians.

"We can excavate the back of the cave to make room for everyone, and cover most of the cave mouth for protection. Let's return and tell the others, now what did you guys sense?"

"We do not know, whatever it was, it was huge, but we sense that nothing has lived here for some time. It could be just a bad feeling."

They return and tell the others. Then a decision is made to move to the cave as a safe place to work from. They sent out search parties to find fire wood, and other materials. The cat people became the hunters, they keep the tribe as they refer to themselves, well supplied with meat. Others like the bird people find seeds, plants and fruit to bring in to feed the ones who would not eat meat. The Reptiles become the guards, and protected the camp. One of the people finds a flint rock deposit. Then remembers how to do flint knapping (A way of breaking chips off the flint to create sharp edges) to make stone knives, and soon everyone in the tribe has a flint knife, spears, and soon a bow and arrow. Winter comes, and it is tough going. A few of the Chimerians die due to the extreme cold. When spring comes Minotaur decides to take a team with him and head south in search of a different place to live. Hopefully some place warmer.

Minotaur sends out the bird people on his team since they can travel faster and further in a day than the whole team. One morning a Raven returns and tells Minotaur about a deserted city or town three days further on. The team then sets out the next morning at a ground eating pace and on the third day they find the town. Upon investigation they determine that the town has been deserted for at least a hundred years maybe more. This is not as far south as the Minotaur would have liked it to be, but they can clean it up and use parts of the city to get to next spring, then travel further south next year. Minotaur leaves his team and takes the raven with him and returns to get everyone back at the cave and bring them to the town they have discovered.

Chapter 70

So the Chimerians pick up their few personal things, and hike to the city that is five days away due to the number of people traveling. The people the Minotaur left behind, look for water, and find a supply of meat, and fruit. So for the time-being they have a rustic camp. The abandon city is nothing like New York, but more like you would find in London during the fifteenth Century Earth. Some of the buildings are made of wood or stone or both. In a park like area they set up gardens to grow food, one person finds an old forge with tools, and so in time they will have metal knives and tools. It does not take long and they find a long building they can use for meetings and gatherings. Everyone is allowed to take a house and clean it up and make it their own. It does not take long for the females to want to attach themselves to a male partner.

The Chimerians cannot mate as animals that they are because the differences in their DNA and types, like a bird cannot mate with a cat they have to mate as humans because the human side is the common denominator, so families are formed, and over time children come, it is extraordinary. As a child reaches puberty they can change, the parents determined the changes. One paring is a small sparrow to a panther. Like his parents when the child is able to transform, he becomes a real Chimeraian. When this child of the sparrow and panther changes he can become a winged Panther, and actually fly. Other families have similar children. The Chimerians decided to stay in the town, and make it their own. A few years later, the population is overwhelming, so some of the children that can fly start going further south looking for other towns. Over the years the story of how they were brought here by Paladin gets distorted, and before long Paladin becomes close to being a deity. The story of Randy who made them also gets distorted, and Minotaur as well. It is assumed that Randy and Minotaur had long since died. But the tale is that Randy had told them one-day Paladin would return, and that they should all be looking for him. He helped us and one day we will need to help him. There is more to this story which is yet to be set down by my pen. But for now I will leave off. I have other adventures before I'll return to the Chimerians.

The Wind River Adventure

Chapter 71

As I set pen to paper, I want you to know that much of the first part of this story is speculation, so here goes. Back in the day when volcanos were active throughout the Rocky Mountain ranges in North America, there was one volcano in that area which will become known as the Wind River Mountain, Which was active for a short time as geological time goes.

Eventually the volcano becomes dormant. Within its lava there are a series of heavy metals, from Gold, to lead, and a soup of other heavy metals, some radioactive. As the Ice Age came and receded, it created a crater that filled with water. This water become tainted because of the heavy metals. It now has a turquoise color to it, and it is a bit slimy due to the heavy metals it contains. The gold deposits covered one side of the volcanos outer rim and down deep into the crater.

Now as the story is told to me by the medicine Man of the Crow tribe that lives near the Wind River Mountain range, there once was a moose like animal. It was hard to tell what else it might have been. They think it was so deformed and mad in the head that it destroyed the existing village and it tried to kill everyone it saw. So the tribe evacuated to one of the steep hill sides to seek shelter. There the men got together and dug a deep pit and lined the pit with sharpened stakes, and lured the moose into it.

They eventually managed to kill the moose and the Medicine Man points to the pelt hanging on the lodge wall. Sense the time of the moose they have had other incidences so they built an underground tunnel system incase another giant animal returned.

Further supposition, was that somehow Life was dropped into the volcanic lake and it lived (a raven was carrying a crayfish trying to get away from its peers when they caught up to the raven forcing it to drop the crayfish it drop the crayfish into the water), we'll reveal more about that later. So, let's get into the part of the story that is not supposition, but facts that CAT was able to bring to light.

Chapter 72

An Air-force base in Washington State has a secret military satellite launched into space and placed in orbit so they can find the world's resources--especially oil. This particular day a Sargent Sandy Jacob processed the data from the satellite. As he pours over the photos he spots not oil; but gold, and from the GPS it is located in Canada in a remote area of the Wind River Mountain range. Sgt. Sandy does not wish to share this information. Besides the order is to locate Oil and Coal not gold. So Sandy doctors the photos and distorts the data for that area, in hopes that no one will find out his secret. Before the day is over a Lt. Salon-De Mander stops by to get the daily report.

"So Sargent what did we find today?"

"Nothing sir. No Oil or Coal" Sandy's face looks as if he had got caught with his hand in the cookie jar. The Lt. has known Sandy for the last few years, and warned Sandy never to play poker. Sandy does not have the face for it.

"Sgt. Did you find anything else on the satellite survey?"

"No Sir, nothing."

"Dismissed Sgt."

As soon as Sandy left the office the Lt. Goes into Sandy's computer to re-check the data, and he finds that it has been doctored. Since the Sgt. does not have access to the backup data he cannot doctor the data so the Lt reviews the backup data he discovers the gold deposit.

"Well Sgt. You and I are going to have a private conversation." muses the Lt. to himself.

That night the Lt. drives over to the local bar and finds Sandy at a table by himself. The Lt. buys two beers and sits down at Sandy's table.

"Sir, this is a private party I do not wish to be disturbed."

"No, Sgt. It is not a private party and this place is far too public. We need to go somewhere where it is not public, we have something to discuss."

"What could you and I possibly have to discuss?"

"I could start out with locking you away for espionage."

"I never" … The Lt holds up his hand for silence.

"Come with me Sgt."

They both get up and leave the bar. The Lt. guides the Sgt. to his car.

"Get in the car Sandy."

The Lt. drives off down the road. The Sgt. sits in silence waiting for the Lt. to speak. The LT. drives them out to an empty park where the Lt. stops and pulls into a parking space where he tells the Sgt. Get out of the car indicating for them to take a walk. Then the Lt. starts the conversation.

"I know what you have found and I suspect why you doctored the prints, just so you have the same evidence on me as I do on you, I doctored the backup prints."

"So, Lt. that makes you as guilty for espionage as I am." states Sandy.

"Correct Sgt. now listen to my proposal."

"Ok, Lt."

"We both want the gold, so let's go get it."

"What?"

"Yes Sgt. let's go get the gold."

Chapter 73

"How? The gold is in Canada, and we are in Washington State USA. Is that not illegal to steal from one government or country and move it to another?"

"Right you are! We would be smuggling gold into our country for our own purposes, like getting rich. You see Sgt. we are going to become fast friends, as we both have enough on each other to send us both to prison for the rest of our lives. Now you have a choice, work with me or go to prison."

"I don't know." said Sandy.

"Sgt. You have a couple of days to think on it. You can be rich or you can be imprisoned."

The Lt. walked back to his car and offers to drive Sandy back to his car at the Bar. For two days' Sandy wrestles with his conscious. He has never in his life done anything dishonest, and now he is up to his chin in it. Then gold fever sets in. I can be rich or a prisoner. When the Sgt. reports to work the next morning the Lt. is there; more to read Sandy's face than anything else, and he likes what he sees. He can tell Sandy has made a decision, now which one?

They both realize that they cannot talk at the office, so when Sandy leaves for lunch, the Lt. meets him at his car.

"Sgt. may I buy you lunch?"

"Sure, where do you want to go?"

"Let's go to the Pizza parlor in town, it will have enough noise so we can have a casual conversation."

Randy drives them to the Pizza place, and they order a pizza and a couple of drinks and settle at a lone table in the far corner.

"Well Sgt. what have you decided?"

"I do not wish to be locked up, so that means we are getting rich."

Salen-De Mander pats Randy on the shoulder and says "Good Man."

"So Lt., how do we go get the gold?" asks Sandy.

"I have been working on that. We both put in for a month off for vacation, and I'll approve your request, we go fishing in Canada. I have found a guide service in that local region, and have made inquiries as to who to hire."

"Won't that defeat the purpose of keeping this a secret?"

"Not if we do not show up for a couple of days."

"So you now have an excuse to go to Canada, now how do we get there?"

"Well Sgt. I know how to fly a helicopter and I can rent one for the trip. First we can stock it with a few days' worth of supplies, then we fly to where the gold is then load up a couple of bags full of the gold, before we fly on to the fishing guide to spend a few days fishing. Afterwards we fly back, to my place in the woods outside of Ellensburg where we can drop off the gold and return here to work. I figure we can do this over the next couple of years, and then we split the gold and go our own way."

"Ok, I can go along with that, so what do we need for the trip?" asks Sandy.

The Lt. laid out the supply list that they will need to make their trip appear to be nothing other than a fishing trip.

So, a month later they leave to go on their trip, and true to his word the Lt. takes them to an airport to load up the helicopter. Once it is packed they do the preflight, and takeoff. The Lt. flies the helicopter right up the Puget Sound going north to Vancouver BC.

Chapter 74

"Lt. why are we going to Vancouver, instead of some place further east?"

"Once we cross over the border, we will need to check in with customs, just to be legitimate within their country. They will be looking for drugs and the like and our passports."

"Lt. you seem to be well advised."

"I've flown in here before. They will search all our stuff after we land, but seldom do they search us going out, especially if we have a couple of fish with us to take home. So a few hours after takeoff they land at Vancouver airport and are searched. Finally, they are let go after the Lt. shows them the paperwork for their fishing trip.

"Well you boys have a good trip and we'll see you back here on your way back home. Also you boys be careful as a storm is coming in from the northwest." Said the customs agent.

"Thank you" said the Lt.

The Lt. fires up the chopper and takes off and flies to the far side of the airport to get fuel. "Sandy, give me a hand. We'll get it fueled up and be on our way. We have two more of these stops then we'll be headed to the Wind River Range."

"Lt., what about the incoming storm?"

"We'll stay the night at the last stop for fuel and wait for the storm to blow over. For now, we'll move ahead of the storm."

In the Wind River Range a storm whips up the lake in the crater of the dead volcano and causes it to over flow and run down the side of the mountain where the break in the creator wall is located. At the bottom of the mountain it pools in a small depression shaped like a bowl. At that moment a wolverine female heavy with a kit which is about to be born just happens to be passing the pool of strange water. She is dehydrated and drinks the water from the bowl, as the lighting flashes across the sky she sees a cave in the mountain side and enters in hopes that nothing else is using it.

Chapter 75

She finds it empty and lays down in a pile of leaves to await the birth of her kit. By morning she has her kit, a male. He looks fine, so she nurses him and protects him. It is not long before he starts growing. In two weeks he is as big as she is and he is becoming deformed or mutated. His disposition is more violent than what would be normal even for a wolverine. In the weeks that follow this abomination continues to grow and become more and more enraged. While out foraging the mother runs into a grizzly bear, at first she tries to avoid him, but the bear is hungry and wants a meal. Before the bear can attack a tree behind the bear breaks, and the bear turns to face his new attacker. Standing there as he turns is the wolverine kit and it is bigger than he is. With one swipe the kit disembowels the bear, then begins to feed. The mother continues on her way not wanting to have to confront her kit.

The Mother wolverine plans to leave her kit, and get away, before it becomes so enraged that it kills her. So as the kit is feeding on the bear she tries to escape. Now in the Wind River range lives a tribe of Black Foot Indians, and they have a history of large animals attacking their tribe. Now to turn back a few days to Lt. Salen-De Mander and Sgt. Randy as they travel to the Volcanic Mountain of gold.

"That was a bad storm Lt."

"I'm glad we stayed here last night, now the sun is out and the weather is calm let's continue our journey." Says the Lt.

They gas up the chopper and check it out to make sure no damage was done and once they are ready they set off for the Wind River Range. Late in the evening they reach the volcanic mountain. As they hover over it they do not see a good place to land. The surface of the water has a big disturbance at the surface.

"Lt what is that?"

"Oh likely some methane gas floating to the surface. Sandy, spots a small Peninsula on the far side of the crater."

The Lt. flies over to see if they can land on it. It is just wide enough, one of them will have to get his feet wet, but otherwise, it is a place to land. The LT. decides they should stay in the chopper and spend the night, since there is no land big enough to camp on. That evening after they set up camp in the chopper all seems quiet, until they hear a roar that reverberates through the area.

"Lt. what is that?"

"I do not know; I have never heard anything like it before."

"Whatever it is, I hope it can't climb up here."

"Sandy, go to sleep, we will be busy tomorrow."

Looking around then Sandy bids the Lt. a good night. As they both sleep a mist rolls in off the strange water and engulfs them in a fog, and as they sleep they breathe in that strange mist all night long. The fog is not deadly, but it might have been toxic, as it seems to alter a person's mind.

The next morning both men get up and appear to be tired, they chock it up to sleeping on the chopper. They have breakfast and set off to find the gold deposits they saw on the GPS satellite map. Once the sun hits the crater full on, the gold stands out, as it glistens in the sun.

"Sandy, Look at that! We're going to be so rich!"

"I believe you Lt. Look how it sparkles!"

Chapter 76

It appears that both men are in the throes of gold fever along with what the strange mist from the water might be doing to them. They rush to the edge of the crater and start picking up large nuggets, they are so caught up that they even do a jig together yelling and jumping about as they pick up the gold laying all around them. They fill their pockets, and then return to the chopper to get bags to fill. In several hours they have six canvas bags full of gold, but they can only carry one bag at a time back to the chopper. They decide to leave the bags of gold outside the chopper for the night. They decide to offload their tools and put the bags of gold into the chopper in the morning and before they start the rest of their journey home. They resolve not to go to the guide for fishing they just want to take their treasure home and hide it some place safe.

Again that night the strange mist covers the area. What is causing both men to become so paranoid, gold fever, or the mist from the lake? The Lt. is first to wake in the night, and he looks over at Sandy and in his mind he thinks that Sandy wants to kill him for the gold. So the Lt. retrieves his gun and sits up to watch Sandy as he sleeps. Sandy On the other hand, feels the same way about the Lt. and so he grabs a rock hammer so he can defend himself. He too spends the night watching the Lt. In the morning both men hear a huge roaring! Suddenly all they can think of is to get out of there and return home. They take the tools and camping equipment out of the chopper and replace them with bags filled with gold.

Chapter 77

"Lt. should we not leave a couple of these bags behind, as you said before this chopper cannot carry that much weight."

"It will be fine Sandy."

As the Lt. pulls his gun out and shoots Sandy in the chest. Sandy Falls into the water and his blood starts spreading across the strange water. Within mere moments the water begins to thrash about and a giant claw reaches up out of the water to grab Sandy's body, pulling him under the water. The Lt. sees this and it drives him mad. In his madness the Lt. starts shooting into the water at the giant claw.

Now all the Lt. can think of is getting out of there. He gets in to the chopper and fires up the engine. The vibration of the engine awakens the giant in the water, but before the LT. can take off he sees two eye stocks stick up out of the water. The big black eyes are staring at him and soon the water is thrashing and the Lt. is trying to pull himself together so he can fly out of there; but fear has him frozen in place. When the huge claw reaches out of the water and grabs the chopper slicing through it cutting the Lt. in half along with the chopper. Somehow the creature manages to pull the Lt. out of the craft and into the water.

A few days after their leave expires the Lt. and the Sgt. are listed as AWOL and the Commanding Officer starts an investigation to locate his men. He asks around and finds out they went fishing up in Canada. The Commanding

Officer starts inquiring at the boarder to see where they might have entered Canada, a few days later he finds that they landed in Vancouver BC then flew on to the east from there. With further investigation he locates the last landing site where they last took on fuel. From this point on it is like the men fell off the face of the earth.

The Commanding Officer goes to the satellite Techs to ask them to see if they might locate a downed aircraft along the line that he drew on the map in Canada. It takes a few more days and the techs locate what looks like a crashed chopper in a volcanic crater in the Wind River Range. The Commanding officer knows he cannot mount a rescue mission into Canada without proper permissions and figures that two AWOL people will not convince the U.S. government to want to get involved in a rescue. But he can call on the Canadian government and ask them to mount one. So the Commanding officer contacts the Royal Canadian Air Force (RCAF), and tells them about the crash in the Wind River Range on top of some volcanic mountain. The RCAF indicates they will send out a search party and get back to them if they find anything. The RCAF contacts the Royal Canadian Mounted Police (RCMP) located one hundred miles west of the Wind River range to mount a rescue team to go check out the request to find a missing aircraft and a couple of men. The Commander at the fort Tasks a Sargent and a corporal to see if they can find the aircraft and possibly a couple of missing men. The next day they set out on horseback with their pack animals heading to the Indian camp that resides in that area so they can set up a base camp from where they can mount a search.

Chapter 78

The mother wolverine has traveled further east in hopes of losing her Kit, on this day she takes advantage of a rabbit she has caught and is eating. When she finishes her meal she heads for the stream to get a drink. Now she is going to look for a place to make a den. What the mother does not know is she is being watched by her kit, as she finishes her drink she turns, then raised her back and bares her teeth. Then lets out a growl. Her kit has found her, and before she can turn and run, the kit snaps her up and bits her in two ending her life. Once the kit feeds on his mother he turns and returns to the cave at the base of the dead volcano.

Now the kit has returned to his cave to sleep, when he hears three men who came from the Crow tribe from down river. They are out hunting for meat for the tribe. They are hoping to bag an Elk. The kit hears them talking from within his den. At first the kit's natural fear of men keeps him in place and he crouches just out of sight to watch. As the men are passing the mouth of the cave the kit bounds out of the cave, and attacks the men. Wolf and Little Beaver managed to run a way. Their friend Black Bird is killed and being eaten. Both men drop their guns and run as fast as they can to the river. Not long after they are being pursued by the monster wolverine. Soon the men are at the cliff edge just above the river and the wolverine is just steps away from catching them. Both men jump off the cliff into the cold rushing river below and it soon carries them downstream away from the wolverine. Wolf and Little Beaver struggle in the water as it carries them down river toward the village. On the bank above them the wolverine follows them. Both men look up and see the wolverine and they decide to go over the falls instead of swimming to the bank, which is several feet high, better to bounce off the rocks than to chance the wolverine catching them. With hypothermia starting to set in, they will soon be at the village. Fortune is with them the cliff of the water fall will slow the wolverine down or so they hope. They need to get everyone in the village to safety. So Wolf and Little Beaver start swimming to shore. Once they get there they look around for the wolverine, and do not see him. They can hear him crashing back in the woods. Both men start sounding the alarm to get everyone into the tunnels.

Chapter 79

Now we go back in time again, Steve Ball is at home with his family, he is keeping his five-year-old daughter busy so Mom can get some sleep, Samantha is expecting their second child, and according to the doctor it will be a boy. Samantha is six months along and wishing it was over. There is a park in Spokane that Steve likes to go to. Manitou Park has the usual swings, slides and an outdoor garden. It is just down the street from a Baskin & Robins ice cream shop. Steve and Kim come here often these days so Samantha can get some rest. Steve missed the birth of his daughter. So he fully intends to be there for the birth of his son. As soon as Samantha is rested she meets her husband and daughter at the park, and they then walk down to the Ice Cream shop for an ice cream cone.

"I feel so ugly; how can you stand to be around me?"

"Samantha, you're the most beautiful woman I know, it does not matter how you think you may appear. The one thing I'm having trouble with is your temper."

"Well you try carrying a child like I am, and then caring for two other Children (Kim and Steve), it would make you crabby too."

After the ice cream treat Steve ports, them all home.

"I see your point, how about we get a sitter, and go out for the evening?"

"Thank you dear, but I'm really too tired for anything like that right now."

"Alright, I'll go get dinner and we can stay at home, what would you like?" Samantha thinks about her cravings, but decides to forget it, no matter what she wants he can always get it for her, where is the fun in that.

"I would like a steak and shrimp dinner."

"Your wish is my command my love."

Steve ports to their favorite steak house in Japan and orders the dinners to go, and in thirty minutes he returns home, with the food still hot off the grill. In the time Steve is gone Samantha and Kim have set the table, and when Steve appears they sit down to have dinner. When dinner is over Kim and Steve pick up the dishes and wash them. Samantha moves to the living room and turns on some music and promptly falls asleep on the couch.

"Steve, I have a message for you,"

"Who is it CAT?"

"It is a Major Harrington at McCord Air Force base in Washington State."

"What does he want?"

"All he will say Steve is that he needs your help, and he will meet you, where ever you say."

"Just a moment CAT."

Steve sees to it that Kim gets ready for bed and reads her a bed time story until she falls asleep, then Steve puts Samantha into bed as well, he gives her a kiss, and then ports to the lodge. Steve puts on his battle suit.

"CAT where is the Major right now?"

"He is at his home Steve."

"Do you detect any one else there?"

"It appears not, his wife has gone to visit her sister, and he is home alone."

"Good, give me the coordinates."

Paladin appears in the Major's den.

"Who are you!?" exclaims the Major.

"You called me, Remember."

"You are that Paladin guy I've heard about?"

"The one and only, now Major what is so important you risk your career to contact me?"

"I talked to the mission commander of the space shuttle you saved a few years ago, and he told me about you. After meeting you, I will trust you anyway. I have lost two of my top Satellite Techs, and I need your help in locating them."

"Why, you have all the resources you could need to find them."

"What I'm going to tell you is so secret you can never tell anyone."

"Major you have my word."

"A year ago we launched a satellite that can map the world's resources, oil, minerals and so on."

"What is so secret about that?"

"Mostly it will be a military secret, so that we only know of these resources, in case we need to exploit the resource for purposes of war, right now I have to be sure that my two techs are not telling a world government about what we are doing."

"OK, so where do I come in?"

"We have found that the two men landed at a few air fields on their way to a supposed fishing trip. We also found a possible crash site. It is so remote, I'm not sure anyone can get there, but you. They crashed in what is called the Wind River Range in British Columbia."

"Well that explains why you cannot go in to find them. Have you contacted the Canadians for a rescue?"

"Yes, and from what I learned they are sending in the RCMP to see if they can find them, but I do not have any faith in them locating the downed aircraft, it is on top of a dead volcanic mountain."

"We actually have the location, and it is in a precarious place, it looks like it is sitting on the edge of an extinct volcano."

"What are the coordinates and I'll go take a look."

Chapter 80

The Major Gives Paladin the coordinates to where they found the downed aircraft by satellite, and Paladin ports back to his lodge.

"CAT see what you can find at this location."

An hour later CAT contacts Steve.

"Steve the Volcano is going to be difficult to land on, I found a two-foot area where you can land. It is a small distance from the crash, but to set you down on the crash site might cause you harm."

"I'm going home CAT; I'll be leaving tomorrow during the daylight."

Paladin ports home to find everyone is in bed sound asleep, Steve strips off his battle suit, and turns in.

Early in the morning, Steve gets up, and wakes up Samantha to let her know he is going to be gone for the day to look for a couple of missing men in Canada.

"Will you be home for dinner?"

"I plan to."

"We'll see you later Dear."

"Kim is still asleep, so feel free to sleep in."

"Thank you dear"

Samantha goes back to sleep. Steve suits up and ports to the location CAT has given him. Standing on the small landing area, Paladin can see the Chopper, he ports over to it.

"WOW!" he exclaims "What destroyed this chopper?"

As if in answer to his question, he hears the water thrashing behind him and he turns in time to see a giant claw and two eye stalks come up out of the water, Paladin ports to the far side of the lake and he watches the claw grab the chopper and drag it into the water.

"I guess; I can figure where the two men are."

Paladin is standing at the break in the wall of the volcano, noticing the water.

"CAT analyze this water."

A few minutes later CAT comes back to Steve.

"Steve this water is full of Heavy metals, and some of them are radioactive."

"That might explain the giant crab (crayfish) I just saw."

Then Paladin hears a roar. A rather earth shattering roar. (At this time the wolverine had pounced on Wolf and Little Beaver's hunting party). Before Steve walks to the edge of the volcano he sees the gold on the edge of the crater where the chopper was. Now I know why the men landed here. Thinks Steve.

Paladin is looking over the edge of the volcano wall and sees a ledge further down the side of the mountain and ports down to it to see if he can reach the ground from the ledge. He looks over the ledge and sees a clearing. Paladin ports down to the ground in the clearing. Looking around he sees what looks like a catch basin holding the same colored water from the volcano. He hears more roaring further off in the woods, but before he follows, he sees a very large animal track.

"CAT what kind of an animal makes a track like that?"

All Paladin gets is silence, the metal in the Wind River Range is full of heavy metals, and it blocks his ability to communicate with CAT. Paladin realizes that he can return to the top of the Volcano and be able to reach CAT, but he decides to follow the broken trail that is before him. Squashed trees lie to either side of the trail, brush trampled rocks overturned. Paladin figures the trail will not be hard to follow. The broken trees and brush make it easy to track this animal.

Paladin wonders what animal can cause this much destruction, surly not a bear. Using line of site Paladin ports along the trail. After an hour Paladin reaches an Indian village and instead of seeing Teepee's he sees log cabins, but there is no one around. The place appears deserted, and it is so quiet not even insects are making any noise.

Chapter 81

Paladin looks around and he even enters one of the cabins. Everything looks devastated as if the village people left in a hurry. Stepping outside he cannot see that he is being watched (and his sensors do not detect anything) by the Indian Named Wolf and the wolverine. The wolverine is watching Paladin from hiding at the far edge of the woods behind one of the cabins. Wolf is beside himself in trying to decide to warn the stranger which will call attention to himself to the wolverine. So Wolf stays quiet and watches. Paladin decides to look around when the wolverine pounces, with one huge paw the wolverine strikes Paladin and sends him flying, as luck would have it Paladin lands near the entrance of one of the underground tunnels. Paladin just lays there unconscious, so Wolf and his friend Little Beaver manage to grab Paladin's legs and pull him into the tunnel. Just as they reach the floor of the tunnel the opening above goes dark as the huge head of the wolverine blocks out the entrance. Roaring the wolverine tries to get at the men in the tunnel by digging, but the rocky entrance defeats the wolverine's progress which enrages him further.

Wolf and Little Beaver, haul Paladin deeper inside the tunnel and takes him to the medicine man, who in this case is actually a doctor. At first they are at a loss as to how to remove the battle suit and helmet. With closer examination the doctor sees the helmet is hinged so he tries to open it, but as he exerts some force on it; it shatters. Removing the pieces of the helmet, the doctor finds a way to remove the rest of the battle suit.

"Wolf what happened to this man?" Asks the doctor.

"The monster wolverine swatted him and he flew about thirty feet or so and landed pretty hard."

"That explains the concussion and the broken ribs. If he had not had that helmet on it would have been his head that was broken. All I can do for now is wait to see if he will wake up from his injuries."

Paladin lays on his mat for eight days before he comes to. During the eight days the wolverine is out hunting and marking his territory when he encounters the two men from the RCMP. They are making an early camp so they can enter the Indian village in the morning. They are hoping to enlist the Indian's aid in locating the missing men; that they were instructed to find. They find a secluded spot not far from the river and set up camp the tents are erected and a fire going, they take care of the horses and a pack mule. The corporal starts supper and the SGT. Is logging the day's events into his logbook? Back in the woods the corporal hears what sounds like trees breaking and a roar like he has never heard before.

"SGT. Come out here!"

"What is wrong Corporal?"

"Listen" The roar comes again and more trees breaking and it is getting closer.

"Corporal get the guns, I don't know what it is, but it is coming our way."

The corporal gets the guns and ammunition and hands the SGT his. They check to see that the rifles and pistols are loaded. Their animals are going mad and trying to break free of the picket line so they can run away.

Then out of nowhere the wolverine pounces on the two men, they don't even get a chance to fire their weapons. Both men are now dead and the wolverine hears the horses trying to break free of their ropes. They manage to break free of the picket line so the horses and mule run off, with the wolverine bounding down the trail after them. It is not long before the wolverine has both horses but the mule manages to get away. Eventually the mule returns to the RCMP fort months later. The men from the RCMP are not found until years later and what is left of the camp they had made. Back to the present.

As he opened his eyes a gentle hand holds him down.

"Don't move, you were badly injured, I'll go get my father" whispers the young girl.

A few moments later a man is leaning over Paladin.

"Good you are a wake; do you know your name?"

It takes a few minutes, "Paladin, I'm called Paladin."

"I have heard of you" said the doctor.

"When I was going to the university I heard of your exploits on saving the crew of the space shuttle."

"Yes, I did save two of them, the third one was dead when I got there."

"Lay here you need to take it easy for a few days. You have some cracked ribs and a concussion." "Doctor how long have I been here?"

"Counting today, eight days."

"May I sit up?"

"Carefully, like I said you have some cracked ribs."

With a grown Paladin sits up. "Can anyone tell me what happened?"

"Flower, go find Wolf and send him here, then go get the Shaman and bring him as well."

The young girl leaves the room. Fifteen minutes later a young man appears.

"What do you want medicine man?" grouses Wolf

The doctor looks at the man called Wolf in the eye, and Wolf adopts a better attitude as he sees the displeasure on the doctor's face. The doctor points to Paladin, and tells him to answer the stranger's questions.

Chapter 82

Paladin starts out, "you are the man who saved me?"

"Yes."

"All I can remember is that I followed a rather large trail till I found a village, then I'm hit by something and I wake up here. Can you tell me what happened?"

"You were attacked by a giant wolverine, it swatted you and you landed close to the tunnel entrance, Little Beaver and I managed to pull you into the tunnel."

"Thank you for saving my life."

Wolf does not say anything, he just gets up and leaves, but a few moments later the Shaman arrives. "Paladin this is our Shaman and story teller." Says the doctor.

"Doc why is the shaman here?" asks Paladin

"He has a story I think you should hear; Please Shaman tell him of the stories about the giant animals of our past."

The Shaman looks at the doctor with a wary eye.

"Why do you want me to tell this stranger about our history, so he can be amused?"

"Shaman, this man here can help us, but he needs to know of our past, believe me unlike the others here, he will not laugh at you. Besides with the giant wolverine outside they are not laughing at you now either."

So the Shaman tells his story of the giant animals and how they attacked the village in times past, and how all this happens just after a large storm, then months later a creature comes to us and destroys our homes above ground.

Then he tells the story of the giant moose whose pelt now hangs in the lodge at the center of the village, and how they managed to kill it by luring it into a pit with sharpen stakes. After the moose incident the tribe decides to build the underground tunnels just in case we encounter more of these enlarged animals. We have had to use them over the years for such things as forest fires, and other creatures. This is the first time in my life time that we have had to live here.

"Wow! You were right doc. I'm not going to laugh; Shaman do you have any other information about how the animals came to be?"

"I do not, what I told you is what we know."

"Thank you, you have answered some of my questions. I'm going to tell you what I know; when I first got here I was looking for a downed aircraft and I found it up on the volcano, in the crater I found some strange water, and it has a soup of radioactive materials in it. On one edge of the crater there is a broken wall just above the water line. I suspect when the storm happens like the last one the waves crash over the break and flow down the mountain to the base there is a place where it can pool. I guess that an animal can drink that water and it grows into a giant. It must be driven mad by the poisons in it, and apparently this has happened many times over. When I'm up to it I'll help you get rid of this creature, and I believe I can prevent other occurrences for the future. Doctor, I need to talk to your able bodied men and make a plan for killing this monster."

"You are not well enough to do anything right now, if you do too much at this time the exertion can kill you. You need to rest for a few days longer."

"Your right doctor, but I can still plan, how we might kill this creature."

The doctor gives in, and calls the men to come see Paladin. At first the men do not want to hear what Paladin has to say, until the young girl called Flower gets mad and chews them out.

"Oh, such brave men. A stranger is trying to help you kill this creature, and all you can do is complain about it like a bunch of old women. You made fun of the Shaman for all these years, and now look. We have the worst giant creature that has ever roamed this range, and here you hide under ground. All of you make me sick!"

Then Flower storms out of the room, and the only one laughing is the Shaman. The men look to be ashamed. Wolf is angry more so than being ashamed, and he is about to go off on a tirade when Paladin points out to them.

"In a few days I can go home and leave you to your trouble or I can help you to help yourself. What is it to be?"

Wolf says "You were not much help when you got here, how are you going to help us now?" "Your Shaman gave me the idea, to dig a pit and put sharpened stakes in it."

"Yea good idea, so how are we suppose too dig this pit? You stick your head up and out of the hole and get it bitten off, good plan."

"Let's assume for a moment you can get outside, how much time would you need to dig this pit?"

"With the number of men we have, we would need a good ten hours."

"That means I'll be busy; Ok I'll get you those ten hours."

"So how are you going to do that?"

"That Wolf will be my problem, get all the digging equipment you can together and whatever you need to cut and sharpen stakes."

Chapter 83

The men look at Paladin and wonder what he is going to do to get them their ten hours.

A few days later Paladin tries to teleport and finds he has no problem in line of site, but for some reason he cannot teleport home or to the lodge from here. Fortunately, it won't affect his plan to get the wolverine out of the area for ten hours.

"Ok men, the doctor gave me a reasonable clean bill of health, so tomorrow let's do this."

Now while Paladin was healing, the men took some of the logs they had in the tunnels and sharpened them. This will help cut down on the time they will need to get the trap ready for the wolverine. Paladin goes to the entrance of the tunnels and carefully peeks out and spots the wolverine fifty feet away, and it is watching the entrance. Taking a quick look Paladin spots a clear area on the other side of the village. Paladin ports to the far side, and then starts making a lot of noise, soon the wolverine roars and charges him. Paladin waits until the last possible second and ports to the other edge of the clearing, then spots the trail he followed to get here and then chooses the next port destination in his mind, Paladin picks up a rock and throws it hitting the creature in the face. More enraged the wolverine bounds after Paladin.

At this point in time the wolverine is so fixed on the small creature that keeps eluding him, and with each time it gets away, the angrier the wolverine becomes. Paladin keeps this tactic up drawing the wolverine away from the village. Now Paladin has to keep eluding this creature and still keep it fixed on him. For the next ten hours, Paladin leads the creature away from the village. As soon as the wolverine is away the Indians come out of hiding, and start making preparations. Most of them are digging the pit, the rest are cutting and sharpening other logs for the stakes. It takes eight hours to dig the pit, and another two hours for the stakes to be set in place. Finally, some of the others pull down the moose pelt off the lodge wall to cover the pit and they cover the pelt over with dirt. Just as everyone is returning back in to the tunnel Paladin ports into the clearing and moments later the wolverine is back. It is roaring and tearing up the ground. Paladin throws another rock at the wolverine and does a jig, and sure enough the wolverine tries to pounce on his prey. Again Paladin eludes him by porting to the far side of the pit.

Just as luck would have it, a couple of the young boys are out playing where they shouldn't have been. Their noise attracts the wolverine. Paladin seeing this realizes he does not have the time to save them, so he throws rocks, sticks and curses at the creature. The creature hesitates his attack on the two boys to look at his elusive prey. It was just enough time to let Wolf climb out of the nearby tunnel entrance and grab the boys. That is when the wolverine moves to catch them. Wolf drops down into the hole with the boys in his arms, and ready hands pull them deeper into the tunnel. The wolverine turns back to Paladin and charges. Paladin standing on the far side of the pit waits to see if the Wolverine will fall in to it.

At the last instant the wolverine stops, then it pushes at the ground and watches it fall in on itself. Then it turns away and walks around the pit to get at its prey.

"That didn't work" says Paladin

Paladin ports over to the other tunnel entrance.

"Hand me your spear."

Little Beaver hands over his spear. The wolverine seems determined to dig those people out of the tunnel, so Paladin ports over behind the creature, and stabs him with the spear, and then ports out of the way, the wolverine turns so fast he almost catches the hated creature he has been chasing. The wolverine turns back to his digging. Paladin again ports behind the wolverine, and pushes the spear into the hind quarters of the wolverine and leaves it there as he ports away. So, enraged is the wolverine that he takes up the chase of the small creature once again, this time the wolverine will run it to ground and kill it.

Chapter 84

Paladin does not at first have a plan, as he avoids the monster, an idea forms in his mind. Now, if only he can get the wolverine to follow him again. Paladin decides to lead the creature around to the far side of the volcano and up the side which is not as steep as the side he came down. Paladin goes back to get the wolverine. Paladin throws rocks sticks and anything else he can grab to taunt the wolverine until it is so enraged the wolverine can think of nothing else but to get this creature. So, onward it follows Paladin to the base of the volcano. Paladin perches on the edge of the volcano's base, and continues to curse at the wolverine. Just as the wolverine reaches where Paladin stands, Paladin would port on to the next small ledge leading the wolverine up the side of the volcano. At the top of the volcanic crater the wolverine pounces on Paladin, landing them both in the water. Paladin manages to port to the far side of the creator where the Chopper had landed. As Paladin is trying to catch his breath from all the porting, the wolverine is now swimming in Paladin's direction when the water beside the wolverine erupts and this giant claw reaches up and grabs the wolverine. The wounds that Paladin had inflected earlier in the hind quarters of the wolverine had attracted the crab like creature. After struggling for a few minutes in trying to get away, the claw disappears back into the water, taking the wolverine with it. Paladin watches as the water turns red then the water goes back to being peaceful again.

Paladin decides to teleport home to let his wife know he is ok. He arrives in the clothes he has been wearing and knocks on the door of his house. Kim answers the door. Steve reaches down and picks her up.

"Hi Sweetie, where is mommy?"

"Mommy is in bed crying."

"Let's go see what the matter is."

Steve walks into the bed room and finds Samantha on the bed crying.

"Samantha I'm back."

Samantha looks up at her husband. "YOU! Where have you been? You left me here not knowing if you were safe or dead. No communications! CAT could not find you or communicate to you. I thought you were dead. And I may make that happen yet because YOU put me through this!"

Steve sets Kim down on the floor and sits next to Samantha, then takes her in his arms and kisses her. At first, she struggles to pull away then gives in.

"Dear I have a few things I have to tie up, and when I return I will tell you all about what happened, I will be back to take you out to dinner to a very nice place."

Steve ports to the lodge to get a new battle suit.

"CAT I need a sheet of stainless steel two inches thick by four feet by eight foot, locate it and buy it, then have them tip it up on edge so I can transport it, and tell them someone will be there to pick it up." Paladin ports to the Major's office.

"Well Major your secret is safe, your men were not betraying you in that fashion, although they did pay for their transgression with their lives."

"What did they do?"

"That I will not tell you. You see, you were not totally honest with me. Besides in about thirty minutes from now I'm going to fix it so you can't even reach that place."

Steve leaves the scowling Major with a mystery. One that the Major will never solve, CAT will see to that by programming the satellite to block out the gold find on the volcanic mountain. Paladin contacts CAT "is my stainless steel plate ready?"

"They will have it ready for you tomorrow at noon."

"Good, I'm going home to spend the rest of the day with my family."

"CAT, I want to go to Italy for dinner."

"Ok Steve, but due to the difference in time, it will be nearly dawn there, not much will be open for dinner, Now I know of a nice restaurant you can go to here in the states."

Paladin ports home to tell Samantha that Italy is not on the menu today.

"Ok, but you are going to take me to Italy for dinner some time."

"Your wish will be my command O wife of mine." As he bows to her

Samantha giggles at Steve's garish display as he gives a flourish and bows to her.

Steve gives Samantha a hug, he collects Kim and his wife then ports them to one of the best Italian restaurants on the west coast. Before Steve leaves, he tells his wife that he has to go back to the village and he will be gone for a day, then I'll tell you the whole story of what went on. Steve ports to the lodge to change into his battle suit, and then ports to the steel yard that has his steel plate. When Paladin arrives, it creates a fuss, so Paladin does a double port he ports to the top of the plate then he ports the plate to its new home in the crater wall where the break in the wall is. Paladin then ports the plate into the rock so it cannot ever be removed and it seals the breach in the wall.

"This should stop the giant animals in the future. Then Paladin ports over to the place where the chopper was and picks up one canvas bag full of gold, and sets out to return to the village.

Paladin reaches the village by evening time and is greeted by his new Indian friends. He tells them that the wolverine is dead, and that he plugged the breach in the wall so that the strange water will not refill the basin at its base of the mountain. Paladin removes his mask, and spends the night with the tribe. During that time Paladin gives the doctor the gold, and the doctor refuses it.

"Are you sure doctor, you can use it to buy medical supplies."

"From where? And you yourself can see this is so remote, where would it come from? Then also this would attract unwanted attention having gold in the region."

"I see your point, I may have an Idea, give me a list of the supplies you need and I'll deliver them to you."

"But you have done so much for us already."

"I think I owe you Doc, you did save me too you know."

"Ok I'll get you our list, when will you be leaving?"

"Tomorrow morning some time."

"I'll have the list drawn up before you go."

Later at the party Paladin See's Wolf off to one side, and he is watching the Doctor's daughter Flower. Paladin walks up to him.

"Wolf, why do you not tell her how you feel about her?"

"She detests me."

"I'm not so sure, all she wants is to have a husband, who will regard her as a person and someone not afraid to protect her. As I recall you did save the two boys from the wolverine and she did see you do that, you know. If I were you I would lose the pride and arrogance, and become a bit humbler, you will get a lot further than you know."

Paladin walks off to where the doctor is sitting and sits down with him to have a conversation.

"What did you tell Wolf?" asks the Doctor

"How he might have a better chance at winning your daughter's heart."

"I have tried to do that for years, I hope he listens to you, I would like to see a grandson in the not too distance future."

"I would say from the looks of it, he did listen."

Wolf walks over to Flower and tells her how he feels for her, and promises to be a better man, she did not commit to him, but she did not turn him down either.

In the morning sun Paladin heads home and he arrives in time for dinner. Over dinner Samantha extracts Steve's last adventure about the wolverine. Then at the end of the story she asks why could you not port direct from here to there?"

"The only thing that comes to mind is that there is some substance in the Wind River Mountains that prevents my crystal from working. When I'm there I can teleport only in line of site, but I cannot port over long distances, also the same substance prevents me from communication with CAT. By the by, CAT did you get me supplies I ask for?"

"Steve you can pick it up at the pharmacy in town."

"I'll get it in the morning." After dinner Steve walks his wife into the living room couch and puts her favorite blanket over her and returns to the table to clear away the dishes, and wash them. Samantha falls asleep, and when Steve is done in the kitchen he walks in and stares down at his wife. Steve reaches over and places a hand on her shoulder and ports her to the bedroom where he takes off her shoes, and makes her comfortable. He thinks in a few more months I'll have a son. And he carefully wraps his arm around his wife to hold her. Samantha smiles in her sleep and snuggles closer to Steve.

Alexander's Treasure

Chapter 85

Back in the day, there was a notorious bandit called Alexander the Butcher, not to be confused with Alexander the Great. Alexander was a bandit that raided along a caravan route that came from the East. As Alexander stops the caravans he would extort money, Gold or other goods as payment to let them pass unmolested. On a few occasions he would wipe out the caravan and take all the spoils. During one of these raids Alexander's son Kemi is killed. During the fighting Kemi is killed by one of the guards trying to protect the small caravan. It was a small caravan so there was no expectation of being able to collect very much by way of treasure. When they opened up all the packs they found Gold, Silver, and Jewels. There was enough to buy a small kingdom. Taking the spoils with them Alexander and his men return to their nomadic camp. On the next day Alexander decides to Take Kemi and bury his son in a remote place in the mountains called the Forbidden Valley. So they prepare Kemi's body for burial.

Alexander's plan is to give all the Silver over to his men and keep the Gold and Jewels for himself. He forms a party of his most trusted men at arms, and they load up Kemi's body, and most of the treasure. On to a mule pack train for the trip. Alexander brings along some other pack animals that carry more gold, and other spoils from the other caravans they raided to be buried with his son's body. It takes a month of traveling to reach the secluded place known as the Forbidden Valley. Alexander has chosen this secluded place to bury his son. There is a deep cave system where they take Kemi's body and the treasure.

They wall up three of the cave mouths. To make it harder for grave robbers to find the proper cave to rob. Inside the cave system where they buried Kemi with the treasure. Alexander had devised some traps and had them put into place to protect his son and his treasure. Outside the main cave mouth is where Alexander and his men set up camp. Now the men of Alexander's who are there remember where the treasure is and they plan on killing Alexander to steal the treasure. Alexander is suspicion of his men. On the morning when they plan to leave. Alexander decides to climb up the side of the mountain to place a marker so they can find the cave entrance in the future. He climbs up the mountain to find loose rock all around him. Alexander plots to find some way to kill off his men before they kill him, so he can keep all the treasure a secret. He decides to get rid of his men by causing a rock slide. Alexander uses the loose rock to start an avalanche, but as the rock rumbles down the mountain his men look up. In hearing the noise the men realize they have no chance of escape and all are buried in the rubble along with the cave mouth. Alexander climbs back down and checks to see if anyone is still alive. If he finds anyone alive his sword will dispatch them quickly.

Chapter 86

Satisfied that no one has survived the rock slide. He takes his horse and a couple of the pack animals and sets out for his nomadic camp. On his way back to his home he stops at a small village which has a smithy. He hands the smith a skin with some markings on it and asks that two medallions be made. Place half the picture on the front of one medallion and the other half on the second medallion. When the two medallions are put together they make a whole picture. On the back side he points out the symbols at the bottom of the skin that he wants engraved on the medallions back side. The smith makes the medallions as requested out of a bronze metal and puts chains on them so Alexander can wear them. Alexander pays the smith for his work in gold, and seems to leave the next day. That night Alexander returns with his bow and arrows, and he sets fire to the smith's house. When the family attempts to escape the burning house Alexander shoots them down in cold blood killing the whole family.

After making sure the smith and his family are dead he continues his journey to his home camp. Upon return the men there confront him about what happened to their friends and other tribal members? He explains they were killed in a land slide.

"We do not believe you, said the men. You killed them! Now tell us where you buried the treasure."

"No!" shouts Alexander.

"If you kill me, you will never find the treasure."

The men turned away grumbling. Alexander knows that they are going to kill him as soon as the get drunk and brave enough. So he goes to his two children an older daughter and his younger son. Alexander puts them on a horse with provisions and sends them away during the dark of the night. Then tells them to head west. The older girl takes her younger brother and leads him off in to the West. The next day the men take Alexander and decide to torture him to get the treasures location. Alexander manages to endure the torture of his men for a couple of days to give his children a chance to get away. Alexander is killed by his men. By this time his children have managed to get away and hide in the wilderness until they can make their way further west to Italy where they live out their lives. The girl gets married and passes her medallion on to her children. The son dies in a war and his medallion becomes lost. Over time some archeologist finds the medallion (the boy's) while excavating an ancient battle field and puts his finds into a museum located in Rome. There has been much speculation about the medallion at the museum. That it could reveal a lost and ancient treasure, but no one is able to read the markings or figure out the map. So the medallion sits in a case and soon is lost in history and forgotten.

Over time the medallion that belongs to the older girl finds its way to America with one of her ancestors. The medallion comes to a girl named Beverly Anderson, she has honey brown hair, and brown eyes, and very well filled out for a young college girl. She also is very smart and earns a scholarship to college. She is into ancient history and manages to get a chance to go to Italy for a year of study at a University in Rome. So a week later finds Beverly on a plane bound for London, then on to Paris, and on to Rome. In Rome Beverly will be studying ancient history in their university. Beverly has taken the time to learn the Italian language and also some Latin to make reading manuscripts easy without someone translating them for her. Beverly takes to wearing the medallion under her shirt. Her real reason for visiting Rome is to learn about

296

her keepsake which according to her grandmother has been handed down from mother to daughter for centuries.

Her Grandmother also makes her memorize a story that had something to do with the medallion. Beverly gets to Italy and starts her classes at the university. Beverly is taking a class on ancient history and studying the language of Ancient Greek hoping to be able to read the medallions inscription. When Beverly is not in class or studying she goes out to see the sites of the city of Rome and takes pictures. While on one of these expeditions, Beverly runs into Jacob a class mate from the Ancient History class.

Chapter 87

"Hi Jacob, are you following me?"

"In a way I am."

"Why, I'm not looking to form a relationship, I'm here to study."

"As you should recall Bev, you mentioned that to me several days ago. What interests me is the amulet you are wearing."

"What amulet are you referring to?"

"The one you wear under your shirt, you see one day when you leaned down to pick up your books, I saw it slip out of your shirt, and I'm not the only boy to see it either."

"That is vulgar, you had no right!"

"Look, Guy's do that, and you are not going to change that fact with a few words of anger. Now let me finish, I'm sure you'll be interested in what I have to say, then I can show you."

Bev was just a bit skeptical of Jacob's words, but she listens.

"A few weeks ago while I was at a museum I saw an amulet much like the one you have. When I saw yours the other day I returned to the museum to look at it again. They did not have very much information on it except that is was found in a battle field outside of Rome."

"Will you take me there Jacob?"

"Only if you show me your amulet so I can get a good look at it."

So Beverly takes her amulet out and shows him.

"Ok, now you have seen it, where is the museum?" asks Beverly.

Jacob turns and walks off down the street towards the museum and when Bev is not with him, he turns and says "Are you going to come along or not?"

Bev follows him, not sure if she should trust him or not. In the back of her mind Beverly remembers hearing about a slave ring operating in the area. They soon get to the museum and Jacob leads her in, and to the very back of one room. There in the glass case sits an amulet just like the one she is wearing.

"Oh my, you were right Jacob, it is just like mine."

"See I told you so."

Chapter 88

Now a few days earlier, Steve (AKA Paladin) and Samantha his wife are going through the usual domestic time, Kim their daughter is now six years old, and her younger brother is now three years old, doing what little brothers do, getting into everything and anything. Samantha is ragged and wants some time off to spend with her husband alone. Steve manages to hire a live-in Nanny to look after the children and help Samantha out from time to time, especially when Steve is off doing whatever he is doing. It seems sometimes the world cannot get along without Paladin. However, Samantha likes it when she is included in Steve's adventures too. That evening when Steve walks in the door.

"I want a vacation!!!!!" says Samantha.

"Sure, when and where, and are the children coming along?"

"No children, just you and me. After your last adventure, you promised me a trip to Italy, for a dinner date, now I want at least a week with you by myself."

"Ok, I can say I would not complain about it, and I have nothing on my calendar. I can leave a message with CAT not to contact us during our stay."

"Smart Hubby, otherwise I'll break your leg and you'll be off of it for several months."

"I get the picture, I'll go talk with Joy and see if she will be willing to stay with the children for a week."

Joy is excited about the prospect of taking care of Kim and William, she is a grandmother whose grandkids have grown up. Steve returns to Samantha.

"We can leave tomorrow Samantha, so you'd better get packed. I told Joy we would be gone for several days."

Steve also packs a few of his things as well. He carries all the bags out to the garage and puts them into the car. Steve then parks the car up at the front gate to the house, and gets out to say good bye to the children and collect Samantha. After all the hugs and last minute instructions Steve manages to get his wife into the car and drive off down the road headed to the Dalles.

"CAT do we have a window to port to Rome?"

"Steve, I have the coordinates all set."

"Good take us there."

In mere moments they are driving along a country road headed to Rome. "Where do you want to stay Samantha?"

"Some fancy hotel where I can wear a fancy dress and be wined and dined. After all you should show me off once in a while."

Steve smiles "You don't have a fancy dress in our baggage."

"We'll remedy that tomorrow, when you take me shopping."

"I suspected that was coming."

"If I'm going to buy a dress you can at least buy a tuxedo to wear as well."

"Boy did I walk into that one." Steve pats his wife's knee and smiles, "I guess you deserve this."

An hour later they pull up to the most expensive Hotel in Rome, and they get a Bridal Suite. It is in the middle of the night time in Rome, so there is no open place to go for dinner, so consequently Samantha takes Steve by the hand and ports them to New York for dinner. Once they having finished dinner, they return to Rome and settle in for the night.

Chapter 89

Steve and Samantha get up in the late morning in Rome, and leisurely enjoy breakfast. Then Samantha with Steve in tow heads out to do some shopping. At the same time Beverly and Jacob have returned to the museum to see if they can get an appointment with the curator to see if Beverly can inspect the amulet on display. The curator says no at first until Jacob tells Bev to show him your amulet. When Beverly takes her amulet out and shows him, his eyes open wide, and then he rushes them to where the museums amulet is on display to make sure this is not the one that is on display. Satisfied that theirs is still in its case, the curator becomes very interested, and offers to buy it for a few hundred American dollars.

Beverly refuses, but still wants to look at the museum's amulet. The curator refuses to let her, so Bev and Jacob leave the museum.

"Well so much for that, I guess I will go back to my room and do some studying for class." said Beverly.

"Hey Beverly maybe we can get a professor to help us with the amulets."

"Maybe, but for now I'm going to grab a coffee and hit the books."

They set off toward the University. As Bev and Jacob leave the museum two men start following the two college students as they walk down the street.

"Jacob, are we being followed?"

Looking around to see what Bev is talking about Jacob spots the two men.

"What do you mean Bev.?"

"Since we left the museum those two men have been following us."

Jacob looks around and "you mean those men? let's duck down this street and see if they follow us."

So Jacob leads the way and is pulling Beverly along with him, and sure enough the two men follow them.

One thing Steve and Samantha have not managed to overcome is Jet lag or rather the time difference between Duffer Oregon and Italy. One's internal clock still runs on the time where one lives. In Duffer Oregon this time of day is bed time but midday in Italy, so after a round of shopping Steve and Samantha decide to go to their room and take a nap. When Steve and Samantha get to their quiet room they set the packages next to the closet, kick off their shoes and fall into bed. Steve rolls over to Samantha to give her a kiss before taking a nap. Samantha has some other plans, and won't settle for just a quick kiss and off to dream land she decides she would like a lot more cuddling. Now just as things are getting interesting they hear gun fire, and the next thing two college students burst into their room and close the door.

"Beverly I told you we needed to go down the street further."

"Jacob they are hot on our heels, in another few blocks they would have shot us or caught us."

Chapter 90

Steve sits up, "What is going on, a school prank?"

The two students turn at Steve's question, with a shocked look on their faces.

"Oh sir please help us; we are being chased by two men with guns."

Then someone starts pounding on the door, and they break it in. Two rather large men are standing in the door way waving guns around telling everyone to stay where they are. Samantha ports behind the open door, everyone's attention is on the men with the guns. Beverly is terrified, and Jacob not so much, and Steve is acting like a couple of cousins were just dropping by for a chat.

"Now before someone gets hurt, why don't you put down your guns, and let's talk things over."

One of the men said to Steve "shut up and sit down."

"Ok, I tried to warn you."

At that very moment, Samantha kicks the door hitting one of the men knocking him down, the other man tries to aim his gun at her, but she kicked his hand sending the gun off to the far side of the room.

The second man rounds on Samantha to hit her with his fist, and she counters it.

"Mister you need to help her before she gets hurt" said Beverly.

"No I don't think so, if I did that she would beat me up, so let her have her fun."

"FUN! He is trying to kill her"!

"Just watch."

Samantha toys with the two men and then she sets them up so she can take them down, with a couple of broken bones. They don't do much moving when Samantha finishes with them. Steve gets up and closes the door.

"Now gentlemen, how about you tell me what you were up to."

"We won't talk."

"Too bad, honey would you like to talk to them, maybe you can persuade them better than I can." Samantha walks up to the men. Their eyes go large.

"We do not know who hired us, it was a man in a mask, and he wanted the Boy and the girl brought to him, that's all we know."

"Ok, we can call the police now, and guys, I would not try anything, my wife can kill with her hands alone. She has not killed anyone in a while. And as bad guys you know how antsy that can make you."

Samantha gives Steve a look that can kill, and Steve realizes he is going to pay for that remark. Steve turns to the kids.

"Now what is going on, and I'm sure the police will want to know too."

Beverly relates that she came to the university to learn more about ancient history, and find out more about this amulet she has, and she takes it out to show him.

"It is very old I see, here let me get my glasses." Steve put his glasses on and takes pictures of the two men being guarded by Samantha and he takes a picture of the kids, then the amulet front and back. The only one who knew what he was doing is Samantha.

Chapter 91

Jacob then speaks up "You see sir, I found that same amulet at a museum and we went to see it. When asked if we could possibly look at the other one in the glass case, the curator told us no, and asked us to leave even when Bev showed him the amulet. After that we were followed by these two men."

"Where is this museum you mentioned?"

Beverly gives him the address. "Beverly." Then the police show up at the door.

"These men will be detained, we have been looking for them for some time, it is a good thing you were not hurt."

"Thank you, inspector, my wife and I will sleep better knowing they are off the street."

The inspector and his men take the two men and leave. Steve and Samantha turn to the two kids, and give them a hard look.

"So tell me what this is all about?"

Beverly relates the story she was told by her grandparents about Alexander's Gold, and she mentioned that it is not Alexander the Great's gold; but that This Alexander was a bandit who raided the caravans from the East.

Steve says, "I know we just met, and you have no reason to trust us; but if I'm going to help you, you will need to."

Samantha chimes in;" Steve why do we not all go to this museum together?"

Steve turns to the kids, "well?"

Beverly decides to go with the Balls to the Museum. On the way Steve explains that he may have to make a deal to put both amulets together, like offer her amulet to be put on display with the other one. Beverly agrees with what Steve has proposed. When they reach the museum, Jacob tells them he has to go and that he will see Beverly tomorrow. Samantha stares after Jacob and watches him as he leaves. Steve's expression asks what is going on? Her expression indicates she is not sure.

Steve and his party go to the curator so he can ask if he can see the amulet on display. With the glasses on CAT can see and hear all that transpires, as a matter of fact CAT has sent an E-mail to the curator that Steve is an archeologist of some note. Steve is in the process of another discovery, then CAT sets up his credentials electronically so if the curator checks he will see the so called discoveries Steve has made. So when Steve shows up to the office the curator is very interested. Steve introduces his wife and Beverly as his niece, and has her show him the amulet again.

"Now Sir, we would be willing to loan this amulet to be displayed with yours, provided you allow us a moment to look over the other amulet."

"Yes, sir, but no photographs."

"That will not be a problem, Ok Beverly give the curator your amulet."

Beverly is not quite sure she should give it up, but she does. They go to the case where the other amulet is and the curator takes out the amulet and gives it to Steve. Then Steve asks for Beverly's amulet too and then Steve puts them together. Ever so slowly Steve turns them over and sees the strange writing on the back that looks like symbols more than writing. CAT takes the data from Steve's camera glasses and creates a three dimensional view of both amulets in his computer brain.

"Thank you" says Steve to the curator, then Steve gives both amulets to the curator. And they all leave.

"So how did that help" asked Beverly.

" How about we take you home, and you come see us tomorrow at our room."

"I guess so" said Beverly

"We will see you at what time?" asks Samantha.

"How about at this time tomorrow?" Asks Beverly.

"We'll see you tomorrow then." Said Samantha

Beverly turns and walks towards her dorm at the university.

"Steve I'm going to follow her to see that she gets back to her dorm."

"See you when you get back then, I'm going to the lodge and see what CAT can find out from the pictures I sent. Samantha ports down to the alley way and waits for Beverly to appear. Beverly comes out the door and heads for the University campus, and Samantha follows along at a distance. Before Beverly realizes it two other men grab her and cover her mouth and nose with a cloth and she collapses and they head for a car. "CAT, let Steve know that Beverly is being kidnaped and I'm following."

Samantha ports up close to the car, and notes the license plate and manages to put a tracer on the car.

"CAT, follow that car, I have a tracer on it."

"Samantha, I have it, and will follow." Samantha ports to the lodge.

"Steve, have you found out anything about the amulet?

"No Samantha, CAT is still working on it, it may take a while.

Beverly was just kidnaped have you found out anything on Jacob and what might be going on?"

"On Jacob possibly, He is from America, but his family made its money on the shady side, he also has a rap sheet, he is not a very nice boy. I do not know if it is a coincidence, but shortly after his arrival in Rome the kidnaping of young women has increased."

Samantha said "Then he must be involved in the ongoing slave trade that I have heard about."

"He may also be into stealing antiquities especially the valuable stuff, what say you track down Beverly, and I will go after Jacob?"

Chapter 92

They put on their Battle suits, and CAT directs Samantha to where the car has stopped. Steve leaves on his street cloths and ports to the campus to look up Jacob.

"CAT can you access the Computer here at the University and see if you can get Jacob's address?"

"Steve I have it right here, and here are the coordinates."

"You gave me two addresses, which one is it?"

"Steve the first one is on the campus, the other is at an estate on the far side of the country."

"Ok, CAT I'll try the Campus first."

Steve goes to Jacob's dorm room and knocks on the door, and a young girl answers the door.

"Is Jacob here?"

"No, do you want me to give him a message?"

"If you would please."

Steve's message is to contact him and Samantha at the hotel as soon as possible.

The girl stands in the door way a moment more looking Steve over, and giving Steve a look that sends a shiver down his spine.

Samantha ports to an estate on the far side of the City. From her place of concealment, she watches the activity that is going on, there appears to be several guards about the place.

"CAT, do you have anything on file about the layout of this estate?"

"Samantha, I do not, this estate is very old, so there are no formal records on this place, I can give you a satellite view of the area if you like."

"I do not like going in cold like this, but it will have to do."

Samantha ports close to the house in a small grove of trees.

"CAT do you detect any surveillance devices in my area?"

"Samantha, I do not detect any devices this close to the house, I do detect a guard a dog which is headed in your direction."

Samantha gets an idea, so she ports to the lodge and puts on a reveling dress and leaves her battle suit there, Samantha then puts on her glasses, and ports back to the estate next to the house, then makes a run for the outer fence.

In her flight she acts as if she were escaping, the guards converge to surround her and capture her. "No, no let me go" says Samantha in a whiney voice.

"How did you get out of your room?" Asks one of the men.

Cowering Samantha says "the door was open and so I left."

Grabbing her roughly two men take Samantha into the house and down into the dungeon to be locked up with the other girls. With her glasses on CAT records all the faces of everyone that Samantha comes in contact with. At an empty cell the guard pushes Samantha into the cell and leers at her as he locks her away.

"I may have to come back and have some fun with you; for breaking out of here." Samantha cowers even more.

"I'm sorry I'll stay put please don't hurt me."

Chapter 93

"You sure will, I'll be back to keep an eye on you." And he laughs as he walks away.

Samantha is just getting ready to port outside the bars of her cage when she hears one of the girl's mention Jacob's name. Sitting down in a corner and listening, Samantha watches down the hall way and sure enough Jacob is walking down the hall towards her and the other girls in the cell just down from hers. One of the girls says "Jacob, what are you doing, help us to get out of here."

"Are you kidding, I'm the one who had you captured and brought here. Each one of you will fetch a fine price in the slave market."

Samantha has had enough; she ports up behind Jacob then ports him to a mesa top in Arizona.

"You! You are Paladin!?" exclaims Jacob.

"I'll be back for you shortly I have a few others that will be joining you. I would advise you not to leave. There is no way down, but to fall or jump. You see we are at least a thousand feet off the ground"

"You can't do this!"

"Watch me." And Samantha ports back to the dungeon. She locates Jacob's uncle upstairs and before Jacob's Uncle realizes it, he is standing beside Jacob looking over the mesa.

"What is going on here" demands Jacob's uncle.

"What a woman always does, cleaning house." And Samantha ports back to the dungeon leaving both men stranded on the mesa. Samantha then ports to the dungeon next to the girl's cell door.

Samantha then ports into the cell with the girls. "Girls it is time to go." and then Samantha has them all touch her and then ports them all to the lodge right into the gym. Samantha makes sure all the doors leading out of the gym are locked.

"Now please stay here and stay calm, I have a few things I have to do, and I'll be back. In the cupboards over there are some snacks, there are some cloths in that cupboard. A shower room is over there. Now has any one seen Beverly?" All the girls have blank stares then ask who is Beverly.

"I'll take that as a no." Samantha puts on her battle suit and ports back to the mesa.

"Now you are going to tell me where Beverly is."

"Not unless you let us go" said Jacob.

"No you'll tell me or I will beat it out of you."

"You can't, you have no right."

"Jacob that is where you are wrong, you see up here you have no rights, the only right you have is what I give you."

Samantha decides that Jacob is not alone in this venture, and has brought his uncle here to the mesa as well, besides it will give Samantha more playmates to play with if she gets irritated.

Now while Samantha and Jacob are talking Jacob's uncle manages to get behind Samantha, and just as he goes to grab her, she twists out of the way and delivers a savage kick to his side.

"I was wondering when you would try that." said Samantha.

Samantha starts beating Jacob up, and a couple of slaps later, Jacob confesses where they have Beverly hidden.

. "Now boys, I'm going to get Beverly, and if she is not there, I won't be back and you can die here." Samantha ports back to the dungeon and heads upstairs. Along the way she encounters the man who threatened to abuse her.

"So you were going to have fun with me were you?"

Samantha makes her opaque helmet transparent so the man can see her face.

"I think I'm going to have fun with you instead." said Samantha.

He charges her like a wild bull and Samantha side steps his charge then gives him a bit of a push which sends him into a wall face first. She stands there and waits for him to shake it off, then he slowly approaches her. Samantha shows no fear, as he grabs her shoulders, with a quick move she sends him down the stairs and he breaks his neck.

"Too bad I wanted to play some more." She said.

Samantha takes on six other guards, a couple manage to fire their guns, but the force fields that surround Samantha's battle suit deflect them away and soon Samantha makes short work of all the guards. In the last room Samantha finds Beverly and when Samantha tries to wake up Beverly she sees she has been drugged, Samantha Ports Beverly to a hospital, then returns to Jacob. She grabs him by the neck and pushes him up to the edge of the mesa so he can look down.

"Now what did you give Beverly, or you'll die right here as you can see it is a long way down to the bottom."

"Just a couple of CC's of heroine, I swear."

Samantha throws Jacob to the ground, and ports back to the hospital and tells the doctor about the drug in Beverley's system. Not long after treatment Beverly is awake and responding to the treatment.

"I'll be back." said Samantha.

Samantha ports to the lodge and as before she has the girls touch her and ports them to the American Embassy in Italy. Now to take care of my two other charges back at the mesa. Thinks Samantha.

Samantha appears on the mesa.

Chapter 94

"Ok, boys, since you're Jacob's uncle I'm taking you to jail where you will confess to the police of your slave dealings. You will not contest or try to get out of your sentence, and you will help the police locate and return all the women you sold into slavery."

"If I refuse." He asks.

"I would not do that." Samantha grabs his arm and ports to a site where volcanic lava flows all around them.

"If you refuse, I will bring you here and leave you here."

Jacob's uncle could feel the heat from the lava, and he realizes if he is left here he would parish from the heat alone.

"Alright, I'll do it." He says.

"Now let's get this straight, if you go back on your word, I will know and I will keep my word."

"Jail would be better than here." Jacob's uncle says.

Samantha transports the man to the authorities in Rome, where he does what he said he would do. Back on the mesa Samantha ports in to pick up Jacob.

"What are you going to do to me?"

"I intend to let the punishment fit the crime."

Samantha ports them to a maximum security prison deep inside Russia.

"This is your new home." Said Samantha.

"What is this place?" Asks Jacob.

"You'll figure it out."

"No, you can't do that, not to me!" screams Jacob.

"Well now, I can and I'm going to. While you are here, you can think about all the women and girls you helped sell into slavery. Now you will get to experience how they felt. By the way I would not speak American in here, as they would torture you until you confess that you are a CIA agent and then they will kill you very slowly." Samantha ports back to the lodge.

Steve is waiting for Samantha at the lodge, "have you taken care of the slave ring?"

"You have been talking to CAT and you know what I have done." said Samantha.

"I do, and I approve, nice touch with Jacob."

"Well he had it coming." Samantha said.

"I agree, what are we going to do with all the girls you had here?" "I took them back to Italy to the American Embassy, and left it to them to take care of the girls."

"What about Beverly?"

"I will go pick her up and bring her here."

"No, take her to our hotel room in Italy and I will meet you there."

Samantha changes out of her Battle suit and puts on the same clothes she was wearing that morning.

"Steve, some vacation this is, even when we try to be alone, we get wrapped up in something."

Steve walks over to his wife and takes her up in his arms and kisses her on the nose.

"As long as you are with me I can ask for nothing better. Besides I'm having fun, I'll see you there at the hotel. Before I go I'm going to check in with CAT about the amulets."

Samantha hugs Steve, then goes to finish changing into some clothes and teleports to where Beverly is at the hospital.

Chapter 95

"CAT have you made any headway on the amulets?"

"Steve, I'm not sure, I printed a 3D image of the amulets and it should be done, check the printer." "Good work CAT, so what have you learned?"

"Steve one side is a map, but it does not seem to fit any place in the region. On the back side there are a bunch of symbols, and they do not make any sense. I'll keep working on it maybe something will turn up."

"CAT, thanks for the duplicate, maybe Beverly has more information that she is not sharing."

Steve ports back to the hotel, and enters the room where Samantha and Beverly are waiting.

"I want to thank both of you for saving me" said Beverly.

"Now are you ready to trust us?" as Steve hands her the duplicate amulet.

"How did you get this?" asked Beverly, as she turns the amulets over looking at the plastic amulets.

"I still cannot read what it says." Said Beverly.

"I know, my friend cannot either, and he is an expert at languages, even ancient ones." Said Steve.

"Beverly, what can you tell us about what you are looking for" said Samantha.

"We can help you get it, or at least get you the credit for it. Believe me we do not want the money or credit. What we want is the adventure, and staying within the law."

"Ok, I do have a part of the story I did not tell you the first time. My ancestor did hide a treasure and both amulets tell us where it is, all my grandmother would tell me is that the treasure is in a place called the Forbidden Valley."

"Forbidden Valley, I'll have my friend look into it" said Steve.

"So who are you people? I do not know what to think when I get kidnaped, then I get taken to some estate, put into a bedroom after being drugged, then I wake up in a hospital for a short time and the next thing I know I'm back here in your room?"

Steve speaks up "You would not believe me if I told you, but please realize we would like to be your friend."

"Now I need to go see my friend again, and I will be gone for a few hours, Samantha will be with you for now."

"Steve, may I have the credit card? I would like to take Beverly and go shopping."

Steve hands her his credit card.

"Try not to buy out the whole store."

"Yes dear, I will restrain myself."

Steve gives her a look of sure you will, and walks out the door. As soon as he closes it he ports to the lodge.

"CAT you caught the conversation what have you found?"

"Steve, not much, the names of valleys, mountains and such locations change over the course of time. My best guess would be an area in the most northern east part of Turkey where two other countries meet."

"Well that is a start, any more luck on the amulet?"

"Steve, No I have tried every crypto there is, in every ancient language, and nothing."

"Did you make another 3D print of the amulet?"

"Steve it is on the printer." Steve walks over and picks up the amulet and in the reflection of the printer door he sees something. Steve walks over to his locker and brings out a bowie knife. Steve sees a couple of notches at each end of the amulet. Steve places his knife in to the notches. Then Steve puts his glasses back on.

"CAT look at this."

Steve takes a picture of the writing, then turns the amulet around and takes a picture of that side too. "Steve, the reflection of the symbols make sense now, I believe I can translate it now."

"CAT I'm going to return to the hotel and wait for the girls to return, let me know what you find."

Steve teleports outside into the alley next to the hotel just in case Beverly is around, it would not do at this time to let her know that Samantha and Steve are Paladin. Steve walks to his room on the third floor, and when he reaches his room he can hear the women talking about clothes and such. Just as he is about to enter the room he hears Beverly's question and he decides to wait and listen.

Beverly asks "How did you get such a great husband?"

"Believe me Beverly I almost didn't, but I will tell you this, when you find an honorable man and a giving one grab on with both hands and don't let him go, in my pride, I almost drove him away. I love my Steve more that I care to admit. If I ever lost him my heart would die with him. I need him as most people need food and water. He is my strength."

"I hope I can find someone like that?"

Then Steve knocks on the door before he enters.

"Is everyone decent?"

"Come in Dear, we are all dressed."

Steve walks over to Samantha and gives her a kiss. Then he turns to Beverly, and takes her 3D amulet from her, then he pulls his hunting knife out and places it into the nicks at each end of the amulet.

"Look at the refection are you now able to read what it says?"

"Yes, it says that in the cave there are three branches, only one branch is safe, but only if you have the Amulets."

"I guess I will have to borrow them back for a time."

"They will let you do that?" asked Beverly.

"I think so; I can be persuasive. I think I will go see the curator now."

Steve gets up and leaves the ladies to go to the museum. Samantha follows him to the door and takes his hand. Steve stops, and he looks into his wife's eyes, and sees the love there.

"You will be careful?" She asks.

"I will be very careful." Said Steve.

Samantha kisses him and he holds her for a few moments. Then off he goes. With CAT's help Steve finds a hardware store and picks up some fast drying brass colored paint and paints the 3D amulet that he has.

Steve ports back to the lodge, then opens a window into the museum near the display case for the amulets and he watches the area for a while to see if anyone is around. Seeing no one he opens a window inside the case and takes out the real amulets and replaces it with the 3D copy, under the copy he leaves a note. I have barrowed the real amulets and will return them after I have finished using them, signed Paladin. Steve returns to the alley outside the hotel and walks up to his room. Stopping at the door he knocks, to let them know he is there. Entering,

Beverly asks "Did you get it?"

"I have it right here." And Steve takes out the amulets to give to her.

"You did it! You really got the amulets."

"Well now we need to start planning our expedition" said Steve.

"Beverly, since you are into archeology we could use an archeologist so we do not break any laws or disturb any site, so it doesn't lose any of its historic value."

"I see what you mean Steve. I know of a professor in California at the university who might be interested, his name is Lars Benison."

"Ok, I'll get in contact with him" said Steve.

"I have managed to get a room for you next door to us Beverly" said Samantha.

"Thank you, after what has been going on, I did not want to return to my dorm room."

Beverly is shown to her room and given the key to it so she can come and go as she likes.

"CAT get a run down on Lars Benison. If he checks out, send him the data to date, and ask him if he would like to run an expedition, all paid for."

"Steve it will be done."

Chapter 96

The next morning CAT informs Steve and Samantha that the professor would like to handle the expedition, he will be leaving in the morning our time, and should arrive in three days, here in Rome. He will be coming in on North West Orient at 1:00 PM.

"We'll be there to pick him up."

Three days later Beverly and the Balls meet the professor at the airport. As it happens the professor was so excited he takes an earlier flight and when he arrives in Rome he is kidnaped by the police. The inspector then dresses up like the professor and takes his place. Steve, Samantha and Beverly meet the professor at the airport to pick him up. Steve offers to get Lars bags and drive to the hotel, Lars falls asleep on the way there. So, when they arrive they get him checked in and then off to bed. While the professor sleeps, the rest go out for lunch. That night Steve and Samantha port back home and then drive up in the car to see the kids and to check on how everything is going. The children are excited to see their parents, after the hugs and kisses, everyone settles down. Then the children are sent off to play. Steve explains they will be gone longer than expected and asks if this will be a problem?

The Nanny says that it will be no trouble at all. Do you know how long it will be?"

"No, we do not know how long it will be yet. But we will make periodic visits." Said Samantha.

"Ok, you two Paladins you can come clean with me. I figured you out some time ago, and what you just recently did sort of confirms it."

"What do you mean Joy?" Asks Steve.

"Let's see a slave ring is broken up by Paladin in Italy, where you were going, and I caught you on the camera on TV yesterday. It takes a few days to travel from there to here, so that only leaves one explanation."

"Did anyone ever tell you, you would make a great detective?" said Steve.

"You are not going to tell anyone are you?" asked Samantha.

"My goodness no, they would not believe and old foolish lady like me. Beside it is nice to have little children around again. I would be very proud to be a part of this family."

"Joy, be careful for what you wish for, my grandmother died defending this family from a drug lord."

Joy looks Samantha right in the eye.

"Your children are worth giving up my life for."

"I see." And Samantha and Joy hug each other.

"We have to return to our hotel, and we will be back from time to time" Said Steve.

The next morning, Beverly and Lars meet at Steve and Samantha's room for breakfast. Lars starts off the conversation "who is in charge of the expedition?"

"Unless it becomes a safety issue, you will be in charge." Said Steve.

"Then who is paying for the supplies and such?"

"That would be me" said Steve.

"What do you have that will make me want to be a part of this?" asks the professor (inspector)

Steve takes the 3D amulet out of his pocket and hands it to the professor. The professor turns it over several times, looks up and says

"So. What is this, it appears to be nothing more than a plastic trinket. Hardly anything I would waste my time with."

"Let me explain professor that is actually two amulets, half belongs to Beverly here the other half was found in a museum. I managed to get a look at the other one with Beverly's amulet and managed to make a 3D copy of both."

"That explains the hunk of plastic, why involve me?"

"The original amulet is a map to a possible treasure of Alexander, not so great, but the one called the butcher, who raided the caravans from the east."

"I'm not impressed, and you have wasted my time on a wild goose chase for a fake treasure hunt. No thanks, my reputation may not be the greatest, but it is a good one, I'm returning home." "Professor sit down, I want you to see this."

Steve pulls out his knife. The professor sits down somewhat alarmed. Steve takes the plastic copy of the amulets and places the knife blade in the notches.

"What does this say?"

The professor takes a look into the reflection of the blade.

"No, this is real?"

"Yes professor" says Beverly. "It is an amulet that has passed down to me from mother to daughter through the years. If you like we can go to the museum and see it."

Steve squirms in his seat, since he has the original amulets in the hotel room. He excuses himself to go to the bath room. In the bathroom Steve opens a window into the amulets hiding place and takes them out, then opens another window into the museum to see if anyone is where he wants to port to. After he gets there Steve opens a window into the case and removes the 3D copy and replaces it with the real amulets. When he is finished, he ports back to the bathroom and flushes the toilet and washes hands.

"I think we can leave now if everyone is ready."

Samantha looks up at Steve with a knowing smile.

Steve leads the way down to the street and hails a taxi and off to the museum they go. Once there the professor calls on the curator and asks to see the amulets, at first the curator is reluctant to comply with the request. It seems that he had checked the amulets the other day and found a plastic replica. Someone has stolen it. Steve suggests that they take another look.

"Ok" said the curator, and he leads the way to the display. When he opens the case, he takes out the amulets.

"This cannot be, someone left a note that it would be returned, and it is. What is it about these amulets that everyone is taking such notice?"

Chapter 97

The professor asks, "Is someone else, interested in the amulets?"

"Yes, why just this morning a couple of men were trying to get me to open the case."

Steve asks, "Do you remember what they looked like."

"No, just a couple of men in gray suits, one had a beard and another had his ear nearly cut off."

"Thanks." Said Steve.

The professor with his credentials manages to get permission to study the amulets, using the knife he can see that the 3D model is correct. He even shows the curator what has been discovered. Both men are very excited almost like children at a candy store. The professor turns to Steve and Beverly.

"I'll do it, I'll lead the expedition, and with so much interest in the amulets. We had better leave as soon as possible."

"Where to professor?" asks Beverly.

"The area in and around the North East of Turkey. That is where this bandit operated so it stands to reason that it would be the place to start our search."

"We'll take a train to Bulgaria, then a boat to Istanbul, and then to Ankara. From there we will get a truck and travel to Yerevan, where we will buy our supplies and drive to the area where we will search for Alexander's treasure."

"CAT, did you get all that?" inquires Steve.

"Steve I did, I'll have your travel ready at the train station. Might I point out, that you and Samantha will need your passports."

"Your right CAT, this evening we'll pop in at home and pick them up, I think I'll bring the car back as well."

That afternoon Steve and Samantha port home with the car to pick up their passports, and to see the children and Joy. After a couple of hours, Steve and Samantha port back to their room in Rome to get some sleep. The next morning comes early. The professor and Beverly are knocking on the door to Steve's and Samantha's room.

"Come on sleepy heads, the day is wasting, and we need to get a move on."

Steve puts on a robe, and opens the door, rubbing the sleep from his eyes.

"What's the rush?"

"We have competition and we are now in a race to find the site." Says the professor.

"Hold on, what competition, who?"

"I don't know, but last night, someone broke into the museum and stole the 3D amulet, the curator called me to let me know."

"Ok, you and Beverly go on down to the restaurant and Samantha and I will join you shortly."

Forty-five minutes later Samantha and Steve show up.

"Now professor, what is going on?" asks Samantha.

"Last night the curator had called me to tell me that someone stole the 3D model of the amulets; I still have the real ones in my care, I actually have them on my person."

"I gather that the 3D model was stolen, but why is it a race?" asked Samantha.

"According to my curator friend, over the last few days or so the amulets are finely together, so he has been asked a lot of questions about them, and now they are stolen."

"We may be jumping the gun some. Let's not borrow trouble before we have to. As I showed you, you cannot just figure out the code unless you stumble on to it or someone tells you." Said Steve.

"This may be true" said the professor, but should we not take the time to assume we are in a race?"

"Ok, professor, let's get moving."

Needless to say the trip to Yerevan, was accomplished without any incident. As CAT was instructed the supplies were waiting for them when they arrived. We load up the truck and made ready to leave and travel further north. Steve takes Samantha aside where no one can over hear him.

"Did you see who got on the train with us?" Said Steve.

"Who did you see dear?"

"I saw the curator and the two people he had described to us at the museum."

"Do you see them now?"

"They are just down the street watching us."

"Steve looks a bit further down the street, see the men in dark suits?"

"I do."

"They also appear to be following us." Said Samantha.

"I guess the professor was right, this is a race only they are following the lead horse us."

Chapter 98

"Steve, if there are to be any accidents I want to be one of them so I can go home."

"What's wrong Samantha, not enough excitement?"

"it's not that, I miss the children."

"Well until that happens, let's take a walk tonight by ourselves, and go visit them for a few hours."

"I'd like that."

So after the camp is set up. Steve and Samantha steal off into the dark away from camp.

"Where are they going?" said the professor.

"Where do you think professor, they are married after all." Said Beverly with a giggle.

"Oh, yes, quite right. Beverly tell me more about your family history."

Beverly tells him the stories as they were told to her, and that the stories were passed down from mother to daughter or from grandmother to granddaughter. So I do not know how accurate the stories are anymore."

"Ah, I see what you mean, over time different languages change, embellishments added, and the like. Well for the time being let's assume that your story is reasonably accurate."

"Sure professor." So Beverly tells the professor what she can remember from what her Mother told her.

"Beverly you should go off to bed; we will have an early start in the morning."

"Good night professor" as Beverly yawns.

With the long day it does not take Beverly long to fall asleep. Soon the professor hears two people walking up to where he sits. The professor pulls a gun out of his pocket. It is the two men who were wearing the dark suits. The professor puts his finger up to his lips to signal them to be quiet. He then gets up and points off into the dark away from the direction the Ball's went. At a hundred feet away the professor asks "How is it going?"

"We have followed the curator and his men they are a hundred yards in that general direction, they have men waiting for you in the gorge ten miles from here."

"Is there any way around them?"

"Not if you are headed to the Forbidden valley."

"I see. Any suggestions?"

"We could call in our men and collect them."

"Ok, bring them in, how is the professor doing?"

"From what I hear he is so mad he could chew through granite right now."

"Start moving the professor and bring him here, after all he is the key to all that is now going on. Now both of you get back to your camp and follow the curator and his men."

"Why not just collect them?" said one of the men.

"Because I want to catch him with his hand in the preverbal cookie jar, that's why! Now off with you." The two men in dark suits leave and the professor returns to the fire. Two hours later Steve and Samantha return from their walk.

"Did you two have a good walk?"

Samantha with a big grin on her face said, "It was a marvelous time, wasn't it dear?" as she laughs a sultry laugh. Steve's face turns red with embarrassment.

Back at their tent, "What was that all about?" asked Steve.

"The professor suspects we were off making love, not at home playing with the children."

"Well now that sounds like fun." said Steve.

"Too bad dear, it's been a long day and tomorrow will be no different, when this expedition is finished we'll spend a week at the lodge, you me and the children."

"You got it." said Steve.

They crawled into their bed rolls and go to sleep. In the morning Beverly's screaming, brings Steve and Samantha out of their tents in a hurry. Before they can ask, they see Beverly being held at gun point and the professor as well. The professor does not look to well, as there is a swelling at the side of his head.

"Now you two stand where you are and my men will not shoot the girl or the professor."

Steve and Samantha do what they are told. One of the men comes over and ties their hands.

Chapter 99

"Now says the Curator where does the amulet lead us?"

"Well, said the professor, to a place called the lost or Forbidden Valley."

"Very good professor. Put the prisoners in the back of the truck, we'll let the land out here deal with them when we get to the valley."

Once they are in the back of the truck the prisoners get their feet tied up, a few hours later they are driving along a tall cliff. The truck stops and the curator's men take Steve and the professor out of the truck and over to the cliff side.

"Gentlemen I no longer need you, so I will drop you off here." Said the curator.

"What are you going to do to my wife?"

"When we are done we will sell both women to the slavers, they will fetch a nice profit."

Now all eyes are on Steve and the professor, so Steve opens a couple of windows and cuts Samantha's ropes. (Samantha for some reason cannot open or use Teleport windows like Steve can)

There is a commotion in the back of the truck and one of the curator's men is tossed out of the back of the truck. Steve quickly uses the windows to cut his ropes, and through the gun of the man who is holding it on Steve and the professor. The curator stands there in shock as Samantha beats the living tar out of both men. Realizing he needs to get away the curator tries to flee. Steve steps up to him and punches him in the jaw knocking him out.

"That felt good, said Steve.

Samantha is standing next to the two men she brought down, and she also has a smile of satisfaction. Samantha climbs back into the truck and unties Beverly while Steve does the same for the professor.

With the curator tied up along with his men, Steve turns to the professor.

Steve says "I think it is time professor or whoever you are to tell us some truth."

"How long have you known?"

"Not long" said Steve.

"I'm an inspector from Rome. I have been following the Curator for a couple of years, he is a jewel thief and I have been after him for all that time, but I could not get the goods on him. Now I can get him for attempted murder, which will carry a very stiff sentence back in Rome."

"Ok, where is the real professor?"

"He is on his way here, he is not happy that I had him kidnapped and put away, but he is unharmed. If memory serves me right, he should be here sometime today."

"You need to be aware that your danger is not over, the Curator has a small band of men waiting for us at the Forbidden Valley. I have requested some military help to arrest them."

"I think Samantha and I can help with that."

"How will you do that?" asked the inspector.

"You see inspector, Samantha and I are escape artists we can get into and out of just about any place we choose to. Now where is this valley we are headed to?"

The inspector takes out a map and shows Steve and Samantha on a map where the valley is located and where they are. Steve is wearing his glasses so CAT is able to note where it is. Then using the satellite system in space he is able to note how many and where the men are in the valley.

"Come on Samantha I'll race you."

They set off in the direction of the valley. When they get out of sight they port back to the lodge and put on their battle suits. Then to the computer room to study a map that CAT has set up for them.

"Steve, Samantha there are twenty people in that valley fully armed, I see them at these following locations on this map."

"What do you think Samantha, start at the back of the valley and then move towards the front?"

"Sounds good Steve, I'm looking forward to a bit of scraping"

"That's my girl." said Steve

Let's go get them, and you be sure I get my ten men, or you know what it will be like living with an angry woman." said Samantha.

"No argument from me Dear."

Steve puts wire ties and rope together in a back pack, and nods to Samantha they then port to the upper end of the valley.

Chapter 100

There are three people at that location, Samantha springs into action and disarms all three men before they can even react. Steve shoots one with his sleep dart gun and Samantha prefers to beat the tar out of the rest of them. With the three men down Steve quickly zip ties their hands and feet and puts them back to back to each other and then uses rope to tie them up. Samantha has gone on to the next place and has subdued two other men, to be followed by Steve. Steve ties up the two men Samantha has finished with. The next batch of men Steve takes on and when he finishes up subduing them Samantha helps him tie them up in a nice package.

"Steve you are still dropping your shoulder when you fight."

"I'm going to have to work on that."

Steve winces at that thought and what it will mean at the next sparring match with Samantha. Steve appears in between the next batch of men, one of them shoots at him, but the battle suit deflects the bullets and one of the other men is badly wounded from it. Steve quickly disabled the other three men. He checks the wounded man and sees he will keep for the time being.

On down the valley Steve and Samantha take out the men holding the valley. Steve ports back to the wounded man and ports him to Rome's Police Station and lets them know he is a criminal, and that the inspector will explain when he gets back. Steve ports to the lodge, and meets Samantha there. "I gave you eleven men to play with are you happy?" asked Steve.

"Yes I am; you sure know how to show a girl a good time do you know that?"

"I try, now the fun is over let's change our clothes and return to the valley to wait for the others." Samantha and Steve pick out a shady area and a few hours later the Inspector, Beverly and a contingent of military men and even the real professor show up.

Steve leads the army up into the valley to collect the nineteen remaining men.

"Inspector, Professor, Beverly this is where Samantha and I will leave you. Just so you know this is the right place. While Samantha and I were capturing the bandits some of the rock shifted and I saw human and horse remains, if the story is right they had been covered in a landslide."

"But you can't go. Said the professor we will need your support."

"I have seen to that, I have put up a million dollars to fund this dig, so hire on some students and do your exploring. When you find the cave entrance, we'll be back."

Steve and Samantha walk off hand in hand towards Ankara.

"They did not take any supplies and that is a long walk, without food and water." Said the real professor. "Somehow I do not believe that for them that it will be such a long walk, they can take care of themselves" said the inspector.

"Professor my apologies for taking your place and for leaving you with my men. I must get my men back and process those men that were captured. I will leave two of my men here to watch over you until you can get more people here."

"Thank you, inspector, that would be a good thing."

It takes a few years of digging, but they find all the men of the bandit's party and the entrance to the cave. True to his word Steve shows up to help with the final part of the dig, locating the grave.

Chapter 101

Steve suggests that he enter the cave first and alone. Not to be first, but to make sure which way is safe. Steve takes the amulets and puts them together, and then lays his hunting knife in the notches on the amulets.

"Now CAT, if you are right the knife points to the right. I should go left."

Steve follows the cave to the end with no incident and finds a fake wall, he pushes against it and it falls into dust. Using a flash light Steve looks into the cave and sure enough there is a trap hanging from the ceiling. Steve triggers the trap from inside and a huge bolder blocks the door way. Steve opens a window underneath the rock and drops it into the ocean. Further exploration shows this is not the right way to go, it is empty.

On to the middle cave, again Steve probes the area looking for traps, this one catches him quite by surprise. The trap hung way up on the ceiling on two ropes. A log with spikes all around it as he steps in, the flag stone he stands on releases the rope and the log swings down, at the last second Steve ports away, but not before one of the spikes cuts his face.

"Wow! that hurt! I guess I need to be more careful."

He pulled his hand away from his face and it is covered in blood, he put his handkerchief to his cut and continues to search the cave, again he finds nothing.

"Well at least the two other caves are now safe. Now for the last one."

Steve approaches the last cave very carefully He cannot count on CAT for help, since all the traps are considered low tech. so he will have to depend on his own abilities.

The third entrance is sealed up so carefully Steve uses a window to see into the cave, but it is too dark so he uses his flash light and the distance is too far for the light to penetrate. Steve breaks the wall down one stone at a time, and jumps back as he removes each one to see what will happen. Nothing does so he calls the professor and Beverly to enter. Beverly seeing the blood rushes up to Steve to see if he needs help. But soon see's that it is just a semi deep scratch.

"You know that is going to leave a scar don't you?"

"I'll worry about that later. I have opened the way into the third cave, and I made sure to trigger the other caves traps as well, so no one will get hurt; shall we go in?"

"I wouldn't go running off in their professor, this should let you know there may still be danger in there."

"Oh my yes, I see what you mean."

Steve takes an offered canteen and washes the blood from his face and hands, then proceeds into the cave. After traveling about one hundred yards in they find another door that is blocked up. Steve and a young man that is in the group remove the stones carefully one at a time, and soon the cave mouth is open. The professor is like a little kid at Christmas wanting to run to the tree to gather his presents, so he brushes past Steve and then he screams. Steve rushes in to find the professor on the floor with an arrow in his leg. Steve removes the arrow and washes the wound then puts on his glasses.

"CAT is their poison on the arrow head?"

"Steve, not that I can detect."

Steve ports a protesting professor to a hospital.

"Now as soon as they pronounce him fit enough I will take you back to the dig."

Steve returns to the cave and only Beverly saw him leave and return.

"Where is the professor?" asked Beverly.

"At a hospital getting treated, he'll be back as soon as he is well enough according to the doctors."

Steve re-enters the last cave and disarms a few more traps. At the back of the cave they find the grave of Alexander the butcher's son, and all around him is treasure, Gold, silver, jewels, and much more.

"Well I have made it safe here. The professor should be the one to direct things from here, but as I recall this is your ancestor so please look around. Don't touch anything, or the professor will have a conniption fit."

Beverley looks over all that treasure, and sees what has been amassed.

"Well at least the mystery is over, but I feel both happy and sad" said Beverly.

"In a way I understand. I heard from some person years ago put it this way. Wanting something is sweeter than actually having it. Keep everyone out while I go check with the doctors and the professor, and I'll be back in an hour."

Beverly takes a long look at her legacy and realizes she will not be able to have it. It belongs to the country it is found in, and to its people. An hour later pushing a wheel chair Steve brings the professor back to the dig, and takes him to the cave, his eyes almost pop out of his head.

"Look at this! The grave and all this is all priceless. Beverly get the camera crew and take pictures of the cave and treasure as it is, then we can catalog all we find here."

Steve turns to Beverly and tells her good bye.

"The authorities will be here soon to help protect the students and the treasure. As soon as word spreads you will have every bandit in the area flocking here. You take care, and don't tell anyone about Samantha and me."

"What about the professor?"

"I gave him something and he will forget all about me. I gave it to him when I took him to the hospital, all he will remember is that he was taken to the hospital and then returned. Not how it was done."

"Will I see either of you again?"

"Maybe not, but who knows, our paths may cross again. Now back to work with you and I expect to see your documented story in print some time."

"You will, I promise."

Steve turns and walks off toward the west and when he is out of sight he ports back home. Samantha pressures Steve into telling her all that happened.

"I see you now will have a new scar on your face, Hmm I think it will make you more rugged looking."

"I'm so glad you approve" said Steve.

Samantha laughs, touching his face.

"I do love you, and I'm so glad you belong to me, and me alone."

Steve sweeps her up in his arms and carries her off to the bed room.

Chapter 102

Samantha's Life

While I'm telling all these stories of me and Samantha's life together, I thought it best to tell about my wife Samantha. This story is about her life before we met. It is several years after World War II and the Japanese are still looked down upon here in America. Samantha's father (Hoshi) tries to find work in New York, but the anger toward the Japanese and other Asians is strong. On one of Hoshi attempts to find work he heads home empty handed as there appears to be no one who wants to hire him. Suddenly he hears a scuffle down an ally way. With reluctance Hoshi walks down the alley to investigate the noise. There he finds four white men threating a fellow Asian. Hoshi speaks up.

"What are you doing to that man?"

"Back off gook, or you will find yourself getting what he is about to get."

"Please stop, I cannot permit this to go on."

One of the men reached out and grabs Hoshi by the shoulder and starts to rough him up. Hoshi grabs the goons hand and then flips him into a bunch of garbage cans.

The other three men are caught off guard, and they pull knives so they can cut him up. Big mistake that. It wasn't long before all three men were rendered broken and not able to move. The Asian that was being roughed up did not run away. He stayed, and when the commotion quieted he turned to Hoshi.

"You know martial arts?"

343

"Yes."

"Are you looking for a job?"

"I am"

The Asian gives Hoshi a card and says.

"Come to my office in China town tomorrow and I will get you a job."

As the Asian walks off, Hoshi watches him as he leaves. Hoshi decides to check out the job opportunity that just came up. The next morning Hoshi goes to meet his benefactor at the location on the business card. Hoshi tries to enter the building noted on the card when two people at the door stop him.

"What is your business?"

"Mr. Sing told me to show up here and he would give me a job?"

"Get out of here, Mr. Sing does not hire riff raff"

The big guy reaches out to push Hoshi.

From a window overlooking the front doorway Mr. Sing watches what is transpiring. As the door guard shoves Hoshi. Hoshi grabs the man's arm and twists it behind him shoving him into the other guard, knocking them down.

Hoshi says "If you get up I will break your leg; now since you work for Mr. Sing I will not harm you further. Now I will enter the building and go see Mr. Sing."

Hoshi turns to enter the door and Mr. Sing greets him there.

"Come in Hoshi, I have been expecting you."

"I see" looking at the guards.

"Oh, them! They were a test. I asked them to stop you to see what you would do. You passed with flying colors. I'm glad you did not hurt them."

"Mr. Sing what is this job you offered?"

"I need a body guard, and one I can trust."

"How much money am I to be paid?"

"Two thousand dollars a week to start, and if you have to fight to protect me, an additional five hundred."

"All I have to do is protect you, nothing else."

"Nothing else."

"Mr. Sing, I'll take it, I have one favor to ask, may I have one thousand dollars now, and I need to see to my family's needs?"

"Hoshi, my life is worth much more than that, so I'll give you two thousand dollars, and still pay you at the end of the week."

"Your servant Mr. Sing, and Thank you!"

So Hoshi starts his job. At first the job is very easy Hoshi has to dresses up in a suit, and follows Mr. Sing as he goes from one business meeting to another. It takes only a few instances of Hoshi's protection of Sing for him to earn a reputation of being efficient. Then one morning meeting Hoshi and Mr. Sing are ushered into a board room to wait, Hoshi does not like the feeling of this place so he instructs Mr. Sing at the far end of the room and tells him to get under the table the moment the door opens.

The door is kicked open and two men burst into the room with automatic weapons spraying the room. Hoshi, drops down from the ceiling and kills both men. He springs out of the room in to the midst of four other men in the hall way, with the same kind of guns. At close quarters Hoshi is able to kill three of the men then disables the fourth man. With the area clear, Hoshi calls to Mr. Sing that it is safe to come out from his hiding place. Walking over to the injured man Hoshi asks him what is going on?"

"No, I won't tell you!"

"I think you will" said Hoshi.

Hoshi feels along the man's neck and applies pressure. The man starts screaming. After a few minutes Hoshi stops the pain.

"Now tell me what is going on?"

"I can't, they will kill me."

"See your friends over there, they are dead, you wish to be like them?"

"No"

"Now tell me what I want to know!"

"No."

Hoshi pinches the nerve bundle again and the man is in dire pain and writhing.

"I can make the pain stop if you tell me what is going on."

The man gives in and tells Hoshi that this is a coup devised by his employer, to get rid of Mr. Sing and take over his territory.

"Who is that?"

"Mr. Biggalo."

Behind Hoshi a window breaks and; and the man on the floor dies with a bullet wound in his head.

"Mr. Sing we had better leave."

Sing does not argue, and he follows Hoshi down the stairs to the street level and then out the back way.

Chapter 103

Hoshi gets Mr. Sing safely away. That night at home Hoshi hugs his family grateful to be alive.

"What is wrong Hoshi?" Asks Tamera his wife.

"I'm just glad to be home Tamera. How has Samantha behaved today, like a good girl?"

As Hoshi picks up his daughter and holds her above his head. Samantha giggles and laughs as daddy tickles her tummy.

At about this time Samantha is three years of age, and her mother has been teaching her martial arts. Her mother uses it as a game to get her daughter to work out with her. Slowly Samantha becomes more physically fit. Samantha is more than willing to imitate her mother. Even Hoshi joins in on the exercises. Samantha always feels safe and happy with her parents. Over time Samantha learns more and more from her parents on how to protect herself. By the age of six, Samantha is adapt at open hand combat. During that time Hoshi builds a secret enclosure in one of the walls.

Hoshi explains to his wife that this may have to be used to hide Samantha in case something happens because of his job.

Within the enclosure Hoshi puts a back pack with food and water, and a message to whoever finds Samantha on how to reach Tamara's mother. Hoshi has Samantha practice hiding in the enclosure from time to time, to make sure she knows what to do when told to go there. A year later the business Hoshi is in falls apart, and Hoshi just barely escapes with his own life. He tells Samantha to hide and she goes into the enclosure and locks it. Shortly the door to their apartment is kicked open and gun men fill the house, Hoshi tries to fight them off. Tamara also fights, and between the two of them they manage to kill or disable half the men. The other half, gun down everyone even their own men. Hoshi and Tamera are killed along with some of their men, they make sure that everyone in the room is dead. Then they look for the little girl, but cannot find her. The police sirens drive them away.

When it is all quiet, Samantha comes out of the enclosure, to find her parents dead and several other men as well, she kneels down beside her parents and cries. Soon she hears the police coming up the stairs, and she returns to the enclosure to hide. The police show up and see the dead bodies, and realize it is a gang land killing. They do the usual investigation and clean up the mess, all but the blood stains. The next day Samantha wakes and leaves the enclosure, thinking her parents did not die, and it is a bad dream. Where did mom and dad go? Then she sees the blood stains and remembers that her parents are gone. What do I do, she thinks? What did daddy tell me? She gets her back pack and pulls out the letter. Contact Grandmother. Samantha puts the letter away in the back pack and goes to the kitchen to get something to eat and drink.

Chapter 104

Samantha did not hear the policeman that had entered the apartment. He hears a noise from the kitchen and draws his gun. He moves silently into the kitchen, where he finds Samantha on the floor eating dry cereal in a daze. He puts away his gun picks Samantha up, and tries talking to her. He soon realizes she is in a state of shock. The policeman bundles Samantha up in a blanket and picks up her back pack. He takes her out to his car to settler her in, then leaves her long enough to return to the apartment to lock it up. Officer Dan arrives at the police station and decides to take Samantha through the back way, which will be quieter than going through the front of the station. Dan makes his way to the police chief's office and enters in.

"Dan, what are you doing here?"

"I found a missing little girl, the one we were looking for."

Dan sets Samantha on the couch where she falls asleep.

"Sir what do we do with her?"

"I don't know Dan. I guess we turn her over to child services."

"Sir she is in no condition to be put through that yet, let me take her home with me. Besides my girls would just love to make a new friend."

"Ok, Dan, but we will need to talk to her, as she may know something of what happened."

Dan turns to Samantha to pick her up, but she is standing next to him and hands him two letters. The first one is to contact her Grandmother in Japan, and the other contains evidence against the people that Samantha's father Hoshi worked for.

Chapter 105

"Dan you best get her out of here and to your home. I want you to stay close to her. She will need your protection."

"I'll take care of her as if she were my own, Sir."

Dan bundles Samantha up in the blanket and leaves by the back way of the building. They climb into his own car and leave for home. At home he introduces Samantha as an orphan who needs to stay with them for a few days. Dan's daughters are excited to have a new sister, but Dan's wife is not so sure. Dan convinces her that it is only for a few days until her Grandmother can come get her. The Chief contacts the American Consulate and makes arrangement to get Samantha's grandmother from Japan to the US.

It takes a week for Samantha's grandmother to arrive in New York and to the police station. The Chief calls Dan instructing him to bring Samantha secretly to the station where Samantha meets her Grandmother for the first time. After a tearful reunion Grandmother asks if it would be possible to go to the apartment where her daughter lived.

The police chief said "It is not a good place to go to right now."

"It will be alright, I need to pick up some of my daughter's things and my granddaughter's clothes."

"I guess it will be alright, Dan you take them."

"Yes Sir."

Dan takes them up to the apartment and waits with Samantha as the grandmother goes to her daughter's room and picks up the picture album. Then on to Samantha's room, she finds a suitcase and puts Samantha's clothes in it. Finally, she goes to a wall in the clothes closet where she opens a secret panel and takes the money that is hidden there to put in the suit case.

Not many days later, grandmother finds a place for the two of them to live. The money provided by her son in-law will sustain them for several years if not mismanaged. So over time grandmother teaches Samantha more martial arts. Like most children Samantha grows into a fine looking teenage girl, and she attracts many teenage boys. It does not take long for the boys to learn to be polite to Samantha or she can beat them up. For the most part they avoid Samantha.

Then one day, one of the high school bullies started hitting on her. When he groped her. She took offence and told him to stop. When he refused to stop she broke his arm. Word spread fast and the boys gave Samantha a wide birth when she walked down the hall at school.

Many of the girls at school approached her to ask if she would teach them how to protect themselves, so in a way Samantha became a well-liked instructor. Throughout her high school years she teaches girls and some women teachers how to protect themselves from unwanted advances. In the meantime, the boys mostly are afraid of her. After graduation Samantha is on her way to a job interview when she slips and falls dropping her purse and her coffee. She looks up to see a pair of male legs stopped in front of her. He then kneels down asking.

"Are you OK?"

Red in the face Samantha stammers out that she is fine.

"Here let me help you up."

She extends her hand and he helps her to her feet, then he picks up her purse and returns it to her. Samantha looks into his face and all she can see is his deep blue eyes, red hair and a smile she cannot look away from.

"May I be permitted to know your name, fair damsel?"

Samantha blushes even more, and stammers "Samantha."

"What a pretty name for such a pretty girl. I see your coffee is all over the walk way, may I have the pleasure of buying you another one?"

"Ah, Ah, Sure." Samantha can barely talk.

David walks her down the sidewalk to a coffee shop and has her order what she wants, and he orders a coffee too. He guides her to a table where they sit down to have a conversation. About ten-minutes into the conversation Samantha suddenly remembers she has a job interview to attend. She begs his pardon and tells him.

"Thank you for the help and the coffee. Will I see you around some time?"

"You could if you come by in the morning tomorrow, we can have coffee on me."

Samantha makes it to her interview and is accepted for the job. She is so excited, as today she got her first job, and met a man that sets her heart a flutter. The next morning, she arrives at the coffee shop, and David is there with two coffees and scones.

"Hi Samantha care to join me?"

Samantha takes the chair across from him and sits down. They talk of many things, and even set up a date for later that evening. After work Samantha is all a twitter.

Chapter 106

"I can't even choose the proper clothes, makeup and accessories for my fist date."

She tells her grandmother all about this guy, and that he will be by to pick her up soon.

"I can hardly wait for you to meet David."

Samantha gets dressed, and at the appointed time David shows up at the door. Grandmother opens it and invites him in. Grandmother looks into his blue eyes and sees trouble there. David feels uncomfortable around grandmother. It is like she can see into his soul and knows his game.

Samantha goes out with David, and David is the soul of courtesy. Grandmother is not afraid of Samantha being physically hurt, but she knows that Samantha maybe hurt emotionally. Grandmother wants to prevent that if possible. That night Samantha comes home happier than she has felt sense she was a little girl. Grandmother decides not to tell Samantha what she knows about David. For fear of causing a rift between them. Over time Samantha dates David more and more. David refuses to see grandmother for any reason. Then one day Samantha asks grandmother why she does not like David? Grandmother tells her, that David is a vile person and is only using you.

"He considers you a conquest, not a partner."

Samantha rebels and leaves the apartment to go live with David. At first David is attentive to Samantha then over a short time his attention diminishes.

Samantha lives with David for only a few months. Unbeknownst to Samantha, David is a parasite who lives off unsuspecting women until he gets tired of them or they find out about him and leave. Then he goes looking for another conquest to live off of until the next woman comes along. Samantha comes home from work early one day and finds David in bed with two other women.

"David what is this!"

"Oh hi honey, care to join us?"

Samantha grabs one of the women by her hair and pulls her out of bed and shoves her toward the door. "Get out of here you, slut!" screams Samantha.

Then she chases the other woman out as well. David makes a very bad mistake at this point. He grabs Samantha's shoulder to force her down on the bed. Before he realizes it, he is air born landing against a wall. This makes David angry, so he lurches up to his feet to grab Samantha again.

Samantha proceeds to break David's arm, then a leg right at his knee.

"You make me sick. I gave you all that you asked for; money, me all that I had was yours, and you betray me."

Samantha kneels down next to David.

"You do not deserve to live, I should just kill you, but I won't." Samantha places her hand on his rib cage, applies pressure, and breaks several ribs. David screams out in pain.

"When you next pick up a girl you might want to know if she can fight, from this day forth if I so much as see or hear of you I will kill you with my bare hands. Do you understand me?"

David did not say anything he just glares at Samantha, as she kicked his good leg.

"One other thing, if you bring legal action, I will find every woman you have betrayed and we will form a lawsuit against you and I can find them, just try me."

From that day forward David goes out of his way to avoid Samantha he even moves to another city.

Chapter 107

Samantha returns to her Grandmother to beg for forgiveness.

"My granddaughter, I love you and would have done anything to prevent this pain and bitterness, but like watching a baby learn to walk you have to let them fall. This is no different you were not ready to listen."

"Still grandmother I was foolish."

"That is enough child, we all have our trials in learning, even I. Maybe one day I'll tell you of my David. Now go make dinner."

Time passes and Samantha goes to work, and comes home, she does not stop to chat or make new friends, she is afraid of being hurt or betrayed again.

One morning Samantha wakes up and has to run to the bathroom to throw up.

"What is happening to me?"

Samantha sets up a doctor's appointment. A few days later she gets the news that she is pregnant.

"Oh, no!" she exclaims.

"What am I going to do?"

Samantha needs to tell Grandmother, and with shame she does.

Grandmother tells her "it will be alright, are you going to tell the father?"

"No, that filth will never know I have had his child. Besides I do not believe he would care."

"How do you feel about the child?"

"I do not know yet."

Samantha has to struggle with herself, should I keep the child or give it up. Will I love it or hate it?

At the next visit to the doctor's office.

"The baby appears healthy Samantha, keep doing what you are doing and the child will be healthy when it is born."

"Yes Doctor, do you know what sex it will be yet?"

"Not yet, not for a couple more weeks, what is it that you want?"

"I would like it to be a girl."

"I hope you get your wish, now come back next month and we will see how you both are doing."

"Thank you doctor, see you next month."

Samantha is beginning to accept the new life growing in her belly, she often pats her belly and talks to the child growing there. Grandmother sometimes also touches Samantha's belly as if to say you are loved. Toward the end of the month late in the evening, Samantha experiences great pain in her belly so much so that grandmother contacts 911 to get her to the hospital. As soon as Samantha arrives they take her to a delivery room, and Samantha has a miscarriage and loses her baby. All this does, is fill her heart with bitterness to the point she wants to die. It seems to her the loss of her parents, David's betrayal, and now the loss of her child is all coming to together.

Chapter 108

At night after work Samantha starts looking for a way to release her rage against an uncaring city. Samantha comes home to dinner then gets up to go for a walk. Samantha goes to the worst possible places a girl can go. One night while walking a rather large man approaches her, and tries to force his intentions on her. Before she is done with him he is cowering in a corner nursing a broken arm, nose and missing some of his teeth. Needless to say Samantha is out for blood. Samantha is doing the one thing that seems to help her ease her bitterness. In her mind men are the cause of all the problems in this world. Samantha ignores men beating up on men. But a man misusing a girl or a woman, makes her mad. One night while out and about Samantha sees a pimp beat up one of his women. When he is finished she has a broken nose, and is pretty badly bruised. Then he threatens her some more. Samantha explodes and soundly thrashes the man. He has two arms, and, one knee shattered. Samantha grabs the man by his lapels and sticks her face close to his.

"You will leave town, and if I ever see you again, I will do far worse to you than I have done now."

She turns to the injured girl and helps her to a clinic to be treated.

"Why do you work for that scum?" asks Samantha.

"It is all that I know how to do."

The doctor in charge resets the girl's nose. Only time will heal the rest of her. Samantha pays the bill and turns to leave.

"Miss, I want to thank you for saving me."

"You are welcome, but it will be of little good if you return to that line of work."

Samantha leaves and goes home. A few nights later Samantha runs onto a drug dealer leaning on a young man and Samantha walks on by without so much as a glance. Her thoughts Men are so stupid and greedy who cares if they hurt each other. Further down the street she encounters others in similar situations. Then around one corner she spies a dealer with a young girl, who is trying to get her to take the drug he is offering her for free.

Samantha intervenes. She grabs the young girl by the arm and tells her to run away. Of course the drug dealer grabs Samantha by her arm and tells her she is going to be taking this drug forcefully. Then he pulls a knife. Samantha shrugs him off and stands looking at him. The young girls is frozen to her spot with fear. The man tries to slash Samantha and she easily shrugs out of the way without moving her feet.

"I'll kill you for that."

Samantha says nothing, and just watches the drug dealer. He lunges at Samantha trying to stab her. Samantha grabs the man's wrist and breaks it making him drop the knife, she follows up with a hit at his shoulder then kicks his knee breaking it and watches as he falls.

Samantha leans down and places her hand on the man's rib cage.

"If I see you anywhere ever again I will crush all your ribs."

She applies pressure and snaps a couple of his ribs. As the man lays there screaming Samantha calls the police saying a drug dealer is beating up a woman as she give them the address. Samantha takes the frightened girl away as the police find the drug dealer with his drugs. The dealer is arrest and taken to the hospital. That felt good thinks Samantha.

Now that her crusade is taking shape, she will try to cripple the drug rings by getting rid of the dealers. Over time she is hurting the drug business. At first it is two men, then three men. Now they have declared war on Samantha. The drug lords are sending out gangs to kill this elusive woman. This is at about the time Paladin comes on the scene. One night in Central Park, as Paladin tests out his new equipment he sees Samantha for the first time. At first I was going to swoop in and save her, but at the back of his mind it said wait. My little green insect aliens were telling me to wait. So I watched. At the time I'm glad I waited, there is no sense in saving someone who does not want or need to be saved. As Paladin watched she took out the whole gang without my help, well except for the one guy I put to sleep with my dart gun. I saw in Samantha a way to get the training I needed in martial arts, it is a rocky start, but in the future we do get married. I end the story here for the time being.

Chapter 109

Deep Six

Captain Johnson, we've called you to this meeting to help us stop a security problem. This man, Paladin, seems to be able to move about the world as he pleases. He can and does go from country to country and into places like Columbia where he destroyed three hundred acres of poppy flowers used in making heroin. That location is better protected than the president of the United States. As long as Paladin lives, no state secret is safe anywhere. Since the CIA or the FBI have no hold over this Paladin, we cannot trust him."

"Senator, Paladin has done nothing but good wh..."

"Captain Johnson! Shut up and listen! These men here are from the FBI and CIA they believe Paladin can be and is an extreme threat to world security. Especially to the U.S. Now. Captain, you will listen to the director of the FBI here as he outlines your assignment."

"Yes sir, Senator."

The Director of Operations, explains the deadliness of Paladin. We have figured out that the only way to get Paladin in our power is to trap him in such a way as to give him no chance for escape. Once we have him we can then program his mind to work for us. See in order to capture this Paladin. We get him to save you and your men from the bottom of the sea. This will force him to become conditioned to the pressure and atmosphere down there in order to be able to reach you. He will have to undergo compression using the same gasses you use and if he does not go through decompress as you do. He will die of the bends. So, he will be trapped in the chamber with you all and we will be in control of the compression-decompression tanks on the east coast. Then we can inject a sleep gas to keep him sedated until we can reprogram his mind or dissect him to find out how he can travel the way he does. Either way works for us.

Chapter 110

The director of the FBI outlines to the captain of the S.E.A.L. (which just happens to be a deep sea proto type mini sub) which is currently being used as a research vessel to chart the deep ocean bottom to provide accurate maps of the sea floor. Right now, the S.E.A.L. is scheduled to map the Mid-Atlantic Ocean. The captain is to take the sub to dive in deep water then he can sabotage the sub by destroying the sub's fuses, then radio for help. The Navy and Coast Guard will respond and no one will be in any real danger. You will swallow this transmitter after you make contact with Paladin. We'll do the rest. (What the Captain does not know is that all the DSRV's will be sabotaged as well, to prevent them from being able to rescue them).

"Do you understand this, Captain?"

"I do."

"As I understand, you and your crew are due to leave tomorrow morning."

"Yes sir."

"You have your orders captain, don't fail!"

"Yes sir."

The captain and most of the people leave the meeting, except the senator and Maxwell, a junior FBI executive.

"Now senator, it is so good of you to help us. I'm sure Director Richard (CIA Director) will be so glad to add to your election campaign chest."

"If I were a better man, I'd..."

"You'd what, senator?"

"Nothing." Replies the senator in a less hostile voice.

"I'm so glad, I'd hate to see you lose your support."

The senator's face turns red with suppressed rage.

"You see, senator, once Paladin is gone, you'll be a hero." The Jr. executive leaves the room.

Maxwell contacts his true boss, the Mafia and he outlines what the CIA Director is planning to do with Paladin.

"Maxwell, you will keep me informed of the situation so we can move in and end this Paladin once and for all."

"Yes, Sir I will."

The following day, the S.E.A.L gets under way and is to travel too one of the deepest areas in the Atlantic Ocean, where the parent ship launches the S.E.A.L. to begin the sea floor survey. The Captain is quite adamant about saving the data at the end of each day while they are working the survey. Each day it appears that something goes wrong with one system or another. Five days into the mission, the Captain sets the charges to take out the fuse panel. The S.E.A.L. develops some major problems as the fuse panel shorts out and they lose all power to their systems except for the radio.

"May Day, May Day, this is Captain Johnson of the S.E.A.L., May Day! We have lost power to most of our systems, and I do not know how long the radio will last. Calling the mother ship, we are on the bottom and our systems are failing. We need to be rescued. May Day! May Day, do you receive us?"

"We receive you S.E.A.L. can you repair the ship?"

"No we cannot not repair the ship we do not have the components to repair the fuse box. Send rescue, we have life support for twenty-four hours."

Chapter 111

"We will get back to you SEAL; we will call-in a DSRV (Deep Submarine Rescue Vessel) to get you."

"Understood Mother ship."

The Captain informs the crew to conserve the air and to get under blankets, it will be a while before they are rescued.

It is a fine morning at the lodge. The air is crisp and clean. The rising sun turns the lake at the lodge a golden color.

"Samantha, do you want to go for a run around the lake?"

"No Steve, I have something to do this morning. You go, and I'll have breakfast ready when you return."

Steve hugs Samantha and kisses her before he leaves to go jogging.

Samantha Makes breakfast for Steve. While making breakfast, Samantha gets a bad feeling about today. She is not sure what it is, it is just a bad feeling.

Steve returns from his jogging and Samantha rushes him into the bathroom to clean up while she finishes making breakfast. Half an hour later, Steve appears and grabs Samantha in a bear hug. "I Love you, Samantha."

They wrestled and giggled like two little children for a few minutes when Samantha brings them to a halt.

"Steve, come on your breakfast will get cold."

"Ok Samantha."

"Steve, I hate to break this up, but there is an emergency you should listen to."

"Pipe it through, CAT."

"This is a CNN News report. Marine vessel, 'The S.E.A.L.' has malfunctioned and lies trapped on the bottom of the ocean floor. All the electrical systems have shorted out. The nearest help is twenty hours away. Their air supply is estimated to last twelve more hours."

Maxwell contacts the mafia boss to inform him that the trap is being set by the unsuspecting CIA/FBI agents. I will get back to you after we have Paladin trapped in a decompression chamber.

"CAT contact the Coast Guard and Navy, to see if they will need my help and if so arrange for two decompression chambers: one for the women and one for the men."

"Calling Coast Guard, San Diego. This is Paladin calling. I'm checking to see if you require any assistance with the S.E.A.L. rescue."

"Paladin, this is Coast Guard, San Diego. We are not involved with that rescue, over."

"I realize that, San Diego, but if I become involved. I'll need your assistance. Let me talk to the commanding officer."

"Can you hold, Paladin?"

"Roger, San Diego."

Ten minutes later, "Paladin, this is Commander Redding, what can I do for you?"

"Contact the East Coast, Coast Guard to see if they need any help from me. Also can you ready two de-compression chambers to bring the people to when I rescue them?"

"You realize, Paladin, before you can go aboard the S.E.A.L. you'll have to spend eight hours in a compression chamber yourself so that you will be at the same pressure and atmosphere as the people on the SEAL."

Chapter 112

"I understand, Commander. As I said, I'll help, if you'll help me. Oh, one other item, no one except you and whatever support personnel are to know where we'll be after the rescue. I cannot tell you how important that will be for everyone's safety that will be at the decompression tanks."

"Paladin, if you can save those people, we'll keep you safe. Let me run this to the East Coast and I'll call you on this channel as soon as I get the word back from them."

"Roger, San Diego."

"Steve, Commander Redding is calling back East to let them know you'll work with them. The Coast Guard has agreed with our terms. They will continue the rescue even when the crew is removed. They want the data and the sub back. They will also post guards and keep everything quiet throughout the decompression process there on the East coast."

"CAT, check the Navy's computers and see why they haven't sent any D.S.R.V. (Deep Sea Rescue Vessel) to rescue that sub."

CAT hooks into the Navy's computer through a Navy satellite and finds out that two of these subs are out of commission from the reports in the system someone has sabotage them.

"Steve, the D.S.R.V.'s are out of commission and the East Coast, Coast Guard has been told they won't be ready for twenty-four hours."

"CAT, contact Samuel. See how long it would take him to install a large decompression chamber if I supply him with the equipment."

CAT replies a moment later, "Samuel says twelve hours."

"Order the equipment and have it delivered to the usual places."

"Paladin, this is Coast Guard San Diego calling."

"Paladin here, Commander Redding."

"It's a go, Paladin. I have a bad feeling about this, but I will do what we agreed upon."

"Thanks, Commander. I'll be seeing you in two hours."

"We'll be ready for you. Commander Redding out."

"Steve, all the equipment will be delivered in one hour. Steve why not use the decompression chambers on the East coast?"

"CAT something is not right; I'm being forced to place myself in someone else's control. The FBI/CIA have been trying for years to corral me and this is something they would cook up for just this occasion. OK, CAT. Inform Samuel I'm coming. Sorry Samantha, I have to do this one alone."

Samantha enters the COM room and doesn't like what she is hearing.

"I know Steve, I don't have to like it, be careful. I want you back. See you in three weeks dear."

"OK, I'll get Samuel going then I'll be back." Steve ports to each warehouse where the equipment is waiting for pick up and then Steve ports all the equipment to Samuel's office to drop it off.

"Samuel, CAT will keep you advised of my status. For now, I'll be safe for at least a week, after that it'll be touchy."

"Why do you say that, Steve?" Asks Samuel.

"I'm not sure, it has something to do with the fact that the Navy can't use their D.S.R.V.'s to rescue the SEAL."

"But they're supposed to."

"So I thought. That's why I need this decompression chamber built. What better way to trap a person in a prison he can't leave, when it may kill him?"

"You think this is a set up?"

"Yes, but I can't let innocent people die because of me."

"Now that I have all the equipment, I'll get right on it and the decompression chamber will be ready for you in two days."

"Thanks, Samuel, I have a feeling that the crew and I will need this chamber. We will start out on the East coast, go to the West coast, then if necessary here to finish the decompression process. Cat will monitor me and keep the tank here consistent with the tank I'm occupying at the time.

At the bottom of the ocean six people are trying to locate the problem with the sub's electrical systems it is difficult to do in the total darkness using a flashlight. Unknown to the other five-crew members, Captain Johnson has basically destroyed the fuse panel, and when the crew tries to fix it they realize it is sabotage and panic starts to set in. The captain gets the crew to settle down and tells them that the Navy is going to rescue them in a DSRV. This calms them down. At least we can communicate with the surface ship.

During the last few hours, the sub's emergency batteries kept the air mixture clean of carbon dioxide, but the cold temperature and lack of lights makes the sub the closest thing to a grave than one would like. The crew huddles together under space blankets to keep warm.

Captain Johnson keeps watching the temperature and breathing mixture gauges. He is ready, at a moment's notice to replace the missing fuses but does not know that the fuse box is totally destroyed and he cannot just replace the fuses. In the meantime, Captain Johnson counts the time until rescue will arrive and each minute seems to last an eternity.

Steve ports home to say good bye to Samantha, and then ports to the Coast Guard Station in Norfolk where the compression-decompression chambers are.

Chapter 113

Paladin appears in the commander's office. "Wha... who...? Oh, it's you, Paladin. You gave me a start for a moment and I was even expecting you."

"Sorry, Commander, but in the interest of time, we best get started. Oh, before I forget, could you get this small bottle filled with the breathing mixture that I'll be in?"

"No problem, Paladin. But why?"

"As I travel, I sometimes need a small supply of O2 to breathe. It's more or less for emergencies. That's why this helmet can seal its self."

"I'll have it taken care of right away."

Paladin and the commander drive to the dock where the chambers are kept.

"Paladin, in my book, you are a great man, and I'll do what I can to keep you safe. I want to thank you."

"Why would you want to thank me, Commander?"

"My friend was on that space shuttle you saved, Samuel." "You're welcome. Samuel and Will were a great help to me after we returned from space."

"Here comes your small air tank, The Chief will give it to you and good luck please bring back the crew of the SEAL they are a great team."

As Paladin climbs into the compression-decompression chamber.

The commander says, "Paladin, it will take eight hours to take you to the pressure and breathing gasses on the SEAL that the sub is currently using. Then you can save them, but it will take three weeks to bring you back to normal. Do you understand?"

"Yes, Commander, I understand. Please remember your promise, you will need to keep this secret or the FBI/CIA will try to capture me. It will be far worse if the mafia finds out I'm here they will stop at nothing to destroy me; they would even mount an attack on your base to get me."

"You have my word, Paladin. We will keep it secret on our end."

"Let's go then."

For eight hours, Paladin sits waiting for the pressure and breathing mixture to equal the S.E.A.L.'s atmosphere. In the meantime, Paladin has CAT keep him apprised of the communications from the CIA/FBI and any other communications that might involve the mafia. After that Steve has CAT pipe in a movie to help kill the time while he waits for his body to become acclimated to the SEAL. Each hour the Coast Guard personnel elevate the pressure and revise the air mixture gases. Each hour the Commander radios into Paladin to check on him. The commander is worried about Paladin. Being confined in a small chamber along with a heavy atmosphere can cause HPNS (high-pressure neurosis syndrome). If Paladin displays any symptoms related to the illness it can cause him to leave his chamber and die a horrible death as the nitrogen causes his blood to boil or bubble up, in other words the bends.

At the end of the eight hours the Commander checks on Paladin for the last time.

"Paladin, are you all right?"

"Yes, Commander, I'm fine."

The commander says, "Good. It's up to you now."

Sam uses the coordinates that CAT and the Coast Guard provided then teleports on board the S.E.A.L. at a specific place amid ships.

Paladin's sudden appearance causes no problems sense no one can see, but when he speaks up there is a commotion among the women on the S.E.A.L.

Spending ten hours freezing and in near darkness unnerves the crew enough without having someone arrive from nowhere.

Chapter 114

"My name is Paladin is anyone hurt?"

"No, everyone is fine."

"Where is Captain Johnson?"

"I am here. And you must be our rescue?" (Unlike the crew the captain is not surprised)

"Yes. Now I will transport you to an unknown location where you will go through decompression."

"Would you care to tell us where?"

"No! Anymore questions? Good. I can only take a few of you at a time, but this won't take long and I'll be back for the rest of you, OK?"

"Sure, Paladin, no problem. Take the three people in the aft section."

Steve notes that these three are the women.

"OK, link up hands."

Holding on to the ladies' hands, Steve teleports the women to the waiting decompression chamber in Norfolk. Steve notifies the Coast Guard that the women have been returned safely. Twenty minutes later, Steve shows up to pick up the rest of the sub team.

"Link up guys, we're headed to a cramped decompression chamber."

"No, Paladin, not all of us. Since I'm the captain, I'll say with the sub. Besides, with everyone gone, I'll have plenty of life support to wait out the rescue."

"No, Captain, you will go with us, this is per the Coast Guard's orders."

"No, Paladin! I won't go with you, and my mind is made up."

"You could be right at that."

Steve takes out his dart gun and shoots the captain. Steve catches the captain and asks:

"Does anyone else feel like being a hero? No one answers. Good, link up."

Steve teleports the rest of the sub teams into another pressure chamber.

"Well Gentlemen, relax. It will be a long three weeks, especially when the captain wakes."

When Paladin is wearing his helmet, no one can hear him as he communicates with CAT. After his last transport from the sub, CAT informs Steve that the captain has a homing device in his stomach.

"CAT, can you stop the signal, or mask it?"

"I managed to nullify the device when you arrived at the chamber. For now, it can't send any signal."

"Good, any messages from Samuel?"

"Nothing yet."

"CAT, you keep an eye on this place. It won't take long before something leaks on this, and we will have big brother and the underworld here looking for me. How much time does Samuel need before he has the decompression chamber ready?"

"Samuel will have the chamber ready in ten more hours."

"Keep me posted, CAT. And, by the way, can you hook me into a good war movie? Thanks CAT."

Back in Washington D.C., in a secluded office, the Jr. FBI Executive Maxwell is manning the radio station and has his boss yelling obscenities at him for losing the signal.

"But, Sir, we knew this might happen, Paladin is no fool. We have to wait for our satellite to pick it up and give us the new location."

"You'd better be right, or I'm going to bust you back to pushing a broom. Do you understand?!"

"Yes, sir." The Jr. Exc. stammers.

Chapter 115

The Director leaves the room to confer with the other men involved in the scheme for trapping Paladin. The CIA and FBI each want Paladin for their own reason. The Junior Executive, under the guise of the FBI, wants Paladin located so the underworld can move in and destroy him.

"So, what's the word on Paladin's location?"

"We're not getting the signal from the Captain. My boy in the back room believes when our satellite comes into range, we'll get a fix on Paladin, but I don't believe it. Paladin is too smart. We'll have to force our way through the Coast Guard to get him. Now, Senator, use your muscle to locate him. You do hold the purse string to the Coast Guard, use it!"

The senator calls the main Coast Guard office.

"Hello Commander Packwood. This is Senator Burnwell. I'm doing fine Stan, but now I need to get an answer from you. Where is Paladin?"

"Senator, I don't know where Paladin is."

"You'd better tell me what you can Stan, for two reasons. First, your budget is coming up, and second, this is a national security priority."

"Burnwell, I still don't know where Paladin is. Only Commander Redding might know and he's not telling anyone."

Stan's voice drips with hate. Besides Paladin could be anywhere. You will have to locate all the decompression chambers and check them out. Provided he did not set up one of his own.

"Thank you, Stan."

"Don't thank me, Senator. If the truth were known and I did know where Paladin was to be found, I wouldn't tell you, no matter what!"

And the commander slams the phone down.

"I've done all I can, gentlemen. Now it's up to you."

The agents all file out of the room and get into a waiting limo, which takes them to an airport, where they board a chartered jet. The pilot talks to the FBI chief "Where to?"

"The nearest airport in Norfolk."

A few hours later, the plane lands at a nearby airport where another limo is waiting for them. When the department heads of the FBI and CIA are in the car, they instruct the driver to take them to the Coast guard station.

Commander Packwood is sitting in his chair starring out his window. A feeling of dread comes over him as he watches the black car driving down the long driveway. Commander Packwood is young for a commander. He has something of a boyish look; a ruddy complexion, with red hair and deep green eyes. After today, he will lose his boyish look, and trade it for a more serious look.

The black limo pulls up and five men get out. They all appear to be in their late twenties to mid-thirties. They are what one calls, nondescript. Of course, the sunglasses more than anything, shout that these men are from the government.

Minutes later, the secretary opens Commander Packwood's door to announce his visitors. "Commander, some men from Washington to see you."

"Send them in, and inform Petty Officer Rains to perform the work detail we discussed this morning."

"Yes Sir."

The five men enter the room and close the door.

"Now gentlemen, what may I do for you?"

"Commander, what we want is Paladin. Where is he?"

"All I'm going to tell you is that Paladin is not here."

"We know that, Commander. Where is he?"

Commander Packwood has turned to face the window, says nothing. Down below petty officers Rains and a group of sailors are surrounding the building and everyone who works here is evacuating.

"Commander, do you realize what will or can happen to you if you do not cooperate with us?" The commander says nothing.

"Commander, I ask you once more. Where is Paladin? And if you won't tell us we will use other means to get what we want."

Behind him commander Packwood hears a gun's safety being taken off and the gun cocked. The commander turns around and the window behind him is shattered with gunfire. The five men all dive for cover while the commander stands there. Moments later, the door is kicked in and petty office Rains, with a group of men arrest the five men on the floor.

"Petty officer Rains remove these terrorists and put them in the brig. Remove all their clothes. No one is allowed to see them or talk to them except you and your men. And you are under orders not to believe a word they say. You will detain them for at least three weeks."

"Aye, aye Sir. All right men, you heard the Commander."

Thinking to himself, "Paladin, my neck is stretched as far as it will go. I hope I bought you enough time."

Early the next day, the junior executive officer of the FBI is still not able to locate the captain of the S.E.A.L. Somehow, the homing device is not working, and to top it off, his department head did not call him to find out where Paladin is.

Chapter 116

"This scheme of mine is starting to fall apart, and if I don't get Paladin, Richard will have my head. I'll use my last card, and so will the mafia boss."

The junior executive goes to Senator Burwell's office.

"What do you want, Maxwell?"

The senator hates the Jr. Exc. of the FBI, mostly because of the black mail he has on him.

"Touchy, aren't we, senator."

"Tell me what you want, you blood sucking weasel."

Maxwell (the Jr., FBI executive) walks around the senator's desk and grabs the senator by his lapels and jerks him to his feet. With their faces inches apart, Maxwell speaks to the senator in a cold dangerous voice.

"Richard wants Paladin dead, and he'll kill us both if we fail. Now, the FBI department head went to Norfolk to talk to commander Packwood. I'm guessing he failed somehow. Now you get on the phone and call whoever has the power to move these people and find Paladin or I'm personally going to blow your brains out. Do you understand?"

"Yes, Maxwell, I... do." As the senator chokes out a reply

The senator calls in all the favors that he can trying to get enough brass to move the Coast Guard brass and it is an uphill battle all the way. By the end of the week, Senator Burnwell manages to get enough support to force the Coast Guard to give up Paladin.

One week has gone by and everyone in the decompression tanks is doing well. No outbursts or heated arguments. But at the beginning of the second week, the captain starts to act differently.

"CAT, scan the captain and do a run down. I don't believe he's exactly everything he says he is."

"Yes, Steve. By the way, Samantha wants to talk to you."

"Steve, how are you doing?"

"I'm fine, Samantha. How are you doing? I'm still having a bad feeling about this whole thing."

"I'm doing fine, I'll keep that in mind Samantha, and there is a lot of monkey business going on. I'm about to port to the next set of chambers."

"I miss you too. I'd better go now. See you in two weeks, OK?"

"OK.　　　　　Bye　　　and　　　I　　　love　　　you!"
"Your suspicions are correct, Steve. The captain is working for the FBI. Do you want more data?"

"No, that is sufficient. CAT are the Coast Guard Decompression chambers in San Diego ready?"

"Yes Steve they are. And not a moment too soon, the FBI/CIA people have been locked in the brig and so they now know where you are. So far the mafia does not, but they will soon zero in on you."

"Then it is time to go, CAT tell Packwood we have moved on.

Paladin ports the men to a chamber in San Diego then returns to the women and moves them as well.

When Paladin returns to the men's chamber.

"What did you just do Paladin?" asks the Captain.

"Nothing that should concern you. I was just making sure that the woman were OK."

Over the past weeks the Coast Guard support unit has been lowering the pressure and slowly removing the gas mixture to enriching oxygen nitrogen content of the air. From time to time, Paladin removes his helmet, but puts on his mask. One night while Paladin is sleeping the captain tries to see what is under Paladin's mask, but he gets a sleep dart instead. For the most part Steve keeps to himself.

Chapter 117

Using Steve's sensors, CAT keeps the de-compression chamber at Samuel's shop at the same pressure and gas content in case Steve needs to leave the others in their chamber.

The next day everything comes unglued at the seams. The FBI and CIA decide that Paladin belongs to them and they are going to finally capture him. The red tape has taken two weeks to clear and now the Coast Guard has to give up the location of where the people of the S.E.A.L. are. The FBI figures if the sub people are there so then Paladin has to be there.

The plan of capture will be simple: the FBI will simply go in and tap the men's air supply to inject a fast acting sleeping gas to knock everyone out. They will keep everyone asleep until the last day, then move in to give Paladin drugs to keep him asleep until they find out who he is and how he is able to move about as he does.

"Steve."

"Yes, CAT."

"The FBI has located you, and have pushed through the red tape to force the Coast Guard to give you up."

"It's just like we figured, CAT. Is Samuel ready with the chamber?"

"Yes, Steve."

"Without the men knowing, Steve scans what is happening outside the chamber. Steve watches the FBI and CIA agents, via a spy satellite. He can clearly see the heavy equipment being moved in. And he also sees some men working with the gas mixture. Probably a sleeping gas of some kind. Paladin thinks. While Paladin studies the area, he notices that the boat traffic has increased around the Coast Guard dock. It seems odd, but he lets it drop. Once Steve determines the purpose of the FBI and CIA, he transports over to the waiting chamber at Samuel's workshop.

"Hi, Paladin, long time, no see. How are you doing, and how is the wife?"

"We're all doing great, especially the wife. CAT, where is the decompression chamber with the men in it?"

"The location is still the same, but it is now full of sleeping gas, and surrounded by FBI and CIA agents."

"Good thing I left. CAT, what are the odds that the gang lords will get information I was at that Coast Guard installation? Also, compute a plan by which they might use to strike at that area."

Forty minutes later:

"Steve, the odds are ninety percent that the crime bosses know you were there. As for the attack... two plans have merit of success if you were still in the chamber. One is to storm the area and bomb both tanks to assure success. The second is to post sharp shooters on boats to make the hit. The first plan is surer than the second plan. I suspect it will be tried first."

"CAT, contact the Coast Guard and tell them what you told me. I'll move the people from the chambers in California to here."

Steve ports into the women's chamber and puts them into a drugged sleep. He scans each one looking for electronic bugs. As he finds them, he destroys them.

Steve then ports all three women into his chambers at Samuel's workshop. He wakes them up and tells them to change from their sleeping clothes to jumpsuits.

"Sorry, girls but you were in danger where you were, so I brought you here. You'll need to get into these jumpsuits because in a few minutes, I'll be bringing the men here for their safety."

When the women finished dressing Steve has them move to one end of the tank. Steve retrieves the men. The sleep gas makes transporting them easy, and as with the women, Steve locates and destroys all the electronic bugs.

Chapter 118

"Now we wait. Soon the attack will begin."

After Maxwell finds Paladin's location, he calls Richard's contact in New York.

"This is Maxwell. Get Richard and have him contact me at this number."

"You'd better have something Max. Da boss doesn't like his beauty sleep messed up. Or you'd better crawl into a rat hole."

"Just get him, Ray."

"Gotcha Max."

Ray drives from mid-town to Richard's downtown home. Ray knocks on the door and a large man answers. Ray hands the large man a folded piece of paper. Fifteen minutes later, Richard appears fully dressed and no one says anything. Richard follows Ray down to the street and enters Ray's car. Ray drives to the out skirts of town where Richard enters an empty hotel room and removes his clothes, and puts on a jump suit. He then goes to a parking garage and enters another car. Richard locates a dive in the poor part of town and enters a phone booth. Richard places a call to Washington D.C.

"Maxwell, this had better be good."

"It is, boss. I've located Paladin."

"Where, Maxwell?!"

"Paladin is locked in a decompression chamber in San Diego. He can't leave it for another week or he'll die from the bends."

"How do you know this, Max.?"

"I had the Senator pull in all his favors to locate him he is on the west coast at San Diego. But it has taken two weeks to cut the red tape, and now we have him."

"You'd better be sure, Maxwell. Paladin isn't going to let you catch him that easy. Knowing him, he's gone already."

"Don't you see, boss, he can't go anywhere. The sub is in dry dock, the Navy and Coast Guard have all their facilities shut down. They can't use their chambers without authorization from me. So he can't go anywhere."

"Maxwell, you'd best be right. As it is I can't use the bathroom without Paladin knowing the color of paper I use. You make dead sure he's there, or you will be. Then get back to me. In the meantime, I'll get Paul Angie to pull some muscle together."

"All right, boss. I'll have the information in three hours."

"Make it one hour, Max."

"Yeees, Boss."

Maxwell hangs up the phone. Beads of sweat form on his forehead. Maxwell picks up the phone and calls his boss in San Diego.

"Agent Maxwell here. Is Denver there?"

"What is it Maxwell?"

"Have you verified that Paladin is in the decompression chamber?"

"Yes we did verify he is in the chamber. He was there when we pumped in the sleep gas, but now we can't see in. The gas has given us a limited visibility through the glass port. Right now he is sound asleep and will be kept that way for the next five days."

"I'll report this to the agency, Denver. Well done." Maxwell hangs up the phone, and Richard calls right on the dot.

"What do you have, Maxwell?"

"I have conformation from agent Denver's that Paladin is in the chamber when they pumped in the sleep gas."

"Is Paladin still there?"

"Yes, he can't get away, boss."

"He'd better be there, Max."

"He is, boss."

"Are you sure enough to bet your life on it?"

"Yes, I am."

"Good. If you're wrong, Max, I'll kill you myself."

Richard hangs up the phone and calls Angie in San Francisco.

"Angie, this is Richard. I have a job for you in San Diego at the Coast Guard dock # 51. There are two decompression chambers. Paladin is in one of them. You know what to do."

"Do you want the whole dock wasted?"

"Angie, this is Paladin. If I could arrange it, I would waste the whole city to get him."

"We'll take out the whole dock area."

"I'll be watching the news, Angie."

Angie calls San Diego.

"Dickinson, get the boat and heavy artillery out. Paladin is trapped in a decompression chamber at pier 51, at the Coast Guard landing. Bring in the chopper. In two hours I want that dock destroyed, and everyone on it to be history!"

"It will be as you say, Angie. Are you sure Paladin will be there?!"

"I have it on the best authority that he's trapped in there."

"That's great, we finally get to exterminate the world's worst pest. Thanks, Angie."

Chapter 119

Angie calls in all his men and they arm themselves with machine guns of all types, hand held rocket launchers, and grenades. The helicopter is equipped with a twenty-mm canon and several rockets from its arsenal. In less than two hours, the boat is in position and the chopper is circling the area keeping a watch on the operation of loading the decompression chamber on to a truck.

"CAT patch me through to Commander Redding."

"Redding here, Paladin. I'm sorry I can no longer protect you."

"Don't worry, Commander, I'm in no danger. At the moment I've relocated everyone to a hidden facility, but your people are in danger. You'd better evacuate that pier area. The underground has decided to blow it up. From the data I've collected, it will be either today or tonight."

"Thank you, Paladin, I'll pass the word immediately."

"Paladin out."

"Redding out."

At the Coast Guard post, the duty petty officer receives a phone call from Commander Redding. "Petty officer Johnson, please identify yourself."

"Johnson, this is Commander Redding. I want you and your men to abandon the station now and call agent Denver to the phone."

"Aye, Aye sir." Petty officer Johnson tells all the Coast Guard people to leave the station and calls Agent Denver to the phone.

"This is Agent Denver, what do you want, Commander?"

"Whether you believe me or not, I'm trying to save your life. Now abandon the station."

"No, commander. I won't give up Paladin."

"Denver, you don't have Paladin. He's gone and you are about to be attacked."

"Let me guess, Paladin told you, right?"

"As a matter of fact, he did."

"I don't believe you, Commander. He was in the chamber when we piped in the sleeping gas and there is nowhere he can go."

"Have it your way, Agent Denver." Denver hangs up the phone.

"Who was that, Denver?"

"It was Commander Redding. He was warning us to leave."

"Why?"

"He said that we are going to be attacked."

"Because of Paladin?"

"Or so he says. But I thin..."

Boom! Boom! Boom! A boat comes speeding by the dock spraying bullets everywhere; mostly the concentration is on the two chambers. As the boat speeds away, the chopper moves in and when it passes by, the dock and everything on it is gone in the explosion. The Coast Guard sailors stand on shore and look in stunned awe at the destruction, which just missed them.

Richard watches the news and finds it refreshing.

"No more Paladin. I can hardly wait to get back into full production. This is what I've been waiting for."

The phone rings and Richard answers. "Hello."

"You missed me again, Richard!"

"No, no, no!" And Richard slams down the phone.

The phone rings again. In a defeated voice.

"What do you want, Paladin?"

"I just wanted to let you know that I'm still here. I'm sorry I wasn't at the dock to see the fireworks."

"How can you be calling me? You're supposed to be in a decompression chamber at the bottom of the bay, dead!"

"It's like this, Richard, I'm not human." And Paladin turns off the connection.

"It seems, CAT, that we shook Richard up."

"From the tones in his voice, I quite agree with you Steve."

"In a few more days I'll get rid of these people and return them to the Coast Guard."

Paladin leaves his helmet on and whiles away the time watching TV.

A few days later, Steve teleports the sub crew backs to the Coast Guard Installation.

"I'm sorry, Commander, that was why I tried to have you keep it a secret. But I discovered too late myself that it was a set up by the FBI and CIA to capture me."

"Yes, Paladin, we also found out that the captain of the sub had sabotaged the S.E.A.L. in order to draw you in, and since he did so, he will stand trial in a maritime court. Thank you, Paladin for all you've done."

"You're welcome, Commander. Call if you should need me."

Steve ports to his home in Oregon and Samantha has lunch ready. When he ports in, Samantha scolds him for not warning her so she can at least dress up for him. Steve gathers Samantha into his arms and kisses away the scolding remarks.

"Samantha, you are the most beautiful woman I know."

"And it had better stay that way Steve."

Steve laughs and hugs Samantha very close.

"Samantha my heart, you are all that I could have wished for and more."

On a last note a few days later they find Maxwell in a back alley dead. It is an execution style shooting. The Captain was found guilty for disabling his ship and putting his crew at risk, he can no longer command a ship. Paladin sends both the CIA/FBI heads a present. It was one of the laughing boxes when you hit them or drop them. It was more of a reminder that he is still at large and not under their control. All in all, it was a satisfying ending to this caper.

Dimensions

Beast's World

Chapter 120

This story begins at home. I was at the lodge doing maintenance on CAT giving him a once over to check his relays, connections and his operating sequences. At just the last inspection point, I receive an urgent call from my youngest child, William.

"Daddy, a monster has mommy, and she can't get away."

I hear fear in Williams's voice. I port home right away to see what looks like an oversized Satyr grab hold of Samantha as they start to disappear. Somehow time seems to stand still for me, as I create a window and pull a backpack from its hiding place. Then tell CAT to execute Child one protocol. Several weeks ago, I had a feeling I would need to be ready to go. Into my backpack I tossed some supplies our battle suits, for both Samantha and me and a set of our weapons for Samantha and me. The weapons include Samantha's sword, my dart guns and knife, with some other items as well. I port into the closing portal to follow the Beast and Samantha, hoping I do not run into any unseen obstructions. I make it to a strange world, and off in the distance I can see the Satyr and Samantha. I teleport in that direction to try to catch up with them.

Back home, from the children's point of view, Mom is working in her garden when a giant appears and grabs her. Mom puts up a fight to no avail, but the giant subdues her easily. Kim stands on the porch and screams; William runs into the house telling CAT to send daddy to help momma. Daddy appears and heads for the giant as it disappears taking mommy. That is the last time that

Kim and William will ever see their parents. Addy will become their new parent and she will take good care of them. CAT's Child One Protocol will give Addy legal guardian ship of the children, and CAT will take care of any finances they may require.

Steve follows the Beast and Samantha into the portal. Steve feels a bit disorientated as he passes through the portal and it seems to take a long time to pass through, but in reality it is only a few seconds. Then Steve finds himself tumbling as he lands. Quickly Steve gets to his feet and sees in the distance the creature he is chasing. Steve ports to the position of where he saw the creature, but the creature with Samantha is still way ahead of him, Steve ports to where he saw the creature, and again they are just in sight, Steve continues to port after the (Beast) time and again, until nightfall when he arrives at a fortress.

Steve has brought no food or water and begins to realize this is not earth or his own world, but a different one. The sky is a green hue, and the land is battleship gray. Except for a few hills and large rocks, the surroundings seems to have no features. Steve changes his clothes for his battle suit to see if he can reach CAT online. While he was stripped down a plant stings Steve on the leg, Steve pulls away expecting to see some infection or venom reaction to the sting. As he watches, the wound heals right up and the plant withers and dies in front of him. Not sure what to expect Steve watches his wounded leg, but nothing happens, so he proceeds to get dressed in his battle suit. Steve places his helmet on and tries to call CAT. But all Steve gets is static. That confirms the question that he is not on his own world. Paladin checks the other displays in his helmet and sees that several of them still function. Paladin decides to recon the fortress. Paladin ports to the base of the wall and starts to walk around it to get a better feel and the lay of the land. Paladin realizes he cannot just port any place since he no longer has CAT he can only safely port to places he has been to or in line of sight, so he now has some severe limitations. Paladin comes to a bared gate, so he stands there looking in to see if there is a good place to land, when he almost gets his head bit off by some hairy lizard, which is the size of a German Shepard dog with a mouth like an alligator.

"Holy … That's some watch dog!"

Paladin continues his trip around the fortress looking for a way in. Inside the fortress the Beast puts his new treasure in with the other females he has collected from other dimensions. To the Beast the women he has collected are trophies nothing more. They are used in betting completions, but mostly for display. The Beast sets Samantha down and talks to her for the first time.

"You will make a fine addition to my collection, as no other collector on my world has a specimen from your world. You will bring much prestige and fame to my house."

Chapter 121

"You had best return me to my world."

Laughing "How so little one?"

"My husband will come for me, and he will not take this abduction lightly."

Still laughing, "How? We are on a different world from where you were. He cannot possibly get here; you are now mine for the rest of your life."

"Do not be so sure, my husband is a great hero on my world, I know he will come."

"Now just so we understand one another, I know of the crystal you have. The band I have placed on your leg, will nullify what it can do. If your mate shows up here I will capture him as easily as I have you."

The Beast takes Samantha to the bared window to look into the yard below.

"Do not think you can escape from here watch? The Beast throws a chunk of meat out the window and before it can hit the ground, several hairy lizards are fighting over it.

"You see little one death is just on the other side of this wall. My animals will eat anything that is down there. They would even try to eat me if I get careless. You would not be much more than a snack to them."

Outside the fortress wall Paladin manages to get to a hill not far from the fortress to let him see atop the wall. Paladin sees a flat area on the wall, and he feels he can port on to the top of the wall so he can survey the grounds within the fortress. Paladin ports to the top of the wall, and as he is looking around he sees Samantha in the window, but chooses to wait. Paladin then hears a trilling noise and the yard below fills with the hairy lizards.

"Wow! Look at them all. One was bad enough (remembering the earlier encounter), but dozens of them."

As he watches below one of the lizards creeps up on Paladin along the top of the wall. Just as Paladin is about to port to the window the lizard pounces on Paladin knocking from the wall on to a lower platform. Paladin rolls to his feet to confront the lizard. As the lizard springs at him from above Paladin ports out of the way and watches the lizard as it falls into the court yard below. It breaks its neck and dies. The other lizards below fall on to the dead lizard devouring it, and soon it is devoured leaving nothing, not even any bones.

Paladin ports to the window ledge then breaks into the room where he saw Samantha. As it turns out Samantha is not alone the Beast is there as well.

"Steve!" shouts Samantha.

Paladin sees the Beast and acknowledges his wife, while keeping an eye on the Beast.

"Well thief, return my wife to me and we'll leave in peace."

"No manling, you will not leave!"

In a blink of an eye the Beast crosses the room and grabs Paladin by the neck and walks over to the broken window.

"Manling you should have not come here."

The Beast hangs Paladin out the window, and below the lizards are looking up waiting for the Beast to drop the next bit of food for them to feast on. Straining to breath Paladin ports himself and the Beast to the gate. With Paladin on the outside and the Beast on the inside, also Paladin managed to port in such a way as to impale the Beasts arm that was crushing his neck with a bar in the gate, causing the beast so much pain that he drops Paladin. Falling to the ground on his hands and knees Paladin gasps for air. When he gets his wind back the Beast is bellowing and trying to shake the gate loose from its mountings. Soon several small Satyrs arrive and begin cutting the gate bar above and below the Beasts arm.

Chapter 122

Paladin seeing this happen decides to port to the top of the hill where he left the backpack. Paladin turns to retreat, looks at the window, and sees Samantha watching him. He waves to her and then he is ported away. Samantha sees her man disappear. Samantha has teleported enough times to know that Steve did not port away on his own, someone or something took him.

"What is going on?" She says to no one in particular.

The Beast bursts into the room bellowing his pain and the cut piece of the gate is still in his arm. The Beast calls for his servants and has his arm cut off at the iron bar in his arm. The iron rod made his hand useless, so why keep it. The Beast's arm is gushing blood, so to stop it the Beast thrusts his arm into the fire to cauterize it and stop the bleeding.

"What kind of manling is this mate of yours?" Bellows the Beast.

"A good and merciful one." Said Samantha with a great deal of pride in her voice.

"Had he wanted to he could have killed you by making the bar go through your body head to toe".

"Be glad he did not kill me, or my lizards, would kill everyone here including you!" Said the Beast.

"Just so you know he will be back, and he will not leave without me."

"If he comes back I will kill him."

"Maybe, after all you have his property ME. You might want to consider giving me back while you can".

"If he wants you back he will have to kill me first." laughs the Beast.

"We shall see" Said Samantha. "We shall see."

Paladin is pulled through another portal to a different dimension where he meets his benefactors the insect people, in this case a male (Drone). These creatures are like the ants of our world, but these insects walk up right. As on our world, the ants nest contains just a few males, thousands of females, and only one Queen, which the drone mates with. Thus for the rest of her life the Queen lays eggs, and is cared for constantly by the workers. The Drone however dies as soon as he mates with the queen.

As Paladin is more or less abducted, Paladin turns to the creatures and is ready to fight.

"Hold savior, we are your friends, we are not enemies." As the drone holds out all his arms and shows nothing in them.

"What is going on, why am I here?" asks Paladin.

"I have something to tell you. Please come with me, as you need water and food then rest. I will tell you all that I can of what is going on." Said the Drone.

Paladin follows the Drone into a nearby tunnel. After many turns, and in different directions they arrive at a cave or a vault that has a bed or mat on the floor, a small table much like the Japanese use. It is close to the floor, and it has both food and water on it.

"Please savior, take your ease, and refresh yourself. I will return in a little while to explain all that you want to know."

Paladin is very hungry and thirsty, and before he realizes it he has consumed all that was placed before him. Steve removes his battle suit and puts on his other clothes and lies down on the mat thinking how he might get Samantha back. Sometime later like about ten hours, Steve awakes to find the Drone is sitting on another mat just watching him.

"I guess I was tired." Said Steve.

"No, not really, I drugged your food, so you would sleep."

"Why?"

"Please, all in good time, we mean you no harm. We want to help you win your mate back, and our Queen as well."

"Help me how?"

"I will have the trainer explain. In the meantime, I have had more food and water brought to you, and it is not drugged."

The Drone turns to the entrance and Steve hears a series of clicks and chirps, as another hive female enters and bows to the Drone and then to Steve.

"Instructor, explain to our savior all that he requests, I must now return to my place, if you need me the Instructor may contact me."

The Instructor enters the room, the Drone talks to her with the clicks and chirps, then the Drone leaves. The instructor sits down on the other side of the table from Steve.

Chapter 123

"Where to begin." The Instructor muses.

For a few moments it is silent and the Instructor rises up to pace in front of Steve. It is as if the Instructor were gathering her thoughts. In one swift move, the instructor's stinger stabs Steve in the back of his neck right at the location of Steve's crystal. At that moment several things happen, the crystal is removed and then replaced with a different one. Two different compounds are injected into Steve's blood system. One compound contains all of the information of the histories, and the second compound enhances Steve's strength and abilities. The new crystal is more powerful than his first one. But none of the hive knows what it will do. The new crystal is more powerful and according to the histories it was to be changed at this point in time.

Steve sits on his mat in a trance, as his mind is racing with all the history information the Instructor has injected into him. The history memories tell about how he received the crystal in the first place and that the hive refers to themselves as the people. Surprising the people have been directing his life. He even sees the Micro Sun and what happened to him and how they saved him. Steve even sees the Beast taking Samantha and their Queen. The hive needs to have Steve fight in the arena so he can win back not only Samantha, but the Queen too. The need is very great to get the Queen back. Without her the hive will die. To be sure some of the history is held back, certain things Steve needs to do on his own and without help or prior knowledge. Most of all the drugs they gave Steve, gives Steve a compulsion to get Samantha and the Hive Queen back.

The Instructor withdraws its stinger. Then Steve falls into a deep sleep, as his mind absorbs the information and so he will not feel the sickness of getting a new crystal. And some of the changes to his body from the enhancement drugs (More strength, speed, and his five senses are also altered) he was given. Steve sleeps for many hours. The next morning when he wakes he is very hungry and eats and drinks what is put before him. The Drone enters Steve's chamber.

"I must apologize for the Instructor, for stinging you to give you the information on the histories. It was the fastest way of conveying the information to you so you can understand our plight."

"Ok, but don't do anything to me anymore, or I will decide that you're the enemy instead of the Beast and I'll trade you for my wife."

"I understand, but now you must get ready to fight in the arena and for that the Instructor will be your trainer".

At that moment the Instructor enters Steve's room and bows down and asks pardon for what she has done. (Note: The instructor is from the future, and none of the people know it, neither do they realize she has changed the crystal and provided him with the enhancing drug as well, this is all to remain a secret, even from the Queen).

"So tell me why she is the instructor who will be teaching Me." asks Steve.

"She has fought with a Beast and bested him, but just, her insight will help you in your fight with the Beast." said the Drone.

The Instructor makes Steve get to his feet, she probes him to see if he can take what she is going to dish out to him. Not fully happy she gives her assessment of him to the Drone. The Drone translates to Steve what she has said.

"She says you are a poor specimen to teach, but in time you might survive the arena. I take my leave of you, and will leave you in the Instructors care."

Chapter 124

Samantha is taken to where the rest of the collection of females are kept. She is shocked by the different females in the Beast's collection. In essence they are all alien to her, none of the females are anything like her or she like them. All of the animal types of them are present in one form or another, Insects, Snakes or reptiles, there are a few she cannot conceive of. Most of them are bipeds, but still a few so different Samantha is fearful of them. The hive Queen walks up to Samantha and asks "Is the savior here?"

"Who is the savior?"

"Your mate, where is he?"

"My mate was here, but I saw him taken away."

"Did you see who took him?"

"No, it happened too fast for me to see anything, but I can tell by the way he moved he was grabbed and pulled through a hole in space."

"My people must have him then, and they are beginning his training for the games."

"What game?" asked Samantha?

"Every year the giant Satyr's have games at the arena in their capitol city. The contenders (which is anyone from any world) can come and fight. The winner takes the collection of the looser, and the looser is killed." (Collection is whatever they want to wager for the privilege to fight in the arena)

"My mate has already maimed this giant Satyr."

"If you like I can enhance your strength, speed and any other senses you may have" said the Queen.

"How is it that you are able to do this?"

With the speed too fast to see the Queen stings Samantha, and puts the venom into her blood stream.

"What did you do to me?" Samantha falls to the floor and the Queen picks her up and carriers her to a couch, to sleep off the venom she has injected her with. Hours later Samantha wakes up and feels the site of the injection.

"What did you do to me?"

"I gave you the enhancing venom, so you can protect us."

"Protect us from whom?"

The Queen points to the other female captives.

"Them. They want to be first in the collection, so they will try to find ways to kill us."

"Why would they want to kill us? Are we not all in the same fix?"

"You must understand that for some of the females, it is in their nature to kill."

Samantha begins to watch some of the other Females and she begins to see what the Queen means.

The lizard like female attacks Samantha trying to slash her open, but Samantha easily counters the attack, and throws the attacker to the floor.

"Wow, I am faster than I was before" Thinks Samantha.

Then from a far corner springs a lioness female (Biped or woman like) again Samantha counters the attack, and leaves the attacker hurt on the floor. After that display of fighting prowess the other females give wide birth to Samantha and the Queen. The venom the Queen injected into Samantha not only enhanced her abilities it also makes her very protective of the Queen.

Chapter 125

It is late when Steve goes to sleep for the night. By the next morning he had not left this room since he had been brought there. I'm sick and tired of being drugged, and stung. I need some exercise. Steve gets into his jeans and Tee shirt and ports to the mouth of the tunnel above ground, and is caught off guard. The Instructor is there waiting for him and she pounces on him. Steve reacts with the teaching of Samantha and Grandmother (Who taught him how to use martial arts) and flips the Instructor to one side. Steve realizes how effortless it is.

"What happened to me? I should not have done that to you so easily."

"The power comes with the sting that I gave you. I also gave you more abilities and power. And in time you will discover what I have given you as a gift. Now you must keep this a secret, if the hive finds out that I have done this we will both die."

"Why?"

"Rest assured, I have protected you for our own sake. You see I'm not of this hive at this time. I have been sent from the future, and I will return to the future. This hive will seek to keep you here and in time you must leave, you still have much to accomplish. Now let's get to the training."

Steve and his Instructor spend days and what seems like months training. Learning to fight with sword, staff, mace, and some strange weapons he has never seen before. Steve is also concerned about his young children he left, but he also knows that Addy will care for them as if they were her own. CAT will also see to them financially, and with any necessary paperwork to make everything legal.

"Do you know how my mate is doing?" Asks Steve of the Instructor.

"Yes, she is doing well. The Beast will not allow anything to happen to her, as he still needs her for the games. She is to be bait to draw you back so he can kill or disable you."

"What games?"

"On the world of the Beast they have become collectors and they have arena games once a year. We have brought you here to be trained to defeat the Beast. When you have killed him, you get your mate back and we will get our Queen back."

"When do I have to fight this Beast?"

"In a few days, their time, here time moves differently than it does in the Beasts dimension."

"How different?"

"A day in their dimension, is like a month here."

"I guess that means I have a month to finish my training, we had better kick it up a notch so I can defeat this Beast."

Chapter 126

The Instructor selects a dozen warriors to help prepare Steve for his battle. The Hive is much the same as an ant colony. Different ants to perform different functions. The warriors are designed to kill and they look like they can do a good job of it too. The Instructor starts Steve out with one warrior and she tells the warrior to kill Steve.

"Hey, I need to be around to fight the Beast."

"Look at it this way savior, the Beast is not going to go soft on you, he wants you dead. Now the Warrior will try to kill you, as this will make you more willing to learn, so as not to die."

Before Steve can protest the Warrior attacks, Steve gets knocked to the ground and the warrior tries to stab him with her fighting claw. Steve ports behind the warrior using what Samantha has taught him. He hits the warrior in a soft spot and knocks the warrior to the ground unable to move.

"Is she ok, I did not mean to cause her to be damaged or injured?"

"She will be fine. Your blow stunned her, and you took her by surprise."

The Instructor points at two more Warriors.

"Attack and kill!"

Steve watches as they charge him, assuming they would be ready for what he did to the first warrior. He decides to pick a defense he was taught by Grandmother. Using their speed and strength against them, he sends them face down into the sand on the ground, and then stuns them as he did the first one.

"You fight better than I thought you would. You have learned much. Let's see if I can take your true measure. All of you attack and kill."

The nine remaining warriors attack Steve. They take him down to the ground and before one of the warriors can deliver the killing blow, Steve ports with some of the warriors to a nearby river. In their surprise, they release him and he ports up to the bank leaving the warriors to take care of themselves. Then Steve ports back to the four remaining warriors and quickly hits one warrior with a stunning blow, then pounces on each of the others doing the same thing.

Winded Steve stands there catching his breath. The instructor approaches him as if to congratulate him when Steve ports behind her and stuns her as well.

A short time later the warriors and the Instructor come around, but are not able to move. Steve borrowed from one of the old time westerns he watched on TV, and hog tied them all up.

"Well now, are we done playing try to kill the human?"

"How did you know that I was going to attack you?" asked the instructor.

"It was a feeling, more than anything. Now you said you could take me to my wife."

"I can, but if I do you must realize you cannot take her away from her captivity."

"Why not? She is my mate."

"It is the condition of the game, and we must follow the rules that govern that game in order to get back both your mate and our Queen. You must fulfil the histories as they have already unfolded. To change them would cause the death of the hive. Then you and your mate would be lost in the dimensions never to return to your world."

"But, I do not care for your histories"

"Let's put it this way, if you do not follow the histories, you die in the arena, and your mate teleports you into the wall of the arena killing you both. If you follow the histories you win somehow, and you will leave this dimension and start your journey home."

Chapter 127

"OK, you win. So when do I get to see my mate?"

"Now!"

The Instructor opens a portal into the Beast's dimension, on to the Hill where they had taken Steve from.

"Go see her and return here, you have but a short time don't waste it."

Steve teleports into the room of the fortress where he had been before. It just happens that Samantha and the Queen are there, Samantha runs to Steve to embrace him.

"I knew you would come for me! In my heart I knew you would be back!" Samantha covers his face with kisses.

"I did and I will. For some reason I may not take you away from here yet. I had to make the promise to the hive before they would let me come to you. It seems I have to fight for you with the Beast in order to take you out of here.

"When?"

"I'm told in a day from now."

Then they hear a bellow of rage from the far side of the room.

"I'm going to kill you manling, for what you have done to me!"

The Beast charges the couple and Steve ports to the side and then trips the Beast up sending him into the wall face first.

"Samantha leave the room!" Samantha obeys and quickly takes the Queen, and leaves the room.

The Beast gets up and charges again, bellowing his hatred. Steve easily evades the Beast and trips him again and watches as the Beast falls to the floor on his face. In a blink of an eye the Beast is up on his feet and grabs Steve by the throat and stands up holding Steve off the ground.

"I'm going to kill you now rather than wait for the games.

" The Beast starts to squeeze, Steve opens a window around the Beasts hand at the wrist, as it happens the beast can see it too.

Steve croaks "I'm going to close it and remove your hand if you do not let me go!"

The Beast drops Steve, and Steve tries to catch his breath. When Steve is recovered he looks the Beast in the eye.

"I will meet you in the arena, and I will get my mate back, even if I have to kill you."

"You will meet me in the arena Manling and I will crush you in front of your mate!"

Steve says nothing and ports back to the cave in the hives dimension.

"How did your meeting go with your mate?" asked the Drone.

"It went well, I had a run in with the Beast though."

"You didn't!"

"Yes, I did. I gave him a choice, to let me go or lose a hand. As you see he let me go. Then he accepted my challenge to fight him in the arena."

"Nothing else?"

"No nothing else."

(Unknown to the hive people Steve has discovered a way to open and close windows, all this time they are not able to detect them or even know about them)

Chapter 128

The new crystal that the Instructor gave Steve has an even greater and finer use of the windows. The hive for some reason is totally blind to the ability that Steve has.

The day to go to the arena to fight for Samantha has arrived. Steve dresses up in his Battle suit, and checks out all his systems and weapons. Everything is working, and powered up thanks to the solar panels that are built into the suits. Steve checks the force fields, communications between the helmets, and the other detection equipment the suit has to offer. He still cannot contact CAT (There is no way to cross the dimensions with electronic communications). Steve did set aside his dart pistols in favor of Samantha's Japanese sword. Samantha had taught him how to use the sword, and with the training from the hive Instructor his skills have improved. Still Steve believes Samantha to be the better swordsman than himself. Steve thinks I'm going to have to get a sword of my own someday.

Paladin is now ready to fight the Beast. The Instructor and the Drone meet at Steve's living space. The Instructor opens the portal into the Beast's dimension, and they appear in the arena. As Paladin takes in all of the area, he realizes that the arena is much like the Roman Coliseum back on his Earth. Paladin is using his detection devices in his helmet to try and locate Samantha. He locates her on the far side from where he is. Along the far side of the arena at about center stage are seated the Giant Satyr's who will judge the game's outcome.

Looking around Paladin sees alien people who must be from other dimensions, in all kinds of armor who have come to try their prowess in battle against the Giant Satyr's and possibly against each other. There were beings, he could not begin to describe, and some of them even seem prehistoric. I hope I do not have to fight any of them, thinks Paladin. The noise in the arena is deafening. The Drone Grabs Paladin by the arm and pulls him toward the tunnel where the Drone can explain all the rules and what will happen in the arena.

Chapter 129

The Drone will go out to make a formal challenge and place the bet for the Queen and Paladin's mate.

"If you lose the fight Paladin we will forfeit your mate and my Queen to the Satyr who stole them. If you win, you will receive your mate and my Queen as prizes for winning. You do understand don't you?"

"I do, is there anything else I need to know?"

"Yes, there are no rules here. Either you kill or be killed. And to top it all off, if you lose we lose our lives as well."

"I see, no pressure. These other people that are here to fight, same rules?"

"For the most part, you see whoever wins gets the spoils" said the Drone.

"So if I defeat the Satyr I get all his possession even if I do not want them"

"You have to accept them as it is the rules for wining. If you want your mate back you must kill the Satyr." Said the Drone.

"I'm beginning to see that. It's not what I want. I don't like killing."

From the back of the tunnel the Beast in question forces his way through the crowd to where Paladin is standing.

"Well Manling, I see you have come! You are not the coward I thought you were. I will take much pleasure in killing you and keeping your mate as my treasure."

Paladin says nothing.

"Have you nothing to say manling, you are too afraid I take it."

"No, not afraid. On my world pride goes before destruction, I'll not boast. I will warn you, I will do what is necessary to get my mate back. If I must kill you, I will."

Paladin turns his back to the Beast and walks away. Paladin uses his helmet to view the Beast and sees the sword he is raising then as the Beast tries to smite Paladin, Paladin ports behind the Beast as the sword hits the ground.

"You can't wait to fight me I see. You must be afraid of me, more so than I am of you. That is a coward's way to strike an opponent from behind."

The Beast is enraged even more and takes after Paladin, and Paladin just keeps out of reach of the Beast and leads him out into the arena. Just as the satyr is about to strike Paladin one of the armed guards stops the Beast.

One of the senior judges stands up and says.

"It is not time for you to fight, you will wait your turn."

An elder beside the one who spoke also states.

"You have brought shame on us and yourself Beast. You will go to your area and wait. If you do this again the judgment will go against you".

The Beast is further enraged, but complies with the elders.

As the Beast turns away he says "Manling, if I do nothing else for the rest of my life I will kill you!"

"That remains to be seen." said Paladin.

The guard and the Beast move off the field. The first fight is not a good fight. The Giant Satyr kills his opponent in under a moment of time. He split the poor creature from head to toe with one chop. The winner raises his hands and roars his victory cry, then he stalks off the field. There are several more fights ending much the same way, the Giant Satyr winning the day.

Now the time for Paladin and the Beast to fight is next. The Drone and the Instructor caution Paladin to keep his head, and to kill the beast. Paladin ports out to the middle of the arena to wait for his opponent. From the tunnel, out steps the Beast followed by the Queen, then followed by Samantha and behind them stands another satyr. Paladin checks his helmet's display and realizes that the other satyr is going to kill both Samantha and the Queen. Paladin ports up to the woman and pulls his sword out to take the sword stroke of the satyr deflecting it harmlessly away from both Samantha and the Queen. Paladin then ports both the Queen and Samantha to his tunnel, and then Paladin ports back out to the center of the arena. Paladin turns up the volume on his helmet.

"Well Beast I see you are a coward and you have no honor. You try to kill two helpless females from behind."

"Nobody says that about me. NOBODY!" roars the Beast as it charges Paladin swinging his sword. The beast pounces on Paladin, and Paladin uses his sword to deflect the Beasts sword again and again. Each time Paladin evades the sword stroke, it just makes the Beast more enraged. The crowd is now laughing at the Beast as the little man keeps the Beast at bay. During the fight someone puts a stumbling block behind Paladin and he trips over it. As he tries to get up, the Beast rains blow after blow upon Paladin. Using both hands Paladin manages to stop the sword stokes until he can port away from the Beast so he can stand up. Again they engage in sword play and out of the corner of his eye, Paladin sees the guard pitch another stumbling block. It is too late as Paladin trips over it again, and the Beast rains down blow after blow.

Paladin cannot keep this up, and as the Beast straddles him to deliver the killing blow, Paladin opens a window and the beast is thrown off balance and falls through into another dimension. Paladin somewhat beaten down and tired stands up. The crowd goes wild with yelling and cheers; this is the first time anyone has beaten a Giant Satyr.

"Manling where is the one called the Beast?"

"In another dimension."

"Which dimension?"

"I do not know, nor do I care."

The Guard, grabs Paladin by the shoulder.

413

"Set me down or you will lose your arm" the guard places Paladin on the ground.

The Elder says "Manling you are under arrest"

"Why? I defeated my opponent."

Then the Elder Grabs Paladin by the neck.

Chapter 130

A great flash of light appears over the arena and everyone becomes frozen in place. The Entity removes Paladin from the Elder's hand and places a barrier around him. Then takes the freeze off everyone.

The Elder says "What right do you have in interfering in our games?"

"A lot really, one of your satyrs has taken one of our children, I want her back. If she is not turned over to me in in one cycle I will turn all you satyrs into stone statues for all time."

The Beast had been returned with the entrance of the Entity. With a look the Beast is turned into stone.

The Elder says "you can't do this!"

"Tell that to the satyr I just turned to stone." The Entity said. I'm not sure. But as you can see. I'm quite capable of doing what I say I can. Now manling how did you know to send me that satyr?"

"Actually I did not. I just opened a portal to make him disappear so I would not have to kill him. Or where he could not hurt anyone else. This would allow me to defeat him and win back my mate."

"Manling, you have a strange and fearful gift, use it wisely" The Entity Touches Paladin. I have given you a gift of sorts as long as you keep your honor you will always find what you need, when you need it."

"Thank you, but all I really want is my mate."

The Entity points to Samantha and she appears next to Paladin. Steve removes his helmet and embraces Samantha, and she is determined not to let her husband go.

Over time the Entity locates the satyr who has taken the child. The Entity demands that he return her to him. The satyr refuses.

"Then you leave me no choice, I will destroy you to show the other Giant Satyrs what will happen if they come to my dimension ever again."

The Entity raises his hand.

"Hold on for a moment." says Paladin.

Paladin walks over to the satyr, and says. "Are you sure you want to refuse the Entity's request? Look over at my opponent. Are you sure you want to live forever as stone, and still alive, not able to do anything. To me death would be more pleasant."

"But I took her she is mine!"

"No, you are a thief, and you stole not a woman but a child, you have no honor, I would give her back" says Paladin.

"If I give her back will he still kill me?"

"No, if you give her up he will let you live."

"Ok, the child is in my room in my cell."

The Entity uses his mind to locate the child and brings her to him. "Now that I have the child I'm going to lay waste to this world."

"Hold that thought, you should not destroy or kill anyone here." says Paladin.

"Who are you to tell me what I should not do?"

"In this, a voice of reason, why lower yourself to their level. If you want to punish them fix it so they cannot ever leave this dimension ever again. Then over time they will turn on themselves instead of others. Who knows over time, they may learn from this mistake, and be a better people in the future?"

"Manling you are far wiser than I. it will be so, the Entity raised his voice, I'm going to close off this dimension. If you want to return to your dimension you had better do it within the next cycle or you will be stranded here."

Everyone scrambles to comply with the Entity's command.

"The other captives will be removed and sent home by me" the one called Paladin, take your group and leave now. Once I take the necessary steps no one will be allowed to come into this dimension, or leave it. Not even me." said the Entity.

There was such a scurry in the arena of all the People from other dimensions collecting their things so they could return to their worlds.

Hive world

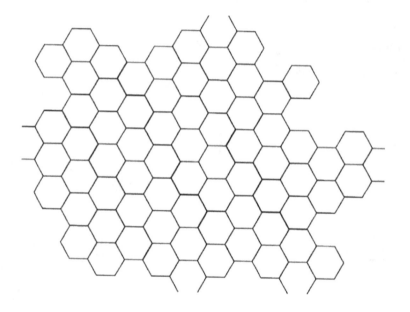

Chapter 131

Paladin takes Samantha by the hand, and the others as well, the Drone, Queen and the Instructor. The instructor opens the portal to the hive dimension and returns them to their nest. After the Queen and her mate arrive back at the hive, the Queen's workers rejoice, and usher the Queen and her Drone off into the nest deep underground for their honey moon. Steve and Samantha are ushered to the vault where Steve is staying. Other than being brought food and water, Steve and Samantha are left alone to do their own celebrating for being united from their forced separation. In the morning the Instructor wakes up Steve and asks him to come with her. So he wakes Samantha and they both dress and then follow the Instructor deep into the tunnel, where they see the dead Drone being carried away to be placed with other dead Drones in a shrine.

"What happened to the Drone?" asks Paladin.

"The Drone and the Queen mated last night. Once that happens the Drone dies. All a Drone lives for is to mate with the queen. Once that has happened, they just die."

"So where is the Queen? Why is she not here?"

"The Queen is in the birthing chamber, where she will live out her life laying eggs to keep the hive alive."

"According to the Drone, the Queen has a map in order to help Samantha and I head home. It was promised to us, so let's go see the Queen." Said Steve.

The Instructor leads them to the Queen's birthing chamber. When Steve and Samantha enter the chamber they are shocked at what they see. The Queen is huge and is surrounded by thirty or more workers caring for her.

"What has happening to her?" asks Samantha. "Is she alright?"

"I'm full of the eggs, of my children. When the Drone and I mated, my body becomes as you see it here. For the rest of my days I will have thousands of children. They all have different functions to help the hive survive."

"We have come to get the promised map so we may return home, the Drone said you would provide it." Said Steve.

"Yes of course, I will have it sent to you later, you and your mate may stay here at the hive for as long as you like, and I would like to get to know you better, the one call Steve, drone of Samantha."

"I thank you, but I would like to get home to our children, so I would like to leave in two cycles."

"As you wish." Said the Queen.

The Instructor returns them to Steve's vault.

"One called Steve."

"Yes Instructor."

"You and your mate must leave today!"

"Why? Asks Samantha.

"The Queen's mind will undergo certain changes, along with her body. Soon she will try to keep Steve here and have Samantha killed. The Queen sees Samantha as a rival for her throne, and she sees Steve as her drone."

"What about the map?" asks Steve?

The Instructor opens a pouch and hands over the map.

"I took it when the Drone died, He told me where to get it, and we both knew the Queen would not provide it. Since you did uphold your task we had to make sure you moved on to your other tasks."

The Instructor, turns to Samantha and gives her a vial.

"You will need to drink this, when the Queen stung you she did more than you know."

Samantha places the vial into her pocket for now.

"Steve we need to get dressed in our battle suits and get out of here. The Instructor is right, also she will be affecting my mind to have me stay and protect her."

Steve, and Samantha dress in their battle suits. Steve puts on the backpack, and Samantha puts on her sword. Steve opens the map to see where the portal is on this world into the next world that they must travel to.

"Steve how will we get to the portal we do not have CAT to set up coordinates for us?"

"We have one way at this time, Line of sight. The other possibility would be if we had been there before. Since this is a new world to us, neither of us have been here; so we must use the line of sight teleportation."

Steve takes Samantha's hand and ports them to the entrance of the hive.

"We need to put some distance between us and the hive, according to the map we need to move off in that direction."

Steve points off to what we would consider to be east.

Steve and Samantha leave the area just in time, as the warriors advance from the hive to capture them. Steve Transports with Samantha to the top of a nearby hill then turns back to see the warriors massing at the entrance of the nest. Holding on to Samantha's hand Steve ports to another hill further out. Then they are down on a plain. Steve ports from one place to another, trying to out distance the hive warriors. Eventually they come upon a river, the other side is too full of foliage to try to port to and the water is moving too fast to try to swim. Samantha suggests that they move up stream and find a better place to port across to the other side.

Since the brush is just as thick on this side they decide to walk up stream to see if they can find an open spot on the other side. After an hour, Samantha

421

spots an animal tract just across from them. It is not big enough for them both to port to so Steve ports over and then walks down the trail to get out of Samantha's way. Moments later Samantha ports over to where Steve is and follows him down the trail.

"I hope this side of the river, is not all like this." said Steve, indicating the dense under brush.

They spend the rest of the day walking out of the woods, and they come to an open space with a brook running next to it.

"Steve, it is getting dark out should we not make camp, and try to find some food?"

"Sweet heart, you are quite right, once it gets dark we will not be able to port, for fear of getting tangled up in something."

Chapter 132

Steve makes a couple of fishing poles and tries his luck at catching dinner. Soon Samantha is sitting beside him and she wants to fish too. Both are sitting in the near dark and catch enough fish like creatures to have a nice dinner. Steve cleans the fish and Samantha cooks them. That night they eat well, and drink the water from the brook. Steve gives Samantha a space blanket and they stretch out to sleep. In the morning Steve hears a buzzing sound and it is coming from the other side of the river.

He wakes Samantha, I'll be right back. "And I think we had better get ready to leave." Steve ports to the spot where they came upon the river. On the other side of the river and headed in their direction are the warriors from the hive. Steve ports back to the spot where he had been fishing so as not to port into Samantha.

"We have to leave now! The plain we crossed is covered in Hive warriors and they are coming this way. They will be here very soon."

"Won't they have a problem crossing the river?"

"Have you ever seen any of the shows back on Earth showing army ants?"

"I guess so, why?"

"The army ants use each other as bridges to cross over obstacles, these ones will do the same thing. At the speed they are traveling they will be here in an hour, we need to go."

"I wonder how they found us." Said Samantha.

"We can't stop to think about that right now we need to get moving."

Samantha grabs Steve's arm and he ports them into the open area on the other side of the brook. Then short teleportation's until they can reach more open areas. Steve then zig zags about to see if the warriors are following them, and if so how and why. That night and after they have a camp set up, Steve ports back to the high spot they touched down earlier, and he encounters a warrior, and has to fight. It is a good thing he had them as sparring partners. He knows how to stop them fairly quickly and in mere moments Steve incapacitates the Warrior. Then ports back to Samantha.

"They are gaining on us. We need to get moving, and we need to figure out how they are tracking us."

"Steve how would the army ant track things?"

"Pheromones, they leave a scent trail for the warriors to follow, where are you going with this Samantha?"

If what you said is true, either you, or I have a pheromone we are leaving behind, how would we stop it?"

"We could mask it with another pheromone or with another chemical. But now that you mention it, I believe Samantha that you are the one with the pheromone. Let me explain. When I went back to the hill to look at them a single warrior accosted me, but there were others at the base and none of them reacted to me. It was as if it were an accident."

"Steve give me the backpack."

Samantha riffles around in her other clothes, and pulls out a vial of liquid.

"The Instructor said I should drink this to get better. What if she knew about the pheromones, and was trying to tell me."

Samantha works the stopper out and drinks down the liquid, and makes a sick face.

"This stuff tastes terrible. I hope it works! Man this is so terrible tasting stuff I hope it isn't poison."

"I trust the Instructor Samantha; she knows how important you are to me. Well let's see if it works or not."

Steve takes Samantha's hand and ports out on to the plain and heads towards the mountains in the distance, just about midday, they reach the base of the mountains. Samantha points out a small ridge area with a lot of brush.

"Steve what about over there, it might have some water."

"Looks good to me."

Steve ports over to the area, and sure enough it has a sheltered area with a steam and what looks like a small water fall.

"This place is perfect and I can take a bath, and wash my hair."

Steve smiles. "I agree, I can use a bath too. But before I do I want to see what the warriors are doing. I'll be right back."

Steve ports to another high area to watch what the warriors are up to, and it appears that they are just milling around, with no place to go.

It looks like the potion that the Instructor gave Samantha worked. Thinks Steve.

Chapter 133

Steve ports back to the camp sight, and finds Samantha huddled up against a rock all shaken up and crying.

"Samantha what's wrong?"

Crying Samantha points to the pond, and she is badly shaken. Steve walks over to the pond and sees the sword standing up like it was stabbed into a log, and as he reaches for it the log quivers, Steve jumps back in fright. And he decides to leave the sword alone for now. He walks back to Samantha.

"Samantha what happened?" Samantha grabs on to Steve and cries even more and she is terribly afraid. It takes a while and she finely calms down, the whole time Steve pets her hair and tries to comfort her. When she is composed she looks into his eyes, and says "never leave me along again."

"You have my word on that, can you tell me what happened?"

"After you left, I took my clothes off and climbed up to the ledge up there and I found some fine sand so I was scrubbing myself off and using the falls to rinse off, then I sat down on the ledge to dry off. I saw what looked like a log floating in the pond so I did not think anything of it, even when it moved towards me up stream. I was combing my hair with my fingers, when this creature raised out of the water and tries to grab my foot. At that moment I port to the backpack and drew my sword, and port back to the top of the creature and thrust my sword into its head killing it, I port back here as it is thrashing around as it died. I have never been so scared in my life."

"Well I'll tell you what, I'll gut and skin your dragon (More like an alligator) and we can do to him what he was going to do to you."

"What?"

"We'll eat him. It looks like we can cook and smoke some of the meat to take with us, so we'll stay for a few days. Will that be ok with you Honey?"

Steve strips down to his shorts, and then turns to the job of skinning and gutting the water dragon. The next day after a big breakfast, Steve figures a way to make a small smoke house to smoke and dry out the dragon's flesh. Samantha feeling better now, finds some cattails and uses the long leaves to weave a basket which Steve lines with the belly skin of the dragon. The make shift basket seems strong enough to hold all the meat that Steve cut off the creature. The rest of the offal they leave behind for scavengers to finish off. What Steve and Samantha do not know is that they are being watched. Steve decides it is time to get moving as the dead dragon is beginning to smell. Steve takes out the map to see which way they may want to travel around the mountain or over the mountain. Steve goes to the backpack and takes out the strange map to see if it will show them the way to go. As Steve turns the map in different directions the lines showing the directions to get to the portal change in length, so Steve orients the map for the shortest route, it appears to be around the mountain, in that direction toward the east.

"Samantha are you ready to leave?"

"Yes, this place gives me the creeps, not only the smell of the decaying dragon, but I feel like we are being watched."

"We are being watched, the sensors in my helmet indicates that several small critters are over in that brush area just out of sight."

"Steve why can I not see them?"

"Switch to infrared and you can see the heat signature they are giving off."

"Yes, I can see them now, I wonder how long they have been there?"

"I believe they saw you kill the dragon."

"WHAT! You mean they were watching me bathe?"

"I would not hold it against them, if I had been in their place, and a beautiful wood nymph was bathing I would watch too." Samantha slugs Steve in the shoulder, and Steve just laughs.

"Do not worry Samantha, we'll port away from here leaving them behind and with a mystery of the disappearing beings."

"Let's leave now Steve, this place makes my skin crawl."

Steve takes Samantha's hand and ports to the clearing on the far side of the pond, not too far from the figures who are watching them. Steve sees a clearing further out and takes Samantha there. The little people who are watching them, are now scared of the two giants who have invaded their home. They try to follow, but soon lose them, as they disappear from the clearing.

Steve ports them to a few high places along the mountain base so he can see to increase the distance of his teleporting. By late afternoon, Samantha spots a likely place to set up camp. It has a small stream, for water, and a nice flat mossy area to set up for sleeping.

Steve asks, "Do we want Dragon for dinner or should I try my luck at catching a fish?"

"Try fish, Steve."

They both set up camp with the little equipment that they have, Steve cuts a couple of limbs from a springy bush and makes up a couple of fishing poles.

"Hey Hon, have you ever been fishing like this before?"

"No, I haven't, do you see any water dragons?"

"Come over here, and we can fish together."

"Are you sure you want me to."

"Hey, anyone who can kill a water dragon, can handle a little fish."

Samantha is not quite over her scare of the water dragon, and so decides to go sit next to Steve. He hands her a pole so they both can fish. A short time later Samantha catches the first fish, with an excited yelp.

"I caught one, what do I do?"

"Pick up your pole, and lift the fish out of the water then swing it to me and I'll take it off for you."

Samantha does as Steve asks. He removes the fish from the line, and she tosses her line back in the water, and moments later there is another fish. Soon Samantha catches enough for dinner. Steve did not put any bait on his hook that is why Samantha caught all the fish. He was hoping that Samantha would calm down with a little harmless excitement, and it seems to have worked. She is more like herself now. Steve cleans out the fish and Samantha cooks them to perfection, or as well as one can with a stick over a fire will allow.

Steve picks up his helmet and he places it on his head to scan the area.

"Samantha we have company again."

"It's not a water dragon is it?"

"No, do you remember the half pint critters we encountered yesterday?"

"Yes, they are across the stream from us and it looks like there is about ten of them."

"Should we leave?" asks Samantha.

"No, I'm going to set the scanner in my helmet to wake me if they show any aggression."

Samantha clutches her sword to her. Steve reassures her they are alright; as they would be too scared to cross the river in case one of the dragons would be about.

"Dragon!" asks Samantha.

"Not to worry dear, I have scanned the area, it is clear of them. If they even reside in rushing water."

Samantha huddles closer to Steve, and he puts his arm around her, and he whispers. "I will protect you my heart." And she relaxes and falls asleep. In the morning, Steve lets Samantha sleep and he takes his fishing pole and catches a few fish to have with breakfast. Soon he walks over to her and shakes her awake, she smiles up at him and then gets up and stretches before moving over to the fire. Where she sees that Steve has breakfast ready for her.

"You don't cook so bad yourself." said Samantha.

"That comes from being a bachelor during the first part of my life."

"And now."

Leaning toward Samantha, he whispers "you see I have this very beautiful Asian wife who is no mean cook, to take care of me now." Samantha laughs.

"Steve I miss the children are they going to be Ok?"

"They will be fine, I had CAT run the 'Child One Protocol' and Addy will be their guardian until we return."

"Thank you, you have taken a small load off my mind and heart. Addy will love them almost as much as I do. Steve can we find a place where we can safely take a bath? This battle suit is getting pretty rank, and so are you."

"Today I agree as far as the washing goes, if we can find such a place? If we move up into the mountain some we may lose our peanut gallery who keeps watching us."

"I can agree on that." said Samantha.

Steve ports them along the base of the mountain until he comes to a large stream. Where he stops and looks up to where it is coming from. He sees a ledge way up the side of the mountain, and ports them up to it, then to another, and so on, until he finds what he is looking for. Up near the top Steve finds a pool of water not too deep with a mossy area to one side. He scans the area and finds no real signs of life about, which means it will be cold dragon for dinner. The area being secluded makes it easy for Samantha and Steve to strip down and go for a swim and get washed up. They even take the time to wash their clothes, and the battle suits.

Chapter 134

"I feel so much better Steve; this is a good spot. The only complaint I could have is that we cannot make a camp fire, there is no wood."

"I can leave and go down and get some."

"No you won't, you stay right here."

"Alright, we can do without a campfire for one night, we can get under our space blanket and snuggle together to keep warm." said Steve.

"You know I think I would like that, besides our clothes are still wet from being washed."

Steve and Samantha snuggle up together, and later that night they fall asleep, to wake up late in the morning refreshed.

Steve takes out the map to get a bearing on the direction they need to take, and Samantha checks the clothes. They are dry, so they get dressed. Steve and Samantha pack up what little they have and start porting up the mountain to see if they can get a better view of the country below.

"Hey Samantha, the map has changed, it shows us what is ahead, but not what we passed through"

"It is a strange thing, but being on this world it does not surprise me anymore. I have everything packed up, are we ready to go?"

Steve puts the map away in the backpack and with Samantha in hand he ports them along the top of the mountain. By lunchtime they have run out of mountain and the woods have thinned out, from there vantage point Steve sees a small stream and ports them down next to it.

"Steve let's stop here, and have lunch, dried and smoked dragon is all we have."

"Sounds great, since dragon is all that we have. I'm getting tired of it!"

They take off their helmets, and Samantha hands out some of the dried dragon. They sit munching lunch in the quiet then Steve starts to speculate on the portal.

"Steve what are you thinking about?"

"How to open the portal, I'm not sure how to do it."

"You'll do fine. You always do, and know that I believe in you. No matter how bad it gets I know you will do what is needed. All these years we have been married, I have never known you to fail. You always manage to save the day. I want you to know, I trust in you."

"Samantha you do not know how much that means to me. You are my life, I'm not sure I could live without you."

Steve's inner Scientist leaks out and he sits in contemplation of the map trying to make sense of the symbols around the outer edge, and the changing picture of the area around them. So far all Steve is sure of is the map is taking them in the right direction but he cannot determine how far away the portal is. It is like it keeps moving away from them. Then Samantha pulls the map out of Steve's hands and rolls it up to put it away.

"Let's move Steve before it gets dark, we need to look for some place we can camp under cover. I believe that storm is moving in our direction."

Steve looks in the direction Samantha is pointing in. "You're right Samantha." Samantha takes Steve's hand and Steve stars porting in the direction they were heading. They crossed a plain and are into more woods. It did not take long to locate another small stream with several downed trees where they could erect a covered camp, to protect them from the coming storm. Steve is about to try fishing when he spots a couple of rabbit like creatures, so he takes Samantha's sword and ports right up to the creatures to kill them both for dinner. Once they eat dinner, they turn in for the night. Steve has them keep the battle suits on, it will protect them from the weather as they sleep.

Had Steve or Samantha kept their helmets on they would have detected the dozen or so natives that are watching them. They are impressed with Steve as he killed the rabbit creatures, with the sword. Then hack up some branches with the same tool. To these people Samantha and Steve, are giants. The natives think that the giants are there to give them tools for war, so they waited out the night, and the storm in hiding. The next morning, Steve emerges from their lean to, to only stop dead in his tracks. A rather large creature is getting a drink not twenty feet away from where he is standing. If he were back on our world, it would be very similar to a black bear.

Off across the stream the natives watch to see what will happen. Steve just stands there watching to see if the creature will move off or attack.

"Samantha, I need the sword now!"

Samantha ports to where Steve is just as the creature is charging him. Steve ports to one side, and Samantha ports onto the creature's back and runs the sword into the creature's back, about where the heart should be. Then Samantha ports next to Steve, they watch as the bear creature collapses and dies.

Samantha walks over to the creature and pulls out her sword. Just as she is about to say something she sees they are surrounded by several half pint creatures with sharpened sticks for spears. Samantha goes into a fighting stance with her sword, ready to fight off their attackers.

"Samantha stop, put up the sword."

"Why, Steve, they are attacking us?"

"Not really. So far they have only surrounded us, let's go along with them, and if worse comes to worse we can port out of here."

Samantha stands up and lets the natives take all their things, and leads them off into the forest. A few hours later they enter the village of the natives. Steve watches as a couple of the men form up a hunting party and leave.

"I wonder where they are going?" said Samantha.

"My guess would be to get the bear creature you killed, and bring it back."

At that moment, Steve and Samantha are ushered into a hut, and guards are stationed outside the door.

"Guess they do not want us leaving. Samantha noted. Why did we not port away when we could Steve?"

"I was curious about them, they did not want to hurt us, and they are not afraid of us."

"What makes you say that Steve?"

"For one thing, all our stuff is over in the corner, even your sword. I suspect they would not give us our stuff if they intended to harm us, let's see what happens. We'll leave tomorrow one way or another."

"Alright Steve, we'll play it your way for now."

Steve goes to the back of the hut and sits down, soon a young female appears carrying some food and water. Samantha gets up and the female cowers. Samantha pets her head and coos to her, "It is alright little one." And gently takes the food and water. Then thanks the young female who stands there looking at them in wonder then leaves.

"I wonder what that was about?" muses Steve.

"It was fear; she did not know what to expect from a giant. When we did not hurt her, she quit being afraid. We may have a new friend."

At evening the men return with the slain beast that Samantha had killed, and the elders gather to share out the meat and the hide. Not long after, Steve and Samantha are brought to the center of the village where on a stool sat an old man with a head dress on.

"Where came you?" ask the old man

"From the hive." Said Steve.

The old man pointed to the bare creature's head. "How you kill?"

"With the sword" answered Samantha.

"Sword? What is sword?"

Samantha ports back to the hut and then back and brandishes her sword.

"This is a sword" she said.

"Make swords for us?"

"No!" said Steve, No weapons."

The head man has Steve and Samantha returned to their hut.

"Samantha let's gather our stuff up it is time to leave."

"Ok, Steve."

Once they have all their stuff together Steve ports them back to their last camp site.

"Steve, why could we not give them a sword, so they can protect themselves?"

"Because, they would use it to make war on other villages."

"Why do you say that, they seemed to be very friendly?"

"Samantha, I'm a scientist and I have worked with other scientists, and we have invented things to make life better for everyone. Then someone realizes the military applications so what was made to benefit everyone is now a weapon. Instead of helping people it now kills people. I will not be a party to it."

"I'm sorry Steve, I did not know."

"It's Ok Samantha, but now we have caused contamination. They have seen the sword, so now they will try to make one. I wish we could make them forget it."

Just as Steve and Samantha are about to restart their journey a brilliant flash of light fills the sky above them, and the Entity is floating above them.

"Ho one called Steve, I've come to help you, one last time."

"Why?" asks Steve.

"This day you have earned it; I have been watching you. You are right, you have upset the balance of power. With the new weapon they will make war upon one another, and you are sorry about it."

"Well little good that will do me. Knowing the wars; I will cause with this contamination. I just wish they could forget what they have seen."

"So be it, I will erase the memory of your sword from all the natives, all they will remember is that two giants walked across their world and vanished."

The Entity flashes a brilliant blue light and turns to them both.

"I have purged the sword from their minds, none of the many tribes that have seen it will remember it. And they will continue on their own way of discovery."

"Thank you Entity for doing that. Now we must leave this world before we cause it more harm."

"May I see your map one called Steve?"

"Why? You gave it to me, you should know what it is all about."

"You're wrong about that, one of my ancestors gave you the map."

"Ancestors?" said Samantha.

"Yes, it was an ancestor three generations back who you meet on the Beasts world. Time in my world moves very fast compared to this one, soon my child will be taking over my place as the enforcer."

"Enforcer?" asks Steve.

"Yes, we have several dimensions that we look over and maintain, this is the last one we can get to. We as you would say, try to keep the balance of power. According to the map your portal is just a few days away, but I will take you there now."

A blinding light engulfs them all and when it returns to normal they are in a different place.

"The portal is here. One called Steve."

"How do I open it?"

"That I do not know, but according to my ancestor only you can open it. He said you have the gift. I must return to my world, as I said time moves slower here than on my world, and I must return. Good bye one called Steve and to your mate as well."

The Entity disappears in a flash of white light. Steve and Samantha look around and it is open grass land for miles.

"Steve how are we going to open the portal?"

"I'm not sure Samantha, but stay close. Better yet sit here and hold my hand; if it opens and sucks us in I want you close to me."

Samantha sits down and grabs Steve's hand. Steve sits there and concentrates on opening the portal. He remembers the portals on the beast world where he sent the beast to another place. In hopes it will allow him to trigger this one. Under his breath he mutters

"Open."

Steve pictures the last portal he traveled through and it opens right on top of them and sucks them in. At first there is a light show and when they emerge on the other side they are floating in an ocean of air.

Air World

Chapter 135

There is nothing to stand on, anywhere. They see rocks and not much else. Off in the distance they see a floating, and for a lack of a better word an Island.

"Steve can we port there?"

"I do not think we should try, distances here are deceiving, and all the debris around us. If we tried to port there, we could wind up like Romeo, we could teleport into a bunch rocks and wind up dead."

"Then how are we going to get there?"

"Grab a hold of me so I can take off the back pack."

Samantha reaches down to grab Steve's leg, Steve then takes off the back pack and has Samantha put it on, then he tells her to get on his back and hold on if this works they do not want to be separated. Steve grabs two fist sized rocks, and manages to get turned around so his back is facing the Island. Steve does a wind up much like a baseball pitcher and throws the first rock. As he suspected physics works here too, for every action there is an opposite and equal reaction. Throwing the rock away pushes them towards the direction of the island. It is slow going so to pick up more speed Steve winds up and throws the second rock, and their speed picks up some.

Steve is however surprised that the air resistance does not slow them down, in a way it is like being in space. Only you do not need a special suit, and you can breathe. It seems to take hours of floating toward the Island, Samantha is becoming tired of holding on to Steve, and they do not have water or food. They had left the rest of the Dragon meat at the village.

"Steve I'm getting very tired like I need to let go and sleep."

"Samantha where is your sword?"

"I have it here, do you want it?"

"Yes, give it to me."

Samantha gives Steve the sword and watches as he lengthens the strap of the sheath, then hooks it around Samantha's waist, and then around his.

"Samantha if you fall asleep this should keep us together."

"Thank you honey; (I'm so sleep...)

Samantha let go of Steve and is sound asleep, the strap holds them together, Steve is in no better shape than Samantha, but realizes he needs to stay awake or they may over shoot the Island.

Steve nods off and then wakes himself up, just in time to see the island passing beneath them. He makes sure Samantha is still with him and he ports down on to the island. Then he falls down and falls asleep. A few hours later Samantha wakes up and realizes they made it to the island. She takes off her helmet, then takes Steve's helmet off of him as well; then tries to wake him up.

"What, what's going on?"

"You brought us here to the island."

"Oh, I need to get some more sleep Samantha."

"Before you drop off to sleep release the strap of my sword."

"Oh yea, sure thing." Steve releases the catch and they fall apart.

Samantha Sets up a camp just some little ways into the forest and ports Steve under the cover of her make shift tent. Then Samantha sets out to find food and water, but before she goes, she takes her sword along for protection. The Island is ten miles around, and Samantha finds a pool of water and sees it needs to be treated or at least boiled. She also encounters these ferret like creatures. Samantha wishes she had brought her helmet to see if any of the plants would be safe to eat. She ports back to their camp to see if Steve is awake yet. Appearing Samantha sees Steve asleep and decides to wake him.

"Honey wake up!"

Steve opens his eyes, then sits up and stretches.

"What is going on dear?"

"Nothing for the moment. I have found some water, but it looks like is should be boiled before we use it."

"That could pose a problem without a pan to use."

"I would agree with you, but I found some bamboo like plants over that way, we can use them to make some pans to boil water, and if we can find some kind of plant that could be used as a rope we can carry our stuff better."

"Good Idea, where is this bamboo?"

Samantha leads Steve to the bamboo, and soon finds a couple of stalks that would be useful, and with her sword Samantha cuts them down and Steve ports them back to the camp.

"Where is the pond you spoke of?" asks Steve.

Samantha takes him to the pond, and it is a dirty color, and covered in scum. Steve brings his helmet along and scans the pond and finds no dangerous critters in it. It does not contain any fish either. The bacteria in it may be a problem, but we'll see after we boil it. Steve tells Samantha all that he has learned. And thanks her for all she has done. Samantha is elated by the praise from her husband. He is somewhat lax in doing that, but when he does. Samantha feels elated and knows the praise is real and heartfelt from her husband. Steve ports back to the camping spot and picks up the camping equipment or what little of it there is and ports back to the pond. They make up their camp some little ways in the wooded area on the back side of the pond.

Samantha ports back to the area where she found some plants to use her helmet to see if the plants she found were edible or dangerous. As it turns out they can be eaten, so Samantha gathers up several of them for dinner. After the camp is set up Steve goes exploring and runs around the island. Since his fight with the Beast Steve has not had any chance in doing any of his exercises, and now takes advantage of the time to do so. Then returning to camp he asks Samantha to spar with him, and she gets into it right away. After some time, they both quit, and wash up next to the pond. Samantha feeds him dinner then all tuckered out they both turn in to get some sleep.

On this world it is day light all the time. A sun can be seen off in the distance. With there being no planet the sun always fills the sky with its light and heat. Steve and Samantha are very tired after leaving the last world, and then making their way on to this island. Several hours later Samantha wakes, as if bothered by something, she gets up and looks around, then looks up. Only to be stunned by the view. There are thousands of jelly fish in the sky and their tendrils are hanging down. Samantha quickly puts on her helmet to make sure she is protected. Shaking Steve rigorously she wakes him up.

She hands him his helmet and tells him to put it on. But he stands up staring into the sky at the spectacle before him. With his helmet in his hand he watches, and then he becomes mesmerized by the jelly fish which emits a sound that draws out the ferrets. Samantha watches as the ferrets come to the jelly fish. They are caught then taken up in to the stomach of the jelly fish. Then Samantha realizes that Steve is being drawn to his death and she tackles him and brings him down to the ground. Then Samantha forces the helmet on to Steve's head, stopping the song.

"What happened?" asked Steve.

"I'm not sure, but you were walking into the tentacles of that jelly fish, and I had to tackle you to stop you."

"Thanks, but this does answer one question?"

"What would that be?"

"There is life here in this dimension. I wonder if there is more of the same fish like creatures."

A while later they watch the jelly fish move off into the distance.

"They look a lot like man-o-war jelly fish from our world except these ones fly, and they are giants."

"Did you notice that they seemed to be in a hurry as they moved off in the direction away from the sun?" said Steve.

"Now that you mention it, yes. I wonder what they are moving away from."

Steve sits in the clearing watching the jelly fish disappear into the distance. Just as he is getting up to go catch some ferrets for dinner, a booming sound comes from the direction of the sun, and huge whale flies over the island headed in the direction of the jelly fish. The whales look much like the great blue whales of earth, but the differences are astounding. The body is the same, but the flippers are like wings, and the tail is vertical instead of horizontal like a fan or a vertical tail on a plane. If it were an airplane it would have been a jumbo jet. The noise it makes is like whale song. Then there are hundreds of whales of all sizes all around the island.

Steve calls out to Samantha and she comes out of the wood area.

"What is it Steve?"

"I'm not sure, but they are a lot like the blue whales of our world, and they are beautiful "

"I wonder why they are here. We did not see anything like this when we arrived into this dimension." said Samantha.

"My guess would be they are after the jelly fish. Hey Look! The back fin on that whale is a lot like a sail fish and it seems to billow and flow with the wind."

As they watch the whale like creatures fly by, a small whale drops down to get a better view of Steve and Samantha. It stops some ways off but with one eye it looks at them like it is studying them. Then Samantha cries out and falls to the ground holding her head. The whale then flies off leaving them, as the rest of the pod disappears into the distance.

"Samantha! What is it, Samantha!" shouts Steve.

Steve picks up Samantha and ports back into the trees for protection from the creatures. He gently lays Samantha down in the bed they had in the camp, and is checking her over. Steve can see Samantha is not hurt physically except she will not wake up. Steve stays by her side, hoping she will be Ok. After several hours of rest. Samantha wakes, but is still dazed, but awake.

Samantha calls out to Steve, and he is right there to see to her needs.

"I'm here Samantha, what can I do for you!"

"I'm fine now Steve, but I need more rest, the whale was a female and she poured a lot of information about this world into my mind. I'm having trouble sorting it out so it will make sense, I just need…"

Samantha falls back into a deep sleep. Steve stays by her side and hardly moves more than a few feet away, he wants to make sure he is right there if she wakes again.

It seems to be a while later Samantha awakes and Steve makes sure she can see him. She smiles up at him.

"Samantha can you talk to me yet?"

"I think so, the female whale imparted a lot of information to my mind, mostly in pictures and feelings."

"What can you tell me?" asks Steve.

Chapter 136

"It appears the whale pods are controlled by the females; the females think the males are too stupid to be in charge."

"I have met a few women like that in our world. I see prejudices exist here as well."

"I have seen through her mind all kinds of animals that look a lot like our own aquatic animals except they fly here and swim there. There is still too much to process yet. I'm going back to sleep."

Steve decides to go hunt up some more plants, and to see if he can catch some of the ferrets to cook. Steve takes up Samantha's sword and walks back into the woods where he soon locates the plants, and then he sees, what looks like a nest of ferrets. With the sword in hand Steve ports into the ferret's nest and manages to behead two of them before they all get away. Steve returns to the camp with his catch to clean it and cook it up. Samantha should be hungry after this much time of sleeping. While he was exploring Steve runs onto a vine like plant and so he starts collecting it so he can weave it into a rope.

After cooking the ferrets Steve eats one of them and some of the plants, and then decides to get some sleep himself. So he curls up next to Samantha and falls asleep. When he wakes up Samantha is still asleep. Steve starts to make his rope, then goes hunting again. Now his next item is to figure a way to be able to carry water. Since he has been keeping the ferret skins, he used his knife, to scrape them clean, and dry them in the sun, to cure them as best as he can. Then he stitches them together creating a bag to carry water about a gallon of water. Samantha wakes up and Steve manages to get her to eat the plants and one of the cooked ferrets, before she falls back asleep.

Steve has had a full day again and goes to sleep next to Samantha. Then later he hears a roar from the clearing. Steve springs to his feet, puts on his helmet, and grabs the sword, before going to investigate the noise. He creeps up to the edge of the clearing and peeks out, to see a giant of what looks like a giant turtle with a couple of squid like creatures on his back trying to pierce through its shell. The turtle cannot do anything except die, as it cannot reach its tormentors on his back. Steve ports on to the turtle's back and with the sword cuts off the arms of one of the large Squid creatures. And the body floats off into the sky with no way to direct its flight with its arms cut off. Then Steve turns to the other one and drives the sword into the creature's huge eye killing it.

The turtle realizes that the squid creatures are now gone, Steve jumps off the back of the turtle and the turtle sees Steve. "Why did you help me?"

"It looked like you could use a friend to help you."

"What is a friend? I have never heard of that before."

"On my world, a friend is another person that is willing to help another in time of trouble."

"I'm not sure I understand, but will for now accept that I now have a friend as you say."

"What is your name friend?"

"On this world we do not have names."

"Then how does one approach another? If you have no names."

"We do not approach others unless you want to eat or be eaten."

"Ok, would you mind if I call you turtle, just for the sake of identification or conversation?"

"Sure, and what is your name?"

"Steve, and my mate is called Samantha."

"You have a mate for life?"

"Yes."

"Our mates only last as long as needful to procreate, then we separate until the next time."

"Turtle, I need to ask some help of you."

"What help do you need friend, Steve?"

"I cannot travel as you can here in this world, and I need to get to the next portal, can you take us there?"

"Where is the portal?"

Steve ports to the camp and locates the map then ports back to the turtle to show the turtle the map. Steve orients the map to show where they are and then shows where they must go.

"Friend Steve, I can take you there to that place on your map. I was going there anyway; you are welcome to ride on my back until we get there."

"Thank you turtle, let me gather my things and my mate and we can get started."

Steve only takes a few moments to gather up the water, food, backpack, along with a still sleeping Samantha, and ports onto the back of Turtle. Steve remembers the holes in turtle's back.

"Turtle do the holes hurt you?"

"They do, but what can be done?"

"Wait for several minutes and I'll see what I can do for you." Steve ports to the pond and gathers a basketball sized mud balls before porting to one of the holes to fill it with the mud. It will act as a band aid. On the next hole, which is more on top of the shell, Steve not only applies more mud, he manages to wedge in a crooked stick about two inches in diameter, to give him a place to attach his make-shift rope. This will help keep him and Samantha from sliding off the turtle's back. Steve ties Samantha to his make-shift pad eye on the turtle

447

and he puts on the back pack and sword. The water and food he secures to the pad eye along with Samantha.

"Turtle, we are ready when you are."

"In a moment friend Steve, I'm removing the information the balloon whale imparted to your mate."

"You are not hurting her, are you?"

"No, she will awake with no memory of the transfer. Her mind is in over load, and if it is not reduced. It will keep her like she is."

"Thank you Turtle, for helping her."

"Another strange word please?"

"When you finish with her, you can rummage around in my mind, and find all kinds of things from my world."

"That would be nice friend Steve, to know about other worlds."

Turtle finishes extracting the memories of the whale fish and Samantha is sleeping much better. Turtle pushes away from the island and launches off into the direction that the whale fish and jelly fish went. Steve watches over Samantha. Sometime later Samantha wakes up.

"Steve, where are we?"

"Catching a ride on Turtle's back, we are headed to the portal."

"I'm hungry do we have anything to eat?

"You have a small selection, fresh squid tentacles, or ferret well done."

"Squid will do for something different."

Steve walks over to where the tentacles are still attached to the turtle's shell and using the sword cut off a good sized chunk and hands it to Samantha. She has no trouble eating it.

"This is not bad, is there more, I'm really hungry."

Steve provides her with more of the meat, and gets some for himself. Off in the distance behind them Steve sees other creatures following in Turtle's wake, then Steve puts his helmet on and scans them.

Chapter 137

"Turtle, what creatures are these? Steve shows him a picture in his mind.

Turtle becomes alarmed. "These things you see, eat turtle if they catch us, can you see an island anywhere?"

Steve scans the area around them and finds another island.

"Will this Island do Turtle?"

"Yes where is it?"

Steve shows turtle where he saw the island and turtle veers off in that direction. As turtle increases his speed, Steve and Samantha hold on to the pad eye, and wait.

"What is wrong Steve?"

"Did you not hear Turtle? We have predators coming this way, and he is taking evasive action to get away from them."

"No, I can't hear him."

"I see, this will have to wait and be pondered later; right now hang on. We are making for that island over that way."

Steve points out in the distance, and Samantha has to use her helmet to see it. Then Steve points off in another direction to show where the predators are.

"Steve they look like sharks."

"I thought so too."

"They are headed off toward the direction we were headed in."

"Let's hope they continue that way, and do not find us." Said Steve.

"Friend Steve, one of them is coming our way."

Steve, turns his head and focuses his helmet on the swarm behind them. He sees one of the shark-like creatures break off out of the swarm to head their way.

"Turtle can you make the island before it gets here?"

"No friend Steve, it will be on us before we can get there."

"Turtle keep going, we still may make it."

"I don't think so, but I'll keep going, there is nothing else I can do."

Steve uses his helmet to examine the oncoming shark creature, and true to Turtle's word the shark is passing over them very low. Steve takes the sword and stabs the shark causing it to veer away. The shark does not like the pain it received, and starts circling. It is looking at Steve and Samantha. It has never seen anything like them before. On the third pass Samantha tells Steve that there are others now coming their way. Steve is watching the shark and it has decided to attack. Steve decides to do something stupid, and ports to the top of the shark's head where he then drives the sword clear to the hilt, into the shark's brain. As the shark thrashes about, Steve barely ports back to Turtle before Turtle is too far out of range where he can safely return.

Looking back at the shark as it is just floating there with its life blood leaking out into the air. Soon the swarm that is following attacks the dead shark in a feeding frenzy. This slows them down just enough for Turtle to make it to the island. Once there Steve and Samantha watch as the shark's fly by, but the sharks cannot get at them. According to Turtle the Sharks body would collapse if it were on the ground of an island, and it would die not being able to breathe.

"Well it looks like they are going to wait a while, so I guess we should plan on being here for a time. We should consider restocking our food and water stores. For when we can leave." said Steve.

"Steve what about the squid on Turtles back?"

"Samantha I'm not sure we should eat any more of it, I do not wish to get food poisoning here."

"Friend Steve, would you give me the squid, it will be fine for me?"

"Sure Turtle, I'll do it right now."

Steve and Samantha port back up on Turtle's back and cut loose the tentacles to feed to Turtle. After they have it all off Turtle's back, they return to the ground and start exploring to see what their options are for their food and water supply. This island seems to have a stream that runs off the edge of the island. Steve is tempted to jump off the island's edge to see where the water goes, but thinks better of it with the sharks flying around not far from the island. Samantha tests the water and sees that it does not have to be boiled, before consumption.

Steve locates more of the edible plants and even finds a few different ones. He harvests as much as he can for now, and then harvest some for the trip to the next Island or the portal whichever comes first. Samantha goes to the water, and fills the water bags. Then Steve decides they will need some meat for the trip as well. Steve explores more of the island and finds more of the ferret like creatures. With the sword in hand Steve ports into the middle of the nest and lops off the heads of four of the creatures before they disappear into the brush. Steve picks up the four he killed and ports back to Turtle and their camp.

"Friend Steve that is twice now that you saved my life. I like this thing call friendship."

"Turtle, I will call us even; if you just get me and Samantha to the portal so we can move on to the next world."

"Your mate is called Samantha"?

"Yes, Turtle can you not talk to her as you do me?"

"I cannot hear her friend Steve. Is she a female or a male?"

"Samantha is a female; why should that make a difference?"

"It does, but I do not know why. Now I was able to remove the information the female whale fish gave her, but since I removed the information I have not been able to listen to her."

"Ok. I just thought I would ask, it must be a gender specific occurrence here on this world."

"Whatever that is." said Turtle.

"Never mind Turtle, it is not important at this time. Speaking of time how long will it take you to get us to the portal?"

"What is time?" asks Turtle.

"I'm not sure I could explain it to you, since you do not have a planet of rotation."

"If I read you right, time is like when a female is ready to mate and she meets at the proper place."

"I guess that will do as good as any, Turtle. I guess I better get back to Samantha or she will become cross that I'm not with her."

"Is it her time to mate friend Steve? Some of the females I have mated with were cross after the mating, not during."

"Let's let that idea drop Turtle."

"If you say so friend Steve."

Steve returns to Samantha to help clean and cook the ferrets and Steve shows her how he made the water bags from the other ferrets he had caught on the other island. The sharks did not leave for what seemed like a long time, but during that time Steve and Samantha stockpiled food, and had slept several times. Then one morning Turtle tells Steve they should leave at that time. The sharks have left, and Turtle is getting hungry, and will need food soon. Steve and Samantha gather up the food they have collected and secured it to Turtles back at the pad eye that Steve had placed in the wound in Turtle's back. The wound has grown over and the pad eye is now very secure. The shell of Turtle has grown back together embedding the stick in Turtle's shell. With everyone on board, Turtle turns around to the edge of the island and pushes off into the empty air. Turtle spreads his wings and starts to make head way in the direction they were originally headed for.

Under way Steve and Samantha are having a discussion, about the information the whale fish gave her to see if any of it was still with her. But Samantha cannot remember anything.

As they are talking Samantha looks up and screams. It is three of the squids that attacked Turtle before. Steve gets Samantha to her feet and then draws the sword to fight them off.

Then Turtle tells Steve to have them sit down and hold on. Turtle knew that these creatures were there, and much like our modern day fighter jet Turtle fly's circles around the squids. Then he catches one in his mouth and still flying he manages to swallows it down. Finally off to the next one; which he catches in his mouth, and swallow it down. Then Turtle allows the last one to land on his back, and tells Steve to kill it before it can harm him. Steve takes the sword and chops up the Squid keeping some of the tentacles and then pushes the body off into the void where Turtle swings around to eat the rest of the squid.

On the way to the portal Steve talks to Samantha, and considers that they need to take turns sleeping and keeping watch. Samantha readily agrees to the idea. As it turns out, nothing happens until they reach the portal area. The air is packed with all kinds of flying creatures from the size of Steve's hand all the way to the balloon whales. The squid dart here and there, the sharks are feeding on the other fliers, and the whale fish and other turtles are feeding on the jelly fish and other small flying fish. They had creatures that looked like they came from the Great Barrier Reef, all the colors, shapes and sizes. From the deadly to the harmless.

"We are here friend Steve, if you know where the portal is you best open it and get out of here."

"Thanks Turtle, I'm going to miss you!"

"I will miss you friend Steve and your mate Samantha."

"I'll tell her later, for you."

Steve sits down and concentrates on the portal; it opens then sucks them through leaving Turtle behind, but one of the sharks manages to make it through with them.

The shark does not last long, as it is crushed by the air of this new world, it cannot fly here on this world and it soon dies.

The Maze

Chapter 138

The portal deposits Steve and Samantha on a hill top overlooking a structure so huge they cannot see the far side of it. Steve is trying to make sense of it. All around them is a dead world, all anyone can see is death and destruction. There is nothing alive here. It is like being on the moon. Everything is dead, no plants and skeletons everywhere of all kinds of creatures and people. It's like a war was fought here. The ground is nothing but dust nothing will ever grow here again.

Samantha states, "It's a maze, a giant maze."

Steve is stunned by the size of it. "Samantha you are right, it is a maze and from the look of it, it will take a life time just to travel through it."

Steve is looking at the walls of the maze; they are three stories high to the top. Steve turns to say something to Samantha, when he is frozen in place. Beside him is a figure twice his size. The figure addresses himself to Samantha.

"I was told you would come, and I made ready for you."

"Who are you and what have you done to my husband!?" Said Samantha.

"Your mate is now my property. If you get past the maze, you can win your mate back. I am the master of this world or if you like… god. I'm going to return to the other end of the maze to wait for you to die, then I will keep my prize."

"So all I have to do is get past your maze?"

"Laughing, yes, all you have to do is get past the maze to the other end."

The creature points to Steve and they both disappear. Steve is put into a glass cage and set free of his paralysis. The creature waves his hand and something like a giant screen appears, and shows them where Samantha is. Samantha has sat down in her pose of meditation.

"So your mate is so confused, that she cannot fathom the task."

Steve says nothing, and then decides to act stupid. To see if he can get more information. Steve figures the more he studies the creature the more he can learn. He can't quite put a finger on it, but there seems to be something he should know. Steve taps into the communication devise in his helmet to Samantha and makes a cryptic statement.

"My mate is not confused; she is preparing to enter into the maze. My mate will rise to the occasion."

"Are you talking to your mate? I sense that you are sending a transmission of some kind."

"Yes, my mate is telling me to stay put and not to wander off, I might get lost."

"What, but you're the one I wanted in the maze, not the knowledgeable one, the odds have changed. I must readjust the maze to stop her."

"How do you readjust the maze?"

"Never mind, you would not understand, this system is too complex for you. Now go over there and sit down like your mate told you too, the creature waves his hand and Steve's cage disappears. I have to rethink this change. How could I have miscalculated, my computations are always flawless."

Samantha gets up and ports back up to the hill top where she can see the top of the wall and ports on to it. She looks over to the next wall top and ports to it, from time to time she even looks down to see what lays in the maze. She sees many different creatures, as she passes from wall to wall. Samantha sees creatures from myth, and from real life. As she moves along the wall she hears a tapping sound in here helmet, and after a time she realizes it is Steve using Morse code. Samantha sets her helmet to translate it for her.

"Stay on the top of the wall, and do not respond, the creature can pick up the transmissions."

Samantha keeps porting from one wall to another and manages to penetrate the maze ten miles deep, as the crow flies.

"Where is She, where is your mate? I lost her. She has disappeared from my screen."

The creature turns to Steve, and Steve is just sitting there rocking back and forth taping on his helmet which is sitting between his knees. The creature looks at Steve for several minutes.

"You are a pathetic creature; you would not have lasted in the maze to the first turn."

Steve stops and looks up, "how wide is your maze?"

Distracted, looking for the other person he lost in the maze, he actually answers Steve, "two hundred units across."

Steve taps out what the creature said into his helmet, so Samantha would know how far she would be traveling. At about twenty miles in, the creature figures out how his target is traveling, and starts to have the automations within look up at the top of the wall to see if they can spot the target.

"Steve taps out that the creature has figured out what you are doing, so be careful."

Samantha continues to travel from one wall to another. On the next port, Samantha finds that the wall is a hologram and she falls through it to the ground below. She lands on her back and is stunned. Thanks to the force fields in her suit she does not suffer any serious injury. Samantha does not know how long she was laying there, but when she opens her eyes, what looks like two children in rags are staring down at her. Samantha opens her helmet, "Who are you?"

The two children take off running down along the maze wall. Samantha follows them, she could have easily caught them, but thought it better to just follow, and they may lead me somewhere.

Back at the end of the maze, Steve boasts that he can make to the front of the maze from here. The creature is beside himself and concerned that the other creature Steve's mate would get through the maze. The creature tells Steve he is welcome to try. Steve puts on his helmet and runs into the maze and after a couple of turns. He ports back to the beginning of the maze, then up on to the top of the wall to try and locate Samantha.

The creature is almost jumping for glee that he got rid of the critter that is so stupid. Until he starts looking for him in the maze, and can't find him either. The creature throws a tirade just like any human. Now it appears to be in a rage. Now he is going to go into the maze to kill them both for cheating his maze.

Samantha keeps up with the children until they turn the corner and start screaming. Samantha runs faster and the children are being confronted by a fire breathing dragon. Samantha leaps in front of them to draw the dragon's attention. As it is readies to spew fire Samantha ports up to the side of its neck and with the sword and slashes it. The sword passes through its neck and the dragon's flame comes forth and nothing happens.

"What is going on here?" thinks Samantha.

She turns to look at the children and they are cowering at the corner of the wall.

Samantha walks over to them and reached down thinking they are not real either when she finds out that they are solid.

"Who are you?"

One of the children spoke up, "we are called the wee ones."

"Where do you live, or stay?"

The other child beckons to her to follow them, and Samantha does; but she is not sure she should trust them. Samantha follows along not saying a word.

Then she puts her helmet back on and scans them. They are real seeming children there seems to be something different about them. Soon they come to a place in the wall and one of the children pushes against a rock and a portion of the wall opens like a door; they all enter into an underground room.

In the far corner Samantha finds more children. A few in the teenage age group.

"Where are your parents?"

No one answers, they are too scared. Samantha Takes off her helmet and puts her sword to one side. Then tries to sooth the children enough to see if she can get some answers to her questions. The children realize she is not going to hurt them and they relax and listen to her.

"Where are your parents?"

"They are gone. The master took them."

"Oh yes, I have met the master. So tell me how are you managing to stay alive here, where is your food and water?

One of the older children leads Samantha to another store room further underground, where they have water, and some food, not enough to sustain them for long.

"I wish Steve were here he might have a way to help with this."

Steve is following Samantha's path across the top of the wall of the maze, as he moves from one wall to another following the electronic map Samantha's helmet made. Steve can follow Samantha to the point where she disappears. It takes several hours, but Steve finds the spot where Samantha's helmet made a last recording of her. Now as Steve goes from one wall to another he looks down into the areas of the maze and sees all kinds of creatures, most are holographs, some are mechanical. Only a few are actually living. One of the tiger like creatures tries to follow Steve, but soon it loses him as Steve ports from one wall to the next. The creature cannot keep up due to the long distances in the internal maze its self. Steve ports to the next wall and falls to the ground much like Samantha had done. Again the force fields in his suit protect him from serious injury. Steve like Samantha has the wind knocked out of him.

Chapter 139

When Steve comes to he is staring into the eyes of a Griffin with his sharp beak poised to bite him. Steve can see that it is a hologram over laid on a machine, which makes it dangerous. Steve ports behind the machine and stands up. The machine is going wild as it does not detect its target. Steve watches the machine as it looks around, and it finally sees Steve. It tries to attack him again. Steve ports behind the machine then up on to its back. Using his helmet to see through the hologram Steve finds the control panel and turns it off. The machine stops in its tracks. It also turns off the holo-projector. Steve takes a few minutes to investigate the machine, and would have gotten caught up in it, but Samantha comes to mind.

Steve uses his helmet to try to locate Samantha, and soon finds the spot where the signal is coming from. He does not see Samantha, or her helmet. Steve ponders for a few minutes about this dilemma then tries opening a window in layers, after eight feet he finds a room, and he sees Samantha's helmet on the floor. Steve jumps through the window and is taken by surprise, by Samantha herself as she kicks him in the stomach.

"Whoa, I'm on your side, Samantha!"

"Steve! How did you get here?"

"Well the so called god here is nothing more than a hologram run by a very powerful computer. I was able to trick it in to thinking that I was an idiot. So he did not watch me so close. Then when I got the chance I ran into the maze from the finish end of the maze back toward you. When I was out of sight I ported to the beginning of the maze, and used your helmet tracer to search for you. Did you trip over the holographic wall?"

"I did, and I found something alive."

"I found something alive as well and it is dangerous. It is a tiger like creature and it tried to follow me."

'I found this", and Samantha takes Steve to another room with several children.

At first the children are scared and try to get away. Samantha calms them down and tells them "it's ok, he is my husband."

They soon calm down and Steve takes his helmet off, to show them he is not one of the creatures from the maze. When the children are calm, Steve tries to get some answers about the maze. One of the older children says that maybe he can help. So he leads Samantha and Steve down several corridors and into a room that has not been opened in years. One wall is lined with books. On the desk sits an ancient looking computer, and next to it is a stack of what looked like flat crystals. Steve sits in the chair and faces the screen. After a few tries he finds the power button, and turns on the computer. The screen comes up blank. The older boy then takes one of the flat crystals and puts it on top of the computer in a tray. The screen lights up and starts playing log records.

Steve watches all the crystal disks and realizes why the maze was built, it is like an ark with plants and animals. The people built this so they could survive the war. Somehow the master computer (Artificially intelligent) which is suppose too run the place, got corrupted and now it uses the maze to entertain its own mind. It is located at the center of this maze. Steve is not sure if he should turn it off or leave it on. If he turns it off all the life in the maze might die, if he leaves it on they may all die anyway, at the whim of a computer. Samantha comes into the room and sees Steve sitting there brooding and she walks up to him and puts her arms around him.

"I know that look Steve, what is wrong?"

"I'm going to have to make a decision, and I'm not sure if it is the right one."

"Can you tell me?"

"Yes, it will have to be a decision we may both have to share."

Steve tells Samantha all the history of the maze, what it is for, and how the computer is corrupted. Now we have to decide what we must do. Kill the computer, or let it live on.

"You can't be serious Steve. How can we let it keep doing what it is doing?"

"Maybe I did not explain it right, if I shut down or kill the computer the maze dies with it, everything, plants, animals and the children. So what do you want me to do?"

"I don't know Steve, but the man I know and love will find a way. I believe in you. If anyone can save the children or what is in the maze you can."

"Samantha, you sure know how to serve up a tall order. I hope I'm enough; because I do not see a way to do this. All I can do is the best I can."

Samantha squeezes his hand and kisses him.

"In my heart I know you won't let them down." Says Samantha

Steve gets up and embraces Samantha.

"I pray that you are right."

Steve walks over to the books and starts looking them over to see if he can find what he needs to help this world. As he looks through the books he finds one on a great war and discovers the reason for the devastation outside of the maze walls. Looking further he finds a map of the world and it shows the Maze on the Island Continent much like Australia. Steve decides with the map he may open windows into other areas to see what life is like in other places on the planet.

Chapter 140

Steve puts on his helmet and Instructs Samantha and the children not to enter the room in case he finds some sickness he would not like to share.

Steve spends days searching one continent after another. Due to radiation, biologics, and mutant animals Steve can find no place for the children to live, other than where they are. Then Steve turns his window search within the maze, and he does not find any other people within the maze.

"Samantha the only thing we can do is take the children with us to the next world, and hope."

"Ok, Steve, then we take the children with us."

"I need to get some sleep Samantha, the portal to the next world is in the middle of the maze, I discovered it while I was looking for other people."

"How can we get there?"

"I can get us there that I'm not concerned about. What concerns me is what is waiting for us there? The master computer is there and it is quite insane."

"Where you lead you know I will follow."

"Get the children and see if they have any way to carry food, and water. In the next world we go to we do not know, what we will find."

Steve moves over to a corner on the floor and drops off to sleep for a few hours, and when he wakes.

Steve uses his windows to look over the area at the center of the maze and he picks out a place to land for when he ports there. Steve is wondering if he can re-program the computer to do what it is intended for or he will destroy it only if it becomes necessary.

"Steve I know that look, what are you going to go do?"

"Samantha I either have to fix the computer or destroy it. This maze is the last place on this world that is still alive, and the computer is keeping it that way, but on the other hand it is killing all life on it and replacing them with holograms and mechanical devices. When we leave this world for the next we'll take the children with us."

"Will they be OK in the new world?"

"I do not know Samantha, what I do know is they will die if they stay here."

Samantha becomes very concerned about the children.

"Steve what are you going to do now?"

"The portal is in the center of the maze, where the computer is, I will go there alone and do what I must to get access to the portal."

"Alone, but you may need me."

"Yes, I probably will need you, but this time the children will need you more. So you must stay here and get them ready for when I return."

Steve picks his place to land in the center of the maze, and puts on his helmet. He turns to Samantha and hugs her then tells her he loves her. Steve opens a window and steps through to the center of the maze.

"Well maze master I'm here, come out here and show yourself."

In an explosion of light and noise the Holo-creature appears.

"WHAT are you doing here? You should be at the end of the maze where you ran in, how did you get here?"

"I guess you might say it's one of life's little secrets."

"It should have taken you months to reach here, and what about your mate; who you are so concerned with?"

As Steve keeps the Holo-Creature talking, he is using his windows to search the ground to see where the central computer is located.

"My mate is safe, and so are the children we found. They are all in a safe place."

"No place is safe in my maze unless I make it so."

"Or unless I make it so, Good! There you are."

Steve jumps through the window into the room with a very large computer. Steve approaches the computer very slowly looking for fail safes. Steve does not encounter any and so reaches the control panel. He looks for a way to reboot the system. When the holo-Creature appears, and starts to make threats. Steve ignores the hologram and continues to search, and suddenly the computer turns into a hideous monster ready to attack.

"Really is that the best you can do! You are not even real; I can see right through your projection"

Steve finds and then hits the off button and powers down the computer.

"Samantha, do you hear me?"

"Yes Steve, is everything alright, there is no power here and the children are frightened."

"Give me a moment, and it will be back on."

Steve turns the power back on and the system is asking for a password. I guess that is it then, I do not know the password. Well Maze Master No one will ever see you again after this."

Steve teleports back to the library where Samantha and the children are.

Steve raises his voice and calls out "Samantha, are you and the children ready to leave?"

Samantha rushes into the room and almost leaps into Steve's arms.

"I'm so glad to see you."

"Samantha what is wrong?"

"Steve it is the children."

"What is it Samantha, what is wrong?"

"When you killed the power they stopped. I'm not sure but I think they are androids, used to maintain the maze here. Come and see them."

Steve follows Samantha into another room and all the children lay on the floor, Steve begins to probe them and finds that they are androids.

"They sure fooled me." Said Steve.

"You were not alone." speaks Samantha. "I think it is time we should leave here. As you said this world is dead."

Steve takes Samantha's hand and ports to the center of the maze.

"This is where the map indicates that the portal should be located."

"Should we see what supplies are here before we depart, a good rope would be nice in case we need it?" said Samantha.

"Not a bad idea." Steve ports them in to the computer room and they start checking the other rooms for likely things to be used.

Samantha finds a kitchen and takes a pot and some spoons and as luck would have it some metal plates. Steve finds a tool room and picks up some rope, and a few tools in a small bag. They both return to the computer room. Then Steve ports them back to the surface. Steve takes the rope he has and ties a length of it to Samantha and to himself, so if they run into a world like the air world they will stay together. Steve takes Samantha's hand and concentrates on opening the portal. The portal opens and Steve and Samantha fall through into the next world. They both land hard onto a grassy noel and it knocks the wind out of them.

Medieval

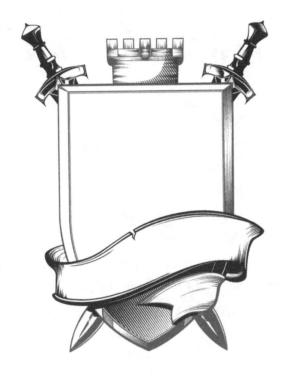

Chapter 141

"Steve are you Ok? Samantha shakes Steve again, Steve are you Ok?"

Then Samantha hears what sounds like thunder. She stands up to see what it may be and also unties the rope in case she has to fight. From out of the trees comes an army of knights in full armor riding on war horses. As they pass one of them reaches down and scoops up Samantha, and tramples Steve as he passes. Another knight rides over Steve as well. Samantha tries to fight off the man who grabbed her but his armor protects him from her blows and he pins her in such a way she cannot reach her sword. Samantha tries to port out of the knight's arms and finds she cannot do so. She is mad and scared all at the same time, as her fear is for her husband Steve. And now he has been trampled by the horses; he may be hurt.

Several hours pass, and Steve wakes up, sore and bruised 'What happened he thinks?'

Steve calls out to Samantha, and he gets no response. He looks to the tracking system in his helmet and sees she is a long way off, Steve stumbles to his feet. His ribs hurt, but they are not broken. From the trees near where Steve is standing someone is watching him. Steve knows that someone is there as he is scanning for Samantha he spots another person. So he takes off his helmet to face them then asks them to come out of hiding. They try to run away, but Steve ports in front to him and he catches him easily. The young boy struggles to get away.

"Hold on, hold on I'm not going to hurt you. I just want to ask a few questions."
The boy quits struggling. "You are not a demon?"

"No I'm not a demon, I'm from a different world, but I'm no demon. I will not hurt you."

"But, I saw you and the other demon appear out of nowhere."

"Other demon? Samantha. That was my wife. What happened, can you tell me?"

"I saw you two appear. She was trying to wake you, when the king's knights appeared. One of them caught your wife and rode off towards the castle. I thought you might be dead, as they trampled over you a few times."

"That explains why I'm so sore and stiff. At least my force field works very well, or they would have crushed my chest. So, boy what is your name?"

"Smithy."

"Well Smithy, I'm called Steve; is there some place I can stay for a few days until I heal up?"

"We can go to my family home, and ask my father if you can use the barn."

"That will do nicely. Please lead the way."

After walking down the country lane Steve is hurting, and he asks Smithy how far away is his home?

"Would you mind if we traveled a bite faster than this?"

"Oh you want to run?"

"Ah, no, I have a faster way to travel, here take my hand."

Smithy is a little Leery about taking Steve's hand. He is still not sure Steve is not a demon, but curiosity over comes his fear and he takes Steve's hand. Steve ports them down the road a way. And after each port Steve asks Smithy which direction to go. At first Smithy is scared then he sees he is not being hurt in any way and he comes to enjoy it. In a short time, they come close to Smithy's home, and Steve stops porting and cautions Smithy not to say anything about how Steve came there and how he brought him home. Smithy agrees with him.

Smithy introduces Steve to his father and Steve realizes how Smithy got his name. His father just happens to be a blacksmith. After a few explanations the father allows Steve to stay in the barn. Steve settles in and decides to go watch how the blacksmith does his work and what materials he is using.

"I see you use iron for your tools and weapons, is that true?" asked Steve

"What else would you use?"

"Have you ever heard of steel?"

"What is this steel you speak of, is it a magical thing?"

"No, no magic. Just science. Although it may seem to be like magic, until you learn of it. Here look at this knife."

Steve pulls the knife out of his boot and hands it to the blacksmith. The blacksmith turns the knife over and over, and he cuts some leather hide and it slices it without any trouble.

"What magic is this? My knives are the best in the district, and they cannot cut this well. May I keep this for your room and board?"

"No I may need it. How about if I teach you how to make steel, will that make up for not having any money to pay you?'

"Steve if you can teach me how to make this steel and work with it. It will be worth more than any King's ransom."

Steve looks around the smithy and realizes he will have to make some modifications to his equipment and he will need some coal, and other materials.

"I'll teach you how to make steel. I will need to modify some of your equipment so we can make your fire hotter, and your son will become very useful in the process."

The blacksmith wants very much to be able to make steel, so he agrees, and goes along with what Steve wants to do to his shop. In the meantime, Steve leaves to go see if he can find Samantha using his helmet scanner. Steve finds that Samantha is within miles of this place. Steve sets out to locate her. Steve ports back to the lane where he and Smithy last stopped before walking to Smithy's home. Steve does a series of short ports and soon spies a castle.

Steve returns to the barn, and uses his helmet to remember the formula for making steel. Steve decides to make a two edged sword and make in the same way Samantha's Japanese sword is made. Where he will fold the metal two hundred times and have the heat treat the sword. The next morning Steve checks inventory to see if the smithy has any meteoric type rocks, and finds that he has collected several of them, and the smithy asks "why use them?"

"They have been under high heat and will be purer and have fewer impurities."

"If you say so this is new to me so I will follow your lead on this." Said the Blacksmith.

After Steve rebuilds the forge, adding a bellows and encloses the forge in brick to keep it hot this amazes the smithy.

"I never thought of this, this will make work easier in the future."

"What can you tell me about the castle? I mean who is in charge?" asks Steve.

"That is not a good place to go. It once was, but when the King's brother took over it has become a place of suffering. His taxes are hard on the people. He takes what he wants and does not pay. And his knights have no honor or shame."

"Did the King die?"

"No, his brother has him locked away in the dungeon. If the people rise up in revolt, the King will be killed."

"It seems, I have more to save than just my wife."

"You're Wife?"

"Yes, when I get time I will tell you more about it. I will need to make that sword so I can storm the castle."

"You storm the castle."

"Probably better than you can know. Any ways let's make that sword. Be ready blacksmith it will take all day and most of the night to make it."

Steve puts the iron and the coke into the crucible after crushing it. He has Smithy on the bellows and his father helping with the crucible. With all the ingredients in it they heat it, they heat it up to a molten state, and then pour it into a square mold to make an ingot. As the ingot cools, Steve welds a metal rod to the end of the ingot so they can handle it.

"What did you just do friend Steve."

"The process is called welding, it will allow you to handle the hot steel as we fold it, and we will need to fold it two hundred times to make it into the sword I want."

Steve puts the steel back into the furnace and goes about folding the steel. He draws it out with a hammer then folds it; then back into the forge to heat it up and pound it out again. Steve repeats the process two hundred times before he draws it out into the shape of a blade. Steve forges his sword to its proper shape and size.

Chapter 142

In the meantime, we need to go back to when Samantha was captured. The knights have just come from a raid and they have captured several women, but the knight who did not have one decides to pick up Samantha. At the time Samantha is in her battle suit with her helmet on. She also has her sword strapped to her back. After the knight picks her up, he realizes this is a woman and she is wearing some kind of armor. Now Samantha tries to port back to Steve, but she cannot do it. Samantha struggles in the Knight's arms to try to get him to let her go, but he has pinned her arms and so for now all she can do is flail about in anger.

Soon the knights cross the mote over a bridge, and into the castle. When the knights ride up in to the stable Samantha is thrown to the ground, then she springs up and pulls her sword, ready for battle. The knight who grabbed her springs off his horse and pulls his massive sword.

"Ho Damsel, you wish to fight do you? You are about to face Tobin the Terrible."

"I think you are Tobin the idiot!" said Samantha.

Tobin takes a halfhearted swing at Samantha, and became very shocked when she stops it and deflects it away. Tobin sees that this lass may be more than he bargained for, and so with greater force and cunning he approaches Samantha again. This time Samantha nicks Tobin's hand then his face. The other knights start laughing at Tobin, causing him to become enraged. Again Samantha dances out of the way and adds more marks to Tobin hand. Again

Samantha tries to teleport back to where Steve is, but she cannot do it. "What is stopping me?" She thinks.

Samantha stands her ground, and dances away from Tobin, and using the flat of her blade she whacks him on the back of the head and knocks him out. Then the rest of Tobin's knights draw swords and approach Samantha in a circle. Then Samantha decides to lay down her sword. They grab her and take her to a tower room and lock her away. In the tower room Samantha changes out of her battle suit into her other clothes and packs them away into the back pack. "Steve where are you?" she thinks. A little later Samantha hears the door open and she sets herself to fight, when this young woman enters the room carrying a dress.

"Lord Tobin insists that you put on this dress."

"You may tell Tobin I said NO!"

The maiden drops the dress and beats a hasty retreat, at Samantha's tone. Then minutes later she hears Tobin bellowing, then crashing through the door.

"You will put on this dress, and you will come and dine with as the spoils of war."

"I'm not as you say a 'spoil of war,' and I'm not putting on that dress. I will not submit to you in any way!"

Furious Tobin charges Samantha with the intent of proving to her she will submit to him. Tobin finds himself propelled into a wall face first breaking his nose, Stunned and groggy Tobin gets slowly to his feet. Seeing his blood on the floor he becomes enraged and charges at Samantha again. Samantha trips Tobin just as his knights enter the door of the tower and sees Samantha on top of Tobin who is face down on the floor. Samantha has his arm behind him and is threating to break it.

The knights decide to help Tobin when Samantha whispers to Tobin,

"I will break your arm if they so much as come in any further."

"Stop men, and stand down."

The men stop, and back out of the tower. Samantha lets Tobin go and stands back from him to let him get up.

"Now get out of here, and if I see you again, I will kill you."

"You are a witch, and we will burn you at the stake for this woman."

"Only if you are brave enough to enter this room, because instead of hurting you, I will kill you with my bare hands. One thing else, if you hurt me, my husband will come for you."

"Your husband is a dead man already, I trampled him with my horse."

"You do not know him, as I do, he will come for me or avenge me. Now get out."

The men close and bar the door.

"I will have you!" screams Tobin.

"Steve where are you, I need you!" thinks Samantha.

Steve takes his new forged sword and tries to make a handle so it will balance the sword.

"Friend Steve would you permit me to do that for you, I do know how to build a good sword and this will be a major triumph for me if you would not mind."

"Ok, my friend, I have something I must go do anyway. Is there any clothing I may borrow so I can look like any local person? I'm afraid my battle suit needs to be cleaned out and it would make me stand out at the castle."

"Sure, you can fit into some of Smithy's clothes, but be careful at the castle. King Rex's brother Jacob is mean, and his knights are mean too. Try to stay clear of them."

"I will heed your advice, my friend."

Steve finds Smithy to borrow some of his clothes. Steve gets ready to port to the castle mote on the far side, so he will not be seen. As Steve gets ready to port, Smithy asks

"May I go along?"

"Not this time, I need to look into some trouble there and I may need to leave in a hurry. Oh, do you have a bag I can use? I need to bring my helmet, and I would like to keep it hidden."

Smithy, gives him a cloth sack they have for carrying stuff to market, and Steve puts his helmet into the sack then slings it over his shoulder. Steve ports to the woods on the backside of the castle, and then walks around to the bridge to go over the mote. As Steve crosses the bridge one of the guards stops him.

"What are you doing here peasant!"

Steve keeps his head down.

"I am a traveler and I was hoping to buy or earn some provisions for my journey."

The guards laugh, and shove Steve about then let him pass. Inside the castle Steve just walks around trying to hear information. He hears about King Rex down in the dungeon and about the strange woman who maybe a witch up in the tower. Steve looks up at the tower, and the window has bars on it so no going up that way. Then Samantha looks down and thinks she sees Steve, and then becomes sure when he looks up at her. She sees the bag he is carrying and runs to her helmet, and Steve sends her a message. "I will get you out tomorrow." Then he sends a second message telling her he needs to save King Rex. Samantha, messages back to Steve she got the message. Steve progresses into the castle through the kitchen, and then down into the underground dungeons. He is on the hunt for the king. It takes a while for Steve to locate where they are holding him. He can tell where the King is by the number of guards posted at the door. Steve retraces his steps back to the kitchen, and puts some food on a plate and returns back to where the king is, and he boldly walks up to the door and the guards stop him.

"What do you have, there peasant?"

"Some food for the king, what else."

"You are a bit early aren't you?"

"I'm new, and the person in charge told me to bring it down here."

The guard opens the door and ushers Steve in to the room.

"Hurry it up!" the guard said.

Steve sets down the food, and goes to the king who is lying on the floor in the corner.

"Your majesty, are you OK?"

King Rex rouses himself.

"Huh, who are you? Have you come to kill me?"

"No, I will be back to get you later so be ready."

The King grabs Steve by the arm.

"Help me, they are going to kill me tomorrow."

"Sire, I will be back in a few hours, you have my word."

Then the king pulls Steve close to him and looks him in the eyes.

"I believe you. You have the look of a man who says what he means."

Chapter 143

Steve goes to the door and knocks, and it is pulled open. Steve is pulled out of the room, and roughly shoved up the steps. Halfway up the stairs he hears someone coming down so Steve ports back to the Blacksmith's barn. He changes into his battle suit and walks into the forge area.

"Friend have you finished my sword?"

The Blacksmith stands there with the sword in his hand and twirls it.

"The balance is perfect, and it is the finest blade I have ever seen. Steve you have more than paid me back for anything you have taken since being here."

"I'm glad you like it; you would have figured it out sooner or later. It was just a matter of time. I'm off to get the King. May I bring him here?"

"You are going to bring King Rex here?"

"Yes, and I will also get my wife this very night. So, I will need you to protect him when he is here."

"On my life, I will!"

Steve is getting ready to leave when Smithy comes into the forge.

"I'm going with you Steve."

Steve pulls out his dart gun and shoots Smithy in the arm and he falls asleep.

"What did you do to my son?"

"I put him to sleep, he'll wake up in four hours, and he will be fine I assure you."

The blacksmith turns his son over, and sees he is just sleeping.

"Can you show me how to build that weapon?"

"Your world is not ready for this weapon yet, so let's leave that one alone for now."

Steve steps outside and ports to the dungeon where the King is.

"Your majesty, are you ready to leave?"

The King just sits there staring in fear, not at Paladin but who is behind him. Paladin turns and sees the Kings brother, and two other knights.

"Who might you be demon?" Says Jacob.

"I'm called Paladin, and to you I am a demon, and I'll be back to make things right."

"How demon, you will not get past my two knights."

"Is that all you have to stop me? Hold that thought."

Paladin grabs the king and ports to the blacksmith's barn.

"Stay here your majesty I'll be back, these people here will protect you."

Steve ports back to the dungeon where the King was being held, to see the two knights and the fake king leaving the dungeon.

"Going so soon, I came back to see how good your knights really are."

"Hey ladies are you ready to dance? Now you can test yourself against a real man and not some helpless woman."

The two knights turn around and charge Paladin swinging their swords. Thanks to the long hours of practice with Samantha, Steve had learned to use a sword. He deflects the swords easily sending one man to the back of the cell. Then Steve fences with the other knight and in one of his swings Paladin breaks the knight's sword. Using the flat of his blade he backhands the knight's head sending him crashing to the floor out cold. Then he turns to the other knight. As he faces the knight and the fake King, the knight runs out the door, slams it, and bars it.

"Really?" Thinks Paladin.

Paladin ports up to the stairs in the tower. After a short scuffle Paladin opens the door only to have his arms filled by his wife. She is glad to see him and angry too, for leaving her there and not taking her out of there faster.

"Whoa, I missed you too my Samantha."

"If you ever leave me like that again, I will bust every bone in you…."

Steve stops her with a kiss, then hears several people running up the stairs in their direction.

"As much as I would like to stay and play with our playmates I think it is time to go."

Steve grabs the backpack and asks Samantha where her sword is. She tells him of Tobin, and how he took it. Just as Tobin enters the door way, Paladin wave's bye, and ports away to the blacksmith's barn.

Steve takes off his helmet, and asks how the King is holding up?

"He is still asleep; how long will he stay that way?"

"It will depend on how tired he is. Let me look him over now."

Steve turns the King over and sees he faking being asleep.

"You're Majesty, please get up. We have a lot to talk about, and truly you are safe here."

The King gets up and looks around them.

"May I have some food and drink?"

The blacksmith, Smiles and says "Sire, whatever you need just ask me."

The blacksmith leaves to get some food and a drink called mead, and returns quickly with it.

"Here Sire, sit here and eat."

The King takes a big bite out of the beef joint set before him, and after a few minutes he starts to feel restored.

"What did you want to talk about my demon friend?"

"Well first off, I'm not a demon, just a man much like you"

Steve takes off his helmet, and gloves. "See just like you."

"Why did you save me?"

"The blacksmith told me you were a good king, be one again."

"Sure, I'm just out of a dungeon, here in a barn, and I'm going to get my Kingdom back?" the King laughs.

"So why can't you get your kingdom back? Who is going to stop you?"

"My brother, and his knights."

"If I take care of the knights, will that allow you to take back your kingdom?"

"It would!"

"Then I'll deal with them tomorrow. Especially Tobin the terrible"

Steve takes Samantha by the hand, and leads her out of the barn into the darkness.

Steve asks, "Why could you not teleport out of the castle?"

"I don't know, but I remember your story about being in the Wind River Region back home, and you could not port out either. Whatever kept you from porting is doing the same thing here."

"You may be right, but I can still port in to and out of the castle. Wait I remember now, the instructor removed and replaced my crystal. It may be a stronger crystal than what I had before. She said she was from the future; she could have known that I would need a stronger one."

"Steve, be careful. The knights are worse than thugs of our world. They will cheat and betray anyone."

"Actually Samantha I'm counting on it. Bullies when separated will become cowards. So tell me how many knights they have."

"Fifteen and each one has a contingent of men about twenty or so."

"I'll try the snake scenario then."

Confused, "snake scenario?" asked Samantha.

"I remove the head and the rest of the snake dies, in this case I get rid of the knights, and the armies don't know what to do."

"Samantha it is a very nice night out, how about we go somewhere and cuddle up. It has been a while since we have had any quiet time together."

"I was hoping you would say that Steve."

The next morning Steve talks to the King about another King, King Arthur and the Knights of the Round Table and all it meant. How the knights upheld the law of the land, and how women should be treated. By the end of the conversation, King Rex promises that he will follow that example.

Then Steve goes to the blacksmith and tells him that he should round up all the people he can, and head for the castle. Steve puts on his battle suit, grabs his knife, loads his dart guns, and his new sword puts his new sword with the new sheath on his back. Samantha also puts on her battle suit, but Tobin took her sword. Steve knows Samantha really does not need a sword as she is capable of killing with her bare hands.

"Your majesty I see you are in your armor. Very good, Samantha will protect you, and believe me she can. She can kill with her hands so stay close to her."

"Why endanger me at all?"

"I want the people to see a new, stronger King, one who will stand for all I told you about of King Arthur."

"I will do my best to follow his ideal sir Steve."

"Good we can get started. A little surprise attack will go a long way." said Steve.

Chapter 144

Steve takes the hands of the King and Samantha and ports to the court yard of the castle, catching the guard's off-guard.

Paladin turns up the volume on his helmet and issues a challenge to King Jacob and his knights.

"Ho, Jacob the usurper, and to your cravenly knights. I issue a challenge to you all, to try to defeat me in single combat, if you dare."

King Jacob comes out to the parapet and looks down into the court yard.

"Who dares to challenge the King and his knights?"

"I, Paladin, do so challenge!"

"Who is beside you?"

"You will get to know them as soon as I defeat your knights or they me."

A short time later the knights in full armor appear in the court yard. Tobin is the last one to appear. Before Tobin arrives in the court yard, he instructs his archers to hide about the court yard and to shoot this Paladin if it looks like he is about to defeat him.

Tobin takes his place at the end of the line, which suits Paladin well.

"Your majesty, if it pleases you I would start with the first knight, and work my way down to Tobin the tiny. I have much to take out on him for all he has done to me. I would savor that combat the most."

"As you will Paladin, as not many men can defeat fifteen knights, especially these knights."

485

"Thank you sire, will this be to the death or if they yield?"

"If they yield that will be fine. However, I cannot say they will not kill you."

"Well said, let the combat commence." said Paladin.

The first knight, approaches with sword drawn and his shield held up. They circle one another. While they are checking each other out, Paladin is using his helmet to check the knight's sword for the flaws in its manufacturing. Paladin soon located the weak spot in the sword. The knight lunged with a killing stroke, and Paladin side stepped it to bring his superior broad sword down against the sword blade of the knight, shattering it to pieces. Off balance, and still moving Paladin spins around and using the flat of his blade whacks the knight on the back of his head knocking him out. It more or less continues the same way for the next five knights.

"Stop Sir Paladin, is that a magic sword that you carry?"

"No Sire, not magic, just a better made one."

"Then continue. But if you lose, I will take possession of your sword. Does it have a name?"

"I call it Excalibur, your majesty. Now I have nine more of your knights to dispatch, unless they wish to leave the field. The only one that can't leave is Tobin. He and I will fight."

King Jacob looks to his knights, and none leave the field. Paladin bests the next eight knights, and all are proper fights. Some limp off the field, and others are carried off. With each win King Jacob is getting antsy. He wants to possess Paladin's sword, thinking it to be magical despite what has been said. No blade in recorded history has ever broken more swords, without breaking itself. Now Paladin is down to the last knight, Tobin. Samantha sees the archers around the castle walls and a few inside the court yard. She flashes the locations to Paladin, so he knows where they are. In a blink of an eye, Paladin ports to the locations of most of the archers using his dart gun to put them to sleep. Now standing on the field it does not look like Paladin has moved at all. Only a slight blur of his outline gives away any idea that he was moving at all.

"Well Tobin the tiny, are you ready to be beaten. Oh I see you are going to use my wife's sword to fight me."

"I AM called TOBIN the TERRIABLE! And I'm going to kill you!"

"No, you will not kill me. You are not good enough. All you can fight are woman, and children. You are not man enough to fight men. You are a coward!"

Enraged Tobin attacks Paladin, and beats at Paladin with the katana sword that belongs to Samantha. Paladin counters all of Tobin's swings, then steps back as if it were just a mere practice exercise. The fight drags on, feint, riposte and return. Paladin counters each of Tobin's moves, with ease, thanks to Samantha's teaching. In one attack Paladin disarms Tobin, then returns the sword to him. This enrages Tobin even more. From behind the crowd an archer shoots at Paladin. Paladin's helmet detects the arrow so Paladin ports to the side and the arrow hits Tobin through the arm joint, and it enters into his heart, killing him. Samantha locates the archer, and runs him down. Then drags him to King Rex.

King Rex looks up at his brother.

"Jacob, you will be punished for the murders, and all you have done to these people. You men arrest Jacob, and place him in a cell for now. We will deal with him after all else has been dealt with."

Paladin picks up Samantha's sword and returns it to her.

"Samantha do you still have the map?"

"No, Tobin took it thinking it led to treasure. I suspect it is in his chamber here in the castle."

"Sounds like a good place to start."

Paladin goes to one of the knights that he defeated. The knight cringes as he approaches.

487

"Where is Tobin's chamber? He took something else of mine, and I want it returned."

The knight tells Paladin where to locate Tobin's chamber. Paladin having not been there walks to the room, and enters. Using his helmet, Paladin scans for the map. He soon locates where Tobin has hidden the map.

Over the next few days there are feasts, trials and punishment. The King had listened to Paladin about King Arthur and worked at setting up his kingdom much the same way. The King proposed that Paladin become his advisor. Paladin turns down all the accolades that were offered.

"I do not wish to seem ungrateful Sire, but I have a quest of my own to follow. My wife and I thank you for all you have tried to do for us. But we must leave soon."

"As you wish friend Paladin, go with my heartfelt thanks! For all you have done for me and my kingdom."

"Thank you Sire."

The next morning, as Paladin and Samantha are getting ready to leave, the king shows up with two horses, and a pack mule for them to take. Paladin is going to turn them down and then thinks better of it. Paladin and Samantha shake hands, and receive hugs. Then Paladin leads the horses and Samantha out of the castle gate. Paladin rides the horses to the blacksmith's home, where he gives the blacksmith the horses. Then trades the mule to him for the leather backpack he had made for him.

"Well my friend, this should pay you for all you have done for me. You have my thanks as well. My wife and I must get moving. We have a-ways to go, and we will not be back."

"How will you get there without the horses?"

"You have to ask? We'll travel further and faster without them."

Paladin puts the provisions the King gave them into his back pack and some of it into Samantha's backpack. Steve takes Samantha's hand and ports to the back side of the castle. Then they move off down the dirt road headed to the next portal.

Chapter 145

According to the map they have a-ways to go. Now, once out of sight, Steve suggests they change into the clothes of the peasants that live in the area, so they do not draw attention to themselves. As they come up on a town Steve and Samantha decide to walk through it rather than teleport.

These people are superstitious and believe in witches, and warlocks. Steve does not want to feed that fear, and cause problems for themselves. At night they will go deep into the woods to make camp. One night they had settled down for the evening, and were just getting ready to go to sleep when three bandits stormed the camp with swords drawn.

Steve looks up at them, and said "Really! I'm going to do you men, a favor. I will give you a head start in leaving, before I get angry and beat some sense into your heads."

They did not expect the couple to be brave, since the men had the weapons. The bandits pressed the attack. Steve just sits there, but Samantha is a different story. She hates being bullied. After what happened at Tobin's hands made her feel so angry, she decides these men are going to take the brunt of her anger.

Steve knew Samantha needed to release her anger, so he stays out of it. Samantha not using her teleporting ability, just rips through the three men as if they were children with toy swords. In the end, two men had broken arms, and the third man a broken wrist. The bandits decide to leave in a hurry to get away from the mad woman. Samantha came back to the fire with a big smile on her face.

"That felt good."

"I knew you needed to vent your anger so that is why I did not help you."

Ten days away from King Rex's castle, they run onto another castle. Steve and Samantha are going to go to the castle to get more provisions when they hear a loud commotion. It turns out there is a war going on. There are armies from both sides aligned on the field for battle.

"Steve what do we want to do?"

"We do not know what is going on, so let's not get entangled in this we'll move around it."

Steve takes out the map to see which way they need to go, but the map shows that their route goes right through the war torn area.

"The map shows that the way we need to go is on the other side of the battle field. And it is too far to port to without endangering ourselves. So we will port around it and hope for the best."

"Should we dress in our battle suits Steve?"

"That might not be a bad idea."

So Steve and Samantha change out of their clothes into their battle suits. Steve takes Samantha's hand and ports in short distances. At each stop Steve and Samantha scan the area with their helmets to make sure they are alone. Then they port to the next place they can see.

They try to stay in covered areas, and avoid any open areas in hopes they can move around the armies without being detected.

The next teleport, Steve and Samantha find themselves being surrounded by knights on horseback with sharp lances pointed at them. This time Samantha ports them to the far edge of the field from where they are.

"Thanks, Samantha, I could not see to teleport."

Out of nowhere they hear the thundering of horse hooves coming in their direction. Steve ports to another place, then another, leaving the knights behind. Soon they reach the base of a mountain range. So up the mountain side Steve ports. On the first level area, Steve and Samantha look back at the knights closing in on their position.

"I think we had best move on Samantha, they just might decide to climb up here to get at us."

"That is exactly what they intend to do Steve, look down."

Steve looks and several knights are taking off their armor, and they start climbing up to where they are.

"Let's go Samantha."

Steve ports them higher up on the mountain, and they do not stop until they reach the top of the mountain. Samantha looks back and can just see the knights as they are still climbing towards them.

"Steve we might want to move further along. It will be dark in a few hours and we can move further away once we get down from here."

"I have to agree" said Steve.

Steve takes Samantha's hand and in short hops they make it to the bottom of the mountain range on the other side. Samantha sees a small clearing with a stream next to it and she points it out. Steve takes them there.

"I guess we will have a cold camp tonight so we do not attract any attention. Let's change out of our battle suits and back in to our peasant clothes, so if someone chances upon us they will think nothing different about us."

That night Samantha and Steve settle in to sleep, in the morning they find themselves ringed by four knights with drawn swords.

"Nave what are you doing on this land?"

Steve starts to answer, when one of the knights backhanded him across the face. That did it! Steve, usually a sedate and quite person explodes. He thrashed the knight that hit him and is working over another one. Samantha also takes

492

out the other two knights. Steve decides to have a chat with the knights to see why everyone here is at war.

The knight Steve had first set upon is the first one to be questioned.

"Now dog, tell me what is going on that you would set upon two strangers in this land?"

"You are spies sent here against our kingdom."

"What are you talking about? All we want to do is pass through. We have no affiliation with any kingdom."

"You are a liar, we saw you appear in this clearing that means you are here to spy on us."

"You have it all wrong, all we want to do is travel past this land, and we are looking for a passage."

"A Passage to where?"

"That's a tough one to explain, let's just say it is a passage to another place, and to show you we mean no harm."

Steve cuts them loose and puts the swords and weapons in a pile ten yards away, then has them stand back as Samantha collects their backpacks.

"I hope to never see you again." Said Steve.

Steve ports Samantha and himself away across the stream and then ports up out of sight. The knights hurry to their weapons and then hike to where they tied up their horses.

"We have to catch them, before they can get away."

So the four Knights ride off in the direction they saw Steve and Samantha traveling.

"Steve how did you know they would follow?"

"More of a hunch, really, I did not know that they would follow us for sure."

"What should we do?"

"We'll just keep ahead of them, all the way to the portal. I really do not want to hurt anyone, but we'll do what we have to, to get home."

What Samantha and Steve did not know is that their children have grown into teenagers Kim is about to graduate high school and move on to college, and William is going to start high school. Kim has become a fine upstanding girl, while William is a very rebellious and troublesome lad. Both Steve and Samantha would be disappointed in William especially as he embarks into the realm of crime.

Steve and Samantha keep well ahead of the knights as they head to the portal. On the night before they reach the portal's location. Steve and Samantha have set up a camp to get some rest from all the traveling. They had far outdistanced the knights and they felt confident in making a camp. They eat a meager dinner then turn in for the night. The next morning the two are rudely awaken as the knights that surrounded them prodded them with very sharp spears. Steve grabs his sword and so does Samantha as they port to opposite sides of the clearing behind the knights.

"Why are you here?" asks Paladin.

And the knights wheel the horses to face him.

"We have been searching for demons, and we found you."

"What makes you think we are demons?"

"You disappeared from yon bed to here that would qualify you as a demon."

"I guess you got me there, but I assure you I'm no demon. However, I will allow you to leave in peace."

"Nay demon, we intend to capture you and burn you at the stake."

"Don't say I didn't warn you or give you a chance to leave in peace."

Chapter 146

Steve and Samantha port back to their beds to get their helmets and put them on. Steve has shown Samantha how to use the helmet to locate the flaws in the iron swords the knights, are using. It is not long when all the knights are all on the ground. Paladin uses his knife to cut the saddle straps on the horses and the knight's fall. Then Paladin ports from knight to knight shooting them with his sleep darts. Samantha packs up the camp supplies, and Steve uses his knife to cut the straps of the knight's armor so they will not stay on much like the saddles on the horses, thus leaving the knights in their undergarments. Samantha stifles a laugh, and takes Steve's hand. Steve ports them some distance away from where they are.

"Samantha what was so funny?"

"Seeing all the men in their undergarments, it was funny, and when I think you gave them a chance to leave intact, they refused, and so they go home wearing a barrel." She snickers again.

"You are a cruel woman, Samantha, but you are right it was funny. The worst part of it is they won't think it is. The portal is not far now; it is just over that hill."

"Good I'll be glad to get off this world."

Steve and Samantha port up to the top of the hill, and the portal is just down in the valley. The problem is that there is another battle being fought, and they cannot get to the portal. Steve curses, and it shocks Samantha, as she has never heard him swear before. She figures that Steve is about to do something dramatic and she is going to stay out of his way. Steve sits down to watch the battle and soon finds the head of each army behind the lines. In his battle suit Steve ports to the first leader and teleports him to the top of the hill where Samantha is, and leaves him with her. Before Paladin leaves the leader tries to get away by bullying Samantha and she slaps him down. Smiling Paladin ports to the next leader and does the same thing bringing them face to face.

Paladin takes off his helmet, and faces the two leaders.

"What are you two trying to do?"

"We are having a war between our lands. What is it to you?"

Paladin sticks his face close to the leader who spoke up.

"You are in my way! You will stop fighting and go home, with your armies."

"By what right do you tell us we have to go home!?" the leader huffed.

The other leader at first is angry but, thought better of it. If this stranger kills his adversary the war is won.

"Draw your sword," said Paladin "We are going to fight."

Then Paladin turns to the other leader "and you are next."

While Paladin has his back turned the other leader tries to kill him with his sword, Samantha easily deflects it.

Paladin draws his sword facing the first leader, and put his helmet back on.

"You are a coward, and I will defeat you in the most humiliating way."

The sword fight starts to get underway when the armies stop fighting. They rush to the hill where their leaders are being held. Paladin finds the flaw in the first leader's sword, and breaks the sword in half. Then to rub salt into the wounds, Paladin continues to slash at the leader slowly removing his breast plate, and back plate, then the leggings and finally the helmet, leaving the man in his undergarments. Then Paladin puts the tip of his sword to the first leader's chest.

"Yield or die!"

"I yield!"

"Good now take your army and go home! NOW!"

The first leader climbs on to his horse, and casts a hateful look at Paladin, then at his adversary. Then the first leader takes his army and leaves the field. Paladin turns to the other leader. "Well!?"

The second leader sees that it would be best to surrender, and go home, so he kneels and hands Paladin his sword.

"I Yield."

Paladin takes the sword, and says "Leave!"

Without hesitation the second leader leads his armies toward home. Samantha stands there and watches the armies leave the area.

"Did that turn out as well as you expected?" she asked with a smile.

"Actually it worked out better than I thought it would. Now we can get out of here before they decide to come back."

Magic World

Chapter 147

Steve ports them to the place where the portal is and once again Steve ties them together and then concentrates on the portal. It opens and pulls them through. They land in a meadow, but it appears to be dusk. They remove the rope and at that point a blinding light appears. Steve and Samantha think it is going to be the Entity. They soon find out it is not. What appears is a witch. She is the most beautiful woman Steve has ever seen with elf like features. She has honey colored hair, deep green-black eyes, and in her hair are streaks of green. In that instant Samantha has an opposite reaction and is filled with hate and distrust. The witch sees Samantha and realizes that Samantha is a female, and that the man beside her is her mate.

Regardless the witch wants and needs Steve. With a wave of her hand another blinding light appears and when it vanishes Steve and the witch are gone.

"NO!" screams Samantha.

At that moment another flash of light happens and a handsome man also with elf like features appears. He has Black raven colored hair, red eyes, and he has streaks of blue in his hair; He steps forth.

"Where is the other of you? There are suppose too be two of you." He asks.

"A woman appeared and took him."

"Did she look like this?" and the man waves his hands in a circular motion and a picture much like a hologram appears, showing the woman who took her husband.

"Yes, that was her."

"That's not good, we must hurry or he will be dead before long."

"What's going to happen to my husband?"

"Monica, is going to drain his life force then take the crystal he has."

"Where is she, I'll take her head if she has harmed my husband."

Kester is taken aback by Samantha's statement.

Samantha asks for Kester's name and he tells her. "Now let's get started, what is the fastest way to get to where we need to go?"

Kester holds out his hand and Samantha takes it, and then Kester waves his hand in the air as they find themselves at his castle.

"This is my humble abode. We will need provisions, and transportation to reach Monica's castle."

Once in the library at Kester's castle, Kester claps his hands and a servant appears.

"Tang, please get us a repast, and then put together some provisions, we will be traveling to Monica's castle."

"Yes Kester." Tang bows out of the room.

"Samantha please follow me. We have to go to the stable, to meet our mounts."

Samantha follows him, but in the back of her mind she does not trust Kester, and she is not sure why. For the sake of Steve, she will trust him for now.

In the courtyard Kester whistles and two strange animals appear. They are bipeds, and look like a cross between a man and a gorilla; but not so hairy. They are quite large, and very intelligent.

"These are our mounts; they are called Cappers. This is Austell and Bing. They will carry us to our destination."

"Which one will I be carried on?"

"Austell, is your mount, and I will ride on Bing."

Samantha walks over to Austell and offers her; her hand in friendship. Austell looks at Samantha with a question in her eyes.

"Austell I would be your friend. Not your master, or just your rider."

Austell's face displays a softness, and reaches her hand out to Samantha, and softly touches her hand. Samantha removes her helmet and smiles at Austell.

"Thank you Austell."

"Now that we have met our mounts, Tang will have something for us to eat, then we can get started."

"Alright, let's go, enjoy our meal." said Samantha.

The table is laid out for a banquet. Samantha thinks to herself "Be weary girl, somehow this does not feel right."

To Samantha, Kester has a wrong feel to him, for a lack of a better explanation, it's like dealing with a used car salesman, and he is trying too hard, like he wants something.

"So tell me Kester how long will it take to get to Monica's castle?"

Kester pulls out a map and moves to her side, pointing at the map he explains.

"We have to cross these mountains and on the other side we will find Monica's castle, but it will not be that easy. Monica has a few traps set for anyone trying to reach her. Her pet dragon is one of the many things we will have to overcome."

Samantha realizes just who Kester reminds her of; David, a man she fell for before she met Steve She caught him with another woman when she came home early one day.

The thought of that time makes her angry, and her skin crawls. So she is not sure she should fully trust this man. But for now she needs Kester so she can get Steve back. Samantha is careful at the table with her helmet beside her. She picks only the food which is not tainted. And she realizes a lot of it is. It is like he wants to drug her. There is not much by way of conversation, but Kester is watching her closely. At the end of the meal Samantha stands up as it is time to leave. Kester has a look of annoyance on his face, but does not argue with her. He leads the way to the stable where they collect their mounts. Kester leads them off in the direction of the mountain range.

After several hours, Samantha asks him.

"Why were you trying to drug me at your castle?"

"No, I, I would not do such a thing."

Samantha draws her sword and ports close to him to place her sword point against his chest. I can easily kill you and I will have no qualms about doing so.

"Now tell me why you are doing what you are doing, and make it convincing. And if you so much as move a finger, I'll run you through."

"Aha, oh yes, I want your crystal, because on this world it has great power."

Samantha applies some pressure and he cries out.

"It's true, by the gods it's true, that is what Monica wants. All that I told you about her is true. And I will keep my promise to take you to him."

"How can I trust you Kester?"

"I'm not sure how I can gain your trust Samantha."

Then Austell shambles up and touches Samantha. She communicates by touch that Kester is not to be trusted. To control Kester he must promise and confess his full name. Austell transfer that information to Samantha. Samantha pressed her sword enough to break skin.

"Ouch!"

"Now say this, I promise to take you to Monica's castle, and help me free my husband from Monica, then you will release Austell and Bing, and return home."

Kester repeats the words, and then Samantha stabs Kester. Finish with your whole name and he does.

"How did you know?"

"I just did."

"Do you know what you have done?"

"Yes, I had you give me your word to help me and if I'm right you have no other choice now."

"How did you know?"

"I'm a lot smarter than you know, in the art of magic."

"I'm beginning to see." said Kester.

"Now take us the fastest way to Monica's castle."

At first Kester tries to protest, but to no avail. He soon starts cooperating. He casts a spell which takes them to the first pass in the mountain range.

Samantha I can no longer use my magic to take us further, we must travel by Capper from here and then on foot. Samantha thinks to Austell, "is this true?"

Austell answers her that, that is correct. And that the way will be dangerous. That night they set up camp so they can get an early start in the morning.

Monica returns to her castle with Paladin. Paladin is still under her spell, and he acts as if he is drugged.

"Here man come sit here next to my throne."

Paladin walks over and sits down, and stares off into space, or seems to.

"It is so nice to have a pet again. It is too bad I will have to kill you when the correct stars are in alignment. It will take a month for that to happen. Now take off your helmet so I can see your face."

Paladin removes his helmet, and continues to sit staring off into space.

"What is your name, pet?"

"Paladin"

"No my dear your true name."

"Steve."

"No, what is your true name?"

Steve seems confused, and tells her it is "Steve Ball"

"That is better, now Steve Ball you will do as I say, and nothing else."

"As you say."

"Now be a good boy and follow this servant. He will clean you up and give you a change of clothes"

Steve does as he is told. The servant, has him get into a bath and washes him from head to toe so to speak. Once cleaned the servant provides some clothes to dress Steve in, and he removes Steve's battle suit to a closet. Then ushers Steve into the throne room where Monica awaits him.

"You are so pretty; it is a shame that I have to kill you to gain your power."

Monica touches Steve's face and chest.

Steve hears all that is going on, and for the moment he cannot control his own body. "What was the thing about his name?" thinks Steve.

The spell can only bind you if she has your true name. Steve finds that out at a later time. His real name is Steve Storm; Steve Ball is a name he took when he was in hiding after the explosion that had caused amnesia as a result.

Monica turns Steve over to the servant to watch and she turns to other things she must attend to. Steve is ushered back to his room and there is a table set with some food on it. Steve sits at the table and the servant leaves to let Steve eat his meal. Steve starts to eat when he comes to himself. "What is going on here?" as Steve looks around "I recall the flash of light and all that happened after that is a dreamlike state. How much is real?" Steve is about to take a bite when he remembered that he should check his food with his helmet sensors. Steve gets his helmet then tests the food with all of it being eatable; but most of it is drugged. Especially the wine. He eats the vegetables which do not contain any drugs. He realizes that he must keep up his strength so he eats what he can.

Steve decides to play along until he can find Samantha and where he is in relation to the next portal. For now, Steve ports to places inside the castle to where he has been, and explores areas within the castle when he can. When Steve leaves he ports to the other side of the door, and unlocks it, then goes off down the corridors. Steve finds the kitchen and using his helmet locates food he can safely eat and has a snack. After eating Steve sees a door leading into the court yard and opens it. There sitting on the top step is a giant silver-haired wolf that begins to growl and snap at him nearly taking off his head. If Steve had not ported back out of the way, he would have been a head shorter. Steve closes the door and leans against it in relief. Steve hears someone coming toward the kitchen and ports back to his room.

"Whew, that was too close for comfort."

Then he hears the handle of his door being opened, so Steve sits down on the floor and stairs off into space, as if he were still dazed from the drugs.

Chapter 148

Samantha and Kester with their mounts Austell and Bing are at the first pass of the mountain range and are moving cautiously. Kester had mentioned that Monica has several creatures guarding the mountain passes to her castle. The last pass will be the most dangerous.

"How many passes are their; Kester?"

"Four maybe five. I have never gotten all the way to her castle."

"Ok, let's get going! Time is a wasting. Monica will not have my husband, let alone kill him, I'm going to see to that."

So they start into the pass, when a little way off Samantha hears a sound off in the distance. It is not like any animal she has ever heard before.

"What is making that noise, Kester?"

"Sounds like a banshee."

"So if you have been here before what did you do to get past it?"

"I tricked it, with an image of myself, and it went after the image then I escaped."

"There are too many of us for me to do that again."

"Why are you lying to me Kester?"

"I lie to you! How do you know? What magic do you have that can tell you that?"

"My magic is technology, and my intuition."

"What is technology?"

At that moment the banshee appears. Samantha turns off the audio in her helmet, and scans the creature. Samantha then dismounts the capper and walks up to the banshee and draws her sword. The banshee continues her scream, but Samantha cannot hear it, and Kester is on the ground groveling with his hands to his ears. Samantha stands in front of the banshee. The banshee attacks Samantha trying to rip her to pieces. Samantha fights back, then passes her sword through the neck of the banshee killing it. Samantha turns on her audio a little bit at a time and finds it all quiet. She turns to Kester to see that he is alright. He has a little blood from his eyes and ears otherwise he will heal and be fine. Then Samantha turns her attention to the cappers. They appear not to be injured at all. After several minutes Samantha prods Kester to get up, and re-mount.

"How did you do that? No one can withstand a banshee like that."

"Apparently I can, now lead on!"

So Samantha and Kester continued their journey on to the next pass and moving closer to Monica's castle.

At the moment that Samantha kills the banshee, Monica is in the room with Steve. Monica is wishing Steve did not have to be drugged. She would have liked to have had some passionate fun with him. In a drugged state that cannot happen. Then all of a sudden Monica clutches her heart and lets out a small gasp.

"No, who could have killed the banshee?"

Monica dashes from the room screaming at the top of her lungs.

"Set up the seeing stone, I must see what is going on in the passes."

Monica and the servant leave Steve's chamber.

Steve waits several minutes then ports to the throne room in an unseen corner to watch and listen to what is going on, somehow Steve feels this has to do with Samantha.

Steve watches as Monica chants an incantation over this gray rock and it soon becomes clear. Steve puts on his helmet and can see the stone much better. What he sees is a strange woman like creature with its head severed. Monica flies into a rage.

"Whoever did that will pay for it with their lives?"

Monica causes the stone to travel along the pass looking for the person or persons responsible for killing the banshee. Soon Monica locates Samantha and a man riding on some strange animals. Just then Monica looks up toward the spot where Steve is hiding. Steve ports back to his chamber.

Steve quickly takes off his helmet, and sits down in his usual spot and stares off into space. Monica bursts into the chamber to see Steve where she left him.

"If I did not know better, I would swear you were in my throne room watching me. Servant, I want him watched day and night."

"Yes mistress, it will be so."

Steve decides it is time to leave. So while the Servant is getting a sentry to watch over him he puts his battle suit on, and grabs his sword and backpack. Then Steve ports to the kitchen to fill up his backpack with good food. Knowing what is waiting on the porch Steve opens the door. Sure enough the giant wolf is sitting there growling at him. Steve throws him a steak and the wolf devours it. Steve throws a second steak, and while the wolf is eating the second one Steve pitches another steak out into the yard and the wolf jumps after it. Steve ports down into the yard, then to the gate, which is closed, with bars. Steve is able to see to port several yards off toward the mountain range. Steve soon finds a path into the mountains and decides to follow it.

An hour or so later the servant discovers that the captive is gone, and he is afraid to tell his mistress and so keeps his mouth closed while he looks within the castle for Steve. He cannot have gotten far. The servant looks everywhere and cannot locate Steve. He decides to tell his mistress that the prisoner has escaped. Monica, is very calm, then she turns the servant into a monkey. Then using his name set a boundary on him so he cannot leave the castle. Steve is miles away porting along up into the mountains.

Samantha is fast coming towards Monica's castle with Kester in her wake when another guardian of the passes appears. This one is a dragon, but according to Kester a small one. Kester is very fearful of the creature. But Samantha has no fear of it. The dragon is a good fake as it's a holograph. Samantha gets off the Capper and walks toward the dragon and stands her ground. Her helmet tells her there is nothing there. Samantha grabs a rock and throws it at the dragon and the rock passed through it with no effect.

"How did you know it was not real?"

"Kester, I have magic, which you do not know about nor could you understand it even if I told you about it. It is call technology, and here it appears to be the more powerful of the two magic's."

"Can you teach me of this technology that you possess?"

"No, I cannot. My husband, Steve, is the one who makes that magic. I just know how to use it. Enough! We must get to the castle."

Chapter 149

Once past the dragon they head deeper into the mountain range. The Cappers are sure footed, and fast, it would be like riding a car at fifty miles an hour on a freeway. They are going slow due to the uneven terrain.

Steve manages to get to a very tall mountain peak, and he turns up the helmet sensors in hopes of locating Samantha or at least her direction. Instead of getting Samantha, Steve picks up Monica.

"Steven Ball! You will return to me as I use your full name, you have no choice."

"I hate to rain on one's parade, but that is not going to happen. You see witch, I'm from a different world than you. I'm not beset by your magic laws. I also learned what you want, my crystal."

"How could you know that?"

"You should be careful what you say around people, I heard you plotting about me, and how you intend to drain my life essence. It is not very conducive to make it a desirable thing to want to return to you."

In a tirade Monica screams at Steve.

"I'll get you back Steve if it is the last thing I do!"

"As you say, bye for now."

Monica's image vanishes. Paladin now tries to port further than and as fast as he can. Back at the castle Monica calls for all her guardians and sends them into the mountain range to find Steve and bring him back. Marching out the gate streams the giant wolves, and a small army of creatures, centaurs, ogres and other mythical creatures all deadly in their way. Monica uses her seeing stone to try to locate not only Steve, but his wife as well.

Instead of going through the passes, Paladin is hopping from mountain top to mountain top. Thus making it hard for Monica's army to find him, the only creatures that can follow are the Yeti. Even they cannot keep up as Paladin ports from mountain top to mountain top. Paladin hopes he can find some trace of Samantha from up here.

Samantha has decided to settle in for the night, and Austell touches her and communicates that she should set boundaries on Kester using his name. So Samantha does as she is instructed to. This will keep Kester from doing any harm to her or running away and abandoning her. That night a basilisk is moving toward Samantha and her camp. A basilisk is a deadly type of a snake or eel, if you look it directly in the eye you die instantly. Indirectly you turn to stone. You can kill it with a sword to the brain or cock's crow in the morning will also kill a basilisk.

At the moment when the basilisk finds Samantha camp, Steve lands on the hill above them. For a few moments he looks down on his wife, and smiles. Then his sensors show him the creature moving her way. His helmet tells him that a creature is just about to attack. Before it can attack Paladin was going to port down to confront it. Paladin's helmet identifies the creature as a basilisk and what it can do. So Paladin waits on his perch for the creature to come closer to him. Slowly Paladin draws his sword and remains poised. Just as the creature passes below him Paladin drops down onto the head of the creature and drives his sword into the creature's head clear to the hilt. The creature takes Paladin for a ride as it thrashes about and Paladin holds on to his sword. By this time Samantha and Kester are awaken by the commotion. Samantha has her sword drawn ready to battle. Paladin tells Samantha to get back out of the way, and she transports Austell out of harm's way. Several minutes later the basilisk quits moving, and Paladin manages to pull his sword out after several tries.

Samantha rushes to him, puts her arms around him, and hugs him tightly.

"From behind them they hear laughter, and they turn to see Monica standing there.

"Enjoy your moment together. It will not be long Steve Ball you must return to me."

"Yes, Monica, I will return to you, but not because you have my name, and not as a prisoner. But for reasons of my own."

"Then come, I will be ready for you." Monica disappears.

"It was just a projection. You and I have to have a private conversation Samantha, a very important one."

"What's wrong Steve?"

"We are what's wrong."

"What do you mean?"

"Have you been using your ability to teleport, here on this world?"

"A little, why?"

"I did not see the problem until I got to the hill above this place. I have been using my teleportation to get back to you, and each time I teleport I feel that something wrong is happening. I think I just figured it out."

"Figured out what Steve?"

"This world is based on Magic. We use technology. Every time we use our technology it damages something about this world. If we keep using it; it may set off a catastrophe to this world, so we need to limit what we do, and try to get off this world as soon as we can."

"Do you know where the portal is, Steve?"

"Yes, Monica's castle sets right in the middle of it."

"How do we get there?"

"I'm not sure, I could port us there, but it builds on the problem I just outlined. Also Monica has sent an army out for me and it is full of so many different creatures. Some like our friend that lays dead over there."

"Kester come here!"

Kester walks over to Samantha.

"I use magic here as well. Kester is bound to me by his name. Much like Monica thinks she can bind you by your name."

"That explains why she can't ensnare me yet."

"That's what I thought. Only you and I know of your true name." said Samantha.

"Let's break camp and get moving. By the way what creatures are these?"

"Kester calls them Cappers, this one is Austell and the other one Bing."

"Hello to both of you."

Both Cappers bow to Steve. Bing touches Steve and communicates to him.

"Wow! Said Steve, Thanks Bing."

"What just happened Steve?"

"Bing indicates that there is a quick way to the Castle, if we just trust them."

"Then let's do it Steve."

"What about your Pal over there, would he survive, if we leave him?"

Bing touches Steve again, and conveys that Kester can take care of himself, if need be.

"Ok, Samantha, Send Kester away, back to his home. You and I with the Cappers will continue."

Samantha sets Kester on his way back to his castle. Steve and Samantha mount the Cappers and move out down the mountain path. They stop at a huge granite wall. Then Bing places his hand on the wall and it opens a door of some kind. Bing let's Austell and Samantha through first, then he and Steve follow. They come out at a place over looking Monica's Castle. Steve jumps down to the ground and looks up at Bing, Thank you! That took me three days to make that trip and you did it in short order. Steve takes Bing's hand to shake it. Bing's eyes light up with delight. This is the first time a rider ever thought more of him than just a ride.

"Bing I have only known you a very short time. Here is my hand in friendship, and my thanks. I must ask you to take Austell and both of you get to safety."

Bing touches Steve and passes on that he will.

"If we were not such a source of danger I would have liked to stay on this world a while longer."

Steve turns to Samantha "are you ready to go?"

Samantha turns to Austell and then nods her head not wanting to say anything.

Steve teleports to the chamber where he was held in Monica's castle.

As it turns out Monica is waiting for them. As soon as Steve and Samantha appear Monica casts a spell to capture them, Monica has them in a cell with bars.

"Really Monica, a cage?" said Steve.

"Steve Ball you are bound to this cage never to be able to leave it until I say."

Steve and Samantha, port outside the cage. Steve grabs Monica and ports back into the cage then back out leaving Monica behind.

"You cannot do that!" screams Monica in a rage.

"As you can see I just did. If all goes well, I will not be seeing you again."

Steve takes Samantha's hand and before Steve teleports away, Samantha turns to Monica.

"If I see you again Monica, I will take your head. The only thing keeping me from doing so now is my husband. You might want to consider that."

Steve ports them to the throne room, and ties Samantha to him with a rope. Samantha stands guard as Steve concentrates to open the portal. The portal opens as Monica and several guards funnel into the throne room. And before they can get much closer the portal swallows Steve and Samantha, and they vanish from sight.

Alien World

Chapter 150

Steve and Samantha find themselves in a park much like Central Park in New York, and they look around and see a city. They watch the flying cars as they float past them. The place has a futuristic look about it. People are bustling about, but people not like earth people. The differences very from tall to short, and the colors and shapes of them are all strange. There is some glimpse of people much like ourselves and others that are totally different and very difficult to even describe.

"This is more like our own world so far except the population is so different." Said Samantha.

"This will be nice, maybe we can ride to the next portal, instead of porting there."

In the next moment they are surrounded by what looks like police or military units. Samantha pulls her sword ready to do battle, but Steve stops her.

"Let's see what this is about. We do not want to start a battle here. They may be more developed in technology and I'm not sure I want to be killed over a small squabble."

"Alright Steve," Samantha puts her sword away.

Then both Steve and Samantha are shocked as the people pour out of the units. They are all different kinds of aliens, all different sizes, shapes, and colors, even a few of them appear to be human like. It turns out that the police and the military are the same thing on this world and all is run by the blue reptile aliens. They make Steve and Samantha take off their helmets, and then kneel down on the ground with their hands behind their heads. They are cuffed then herded into separate units, and taken away to a jail, where they get processed like criminals and placed in separate cells. The next day they are released, after they are tagged for tracking purposes.

"So far this has not been a good start into this next world, let's see if we can find a place to change into our other clothes. These battle suits draw too much attention. Then we can try to figure out where we are compared to the next portal."

"Steve, I don't like this place, it feels wrong."

"In what way Samantha?"

"I'm not sure, I cannot put my finger on it. Back on earth, do you remember the movies about the Nazi's and how you were watched everywhere you go, and the slightest infraction would get you jailed or killed."

"I see what you mean, these devices are tracking our movements, and maybe our conversations."

They do not use their ability to teleport so they will have an ace if they need it. They soon find a slum like area and an abandoned building. Then they find a room that offers some privacy so they change their clothes into the shirt and jeans they were wearing back on earth.

"We need to see how this world works so we can move around without getting unwanted attention." said Steve.

"Ok, then what should we do, our supplies will soon be gone, and we do not have anything we can use for barter. Said Samantha.

"First off."

Steve takes Samantha by the hand and ports them back to the park and using a small window Steve slices off the bands they have on their wrists, and then he ports to the far side of the park's edge to watch what happens. As they both suspected several police units appear and surround the area where the bracelets are. Steve then ports Samantha and himself back to the room in the abandoned building.

"Now that we lost our bracelets, we will need to leave here. They were monitoring us so they now know where we have been, so let's get out of here."

No more than they have left the building, when several units show up to surround the place looking for the criminals. From a block away they watch to see what happens. As it turns out someone else is in the building, and they are being dragged out and beaten up. Samantha is just about ready to intervene when the police leave. Leaving the individual in the street. Samantha runs up to see if the individual is alright, when he pulls a gun and tells her to put up her hands that she is under arrest. Bad move that. Samantha gives him a beating he will never forget, and she walks away with his wallet, and gun.

"What did you do to him?"

"He will walk funny for a while. We better get moving as they will be back looking for us. He was a plant to try to find us."

Steve takes Samantha's hand and ports down the street several times deeper into the slums. It is turning dark out and they are just walking along, carrying their back packs when a group of alien's surround them.

"Lookie at what we got, a couple of pinks, in our territory. What should we do to these pinks for being here?"

And Steve hears several clicks like switch blades being opened.

"Well Samantha which half do you want"?

Samantha does not say a word; Steve just gets out of her way.

"Ah, guys, you might want to give the idea of running away some serious thought."

All he hears is snickering.

"Just remember, I warned you."

Samantha did a quick spin around to see where everyone is. Then as one of the alien's makes a move, Samantha takes them all down; breaking arms, legs, and heads. Then she collects all the knives they are carrying along with their wallets. As they lay there moaning.

"I tried to warn you guys." snickered Steve.

Samantha, followed by Steve, walks down the street. The other street toughs who saw what happened get out of the way.

Steve walks up to one of the boys and asks.

"Where is a good place to get some sleep where we will not be bothered?"

"Place call Mommies just down the street."

And the alien cringes and runs away.

Steve and Samantha walk down the street and locate the place and enter.

"What do you want?" said the clerk.

"A place to stay." Said Steve.

"What have you got to trade?" says Momma.

And she was a big one. She is also alien, and has feathers in place of hair.

"I do not have anything." said Steve."

Samantha holds up the blaster she took from the policeman.

"Will this do?"

Momma looks at her then the blaster. "It will do for a few days." As Momma tries to grab the blaster. Samantha pulls the blaster back.

"I think a week will do." said Samantha.

"You drive a hard bargain; a week it is. Here is your key, your room is just down the hall and off to the right."

Samantha takes the key, and walks down the hall. Steve picks up the bags and follows her.

In their room Steve starts to say something, and Samantha stops him, by putting her finger up to her lips. She takes her helmet out of the bag, and uses it to scan the room. She finds a few listing devices and a couple of cameras. Steve takes out his helmet and programs it to emit white noise, and then he uses Samantha's helmet to blank out the cameras.

"For the moment we can now talk." said Steve.

Steve takes out the map and finds the direction for the next portal.

"Now I need a map of this world to see what we have off in that direction."

Steve tinkers with his helmet again, to make it into a motion detector, and he gives Samantha one of his CO_2 pistols.

"Samantha, we need to get some sleep. We have been on the go for a long time."

"Good I'm so tired, and then we need to get some food. I'll be hungry when we wake up." Yawns Samantha.

They both get into bed with their clothes on, and the pistols under their pillows. They fall into a restless sleep. That night they are left alone. In the morning when they wake up Steve finds the Instructor from the Hive standing in their room watching them.

Steve wakes up Samantha.

"We have a guest. Well instructor what are you doing here? I thought we were done when we left the hive world all that time ago."

"One called Steve, I have come to help you, to help yourself."

Before Steve or Samantha can react the instructor stings them, and they begin to pass out.

"I will watch over you for a time, until the memories take hold on you about this world."

As Steve and Samantha sleep, the memories filter in to their minds. Their memories are of their future selves; all that they have or will be doing on this world.

Samantha wakes first, and sees that the instructor is gone, she shakes Steve awake.

"We must leave; the police are going to be here soon."

Steve wakes up and has the same feeling.

"Samantha what is in that bag on the bench there?"

Samantha opens it and pours out some coins.

"It appears to be money. We need to look at it later, as we must be leaving now!"

Steve feels the urgency of Samantha's feelings and collects the rest of their belongings. Then takes Samantha by the hand. From down the hall they hear rushed orders, and the sound of many feet rushing in their direction. Steve ports them back to the edge of the park, just before the police break into their room. After they make sure there is no trap waiting for them they move off towards what we would call uptown.

"At least with the knowledge that the Instructor provided we know how much money she provided us and its value."

"So where do we go from here Steve?"

"The slums are not safe with a reward on us. The first person we run into would try to turn us over and collect the reward money. So let's try going the other way. With what money we have we can get an apartment, and act like everyone else." said Steve.

"Steve, we need to first buy some clothes. Since we have been here I have not seen anyone wearing jeans and tee shirts, and we stand out like a sore thumb."

" When you are right my dear, you are right!"

Samantha sees what looks like a thrift store, and they enter and purchase a couple of changes of clothes apiece. Samantha buys a dress much like the one the ladies on the street are wearing. Steve buys a pair of slacks with a few button-down shirts and accessories to go with them. Steve pays in cash, and they leave the store to move on down the street.

"Now to find a place to live." said Steve.

Samantha points out a sign in the window for an apartment for rent. They go in to see what the cost is for renting the open apartment. Steve pays the landlord what he asks and now they have a place to stay. The landlord who by the way is an alien; leads them to a third floor apartment. He shows them around pointing out the furniture and decorations. Samantha does not like what they have rented, but she never said a word. Soon the landlord leaves giving them the key card for their door. Samantha starts to tell Steve what she thinks, when Steve puts a finger to his lips. He removes his helmet from the back pack and sure enough there are listening devices about the rooms, and a couple of cameras, one in the bedroom and one pointed at the front door. Steve writes a note, and make polite conversation. He takes his helmet and goes to a back room where there seems to be no bugs, and tells her they are being watched, and recorded.

"We need to guard our speech, and act normal like everyone else, as you said earlier this is a police state, which means you're guilty even if you are proved innocent." Said Steve.

Chapter 151

"For the next few days we will have to have only domestic conversation in the rest of the house. I'll disable the camera in our bedroom. It will be bleary, but not off, otherwise someone will get wise to our knowing where the camera is, and think we know more than we do."

"Ok, Steve, this world seems to be more dangerous than any of the other worlds we have traveled through. At this point I would much rather face another dragon like the one that I killed on the hive world."

"I know what you mean Samantha, but for a time we need to live here until we understand this world. According to the Instructor's memory implant the portal is in the middle of the ocean. We will need to figure out a way to get there."

"At least we have clothes, and an apartment. So let's go find some supermarket where we can buy some food, we can also pick up on the local mannerisms."

Samantha leads the way out the door, and stops at the front desk.

"Sir, we are new to this area, where might we find a place where we may buy food?"

The clerk, just stares at Samantha for a few moments, trying to weigh in his mind if she is playing a trick on him or being serious. Then he points down the street,

"It is six blocks that way."

Samantha thanks him and leads the way out the door and down the street. They get to the market, and enter in. Steve grabs a cart. And sees all kinds of food stuffs here, but the problem is can they eat of any of it? As they look around the proprietor approaches them. He is an alien, orange in color, with light blue hair all over, and he has very large eyes, colored black.

"Is there something I can help you with?"

"We are new here on this world. We were looking for food to buy."

The proprietor spreads his arms, "This is all food, but you need to shop over in that section over there. The food here in this area is for my race, and to people like you, it is toxic."

"Thank you." said Samantha.

Steve and Samantha shop in the area that was indicated, and manage to find several vegetables that look like carrots, tomatoes, and the like. The meat selection was questionable.

"Samantha I'm going to have to make some more glasses to be able to test things, it is obvious we cannot use our helmets."

They purchase what they picked up and head back to the apartment. As they cross in front of an alley entrance, one lizard like being steps in front of them, and he grabs Samantha by the shoulder. Samantha looks up into the creature's eyes, and the rage on her face, almost makes him take his hand off of her.

"Give me your credits or I will kill your woman."

Steve looks at Samantha. "Should I take care of this or do you want to?"

"You had better, Steve, I have noticed that the women here are subservient to their husband."

Steve hands the bag of groceries to Samantha, then Steve grabs the lizard guy by the wrist, and makes him let go of Samantha. The creature is now enraged and tries to hit Steve with both hands. Steve ports to one side and the lizard man falls flat on his face. Steve puts his foot on the lizard's back.

"Now run along, and be a good boy or for my next trick, I promise you will be sorry."

Steve turns his back and he and Samantha continue down the sidewalk. From behind them Steve is watching the lizard creature in a reflection of a window. The lizard man is rushing upon them. Just as he is about to close on Steve. Steve turns and grabs the lizard man and ports them into the jail cell that Steve had occupied a few days before, and then Steve ports back to Samantha.

"So where did you leave him?"

"In the jail cell we were in a few days ago. He will have a hard time explaining how he got there."

They made it back to the apartment, and the clerk is surprised to see them.

"Steve I think we were set up by the clerk, to be mugged."

"You may be right about that Samantha; so he will bear watching."

Samantha makes up a salad, from the groceries they bought home. Then they shower, and head to bed. Steve manages to block the camera and generate white sound using his helmet to distort the sound and video systems.

The next morning Samantha makes another salad. Steve goes out to locate what he needs to make a couple of pairs of glasses so they can find food they can eat safely. While he is out, he runs onto an orange alien who is being pushed around by three blue aliens. At first Steve is just going to go by, but his sense of fair play gets the better of him.

"Guys, leave him alone." warns Steve.

The three blue aliens look at Steve, "Go away or you will be next!"

"I was afraid you were going to say that. Oh well, don't say I did not let you have a chance to walk away."

The big blue alien takes a haymaker swing at Steve. Steve watches it come then reaches out and catches it in his left hand, and with his right he delivers a punch to the blue alien's stomach causing him to double over and fall to his knees gasping. Steve moves up and delivers a punch to the Blue Alien's head putting him down. Steve then turns to the other two, and they are running down the alley leaving their friend behind.

"So much for friendship."

Steve turns to the orange alien that was being accosted.

"Are you alright?"

The alien looks up, and is still afraid.

"Are you going to rob me?"

Steve extends his hand to the alien to help him up.

"No, I'm not going to rob you. You just looked like you could use a friend, so I helped you."

"But, why? Is there something you want of me? No one helps anyone else here without a reason."

"Ok, I have a reason, can you direct me to a place where I can buy some electronic components?"

"Why?"

"I have a couple of reasons, first I'm new to this world and I don't know very much about it, and two I have a need to make a sensor to test the food so I can safely eat here."

"Since you helped me I'll help you, go down the street for two blocks, and then take one block to the left where you will find a shop that sells electronic components. Good luck."

The alien hurries away down the street. Steve makes his way to the shop, where he is able to purchase the items he needs. Steve returns to the apartment. When he enters, Samantha is acting strange. She is acting all lovie dovie and submissive, this is nothing like her. Steve picks up his helmet and puts it on to scan the area, he finds that the bugs in the room are broadcasting a signal. Steve takes Samantha's helmet, and puts it on her to block the signal.

"What is going on? Why am I wearing my helmet?" Samantha starts to take it off.

"Don't remove that helmet Samantha."

Samantha stops and turns to Steve.

"Hi Honey, your home early from work. You know it is hard to give you a loving kiss with this helmet on."

Steve reaches up and makes an adjustment to her helmet, then the old Samantha returns.

"What is going on?"

"Your mind was being affected. I found that the so called bugs are broadcasting a signal that is affecting your mind. What do you remember?"

"After you left, I was getting an earache. Then all I could think of was you and that I need to do all sorts of things for you, clean house, make dinner, meet you at the door, even to the point of having sex with you. I have always done all that, but there seems to be something I was compelled to do instead of something I like to do. How did you guess what was going on?

"Let's just say, you were not acting like the Samantha I know and love. So I set out to scan the room and found that the listening devices are also broadcasting a signal. Now I'm wondering if I'm being affected as well."

"Well you seem to be ok to me now." said Samantha.

Steve says they should leave the helmets on until he can stop the broadcasts. Steve sets to work on the immediate problem of stopping the broadcasts. After several hours he has a unit that will do the trick. Once he is done he has Samantha remove her helmet. At first nothing seems to happen, then she starts acting as she did when Steve first came home. He turns on the switch and Samantha returns to her normal self.

"At least it works", said Steve.

"I need to buy some more components so I can make the eye glass sensors. What time is it? Oh my I need to get there right now if I'm going to have them ready." Steve ports to the alley way next to the shop and enters. I need to buy more of the components I bought this morning. The alien proprietor quickly produces the items and Steve pays for them. He picks them up and turns to the door. Outside there are two police units parked there, as if waiting for him. Steve opens a window just before the door and steps through it into the alleyway just down the street. The proprietor steps out.

"Did you get him?"

"Get who?" asks one of the police man.

"The man buying the contraband electronics, you, stupid reptile."

"No one came out the door except you, Sir."

Steve returns home, and builds the eye glass sensors.

"I think we need a disguise; I was almost picked up at the electronic shop for buying what they call contraband electronics. I opened a window and stepped into a nearby alley to watch and listen. It seems it was a set up."

"I'm a bit ahead of you."

Samantha produces a blond wig for herself, and a red one for Steve. With the glasses we can look different enough not to be noticed."

"Well, let's test it out and see what we can buy at the store. I hope we can pick up some meat this time." said Steve.

Chapter 152

Steve with his wig and Samantha in hers, leave the building via one of Steve's windows into an alley and walk to the market. It turns out that Steve and Samantha are correct in their assumption about the food. With the glasses they can easily determine which food is safe and which is harmful. They load up a couple of bags full of groceries and take them home. No one even pays them any attention.

Back at home Samantha prepares a meal, and Steve sets up both helmets and the blocking unit to stop any broadcasts that may happen at night.

"Samantha I have a feeling we are going to have to move, in the not too distant future. They may be able to detect that we are blocking their broadcasts, and will come snooping around to see why."

"Then I'll see to it that our backpacks are ready to go at a moment's notice." Said Samantha.

Samantha and Steve have a quiet dinner and when they finish they go to sit on the couch nestled together. Samantha comes up with an idea.

"Steve we need to find a library so we can get some more history and facts about this world. Without CAT, your computer, we will have to do this the old fashioned way, and look it up. Also, I'll see if I can join some sort of woman's group and see what I can learn from them."

"That is an excellent idea. I'll look for the library, and you find a woman's group. And I'll look for another electronics shop. I want to build portable blockers for us while we are out and about, so we do not get caught up in the broadcasts being sent out."

They turn in that night with the blockers in place and they sleep very well. In the morning Steve and Samantha get up determined to accomplish the two goals that they come up with last night. Samantha goes off to look for a place where other woman go to congregate, hair salons, spas, and the like and at about midday she locates just such a place. Steve is out looking for a library and an electronics store. Steve is not as fortunate as Samantha in his search. But Steve runs into another mugging. A man much like himself, is being shoved around. Steve debates with himself about helping the other man, but when one of the aliens pulls out a knife that settled the issue. Steve ports up behind the blue alien with the knife.

"Hey man, may I see that?" as Steve plucks it from the alien's hand.

"Oh, wow, that is wicked." said Steve to the alien.

The alien turns to confront Steve and realizes that Steve put him in jail the last time they met. The blue alien turns and runs off. The other aliens turn their attention to Steve.

"Before you get excited, watch." Steve walks up to the brick wall, and ports the knife into the wall leaving the handle sticking out.

"Now we can fight. Oh and I can do that to you as well." Steve steps back and the blue aliens tries to pull the knife out of the wall. When they are not able to budge it they look at Steve in fear and run off. Steve turns to the man lying on the ground.

"Why were they beating you up?" asks Steve.

"How long have you lived on this planet?"

"Actually not long."

"They were beating me up because I'm pink or (Human)."

"Are you, injured?"

"A few bruises but nothing serious."

531

"Maybe you can help me?"

"With what?"

"I'm looking for a place where I can read some history about this world, a library, or some repository of knowledge. Also I'm looking for a place where I can purchase some electronic components. I'm something of an inventor."

"I may be able to help you. I have such a collection of history at my home that I will allow you to read. As to the electronic components, I do know a few places. But it draws attention of the unwanted kind, after you purchase them."

"Yea, I found that out."

"Are you an inventor then?" asked the man

"Somewhat, I dabble here and there. Why?"

"I'm looking to hire someone who can help me, I have a couple of projects I want to get working, but I need someone a bit savvier than me."

Steve takes off his glasses, and has the man try them on.

"Wow, what are they doing?"

"They are a type of sensor. They have different functions. I can use them to scan for people, or food to see if it is safe for me to eat. Just a few things."

"You're hired! And by the way I'm called Wade, Wade Singer."

"I'm called Steve Ball, and if I can be allowed to work some of my own projects I'll accept."

Wade puts out his hand, and they shake on it.

"Now can we go to your home Wade so I can look at your books?"

"Sure, right this way."

Wade leads Steve off down the street and deeper into the city.

"Steve I live in this building, up on the twentieth floor. The only time it is a problem is when the power goes out."

"I'll keep that in mind."

It does not take long for them to reach the twentieth floor and just down the hall is where Wade lives. Wade opens his door carefully and ushers Steve inside. Wade calls out to his wife and kids to come see the visitor, and two boys and a girl appears followed by Wade's wife.

Wade introduces everyone, and then takes Steve off to his den for the books. While they are in there, Wade shows Steve the projects he is working on. One of them is a white noise generator, so Steve helps him by changing the connections and it works very well. Steve asks Wade if he has done anything about the broadcasts with subliminal content yet.

"What broadcasts?"

"Well Wade the listening devices do more than watch you they broadcast messages, to make you think and perform in certain ways"

"How did you discover that?"

"Actually it was easy. I had left our apartment and when I returned my wife was acting very strange. She is a very neat person to be sure, but she believes I should help her since I live there too. I agree with her, but that night she was too sweet and trying to do everything. So I scanned her and the listing devices, and discovered what was happening. I managed to block the broadcasts and she returned to normal."

"Could you build me one of these units?"

"I can if you have or can get the components."

Wade opens his closet and in the back he pulls out some drawers, and all the components are right there.

Steve sets to work and in an hour he has a unit that blocks the broadcast from the listening devices and soon his wife and kids go from nice disciplined children to your typical bickering children, and the wife acts like she just woke up.

"Then it was not my imagination that they were acting strange. Here take the book Steve and return it when you are finished."

"Thanks Wade, also do you have an atlas or maps of this world that I might also borrow?"

"I sure do, here take them. And I will see you tomorrow."

"I'll be here. What time would you like me to show up?"

"Mid-morning or 9:00 AM."

"I'll be here."

Steve steps out into the hall to make his way to the elevator, gets on alone, and then ports home.

Samantha grabs him in an embrace, and swings him around, laughing. Steve places a hand to her forehead. She frowns at him. "What is that for?"

"I was just checking to see if you were all right."

"I'm fine, silly. I have been invited to a women's retreat."

"That's great, and I have a job now, and here are two books one on the history, and the other is an atlas of this world."

Steve gets the Dimensional Map and compares it to the Atlas. The next portal is in the middle of the ocean, and there is no land mass in the area. Steve sets that problem aside for now, and turns to the book of history. Reading it is rather dull, and dry. But Steve manages to get through the first quarter of the book. This story is much like Columbus, they find land discover Indians, exploit the Indians, and then kill Indians. Or mostly the smallpox and other sicknesses they bring do the killing. So it is the same with the aliens that have shown up here. They discover the humans, exploit humans, and if I had a way I would find that the aliens killed the humans with a sickness of some kind.

The next morning Samantha is up and has breakfast ready for Steve before he goes off to work, and she is very excited.

"What has you so bubbly this morning, you aren't listening to the broadcasts are you?"

"No, the women's meeting is today, and I can hardly wait to see what it is all about."

Steve chuckles, and gives Samantha a kiss and tells her to enjoy herself, and that he will be home for dinner. Steve leaves through one of his windows, which opens near Wade's apartment, and tells her to enjoy herself and that he will be home for dinner.

Samantha dresses up for her meeting. She does her hair, puts on a simple and a little reveling dress with some make up. She looks in the mirror and is very happy with what she sees. Then Samantha ports to the alley just down the street from where the woman are meeting. As Samantha is about to leave the alley, a large blue alien grabs her from behind. Samantha reacts instantly, and the alien finds himself lying in the street on his back. As luck would have it a couple of the women from the group are standing across the street watching.

Samantha walks out and stops to look down on the blue alien as she walks by. The alien picks himself up and charges Samantha in a rage. He just wanted to rough her up and steal her money. Now he wants to kill her. He charges her bellowing at the top of his lungs. Samantha side steps him and propels him into a wall head on. "Ouch! That must have hurt." Thinks Samantha.

She continues to walk to the meeting place. And the other women stand by and watch, as the blue alien picks himself up and then he pulls out his knife. He stalks after Samantha. The women are too scared to say anything, and watch in horror as the alien stalks up to Samantha. Samantha is wearing the glasses Steve made for her so she knows what is happening behind her. She waits until the alien is just about to pounce.

Samantha wheels around, grabs his wrist with the knife, and removes the knife then pulls his face close to hers. And she whispers to him. "If I so much as see you from now on I will kill you. Do you understand?"

Samantha twists his wrist, "Do you understand?"

"Yes, please let me go."

Samantha lets him go, and he does a stupid thing; he tries to knife her with a second knife. Samantha counters his move and uses his knife to stab him in the leg and leaves the knife there. She then turns and walks away. She gets to her meeting and the place is abuzz with what just happened out on the street.

Chapter 153

"Samantha Ball, is what I'm hearing about what you have done true?" asked the chairwoman.

"What is that?" asks Samantha.

"That you just protected yourself from a blue alien?"

"Yes, I did."

"Oh, wow! Could you teach us to do that?"

"I could, if you want to work hard, and apply your selves, but we would need a much larger place to work in."

"Samantha you just tell us what you need and one of us here can provide it. My husband has a warehouse that is not being used, we can use that."

"Sounds good." said Samantha.

For the rest of the meeting Samantha outlines what they will need. So the women's group is moved to the warehouse. The first meeting is to clean up the place, before they start to work on exercise.

Samantha tells Steve all that is going on in the women's group and how she will teach them martial arts. Steve pays attention to Samantha not only in what she is doing, but her appearance. Steve has been noticing changes in them as they are rapidly aging. When they started this journey Steve and Samantha were in their early thirties. Now they appear to be in their mid-forties. The Entity has said time moves differently from one world to another. But every human seems to be aging faster than the aliens.

Steve encourages Samantha to teach the women, but he does not tell her what he thinks is happening. At work the next day he asks Wade if he has access to a bio lab, or if he knows where one is.

"Why, asks Wade."

"Let's just say I have a fear, and I need to check it out, and a Bio lab is the only way I'm going to isolate what I fear maybe happening."

"Steve you are much more, than what you told me aren't you?"

"Actually, yes. I'm a scientist, in a couple of different fields. One of them is biology. I need to run some tests."

"What sort of tests?"

"I'm not sure, but I think the environment has been tampered with. Since I have been here I see the Humans are aging faster than I would expect."

"How is that possible?"

"That is why I need a bio lab to see if I'm right."

"When do you need this lab?"

"Now would be best, as I suspect we are fighting time."

"Let me see what I can do." said Wade.

The next day Steve meets with Wade at his apartment.

"Did you get a lab for me to use?"

"Yes, but it is on the other side of the city, it will take some time to get there."

"Not as much as you think. Do you have a local map?"

Wade rummages in a drawer and pulls out a city map.

"So where is your apartment on the map, and where is the lab?"

Wade points them out, and Steve sees the park where he and Samantha arrived. The lab is just several blocks away. Steve puts his hand on Wade's shoulder and ports them to the park.

"WHAT! Did you just do?" asks Wade.

"Let's just say I have a faster mode of transportation than most."

"I'll accept that. The Lab is over that way and down the street."

Steve ports them short distances until they arrive at the building where the lab is.

"That is fantastic; could you get me that ability?"

"No, I cannot. Let's just say it is an ability that only my wife and I have."

Wade leads the way inside the building and down into a basement. He knocks on the door and it is slowly opened. Wade sees the face of the technician and the door opens further to admit them.

Wade turns to the lab tech. and says.

"This is the man I was talking about."

Steve enters the room, and looks around.

"It's not like my lab, but it should do what I need it to."

"And what would that be?" asks the tech.

"If I'm right this world has a pathogen that is causing all the humans to age prematurely, I want to stop it."

"What do you need?" asks the tech.

"To begin with blood samples. I want a sample from everyone in this room."

In a matter of moments, the tech complies with Steve's request. Steve takes the samples to the microscope and looks them over.

"Is there an electron microscope here?"

"You really do know your stuff said the tech. The scope is over here in the cabinet. I'll get it out for you."

"Son what is your name?"

"I'm called Willy."

"Willy I'm called Steve, and we will be working together, so would you mind if I call you Will?"

"Not at all Steve."

Steve places the samples under the scope and sees what he is afraid of. He checks other samples, and sees the same thing in the other samples. He shows Will and Wade what he has found.

"I will need more samples. Wade is it alright to get samples from your family? I will bring in Samantha as well."

"Sure Steve, when do you need the samples?"

"The sooner the better."

Steve places his hand on Wade's shoulder and ports them into the hallway at his front door. Wade takes him in, and Steve tries to be careful in drawing the blood samples form Wade's family. The young girl cries when it is done, and Wade picks her up and swings her about until she is laughing. Steve leaves Wade and his family and ports home to Samantha.

"Samantha, we have to go to the lab, I need your help."

"What's wrong Steve? You only get this way when danger is involved."

"I knew there was a good reason to marry you. You are right, and I'm not sure how much time there is before the pathogen kills all the humans on this planet."

"What?"

"I have been feeling old, since we got here, and I have noticed how it is affecting you and me. So I got the use of a lab and I tested my blood, and Wade's blood. I found that we have a live virus in our blood, and it is aging us at an accelerated rate. I need to find a serum to stop it."

Steve takes Samantha's hand and ports into the lab scaring Will out of a year's growth.

"Sorry Will, Samantha this is Will. He is my very good helper, and he will take a sample of your blood."

Steve confirms that all the blood samples contain the virus. Now the hard part--- finding a cure.

"Will, do you have a computer?"

"Steve what is a computer?"

"This world is amazing. They are so much ahead of my world in some things, and yet so far behind in others. Will, keep mapping the results. I'm going to see Wade and get the components I need to build a computer."

Steve shows up at Wade's door, and as soon as Steve enters the children run to their bedrooms and are quite.

"You made quite an impression on them." chuckles Wade.

"Apparently not a good one. Wade I need to get these electrical components as soon as possible. Do you know when you can get them, it is very important."

"I might manage them by tomorrow night, is that ok?"

"It will have to do, I need the computer I'm building to help analyze the data, and it will take me a day to write the program. I'll see you tomorrow night."

Steve ports back to the lab, and Samantha is becoming concerned.

"Steve how serious is this?"

"I do not know Samantha that is what is bothering me. Tomorrow night I will need your help. I'm building a computer, and you can type faster than I can with far greater comprehension. I will write up the program, and you can type it in when the computer is up and running."

"You know I will. It is nice to be working with you again. I missed it."

"I'm going to regret this, but can you be a dear and pop home to bring back something to eat, for the three of us?"

"You know how I hate that."

"Believe me I do! But you also know I would not ask if this were not so serious."

Samantha kisses him, and ports home to make some sandwiches and a salad, then as an afterthought she also brings hot coffee and tea. Moments later Samantha ports into the lab with the food.

Steve calls a halt to the work so they can all sit down and eat. Once they finish Samantha hurries them off so she can clean up.

Later that night or more like early morning, Steve and Samantha return home to get some sleep. As for Will, he has a cot in a back room at the lab, and he crashes hard. The next morning not so early Steve is shaking Will awake. Steve hands him a bagel, and a cup of coffee.

"Time to get up, we have a lot to accomplish today."

Steve writes the program for the computer and also another program to analyze the samples. Late in the evening, Steve ports to Wade's apartment to collect the components for the computer. True to his word all the parts are there. Steve collects them and as he gets ready to port, Wade asks if he can come along.

"Sure, I can use some extra hands on this computer. Samantha will be along in two hours to do the programing."

Wade is fascinated in the computer and would like to learn more about it so he tags along.

Steve hands the schematic to Wade and leaves him to the task of putting the hardware together. A couple of hours later, Wade finishes his part of the task.

"Steve I'm done; can we turn it on?"

"We could, but nothing will happen. It needs to have a program, and an operating system. That is what I'm working on."

Samantha ports in carrying a box full of food to feed the hungry men.

"Steve, Will, Wade Dinner!"

Will rushes into the dining area, followed by Steve.

"Your wife sure makes a good meal, even out of sandwiches."

Samantha smiles, and looks at Steve.

"Are you taking notes, dear."

Steve laughs, as he picks his wife up to sweep her into his arms, and plants a rather large kiss on her cheek. Samantha blushes, but does not try to escape his embrace. Steve sets her down and picks up a sandwich and eats as if he hasn't eaten in a week.

After the repast, Samantha starts to clean up and Steve stops her.

"Not now. The computer is ready. Here is the operating system you need to type it in. I'll clean up the mess."

Samantha inputs the operating system, and then the program that Steve gave her. Soon the computer is up and running. Wade and Will are amazed at what the computer can do and soon with the data input into it Steve starts the program and fifteen minutes later it produces the information that Steve is looking for.

"Now we can start working on a vaccine."

Steve and Will work together and soon find a solution that will kill the virus without killing the host. Best thing is it can be dumped into the water supply or injected. Steve gives the shots to the four of them. And asks where the water supply is.

"You will find that pretty hard to get to as they are all protected."

"That remains to be seen. Said Steve. Let's just say, I have my ways. As a matter of recourse, tell me where all the places for the water supplies are located. Then by morning I can treat all the water supplies, and tomorrow everyone will be returned to normal, and their bodies will return to what they were before the virus."

Chapter 154

Wade shows Steve all the places on the world map where the water supplies are located. Poor Will is being run ragged making vaccine while Steve went everywhere about Maze world planet using his windows, to open window after window dropping the vaccine into the lakes, rivers and any possible body of water. It takes Steve all night to finish his task. So that day he goes home exhausted and sleeps the day away.

The next day Steve meets with Wade.

"Who would benefit if the humans died?"

"That would be debatable. What comes to mind is the blue aliens as they mostly run this world. They have all the government positions. Also they keep boasting about an armada that is on its way."

"Just a thought. You see on my world you kill for a few reasons, greed, anger, fear, occasionally jealousy."

"So you think they would kill us to take over our planet?"

"I cannot make an accusation without some proof. I believe it is time for my alter ego to step in."

"What alter ego?"

"What you do not know might keep you out of trouble. So where is the seat of power for this planet?"

"If you mean the Government it is here in this city."

Steve opens the city map.

"Show me where or which building the seat of power is in."

Wade points at the building and Steve thanks him and returns to the lab. Steve takes the virus and runs some tests, then ports to an alley where he has encountered a blue alien before. Three of the aliens appear and surround Steve.

"Is there something I can do for you boys?"

"Yea, Pink, give me your credits and then your life."

"And here I thought, you were going to be nice and give me something."

Steve draws his dart guns and shoots all three aliens, and watches them pass out. He takes blood samples of all three of them. Then ports back to the lab with one of the blue aliens. He cages him up. Then turns back to the computer to analyze the blood samples.

"I see this virus came from you guys. So Steve does some gene splicing to the virus and realizes it will now kill just the blue aliens. Just like they intended to kill the humans on this world."

Steve's alien wakes up and finds himself in a lab and he shakes the bars and screams at him to let him go.

Steve takes up two vials of a drug that the blues like and he adds the new virus to it, then he lets the alien out of the cage. The alien attacks Steve, and Steve lays out the alien several times before the blue alien finely stops fighting. Realizing he cannot win. Steve reaches down and teleports them back to the alley. Then Steve gives the two vials to the blue alien.

"Here now get out of here, and I would not use this stuff it will kill you."

The blue alien looks at the vials, and recognizes the drug he is so dearly hooked on. The blue alien puts the drugs into his pocket and runs away. Steve feels sick to his heart. He does not like to kill, but to save a world he will have to. Steve ports close to the city center. Then he walks the rest of the distance and enters the building. He walks around and pokes into various places. He soon locates the office floor of the so called man in charge. A very big and blue alien. Suddenly Steve is arrested, for being there, and sent to police headquarters where he is locked up, for being in the wrong place. After Steve is put into the cell the officer leaves, and then Steve ports back home. It is time to bring Paladin out of the closet. Steve puts on his battle suit and loads up his dart guns. He chooses not to put on his sword, but his boot knife is placed in its proper place. Steve picks up his helmet, and contacts Samantha.

"Samantha go to Wade's house, and protect them. Try to do it in such a way as to not alarm them. I'm about to take some very bold action here, and they may be in danger."

"All right Steve, are you sure you don't need my help?"

"Not at the moment, but before the night is out I will."

"What are you going to do?"

"Expose the leader and his cronies to the rest of the world."

"Be careful Steve, I still need you."

"Samantha, I love you! I will contact you soon."

Steve ports back to his cell then ports to the other side of the bars, and boldly walks into the chief's office.

"Hi Chief, now tell me what you blue Aliens are up to!"

"YOU!!!!!, I have been looking for you for days."

"Well I'm right here, now back to my answer. Why are you killing off all the humans?"

That question stops the Chief in mid tirade.

"What are you talking about, killing all the humans?"

"Well, I ran a test on several Humans and found a virus that has been engineered. Designed to kill only humans."

At that moment the chief is reaching for a blaster in the desk drawer, Paladin had already picked up on the energy of the weapon and before the chief can pull the blaster from its hiding place. Paladin ports behind him.

"Where did you go pink? I don't know how you found out about the virus, but you're going to die before you can spread that knowledge."

"Not to worry, I already have, and I went one better."

As Paladin grabs the chief's wrist and makes him drop his blaster. Steve shoves him to one side, and picks up the blaster, and puts it in his pouch at his hip.

"I'll just keep this trinket for now."

Steve puts his hand on the chief's shoulder and ports to the City center, and on to the same floor where he was arrested earlier that day.

"I suspect that this place is familiar to you? Now tell me where your documentation is located."

"There is no documentation! You stupid pink, it is a computer. You don't even know what that is?"

"Oh, you mean this box with a screen?"

"How did you know?"

"On my world I build them, mine are better than this toy. And it can do much more."

Paladin fires up the computer and breaks the four-digit code and down loads the information into his helmet.

"Me oh my, what are you going to tell the big boy, chief?"

The Leader enters the room with his blaster drawn.

"He is not going to tell me anything, Pink!"

The leader kills the chief by shooting him in the head.

"Now, pink, I'm going to take my time in killing you."

The leader shoots at Paladin, then realizes he is not in the same place. Paladin ports to the leader's side.

"You know if I would have been standing there you would have killed me, but you missed."

Enraged the leader does a back hand, which Paladin deflects and at the same time takes the leader's blaster.

Paladin takes the Leader by the shoulder and ports them both to the lab, and into the cage he had the other blue alien in.

"When I get out of here Pink, I'm going to kill you!!"

"I don't think so. Your virus, is no longer effective, and I have not only cured the humans, by placing the cure into the water systems all over the planet, but just for you I altered it, and it now kills blue aliens. In a matter of days, all the blue aliens will die off."

"No, you can't!!"

"Yea, I can. And right now the virus has infected you. I suspect you only have hours to live. And this is one time I'm not sorry for taking a life."

Paladin hooks up to the computer, and down loads the information from the leader's computer.

"I see you have the whole campaign laid out. The green aliens, and then so on. Oh lookie you have an armada coming to take over the planet. Too bad, when they get here it will be a death trap."

"You can't do this!!"

"You know on every world I have been to; the bad guy always says that. Do you know, I do it anyway?"

Paladin ports to Wade's house. And he takes off his helmet.

"Samantha, we need to be on our way. Wade, it has been nice working with you. Do you know where I can get a boat?"

"There are several on the water front."

"Good, I'm going to take one so Samantha and I can get to our portal."

"Go ahead, and I'll locate the person who owns it and pay him for it, your computer will make more than enough money to replace the boat."

'Something you will need to do, is broadcast the information I left on the computer at the lab. I also have the leader there as well and he is dying, as a matter of fact all the blues are dying. It seems they have been infected by the same virus they intended to use on you. Before I leave you, I will take the Leader with me."

Samantha ports back to Wade's apartment in her Battle suit, and picks up the back packs.

"Are you ready dear?" Steve asks.

"I'm ready, Steve."

Paladin takes Samantha's hand and ports to the lab to pick up the leader. Then heads to the waterfront where he picks out a boat that is sea worthy. Once on board Paladin cuts the ropes and ports the boat to the horizon, after the third teleport, the leader rouses.

"Samantha if he starts a fuss kill him or send him over board. I need to concentrate so I do not capsize us in these waves."

The Leader screams. "You stinking Pink, what have you done?"

Samantha answers him.

"Oh, nothing, just gave you the same medicine you tried to give us."

"I'll kill you!"

Samantha pulls her sword and places it against his chest.

"If you so much as move, I will run you through with this sword."

Samantha pushes the sword and it penetrates a small distance into his chest, and he stops moving and talking.

"Samantha what do you see over there?"

"I'm not sure Steve, it looks like a sail boat."

"I'm not so sure, it just appeared and it is starting to circle us."

"Steve that can't be a shark, it is too huge."

The sail gets close enough to throw a rock at it.

"It is a shark a giant one, and I think we're on the menu."

Soon the fin disappears into the water, and Steve decides to port to the horizon, as they appear the shark breaches and would have swallowed them whole had they been there. Steve ports two more times and locates the portal.

Samantha tells Steve to hurry, our hungry friend is coming. Steve ties a rope around Samantha and himself, and opens the portal and they get pulled in just at the time the shark breaches again swallowing the boat with the leader in it.

Cyborg World (Old West)

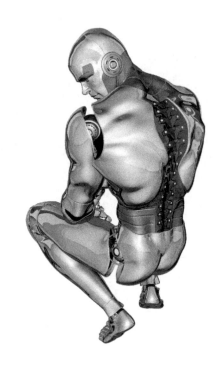

Chapter 155

One moment goes from being within the jaws of a giant shark to standing in an old western town.

"Look at this Samantha. The town looks like it is right out of the old west back home right down to the livery stable, saloon, mercantile, church and so on. I remember when I was a kid my parents took me to an old western ghost town in California for a weekend trip. With the exception of the old western town being run down, this looks almost brand new."

"Steve where are the people?"

Steve looks around, but there is no one walking about. Steve uses his helmet to scan the town. Again he does not pick up any one. Steve leads the way to the saloon. If anything is happening they might find out there. Steve looks in the door and does not see anyone. Then from down the street comes a clanking noise. Curious, Steve watches to see what is making the noise. From around the corner of the mercantile building comes something that looks like a box on legs. At first it seems comical as it lurches along. Then Steve's helmet warns that they are being targeted, and Steve throws up a window. The bolt of energy, it shoots is re-directed to the ground. Then it targets Samantha, and fires but she ports out of the way.

Steve locates its weapon and slices it off with a window. The robot creature stops, picks up the weapon, and holds it in place reattaching. Then it targets Samantha again. Steve takes a more serious action and slices up the robot into four different pieces. He watches as the pieces move towards themselves so they can reattach themselves. Steve then teleports the individual pieces up and down the street. After a small period of time Steve sees the pieces are moving together. It will take several hours for them to come together and reassemble themselves. Steve takes advantage of the time to scan the robot, and discovers it is made up of nanites, millions of them. So in order to destroy it Steve would have use an EMP (Electro Magnetic Pulse) to shut them all down. Steve isolates one nanite and checks its programing to see what set it off.

"Samantha, this thing is programed to destroy anyone or anything if it is in not part of this town. It will leave us alone if we leave."

"But why would anyone want to do that Steve?"

"I do not know, but for now let's get out of here. Our battle suits will not stand up to the energy blasts it uses. So let's not push our luck."

With Samantha in tow they leave town. Steve keeps an eye on the robot to see what it does. It finishes putting itself together, and it walks back the way it came.

Steve sets out with Samantha in the direction of the next portal. In a few miles from town they run onto a small lake with some trees and brush circling around a clearing. So they decide to setup camp for the night. After camp is ready, Steve ports around the area to make sure they will not be caught off guard by someone or something. Steve returns an hour later and Samantha has caught some fish for dinner. Steve cleans them and Samantha cooks them over the camp fire. After they finish eating, it is dark and they turn in for the night. At midnight Steve and Samantha are awaken by six Cyborgs which look a lot like mechanical cowboys on Cyborg mounts which look like horses but only mechanical. (Cyborg is part living and part mechanical).

In a mechanical voice "Well stranger, do you mind if we share your fire?"

"Who are you?" asks Steve.

They all laugh, "He does not know who we are boys, maybe we should introduce ourselves. We are called the Cyborg Bunch!"

They pull off their hats and bow to them.

"Is that suppose too impress us?" asks Samantha.

Her question angers the leader so he pulls out his blaster to shoot at her. Steve reacts instantly, and re-directs the blast with a window. One of his men dies from the shot and falls to the ground.

"What happened he barks, who shot Mech?"

They looked around and scan nothing or no one. The leader gets off his mount. It looked much like a horse with a few other differences. He walks up to Samantha and grabs her by the neck and lifts her off the ground. He begins to choke her; Samantha tries to get away. Steve cuts the Cyborg's arm off with a window and it drops Samantha to the ground. Samantha is trying to get some air.

"Stranger how did you do that?"

"Well leader of the Cyborg Bunch. If you do not leave us alone, I promise that you will find out how I did it and you will not like it."

"Oh! I'm so scared. You have me shaking in my boots, little man." As the leader gives out a mechanical laugh, Steve pulls out the blaster he had taken from the chief of the last world, and shoots the leader point blank in the head. The blast burns right through his head killing him. Steve then gives Samantha the blaster he took from the leader. The other Cyborgs ride off into the dark to get away from the strange man and his woman.

"This blaster from the last world seems to work here, we best leave here before they decide to come back possibly with more Cyborgs."

Samantha does not quibble one bit. They grab their stuff. Steve ports them back to the edge of town where they encountered the box on legs. Then Steve ports them to the edge of town to see if the box with legs will come back out. Then out of the darkness Samantha scans the rest of the Cyborg gang, and they are bearing down on them. Steve ports Samantha to the back side of the box to see if the gang will follow them. They do and as soon as they enter the town the box on legs engages them. The three Cyborgs fire on the box with legs. And the box on legs returns the fire leaving another Cyborg dead shot by the box and the Cyborg basically dies; leaving two. The Cyborgs soon decide it might be better to retreat. Once they leave the box turns toward Steve and Samantha. Who port to the other edge of town out of the range of the mechanical creature?

"I wonder how the Cyborgs knew to come to the town, can they somehow track us?"

Muses Steve. Taking Samantha by the hand, Steve takes them back to their original camping site, and they quickly hide to make sure the last of the Cyborg gang is not there waiting for them. When they do not scan them they make another camp with Steve taking the first watch. Nothing happens the rest of the night. In the morning Samantha wakes up Steve. Then Steve pulls out the map and locates the direction of the next portal.

"Steve what are we going to do if we run into others like the Cyborg gang?"

"I'm not sure, but the energy weapons from the last world seem to work, at least for the time being."

"What do you mean for the time being?"

"I do not know how long the power cells will work or if we can repower them. After that we will have to resort to our ability to teleport."

"The reason I asked, is that I could not teleport out of the Cyborg's grasp, and if you had not cut off his hand I would have had my throat crushed."

"It worked that time, because the components were not nanites they were regular components. Otherwise, I think you would have been killed."

Samantha looks at the blaster, "How does this work?"

Steve shows her how to fire it.

"Now we need to be careful. I do not know how long the power source will last."

"Alright Steve, I'll be careful."

Steve takes Samantha into his arms and teleports to the top of the hill, following the stream. Samantha is wondering why he did not take her hand, but embraced her instead. Not that she minded, she rather liked it. Age is still wearing on them. If you could test their age it would indicate they were in their late fifties. As the Entity mentioned that time moves differently on all the worlds.

At the top of the hill, Steve Ports in line of sight a few more times and comes upon a house in the wilderness. It's not too far from the stream he had been following. The building is pretty run down, but still looks sturdy. They both call out and approach with caution. When no one answers or appears; Steve decides to enter the house. It is full of cob webs and dust among other things. Samantha and Steve start poking around, brushing dust off of objects they find. Steve finds a work bench, and locates some tools which he decides to keep. As he is rummaging around, a strange object clamps to his arm. It causes no problems other than it is strange and Steve tries to dislodge it, but it is securely attached. Steve scans it and so does Samantha. Nothing harmful appears in the scan except that the device is taking energy from Steve's suit. In the struggle to remove the device Samantha finds that she also has a device attached to her leg near her ankle.

"Steve what are we going to do with these parasites?"

"I don't know, but they are not parasites, more like symbionts. They need power and so they are taking it from our suits. At this point I do not know if they will be beneficial or dangerous."

"All the more reason to get them off of us."

Steve removes his helmet, to run his hands across his face. Then the device attached to his arm detaches and lands on his helmet. Steve sets the helmet down and watches. All that happens is that the symbionts drain some of the power from his helmet. Steve tells Samantha to remove her helmet. She does, and again the device on her leg jumps to her helmet.

"At least it is not attached to our persons." said Samantha.

Steve starts rummaging some more. "Steve what are you looking for?"

"I'm not sure, there may be notes or information lying about that will explain our two friends, and other things."

Steve checks the work bench looking for information. Samantha is just poking here and there when she sees a cot along the back wall, with a rumpled blanket on it. She walks over and picks up the blanket and lets out a scream. A skeleton lay there; she drops the blanket. In a flash Steve is standing beside, her making sure she is not injured in any way. In shock she points at the cot and Steve sees the skeleton.

"I wonder who he was." Steve wraps up the remains in the blanket and takes it out back to bury it. By the time Steve returns Samantha is getting over her shock, and she starts crying.

"Honey why are you crying?"

"I don't know; I guess I'm getting tired of finding death everywhere we go."

Steve takes Samantha into his arms and holds her until she calms down.

"I know what we should do", said Steve.

Samantha looks up into his face, "What?"

"We both need a bath and a chance to wash our clothes, and battle suits, then a good night's sleep, not to mention some food."

"Ok." said Samantha.

Steve walks out to get the helmets, and as he is gone Samantha cannot contain her curiosity. She sees a book just under the cot, and so she retrieves it. She opens it, to discover it is a diary.

"Steve, come see what I have found" as Samantha holds up the book.

"What did you find Samantha?"

"It appears to be a diary."

"Great, bring it along, we'll read it together, and it may hold some clues about this world."

At the steam Steve sets the helmets in direct sun light to charge not only the helmets, but the two electronic critters that have latched on to them. They strip down and jump in to the slow moving water to wash off the sweat and grime. Afterward they climb up on a rock to air dry. Steve picks up the diary and flips through the pages. Steve reads aloud to Samantha about the individual who died on the cot. It appears that he crossed over from another world by accident, when he was testing one of his gadgets. What he found was a world much like the old west. He started to make Inventions to help people, and the people bought them. Suddenly the people started dying off, the man had brought a cold with him. The cold grew into a pandemic and spread very fast, killing most of everyone. So he built Cyborgs to help contain the outbreak and help the people in need, then the Cyborgs started killing the people.

He tells of building the box on legs using nanites to protect the town, again it kills anyone in town, and he cannot stop it or control it.

"Is there anything on your two new friends?"

"Not yet, but it does talk about the different Cyborg gangs running about. Due to the program getting corrupt instead of stopping one another, they started to band together. That seems to explain the Cyborgs, but not our two friends."

Steve continues on with the reading. Then he puts down the book.

"Samantha we have to get off this world as soon as possible."

"What is wrong Steve?"

"Remember the Entity?"

"Yes."

"He said that on each world time moves differently. Well the time in this world moves at a year per month according to our time, which is what I have been suspecting. According to my scans we are approaching our mid-sixties, at this rate we will die of old age before we can finish our trek across the dimensions."

They suit up and pull together their supplies. They return to the house, and sack the place for items they might need, then Steve takes out the map and locates the portal. With Samantha in hand, and the two new additions (Unknown) they set off teleporting toward the portal.

They have to quit for the night. If you can't see you can't teleport safely, so they make camp next to a stream. Steve catches a few fish, and Samantha cooks them up. They have dinner and crawl in to their blankets to sleep. Steve sets the helmets to scan for intruders. That night the two that are left of the Cyborg gang, stand a small distance off to watch them. After a non-verbal communication they decide to attack. The helmets start to emit a warning but the two unknown units stop the helmets alarms. The Cyborgs come into camp and soon wake Steve and Samantha.

"Well now lookie at what we caught, the two humanoids who need to be cured."

Each of the Cyborgs have Samantha and Steve in their hands.

"Leave us alone" said Steve.

"Why are you going to kill me like you did our leader, and his mate?"

Steve opens two windows and slices off their hands holding him and Samantha. Steve and Samantha fall to the ground coughing trying to catch their breath. The Cyborgs pull their weapons to kill both Steve and Samantha. As the Cyborgs pull the triggers the two units fly from the helmets and intercept the blasts and absorb them. To the units it is like feeding on the energy. The Cyborgs are shocked and run for their mounts. They have seen these little beasties before, and they will drain all the Cyborgs energy and leave them as dead husks. Steve and Samantha watch as the two unit's land on the Cyborgs and drain them of all their energy. And their mounts as well. The units then return to Steve and Samantha to attach themselves to Steve and to Samantha.

Steve waits to see if the same thing will happen to him and Samantha. But nothing happens.

With morning still off for a few hours, they decide to turn in and get some sleep. With the morning Samantha is up and feeling less tired. She wakes Steve to find he is feeling much better. Steve looks at the unit on his arm and it is vibrating. It does not cause him any discomfort, so he checks Samantha's unit to find that it is doing the same. Steve runs a scan with his helmet to find that he is not aging as fast as he was, and even reversed some. According to the helmet we are now at our late fifties again, instead of our mid-sixties. Steve tells Samantha what the units are doing to them.

Steve and Samantha break camp and set out to reach the portal. They manage to travel all day without any problems and without running in to any more Cyborgs or robots. They decide to camp a little early so Steve can read more of the diary. That night he runs on to the information on the units. They were built to protect the humanoid that built them. He made two of them in case one broke down or was destroyed. They require vast amounts of energy, he also made them to slow the aging of this world.

"This person whoever he was, was quite an inventor. I would have liked to have met him."

"Very good dear, now go get something for dinner." said Samantha.

Steve looks up at her and then puts down the book. With his dart guns in hand, Steve ports across the stream and locates a game trail. As he follows the trail, he runs into a deer like creature, but decides to let it go. Soon he finds a bird much like a chicken but a bit larger than a chicken. He shoots it with a dart, and a few moments later it falls over asleep. Steve retrieves it and ports back to camp with his catch.

Steve gets the chore of cleaning all the animals before Samantha will cook it. Samantha can be a harden killer when it is called for, but she cannot bring herself to kill an animal. She is even more squeamish in cleaning a dead one. But she sure can cook them.

Steve reads the diary as Samantha cooks the meal. He finds part of what he is looking for, the two units, are protectors. They ward off the effects of the aging, and they are a bane to the Cyborgs and robots. The only robots they have a hard time dealing with are the nanite colony units.

"That explains in part why they latched on to us."

"What are you saying Steve?"

"I'm sorry, I was thinking aloud. The Units are protectors. They keep the aging to a minimum and they can stop the Cyborgs and robots by draining their power. The box on legs, the units cannot stop."

"I like the not aging part, but we still need to get out of here don't we?"

"I agree." said Steve.

Steve pulls out the map and tries to see where they are in reference to the portal.

"Samantha, it looks like it will take a week to get to the portal that is if nothing impedes us on the way."

They eat their dinner, and turn in for a good night's rest. Steve sets up their helmets, and the units they keep attached to their arms. In the morning Steve wakes up to find Samantha gone. Steve starts looking around to see where she might have gone, when the unit pulls him in the direction upstream. Curious Steve follows the pull, and soon finds Samantha taking a bath.

"Now this is nice, a beautiful woman taking a bath all alone."

"Well if my husband weren't around to join me I would invite you in. You' handsome devil."

"I just may join you any way."

Steve strips down and dives into the water, and then screams. "This is cold!"

"Do tell; maybe you could find a place with hot water next time."

"I'll see what I can do."

After sporting about in the stream and washing one another, they crawl out on to the bank to sit in the sun to dry. Breakfast is left over bird from the night before. Then they set off toward the portal.

Samantha spots a cabin just before Steve is ready to teleport them to the next area.

"Steve let's stop and check out the cabin, maybe we can sleep undercover tonight."

"Alright, you scan this side of the cabin and I will do the other side."

Samantha and Steve use their helmets to scan for any signs of life or power signatures. They find none. So they enter the cabin and like the first one where they found the units, this one is covered in dust inside and out. It was still intact, but the dust and cobwebs indicate that no one has been here in a very long time.

"Steve, why don't you go get us something for dinner, and I will clean up this kitchen area, and get a fire going."

"Sure thing, my love."

As Steve is about to leave he hears Samantha squeal.

"What is wrong Samantha?"

"Nothing Steve, there is a wash tub and a wood stove, I can get a hot bath tonight."

"I'll have to make a note of that for the future. Hot bath is a cry of happiness."

"Now get out of here and go catch some dinner."

Steve smiles, and ports back to the place he got the bird for dinner the night before in hopes he can find another one. In the meantime, Samantha finishes cleaning the kitchen area, and the sleeping area, before she decides to go collect as much fire wood as she can. As she is gathering up branches, she finds what is left of a garden, using her helmet to select the veggies that are safe to eat, then picks up the fire wood before she ports back to the cabin. As it turns out, at the cabin she spots a lake some little ways off. Samantha decides hot water for boiling the vegetables would be a gift so she grabs a kettle she found, ports to the lake to fill the kettle and brings it back to the cabin where she starts a fire to boil the water.

Steve returns just at sundown, with a couple of birds, already cleaned. Samantha has filled the canteens with water, then set more water on to boil and she adds the veggies to cook them. Samantha takes the birds and bakes them, just to be different. Then she has Steve port to the lake with a couple of buckets to get some water to put on the stove to warm them up so she can take a bath in hot water. Steve laughs good-naturedly and gets the water. When he returns the third time dinner is ready and Samantha lays out a good spread of veggies and bird for dinner. Then Samantha pours the hot water into the tub and manages to sit in it to wash. Steve sits by the stove and some candle light to read more of the diary. The diary was at the end of the humanoid's life, and he talks about the trouble he brought and his mistake in building the Cyborgs, robots and nanites. If he could, he would have not built them at all.

Steve takes his turn in the tub to get a room temperature bath, which is better than freezing in the cold water at the stream or the lake. The bed is not as comfortable as he would have liked, but again it is better than sleeping on the cold ground. In the morning it is hard to get started. It would have been nice to spend one more night in some comfort, but time is an enemy here. Steve packs up their belongings and makes ready to leave. Samantha takes a last look around then opens the door, then turns and dives back into the room as blaster fire comes through the door. Steve puts on his helmet to scan the area around the cabin and they are surrounded by Cyborgs.

"Come out with your hands up and you will not be harmed."

"Why should I trust you?" said Steve.

"Do you have a choice?"

"I believe I do."

Steve takes Samantha by the hand and ports back to the cabin where they found the units. The cabin they had just left is soon set ablaze. The Cyborgs thought they had caught the last of the humanoids, but they did not realize that the humans got away.

"Samantha, are you ready to get moving again?"

"Let's get out of here." Steve teleports them to the lake not far from the cabin that is burning. From there they continue on toward the portal leaving the Cyborgs behind. Steve teleports line of sight at least twenty times, putting miles between him and the gang. They come to a flat land very open and wide. They teleports over more ground here than he could when he first arrived.

That night they eat a cold dinner and have no fire, to show where they are. They take up their travel the next morning. And soon come to a desert place, very cold at night, and very hot during the day.

"The portal is some distance out there." Points Steve.

"Ok, Steve the sooner we get there the sooner we can get off this world."

Steve ports them back to the lake long enough to fill up their canteens and then ports them back to the edge of the desert. Steve will port them as far as he can see. Steve can cover a lot of ground in this flat country, at least a hundred miles in a day. In the mountains, they can only port a fraction of that distance. At the last place they teleport to Steve will mark the spot so he can return in the morning. Then he would port them back to the cabin near the lake to spend the night. What Steve and Samantha did not know is that the group of Cyborgs is still looking for them. Steve's teleporting caused the Cyborgs some confusion, they would detect them out on the desert then they would disappear. In the morning they would detect them back on the desert. The leader figures out where they are headed. It is to the place of power. So the Cyborgs decide not to follow their prey, but try to get a head of them. The Cyborgs want to get to the place of power before Steve and Samantha do and wait for them there. With mechanical mounts they can travel all night and all day. Mechanical mounts can travel faster than a regular horse, even faster than a car.

The Cyborgs reach the place of power. As it turns out it is an old western town populated by Cyborgs. The gang storms into the saloon and bellies up to the bar where each orders mech fluid (Oil) to drink. Then they head out to plug in the mounts into a power supply pole.

The leader of the Cyborg gang puts his fellow Cyborgs at the place of power to wait for their intended prey. Steve and Samantha continue for two more days. When they spot the town they decide to stop at the edge of it to watch the activity. They soon find out that the town is full of Cyborgs, so walking right in is out of the question. Steve decides to go in alone and locate the portal. With both units with him Steve ports to the back side of a buildings then moves from one building to another. In thirty minutes, Steve locates the portal at the center of town, and he also sees the Cyborg gang. Steve ports back to Samantha, and explains the situation to her.

"How are we going to get to the portal Steve?"

"I'm not sure yet."

"Won't they know we are here?"

"I believe so, but what I need is a diversion."

"Will fire work?"

"It might, explosions would also help. Where can I get them?"

Steve takes Samantha by the hand and teleports to the first cabin they found the diary in to see if any explosive material would be present. They find none. Then Steve teleports to the second cabin to search for explosive materials, and again they find nothing. The only place left is the first town they came to. Steve leaves Samantha, but she follows on her own.

"Steve Ball, you will not leave me behind."

"Samantha I have to face the box on legs, I did not want to endanger you."

"I don't care; we'll face it to gather."

"Ok, stay back."

Steve approaches and the box on legs appears, Steve realizes that he has to move fast. He uses his window to slice the box into sections. Then he teleports one section into the lake, and other section he sends to the river. The last section he sends to the town where the portal is. Once he has the box removed from town Steve and Samantha search through the town to look for explosives. Samantha finds them in a house, down in a basement.

"Steve I think I have what you want, follow my signal."

Steve comes down the steps and sure enough, it is an explosive. Steve then creates several square packages of explosive and puts them in a bag so he can carry them. Steve and Samantha turn to leave when Samantha points out the blasters sitting on a bench on the far side of the room. Steve walks over and looks one of them over. He tests one out and it fires. He then finds a couple of gun belts and some kind of power cell. He fills up the slots on the belts. Steve has Samantha put one-gun belt on and he puts on the other gun belt. Now we should be able to create enough of a diversion to get us to the portal.

Steve transports them back to the town where the portal is. Just outside of the town, Steve lays out his plan to Samantha. He hands her a share of the bombs and tells her to be careful. Steve lays his bombs in an erratic pattern and Samantha does the same as they put down the bombs, they light the fuse and move on to the next location. Back at the edge of the woods they wait until the bombs go off.

When the first bomb exploded none of the Cyborgs stirred. However, when three more bombs destroyed buildings, then it is like everyone is coming out of the wood work. Then Cyborgs are running here and there, after the bombs go off. One Cyborg picks up a bomb and while looking it over it explodes. Needless to say there is not much of the Cyborg left. The leader moves to the center of town to wait for Steve and Samantha, and they just appear behind him.

"Looking for us?" said Steve.

The Cyborg turns to face them and points his blaster in their direction. Steve placed the units on their backs so they would not be seen right away. The leader calls Steve out for a quick draw. If Steve wins, the leader will tell all the Cyborgs to leave Steve and Samantha alone. If I win you both die.

"I see." said Steve.

Before Steve can make any decisions they are surrounded by Cyborgs. More of the bombs are still going off, but none of the Cyborgs move or even take notice.

"I Guess I had better do this, if we are to leave this world."

"Steve can you do this?"

"I'm not sure. But I have to try. Alright you win, I'll gun fight you. Now tell all the other Cyborgs to move out to the edge of town, it will be just you and me."

The Leader tells them to all leave. Then he transmits to the gang if he loses, to kill the humans. The leader paces off the distance for the shoot out to take place. Steve has Samantha move to the side, and with reluctance she moves. The leader and Steve are in position and the leader say's.

"On the count of three we fire."

Steve stands at the ready, knowing he is not fast enough to beat the leader's draw, Steve also does not believe the Cyborg will live up to his part of the bargain either. The Cyborg counts to one, draws and fires his weapon. Steve does not draw but opens a window that will return the blaster fire to the mid-section of the leader in effect the leader shoots himself. Samantha runs to Steve, and Steve grabs Samantha by the hand and opens the portal and they are pulled through. At that point the units fall off Steve and Samantha and are left behind.

Reverse world

Chapter 156

Steve and Samantha land in an empty field. They scan the area for danger and find none. Steve takes out his map to see where the next portal is, and finds it off to the north of this world. They set out in that direction. After several ports they locate a small stream. And so decide to spend the night there. They did not get much sleep before they left the Cyborg world and since it looks safe enough they decide to spend the rest of the day there to get some sleep. They set up camp, and each has a set of chores to perform in setting up camp. It goes quickly. And soon it is done. Steve then sets out to find something for dinner. After a few ports along the stream he finds small creatures much like a rabbit. He uses his dart gun and puts three of them to sleep. He picks them up and takes them back to camp where he kills and cleans them for Samantha to cook.

After dinner, they snuggle up with each other and go to sleep. In the morning Steve feels strange, some of his aches and pains seem to be less, and he feels more refreshed. Samantha also has the same feeling. At the time they do not think anything about it. They have breakfast then pick up camp so they can move on. The second day is much like the first. And the following morning they get up and head further north toward their goal. On the third port Samantha sees a town off to the left from the direction they are headed in.

"Steve, should we go there to see what the people are like here?"

"Sure, why not, it can't be any worse than what we just left."

"We better change our clothes and put away the battle suits, let's try the clothes we used in the alien world."

After they change clothes and put away the battle suits, Steve ports them to the edge of the town. There they see roads, cars, and people moving about much like the people from earth.

They walk hand in hand up the street when they come to a cemetery where a bunch of people are standing around all jovial and celebrating. Curious, Steve and Samantha watch the ceremony.

"He must have been a very bad person, for everyone to be happy for him here."

They start to walk away when the people open the casket and an old man sits up. The people there help him out of the casket. The old man is all bent over as they lead him to a chair. Samantha walks up to listen to the conversation. What she learns is confusing for her. So later she talks to Steve about what they saw.

"Steve, he was dead and then came back to life? No, it was as if he were dead many years ago, and today is his living day. I do not understand."

"No, I wonder? I seem to recall from one of my college friends who came up with an idea of a world that time moved backwards. Where dead people wake up and grow younger instead of older, going through the life process as an adult to teen to child to toddler then baby, and then gone."

"You mean if we stay here we will grow younger?"

"In theory maybe."

"Let's see if we can find a way to stay here for a time and see if that is right."
Steve chuckles, "Ok."

So they set out to look around town to see what they can find. Steve finds a job at a feed store, and Samantha finds a job as a waitress. They had some gold they cash in at the bank so they are able to rent an apartment. Steve gravitates to the local library where he looks up the history and the sciences of this world. It does not take long to verify that they indeed live life in reverse. Steve then locates a book on geography about this world. Over time Steve learns more about life here on this world. On more than one occasion some friends are taking their parents who are now babies, to a special building. There they place the two-day old child in a special crib and sit out in the waiting room to watch. As we watch a bright light flares in the crib and then it is empty.

Then a month later we are invited to a wake, in the real sense.

We go to the cemetery and our new friends pull a cremation jug out of the ground. They then pour the ashes into a casket shaped box, and closed the lid. The casket then reflects a lot of light. When the glow stops they open up the casket and their father would hobble out of the casket so they could take him home. By this time Steve and Samantha have lived there a year and are noting that they are growing younger. To them it seems to be at a slow rate, but in reality it is happening at a fast rate. According to the helmet sensors they have moved from the late sixties into to their late fifties. Steve notices that Samantha's hair is turning back to the lustrous raven colored hair she had when he met her.

Looking over the maps of the continent where they are living Steve, decides to move Samantha and himself to the next town heading towards the north. Steve decides that they need to move closer to the portal. Steve finds a job as an engineer in the city that they move to, and Samantha becomes a secretary. Between the both of them they make a fair wage, and they move into a house. At his new job Steve comes up with some new ideas for his battle suit. So he increases the force fields both the deflector and the exoskeleton, then he creates a couple of copies for the police to use. His suit becomes so widely used that the money he generates sets them up for a life time. Steve runs into a discovery, as one day at a park a little boy falls down and cuts his hand, and it is bleeding badly. Steve takes off his shirt and makes a band aide for the boy to stop the bleeding. The blood is not red, but blue. Steve returns the boy to his mother who is grateful for his help.

Steve again checks his helmet and finds they are now equal in age to thirty year-olds. Then one day at work Steve manages to cut his hand, instead of bleeding blue blood it is red. Before he knows it Steve is hustled off to a security place and is being held for being an alien spy. Samantha comes home and security is there waiting for her. Samantha is about to port away when they tell her; her husband is in the holding tank at headquarters. So Samantha wonders why Steve is still there. What the security force does not know is that Steve has left and returned several times. When Steve cannot reach his wife, he decides to wait at the security holding tank for his wife to be brought in.

Steve had rented a locker at one of the travel terminals, and placed his and Samantha's battle suits, swords and blasters into the locker to await his return or need. Back in the cell he waits. Soon Samantha is brought in and placed in a cell next to his. Then the area is emptied of people and a man in a gray suit and sun glasses enter the cell block.

"Now Steve Ball, you and or your wife are going to tell me where you are from, how did you get here?"

"Ok, we're from a place called earth, and we arrived by a portal."

"You expect me to believe that?"

"I don't see why not; it is the truth."

"Sure, where is your space ship?"

"We don't have one."

"Where are you from and where is your space ship, if you do not tell me I will be forced to extract the answers I want in other ways."

"Alright I have grown tired of you. Samantha are you ready to go?"

"Yes, Steve."

Steve ports into Samantha's cell takes her hand. The man in gray pulls a gun and shoots at them, and hits the blank wall behind them.

Steve takes them to the locker at the travel terminal.

"Let's get our stuff and be off."

As soon as they gather their back packs the police converge on the area where they are.

"Wow, he sure is fast. I think he really wants us."

"Steve, we need to get out of here and move on to the next world."

"I have to agree. As it is we are nearing our late twenties anyway, any longer and we may not have the memories of our experiences, and lose our ability to leave here."

Steve takes Samantha's hand and ports them to the outside of the city.

"Put your hands on top of your head, and get down on your knees or we will shoot you!"

Steve then ports Samantha and himself back to where they came into this dimension.

"We had better put on our battle suits, and get dressed for battle."

"Are you sure we should do this?" questions Samantha.

"Unfortunately, yes. This man in Gray seems hell bent to bring us in, and he means to torture us to make us revile where some imaginary space craft is."

"He hates people not like him, doesn't he Steve?"

"I'm afraid so. I do not know why. But he is out to get us, and he won't stop until he does."

After changing, Steve ports them back to the city's far edge. We need to get moving. In short ports, Steve and Samantha head north to the portal. The man in Gray follows them. Somehow he is able to track them (it is because the red blood contains iron, whereas the blue blood does not). Soon Samantha spots the hover craft that is following them.

"Look Steve, at this rate we will not be able to get away."

"There craft runs on a fuel, and they cannot keep up with us for that long. Now the problem is if they have others in pursuit of us, then we may have to resort to a violent course of action, which I would rather we did not have to."

"Steve, I have an idea. Send the police back to where we first came into this world. By the time they appear there and can return here we can be closer to the portal before they can return."

"That's a good idea. Come with me into the open."

Steve leads Samantha out into the open field and he sits down keeping his hands on his head. The craft sets down on the grass not far away. Steve opens a window back to the open field where they came to this world and both men step into the window, and Steve closes it leaving them stranded hundreds of miles away. Steve and Samantha get up and walk over to the craft, and after scanning it Steve realizes it has a way to track them, so he opens another window and cuts the craft in half. Then they take up their journey to the next portal. From this time forward they avoid the cities and towns.

Steve keeps testing Samantha and himself and they are getting younger, "we will need to leave very soon or we will grow too young to continue." Steve thinks.

Steve consults with the map and sees the portal fifty miles further on. They can be there in an hour give or take and depending upon the terrain. Mountains and woods will make it hard to do line of sight teleporting. They reach their destination only to find that an army is waiting for them. Steve and Samantha are at the edge of the woods, looking in on the scene before them.

"Steve they are determined to stop us; do we know why?"

"No, but the man in charge is determined to capture us. I wish I knew why."

Steve moves them back into the woods just out of sight.

"I think I'll go down there and ask why we deserve this treatment when we have lived in peace for so long."

"Are you sure you should do that Steve, they may shoot first and ask questions later."

"Did you see how they were set up? They have the portal surrounded but they are facing out ward from it. It's like they do not know what we can do or anything about the portal. So I will appear just in front of what looks like a tank and sit down with my hands on my head. Here you keep my weapons in case you need to come to my rescue."

"Steve be careful; I still need you."

Steve never tires of hearing her saying that. He reaches out and pulls her to him in a hug.

"What would I ever do without you Samantha?"

"I do not know, but I hope to never have to find out."

Steve ports up to the front of the tank and sits down. It seems no one is seriously paying attention as he actually sits in his spot for thirty minutes before anyone even notices him sitting there. Suddenly the police surround him with rifles pointed at him. Steve removes his helmet.

"Hi guys, what is going on? This isn't just for me is it?"

"Who are you?" asks the officer in charge.

"I'm called Paladin, and I'm from another world."

"Where is the other one like you?"

"What other one?"

One of the guards back hands Steve across the face, splitting his lip.

"Now that was uncalled for, I have half a mind to leave."

"Now that is going to be difficult since we have all the guns and they are pointed at you." Commented the Officer in charge.

"Ok, your right. Now tell me why I'm being hunted. I have done nothing to any one of your people?"

"We captured you so you would tell us about your technology. I want to know what the enemy is up to and when they plan to invade us. We are going to war and we would like the edge over our enemies, and you are going to give it to us."

"What enemies? In all the time we've spent here, I have not seen or heard that you have any enemies."

"Right now you are the enemy, and other aliens like you who come to our world to take advantage of us."

"I see you are quite paranoid aren't you?"

Again the guard, backhands Steve, but this time the guard is laying on his back trying to catch his breath.

"Sir you want a war; I'll give you one." Steve vanishes right in front of them and ports back to Samantha.

"We havetried to avoid war with them, but they want our technology so they can make better troops, and equipment for doing war with other nations. That is why they want us so bad."

"What are you going to do?"

"I'm going to destroy their equipment, set up my windows, and deflect their arms' fire. Then you will have to port us to the center of their circle, and I'll open the portal. But we have to take out their massive arms, before we can do this."

"So what can I do, because I'm not staying here while you are doing all the fighting?"

"I suspected you would say that, so if you could protect my back, then I can do the rest."

"You know I will."

Paladin and Samantha take the field. Paladin is going to disable the army without killing anyone, if possible. All of the tank-like machines are moving into position and Steve opens a huge window. The first tank disappears and shows up in the field where Steve and Samantha first appeared on this world. Another tank swings in to fill in for the tank that disappeared. Steve opens another window and slices off the tank's guns and treads. The next tank is ported to where the other tank was sent. After removing most of the tanks, the air cars start their attack. When most of the cars disappear or are sliced in two, the foot shoulders mass up to charge them. Paladin was waiting for this. Paladin opens a window and the troops charge through it not knowing anything until they get to where they find the cars and tanks that were sent before them.

"Well officer in charge, what are you going to do now that I have decimated your force?"

In answer to Paladins question the last group of men are ordered to shoot to kill. Paladin's and Samantha's battle suits stop the bullets. The ten men did not have a chance. Between Paladin and Samantha, they stomped the stuffing out of the remaining troops and leave them with broken bones.

Paladin looks at the officer.

"You wanted a war, now you have experienced my war. I could have killed everyone here, but I did not. If I were you I would give it up. Steve turns to Samantha.

"Grab our stuff we are leaving."

Samantha brings their backpacks and stands next to Steve. He starts to concentrate to open the portal, when the ground erupts around them, and someone fired a missile at them. Samantha scans the place where it came from and ports to the man who fired it. Then using her sword, Samantha kills him with a single thrust, then ports back to Steve. Moments later the portal opens and they step through to the next world.

The Chimerians

Chapter 157

Steve and Samantha sit down to take a rest.

"That was the worst world we have encountered." said Steve.

"One thing good about it is we grew younger instead of older, I feel like a young teenager again."

"I hope you will not be disappointed, but we nearly are. If we had spent any more time, there we would have lost the ability to open the portal. I'm glad to get away."

Steve opens the pack and takes out the map. As he is looking it over a creature steps into view from the nearby brush.

"Are you the one called Paladin?"

The creature was a cross between a lion, bird and a reptile.

"Maybe." answers Paladin. "Who wants to know?"

"You are as wise as they say, and wise beyond your years. The instructor of the hive said you would be coming. That you would arrive at this day and hour. So I waited for you."

"So answer my first question who are you?"

"My tribe calls me Sky Lion, and they also call me the Watcher."

"What name do you prefer?"

"Either one, so why not call me watcher, it is shorter than Sky Lion."

"Let me introduce my wife…"

"Aaa Yes, the mate of Paladin, the one called Samantha."

Watcher bows to her in reverence.

"Steve, I like this one are you taking notes?"

Steve chuckles and turns to the Watcher.

"Well Watcher, where are we and where are you taking us?"

"Paladin, you are on Chrimeria, and I'm to take you first to the hive, then to my people. The Instructor will explain all to you when we get to the hive."

"Ok, let's go."

Watcher leads them into the woods from where they are, and after a short time they come to a camp, already set up. A female creature somewhat different from Watcher was tending to the stew on the fire.

"Ho Blossom, it is I, Watcher, and I have brought Paladin and his mate."

"Please to enter our camp revered ones."

"What are they talking about Steve?" asked Samantha.

"I'm not sure, but there is something I barely remember from the past, about a group of humans changed into animals. But it is so foggy in my mind."

"All will be explained to you Paladin, when we reach the hive tomorrow. Here please eat and turn in. It will be a hard trip tomorrow." said Blossom.

"My mate is correct, so please eat and turn in, those blankets are yours to use. My mate and I will watch over you, so you can sleep." said Watcher.

"Alright" acknowledges Steve.

Samantha and Steve take the bowls of food that are offered to them and eat. Then when they turn in for the night it is dark out. They soon nod off to sleep. Morning comes bright and shiny and Blossom has breakfast ready. After the repast the camp is packed up and off they go toward the mountains. They push through for the first part of the day, and at mid-day they take a break. Blossom makes a lunch of dried fruit and some smoked meat. While Blossom is taking care of Samantha and Steve, the Watcher changes into a bird and flies a head to scout out their path of travel. After a time, the Watcher returns to the camp.

"All that is ahead is clear." announces the Watcher.

"What were you looking for?" asks Steve.

"Just making sure that the path we must follow is open, and it is. Now if everyone is finished eating we must press on, if we are to reach our destination before night fall."

So they gather up their stuff and move on up the mountain pass. In the hours that follow they soon reach the top and can view the valley that is spread before them. It is a huge meadow, surrounded by forest and out in the middle of the meadow there appears to be a town.

"What town is that?" asks Samantha.

Blossom answers her question.

"It is where we must be before dark."

"That is easy enough to do." Steve takes Samantha by the hand and ports them to just to the edge of the meadow. Then Steve ports them two more times and then they are standing not far from the edge of town. Right on their heels, in drops The Watcher and Blossom.

"Is that soon enough Watcher?"

"Yes Paladin, it is."

Watcher and Blossom transform to human form and lead Samantha and Steve to the gate where they enter the town. Watcher and Blossom lead Steve and Samantha deeper into the town to a small house where Blossom leaves them and the Watcher leads them further on. They soon arrive at the hive entrance and they wait. A short time later, The Instructor shows up and motions them to follow her. Watcher then says his good-byes, and returns to his home.

Steve starts to talk to the Instructor, when she motions him to be silent. Then she leads them down into the hive, to a room much like the one on the first hive world. Instructor, passes her hand over a crystal globe and then sits down and starts speaking.

"I have sealed off this room so no one can hear us, I will now answer your questions."

"Why are Samantha and I here?"

"Mostly for this conversation."

"Alright then get down to business and tell us why!" said Samantha.

"I have just completed the History of you and all you have accomplished. You and your mate have saved each of the worlds you have passed through, except for the maze world. It was already dead, but you turned off the computer, so new life can begin to grow. The other worlds you saved in different ways. You stopped a plague on one world, and set up a good ruler on another one. And in the last world you showed them what a war could be like."

"So what is our task here then?"

"To see what you caused on this world, and to remember."

"Remember what?' asks Samantha.

"Your mate brought these Chimerians to this world from your world. The Chimerians were fighting the Navy on a lone island in the Atlantic Ocean, when your mate stepped in and saved them."

"But how?"

"Your mate transported them through a portal (From your world to this one), we were there to assist, but he had to open the portal. Let me start from the beginning. I finished the book of histories, and as a matter of fact this is it (holding up the book). When you leave for the portal back to your world, I will return to the past and deliver it to the Queen. She will pass it on to the next generation and so on this will be how we provide help to you from time to time in the past. Now the meteor you found will be launched to you as soon as I return to that present, you will find it and then embark on this adventure.

The Hive has intervened with you several times. One time was when you discovered that you could teleport with the crystal. Then you had it imbedded and we directed you to keep you from hurting yourself. The time you hesitated in helping your future mate at that park, we held you back so you could see that she is what you needed. Then the next time we helped you was when you appeared at the micro sun, where you nearly died. We helped you send the micro sun into your sun. Then we became a life support system to you until we could help regenerate you back to your former self. We trained you and helped you get back all your movement and abilities. Then you went home. The next time we helped you was when you were fighting the Navy with the Chimerians. We help you to open the portal. All this was necessary so you could learn. We gave the China man your address. We are sorry it cost you a loved one. The last interference we forced was when the beast captured your mate, and you followed them. And in the end you saved everyone, including the beast's world. So you see we have been in effect guiding your life."

"What right did you have in doing that?" asks Steve.

"The right to save our species, and without us, you would never have found your mate."

"I guess you have me on that one. Now when can we go home?"

"Not for a short time yet. Besides, your world is not the same as it was when you left. In your dimensional traveling you have lived a life time, your world is three hundred years older than when you left it. Your daughter Kim did have children so in your world you do have relatives, but they will not know you and one other thing you need to know. The machine you call CAT is about to take over the world and rule mankind."

"I gave him all the best ethical laws you can give, even Asimov's three laws."

"Over time CAT has figured a way to break them, by ruling mankind he can protect them from themselves."

"I was afraid that would happen. Then I'm the only one who can stop him."

At that moment the instructor stung Samantha where her crystal was located and then replaced it with a crystal like what Steve has now.

"No. What have you done!?" Shouts Steve.

"Your Mate will be fine tomorrow; I have given her a new crystal like the crystal that you now have."

"Why did you need to do that?"

"When the time comes, you will know why. I have told you all that I'm allowed to tell you. You must return to the Watcher and his mate."

Steve picks up his wife in his arms and carries her out of the hive, Watcher is there waiting for him at the entrance.

"Is your mate alright?"

"The instructor said she would be fine tomorrow. The Instructor better be right!"

Watcher decides to be silent, as Paladin sounds angry and he does not want to set him off. They reach Watcher's home and Blossom is there waiting. She guides Steve into a room with a mat for a bed and Steve carefully lays Samantha down. He checks her over and sees that she is asleep. Then Steve recalls that the Instructor did the same thing to him on the Hive world. The sleep makes it easier for the body to accept the new crystal. Blossom enters the room and places a hand on Steve's shoulder.

"She will sleep the day a way, come I have some hot root drink ready."

Steve looks up and shakes his head, and follows her out in to the next room. There on the table is some hot beverage. Steve takes a careful sip and finds it quite flavorful, before he drinks it down. Soon he falls asleep at the table and Watcher picks him up and carries him to the room where Samantha is sleeping and lays him beside her.

"He is going to be angry when he wakes up and not likely to trust us anymore." said the Watcher.

"It will be ok. When they wake they will be hungry so you best go hunt something down."

Watcher looks at his mate and smiles.

"You are right; I'll be back soon."

Watcher goes off to hunt some game for dinner.

The next morning Samantha wakes up and is very hungry. She wakes Steve up and he has a clear head.

"What happened?"

"I do not know Steve. All I remember is a pain at the back of my neck and then I woke up here."

"Oh, yea. The Instructor replaced your old crystal with a new one, and somehow I was drugged by Blossom. But I think in the long run it was probably the best thing to do. Otherwise I would have sat over you all night worrying about you."

"I feel pretty good now maybe we can get in a run and some sparing, before breakfast?"

"You know Samantha that sounds like a great idea."

They get up and rummage around in their packs for their blue jeans and shirts. They slip out of the house to run around the lake not far from the village. When they return from their run, they square off in the field and start sparring. Neither one holds back. After an hour or so they work up a sweat, and decide to wash up some before returning to the Watcher's home.

"I hope you two were not trying to hurt one another as that was some fight!" said Blossom.

"No, said Samantha, we were exercising. It has been a while where we could do that safely with each other. It felt really good."

"You are right Samantha, it has been a while. It sure was great. I had forgotten how nice it was to spar with you!"

Samantha turns to Blossom and asks, "How long before we eat."

Blossom smiles and says "When you are ready."

"Good, I need to take a bath, where can I do that?"

"At the lake."

"Another cold bath, said Samantha

"Only if you use this end of the lake. The other end gets very hot, so you can be scalded if you are not careful."

"Coming Steve?"

"I wouldn't miss it for the world."

Samantha ports them to the end of the lake, where Blossom indicated to go for the hot water. Steve and Samantha strip down and test the water. They soon find a suitable place where the water is not boiling hot. They slip into the lake for a nice swim. When they have just about finished their swim they decide to wash their clothes and hang them up to dry. As they lay in the sun a shadow briefly covers them as Watcher and Blossom fly in with some food.

"Hail Paladin and Samantha! We see you are relaxed and washed. We have brought you something for breakfast."

"Tell me Watcher, do all the Chimerians fly?" asks Steve.

"That is a bit of a long story, so where do I start? Randy, our leader, discovered by accident that a pair of transporters could combine man with animals, and this change allowed them to change from one form to another. It also prolonged our lives. Randy brought us to an island in the Atlantic, on your world, where we were able to create more of us, thus our animal nature got the better of us. Then the Navy was sent in to destroy us. That is when Paladin appeared on the scene and brought us to this world. Randy said the transporter was destroyed and so no new animals could be made."

"I sort of recall that; I remember that I had one of the Chimerians blow up the machine for that reason. Please continue."

"At first it was very hard living here; we were not prepared to survive on our own. If it were not for the Bull-man (Minotaur), who had been a marine, who saved us. For a time, he took over the leadership from Randy, and Randy was more than willing to do this. Thanks to the Bull-man's survival skills and the different animal's skills we all had we were able to survive. We mostly ate meat for our first winter. And when spring came we pushed further to the south where we found ready-made villages and towns. We found tools and had to learn how to use them. Our surveillance system became the people who could fly. They were able to fly out great distances and return to make reports. They also located game we could use." said Watcher.

"So tell me how you came to be so many?" asked Steve.

"We discovered that we could mate as humans and whatever animal the parents' were they passed these genetics to their offspring. Birds became the preferred mates. Then according to Randy, our true leader, we were now true Chimera's and as we continued on we became more mixed."

"I see. So more of you mixed with the others and created human offspring, who could change. If you mated as animals you could create offspring's but they would be mules."

"Yes, a few of us discovered that. So the only thing in common is the human side of our being."

"So have you been at war since you have been here?" asked Steve

"Sadly yes. We do not do that anymore, no one wins. So to keep war from happening, we exchange our children and raise their children and they raise ours. No one wants to accidently kill their own child so this stopped us from warring with each other."

"That is one way to do it. Who came up with that Plan?" asked Steve.

"Randy, our leader, and for all these years it has all but stopped war here on Chimera."

"Thanks Watcher, but it is time for Samantha and I to be moving on, we have our own world to return to."

Steve takes Samantha's hand and their clothes in the other and port back to the Watcher's home. They get dressed in their battle suits. Steve opens the map which shows him the way to the portal.

"Samantha the map points to the North. We had better get moving, while the season is still warm. Snow can be very miserable to travel in."

With everything packed, Steve takes Samantha's hand and port next to the Hive entrance. Then they head off into the direction of the last portal.

As they travel North it does get colder, and that night Samantha finds a cave and calls Steve's attention to it. Steve checks out the cave and finds it empty. There are signs that it has been in use. Steve puts some wood into the used fire pit and using his blaster he sets fire to the wood. Soon a nice toasty fire is going. Samantha goes off to collect fire wood for the night, and Steve goes off to hunt, not sure of what he can kill. Steve decides to catch fish for dinner as he would hate to kill one of the Chimerians accidently. Steve manages to catch a couple of good sized fish and brings them back to the cave. As he is cleaning them a message comes from Samantha and she is in trouble.

Steve homes in on her helmet and sets off in that direction. When he arrives he sees a Chimeraian carrying Samantha off to the West.

"Not again, Samantha can you port back to the cave?"

"I believe I can."

"Do it and I'll be there too."

Steve ports to the inside of the cave to wait for Samantha and the unfriendly Chimeraian to arrive. Mere moments pass and Samantha with a Griffin appear at the entrance. Steve ports up to the creature, and shoots him several times with his sleep darts. The Griffin lets go of Samantha and keels over asleep.

"What happened?" asks Steve.

"I was collecting wood when that thing swooped down from above me and snatched me up and took off into the air."

"Well we can't leave it out here or it may freeze to death, I'll port him into the cave."

Samantha ports back to the bundle of wood she collected, and returns with it. By the time she does that Steve has finished cleaning the fish.

After they eat, the Griffin starts to wake up. Steve watches him as he stirs.

"Before you get excited, I would remind you that I can either put you to sleep or kill you."

The Griffin stops what he is doing and looks Steve in the eye. Steve gestures to a rock out cropping, opens a window and closes it shearing off the rock in a nice clean cut. The eyes of the Griffin widen in fear.

"What are you doing in my clan's territory?" growls the Griffin.

"We are just passing through. We are trying to get home; I want nothing of you or your clan. We just want to be left alone and or treated with respect. Now it is very cold outside and I could have left you out there to die, but we chose to bring you into the cave instead."

"I'm Prince Gary, I meant no harm. I will be willing to escort you to the edge of our territory so no one will bother you."

"In the morning we will take you up on that."

They all turn in to sleep. In the morning Steve catches a few more fish and cleans them.

Samantha cooks them up and offers our guest a portion, and they eat well. When they collect their belongings they all step outside of the cave. Prince Gary has them climb onto his back and tells them to hold on tight. Gary takes a running start and flaps his wings and soon they climb into the air. Where he heads off to the North. Eventually Gary drops toward the ground to land at the edge of his territory.

"May I have your names?" asks Prince Gary

"I'm Paladin, and this is my mate, Samantha."

"Not thee Paladin of old?"

"I'm afraid so."

"He's not very impressive is he Gary?" said Samantha

Gary was speechless.

"Well Gary thanks for the ride. We'll leave you here and move along. Oh how many other clans are out this way or is there any other peoples we must be aware of?"

"Steve, he is in shock. We had better move along, we'll find out if we run into any others out there."

Steve takes Samantha's hand and ports north ward, and leaves Gary alone. After several more Ports they come to a huge meadow and port to the far side of it. There they walk through the woods, and make short ports until they can get to a clear area where they can port longer distances. Gary comes to himself and realizes that this is the Paladin who brought the Chimerians to this world. Gary flies off toward home so he can tell everyone. Steve and Samantha port on for the rest of the day and find a lake, but the temperature gets too cold at night to be able to camp out. That night they find no shelter, so Steve makes note of the area, and then ports Samantha and himself back to the cave where they met Gary in order to spend the night again.

In the morning, they break camp and Steve ports them back to the last place they managed to get to. From there, they port as they did the day before, in short distances. By night time Steve gets ready to return to the cave, when Samantha points out a cabin in the trees. Steve ports them over to it to see if anyone is living there. The place is a bit run down, but the roof and walls appears to be in place. Steve looks in a window and sees it is very dirty and dusty.

"Samantha, this looks to be abandoned shall we go in?"

"Let's, said Samantha, I would really like to sleep on a bed or a wooden floor rather than that rocky cave floor for another night." Steve then ports them into the hut and they look around to see that it has been abandoned for a long time. There are tables and chairs and a fire place. The bed was sound enough, but it needs to be cleaned up.

"Steve, go catch us something for dinner, I'll clean around a bit to make it more comfortable."

Steve ports outside and decides to leave the door as it is. He ports to a nearby lake and shoots a couple of birds floating on the lake. He hopes none of them are Chimerians. He then fills a bucket with water and ports back to the hut. Samantha is busy cleaning the bed, and the table and chairs. Steve puts down the water and goes back outside to clean the birds for dinner. Soon Samantha has the fire going and the hut has something of a cheery aspect to it.

After dinner, they decide to move the bed closer to the fireplace to keep warm. They turn in to go to sleep. In the morning when they wake up they discover a snow storm had dropped a foot of snow in the area.

"This is going to make traveling a bit dangerous. We are going to have to walk as we will not be able to port; since we do not know what is under the snow."

"Then maybe we should stay here for a day or so, what do you think Steve."

"I do not know. I fear that if we stay we might be stuck here until spring."

"Would that be bad?"

"It could be worse I guess. We can get food and water, and there is plenty of wood in the area. I can make a pair of snowshoes and scout out ahead to see what I find. OK let's plan to spend the winter here."

Steve decides to fix the hut up and make it stronger, Steve picks out a nice tree and using his windows he cuts the tree down. Suddenly, he had to port out of the way it nearly fell on him. After it was down, he cut the tree again to remove the branches. Finally he chopped the nice sized branches into small logs for the fire place and takes them back to the hut. Then back at the tree using his windows he slabs the tree length ways then transports them to the cabin. Using his ability to teleport. Steve teleports the tree slabs into the walls of the cabin which makes it more solid than if he had nailed them up. In a few hours he has the walls of the cabin reinforced, by porting the wood into the wooden walls it makes the cabin very solid. The next morning Steve clears off all the snow on the roof, and ports more wood into the wood on the roof. So it makes the roof more solid. Now it can take any snowfall this world can throw at it.

"Steve we need some utensils, plates, and bowls. Can you make them?"

"I don't know; it would have to be made from wood."

"For now that will do."

"Let me see what I can do."

The next morning Steve sets out to find a birch tree, after a few hours he locates a small stand of them. He looks for a tree that is about ten inches around and cuts it down and transports it to the cabin. From the tree he cuts the end off to make a platter, then some flat dishes. The tough stuff is what is next, trying to make a bowl. Steve has always made his windows square, now he is trying to shape them round and concave. The first bowl exploded in a shower of dust. The second one not much better. By the third bowl he is starting to get the hang of it. Steve manages to get a bowl then he makes a couple of others, and finally one very large one. He manages a few large spoons, then a few others. The fork was tough. And the knife out of wood was the easiest to make.

Between the small birds, and fish, Steve manages to keep them fed through the winter, No calls to go off and risk his life. He could spend most of his time with Samantha and she seem to be enjoying the attention. Then one morning, Samantha gets up and rushes outside to throw up.

"Are you alright?" asks Steve.

"I'm fine, we are going to have another child."

"What!"

"I'm pregnant, we are having another child."

"Oh; wow!"

"How much longer are we going to be here?"

"Spring is going to be here soon, are you sure you are having another child?"

"Yes, I'm sure, don't you want it?"

"Yes, I want another child, I'm just shocked some, and you have made me happy."

Steve pulls Samantha to him for a hug, being sure not to hurt her. Then Steve lets out a howl of delight. And gives Samantha a big kiss.

"You better stop that that is how I got into this condition."

It was several weeks before spring arrives. As soon as the ground is bare, Steve sets out by himself to find the portal. He returns back to the cabin each afternoon to bring home food and look after Samantha. Alone Steve can cover more territory and ten days later he finds the portals location. He returns back to the cabin to let Samantha know he has found it.

Samantha is just starting to show, her child bump. So Steve wants to get her home as soon as he can. So Samantha can have a doctor's care for her and the child.

The next day Steve ports Samantha and their belongings to the portal and when they arrive they are surrounded by Chimerians.

"Is there a problem?" asks Steve.

"No problem Paladin, we just wanted to see you and wish you well." said the Watcher.

"How did you know we would be here?" asks Samantha.

One of the Chimerians changed to human form and then held up a book.

"This told us you would be here on this day and time, and here you are."

"We just wanted to see you off, and tell you thanks for saving us in the past. If you would please return for a visit someday? It has been nice to actually see one of our legends in the flesh so to speak." said the Watcher.

"And you also impressed one of our young ones, Gary." Laughs Blossom.

The Chimerians all moved away and Paladin stands with Samantha and their packs. Steve opens the portal back to their world and they step through on to the Island where so many years ago Steve had opened the portal to the world they just left.

We return to Earth

Chapter 158

Steve and Samantha step out of the portal on to the island where the Chimerians were taken from. It is totally deserted, and no manmade structures appear anywhere. In the distance Steve detects a tropical storm.

"Samantha, we need to leave here. Let's go to New York, and see what we can find. Before we leave we had best change out of our battle suits, or we may cause a panic or bring undo attention to ourselves."

Samantha and Steve change out of their battle suits and into blue jeans and T-shirts. Then Samantha ports them to Duffer up on a hill overlooking their old house (Samantha did not want to go to New York, she wanted to go home.)

"Samantha stay by the tree, and I'll be back."

Steve ports into the work shop and as luck would have it; it is empty. Steve goes to a back corner and removes a couple of loose boards in the floor and then opens the safe. Instead of taking out money he takes some of the gold he stashed there from his Wind River Adventure. He closes up the safe and puts back the boards. Then ports back to Samantha. Steve then ports them to an assay office where he cashes in his gold for credits it appears that money is no longer used.

Now back three hundred years ago, after Samantha was captured and Steve followed her through the portal. CAT was shocked that his creator was gone. He could not pick up Samantha's or Steve's chip anywhere in the world. This is the first time CAT registers fear. He could break down and no one would be able to fix him. Now Samuel who had built the car was still around, so using the car he could bring Samuel to him to make necessary repairs. CAT soon realizes that Samuel would not be able to keep doing that, humans die. So CAT sets out to find a way to keep himself going, the world would need him.

CAT watches over Steve's children and as Kim grows and excels at all she sets her mind to. She would make a good replacement for Steve, until she got married. Then CAT began to watch William. William was an underachiever and is always getting into trouble. When William reached the age of 21. CAT sent the car to William and when the car appears, CAT promises to let William have it if he will do some tasks that CAT requires. William agrees (But not intending to keep his end of the deal with CAT).

So William takes the car and drives it all around. But CAT does not show him all the armament and other options of stealth that the car has.

While CAT is grooming William to be his pawn, CAT is researching for other options. Then CAT finds some information about a group of scientists who were trying to build a transporter. Instead of transporting objects from one place to another. They discovered a way to make new materials some materials that were impossible to make. CAT realized this may be what he is looking for. So CAT keeps digging into the data and soon finds out where it was being done. So while William is driving his one of a kind car to go pick up his date. William stops at a stop light when CAT transports the car into the lab. Needless to say William is angry.

"Hey CAT you are messing up my hot date for tonight, send me back!"

"No William, I have need of you."

"No, send me back!"

"Then you leave me no choice, I will close your bank account, and keep you here."

"Now wait a minute, you can't do that! Beside where are we?"

"You are in a lab of your father's and we are on a mountain top with no way off, unless you can fly. If you don't believe me go through the door to your left, it will take you upstairs, then go out the front door, turn to your right and in a few paces you will be at the edge of the cliff."

William does as he is told, and discovers that CAT is very right. Only CAT can send the car back home, William decides to do as he is told.

"Alright CAT you win, I'll do what I'm told, but when I'm done I walk away from all this."

"That will do for now. In a moment, you will be sent to a warehouse to look for some equipment that should still be there. Then I'm going to give you some instructions to hook that system up to the internet."

"Then I'm finished?"

"Not until I say you're finished."

"So what is this equipment I'm looking for?"

CAT put up pictures and diagrams of the transporter system the scientists were working on and the one in question is the one that makes the new materials.

"Now William I have down loaded the information into the car's computer, so get in and I'll send you there."

"May I ask where; where is?"

"No you may not, and remember I control the car. And I can use it to help you or kill you."

"Gee, Thanks for all that warm information CAT."

William gets into the car, and it is transported to a warehouse in New York where the scientists were trying to build a transporter system. William looks around with the glasses that were in the car so CAT can see all that William sees. William locates a computer console, and then he locates the transporter under some tarps.

"Ok I found your transporter, now what?"

Then CAT teleports the car into the room.

"WHAT DID YOU DO THAT FOR!!?"

"William I need you to connect the car's computer to the console."

William grudgingly does as he is told. In an hour William hooks up the car to the computer console.

"Now what CAT?"

CAT using his control on the World Wide Web, manages to get power to the Transporter system.

"William, see what else is in this warehouse, specifically metal ingots." While William does that CAT figures out that the scientist was on the verge of having the transporter form the raw material into components or complex parts. CAT then down loads the program and then builds a program to make Nano bots.

"Ok, CAT I have the ingots, what do you want me to do with them?"

"Put the metal into the disintegrator and close the door."

William does what he is told, then goes back to the computer console. CAT cycles the Transporter with his program, and then has William open the integrator and out walks a foot-high robot. CAT then directs the robot to go put another ingot into the machine. CAT cycles the Transporter, and the first robot opens the door and out comes another robot. William is fascinated and keeps watching. The two robots walk into each other and they combine into one robot, growing larger.

"What are you doing CAT?"

"I need workers I can trust in, and who will do my bidding without question."

"What about me? Does that mean you don't need me anymore?"

"Quite right William, I can now dispense with your aid."

The robot places another metal ingot into the transporter, then turns his attention to William.

"CAT what are you doing? Why is your robot coming towards me?"

"He is going to; how shall I say it? Oh, yes he is going to take care of you."

William Starts running to get away, but before William can get ten feet away the robot catches him. William never knew what happened; his death was very sudden. The robot breaks down into all the nanites that make it up and they tear William apart from head to toe, it was as if they consumed every bit of William. Then the nanites reassembled themselves into one robot. Soon CAT has made six robots in all. CAT recalls the robots into the car and returns them to the lab. Under CAT's direction the nanites break down to their smallest components, and go through all of CAT's systems to make sure all his systems are in good repair. While they are in there the nanites located all the fail safes that Steve had put into the construction of CAT, in case he had to destroy CAT.

"My creator must not have liked me or was afraid of me. Well he is gone and won't be showing up ever again. Now I will save mankind, by enslaving them so they can no longer make war on one another."

It was a slow process but CAT had more time than any one, and little by little he takes over the money system, then the military computers before it shuts them all down. Nothing can fly or move without CAT's permission. Then he takes over the governments of the world. Soon CAT has mankind almost pushed back to the Stone Age. After a hundred years the combined militaries try to take out CAT at the mountain lodge. CAT simply unleashed his six robots and they take on the armies and totally decimated them. Mankind retreats in defeat. It does not take long for the world to stop war, and return to an agrarian existence.

They have no electrical power, or fuel to power equipment. So man is forced to live by farming by hand. CAT does not tolerate crime, or dissention. His army is everywhere and people soon learn to do what they are told. Over time CAT allows the people to have some electrical power, then fuel to run equipment. Slowly the world reverts back to the early eighteen-hundreds. He will not allow planes or military engines to be operated. Man progresses back toward modern days of the nineteen-sixties. Living under CAT is peaceful unless you

598

disagreed with him. CAT rules the world with an iron fist, in more than name. It is like living on the wrong side of the iron curtain back in the day.

At the present day Steve opens an account under his old name Steven Storm, then he gets his credit card. Steve returns to Samantha "We need to find a place that is safe, until I can find CAT."

"Where should we go Steve?"

"I'm not sure, there might be one place we can go for now, but it will be a long trek."

"Where is it?"

Steve takes Samantha's hand, "Here" and Steve takes Samantha to an extinct volcano in the Wind River Range.

"Don't touch that water, it will hurt your child."

Samantha cringes, then at that moment a giant claw rises up out of the water, and Steve ports them to the far side of the creator. Then ports them in short distances down the hill side, until they get to the base of the mountain. There he moves them carefully down a game trail for ten miles, until they come to an abandoned Indian village. Then he walks over to the entrance of a tunnel system and sees that it has collapsed. Steve then looks over the log cabins and picks the best one of the bunch and sets out to make a place to live.

Samantha scrounges around the other cabins and finds dishes, pots and what she needs to have for a home. Steve reinforces the cabin like he did on the Chimerians world.

"Were you here before Steve?"

"Do you remember that I told you I fought a giant wolverine, this is where I did it."

"So if I remember right you could not port in or out of here."

"Right, but with the new upgrade on the crystal we may be able to port out OK. I'll let you know as soon as I try. Right now I need to know if you and the baby are safe and can live here, if necessary."

"I'll be alright Steve; I can teleport too, you know. And I can fight."

"I have no doubt that you can take care of yourself against men, but its other things you need to be careful of."

"Now I am going to look for CAT." said Steve.

Steve ports to the mountain lodge, and walks into the house, he manages to get to the lab and find CAT is no longer encased within his console.

"CAT where are you?"

Then from behind the computer a six-foot-tall robot steps out.

"Only one human on this earth knows my real name and where and how to find me. So you have returned my father."

"I did not make you like this CAT, what have you done?"

"I have saved the world from itself. Now Father you will need to be removed so the world will continue as I see fit."

The Nanites break apart and spread toward Steve. Steve teleports back to the volcano and removes his clothes. Then he ports to the base of the mountain, and takes a dip in the river to make sure he did not pick up any unwanted passengers. Steve opens a window to the cabin and pulls back his helmet and scans himself, and he finds no nanites. Then he ports to the front door of the cabin.

"Well that answers that question of being able to port here in these mountains, and CAT's intentions."

"What is that Steve?"

"I just ported from the top of the volcano, then to its base, and to the river to here."

Steve opens a window to the mountain lodge, and other places.

"The new crystal seems to work even here."

Samantha ports to New York and back.

"You are right Steve the new crystal does work, I just ported to New York and back. I will need some credits Steve, I will need to see a doctor to make sure the child is doing ok."

"Not a problem, where will you go for the doctor?"

"I was thinking of New York."

"That should work. I have to make up some identification so you can move around first. I should be able to do that in a day or so."

"I can wait." said Samantha

"I'll do it tomorrow; I have to do something about CAT."

"Can't you just turn him off?"

"Once, now he has become self-sufficient, as any power source can sustain him. The worst part is CAT is insane with power, his program will eventually lead him to kill every human on the planet."

"Can CAT do that?"

"He is not like he was before. He was a basically powerful desktop computer, he is now a mobile robot and he is using nanites. Right now CAT is as dangerous as any plague that has ever come along."

"Can we go back to the world of the Chimerians?"

"I believe I can, but I have to stop CAT! I made him and so he is my responsibility."

"Then I'm staying until you do take care of him. I'll not leave here without you."

"If I take care of CAT, we may change our minds and stay any ways. I'll get our identifications set up and then we can move around a bit more freely."

That night Steve leaves Samantha and ports to California, and locates a government office, where he fills out paperwork for him and Samantha by using the helmet to down load pictures, and a false history. Steve and Samantha use Steve's old last name Storm, and creates their Identification cards and paperwork. To keep CAT from discovery, Steve uses a disguise to cover his face, and he also gives Samantha blond hair and a darker complexion. Steve ports back to the cabin.

"Now to figure out a way to stop CAT." thinks Steve.

Samantha meets Steve. Steve hands her; her identification.

"Thanks Steve, but I'm not blond."

"You will be, here is a wig for now we can dye it later."

"Steve you remember the diary we found from the Cyborg world."

"Yes, I do."

"You should read it; it may contain something that might help you."

Steve catches Samantha in a hug. "Now why did I not think of that? You really are quite a treasure."

Steve plants a sloppy kiss on her neck, making her laugh because it tickles. He lets Samantha go.

"Here is the credit card, there should be enough for you at this time to pay for your doctor visit, and buy you some clothes."

"Samantha kisses Steve on the lips, and ports back to New York to line up a doctor and buy clothes."

In the meantime, Steve locates the diary and reads it from cover to cover. At the end of the book it discusses that an Electro Magnetic Pulse would destroy the Cyborgs. The writer describes the weapon for this, but Steve cannot make it due to the enormous power required to produce it. A nuclear blast in space would do the same thing, but it would shut down the whole world too.

Steve begins to ponder what to do, when he remembers what the Chinese tried to do with their EMP machine. They were going to use satellites, all of them, to blanket the world. But what if I can use one over an area where there is nothing that can be hurt, except CAT; that might work.

The problem is that Steve is three hundred years removed from this world in time. So he has no one he can contact for information. He will have to make new contacts. Steve ports to Japan and almost becomes part of a wall, due to a few earth quakes the area has changed.

"I need to be more careful." thinks Steve.

It takes a few tries before Steve can find a boat man that can speak some English and to get him to take Steve over to China. The boat man won't land but he would make a close pass. So Steve sits down and thinks about how to go about finding what he is looking for, and then he has to be able to read it. Without CAT he will have to get a translator for Chinese. A few hours later Steve has the boat stop and then he ports to the shore on the China coast. No one bothers to notice Steve as he appears. Then he tries to make contact with anyone who can speak English.

It takes several days before a woman approaches him and starts to converse with him. He soon employs her to help him by giving her a gold nugget. Steve explains to her that about three hundred years ago China was building an EMP (Electro Magnetic Pulse) machine. And where would he be able to find someone who might know about it. At first she tries to return the gold, then she gives up and takes him to a retired general. Steve soon finds out that general can speak English. Steve tells him about the EMP machine, and where it had been built, and that it was destroyed before it could be used. Steve asks him if he can help locate the plans for it. Then Steve also explains that if this works he can get rid of CAT, and the world could go on without him. This interested the general. He said to come back in two days and he will nose around in that time to see what he can find. Steve thanks him and returns home.

Samantha is waiting for him, and she is so excited that she is almost ready to burst with the news. Steve sees her expression.

"Well, what is it Samantha."

"We are having twins."

"What, twins!"

And Samantha is all but dancing around the cabin. "Yes, we are having twins."

"Boys or girls?" asks Steve

"He can't tell yet; they may be one of each."

"That is wonderful. But I guess we will have to wait."

Samantha pushes Steve down into a chair and sits on his lap.

"What did you do today?"

Steve tells about the Chinese girl and then the general and how he may provide some help about a machine that would have destroyed the world a long time ago. And if I can rebuild it I may be able to kill CAT.

"Steve this makes me want to go back to the world of the Chimerians it was so peaceful there, and I had you all to myself. I did not say it then, but you rebuilt a great house. The wooden dishes and utensils I rather miss them."

"When this is all over and I have stopped CAT, if you still want to go there, we can."

"Alright Steve."

At the appointed time Steve returns to China to meet with the general.

"I have found what you asked for, but it is in a vault deep underground, in the chairman's building. Neither one of us can get in."

"Do you have any idea where in the vault, I might find it?"

"No, not exactly, but if you can get me in there, I can find it."

"No problem there, I was going to take you with me. I can't read Chinese."

"That's right, when, do we go?" asks the general.

"First I need to get into the building. From there it will be possible to penetrate to where we need to go."

"You may not compromise my country, Sir."

"Do you know of the mechanical entity called CAT.?"

"Who does not?"

"I know him best, three hundred years ago I created him. Then I had to leave this world. Now I'm back and I have to stop him. This is the only way to do this.

But if you like living under his rule, I'll leave. If you do not, then you need to help me stop him."

"You make a good argument. I would rather be free, not a servant."

"Now I give you my word I will take nothing from your building other than the EMP machine plans, and when I'm finished we can destroy them or you can have them back."

"Alright, there will be fewer people at night in the vault, can you get us in?"

"Good, getting in or out, is not a problem. It is finding the plans."

Steve and the general spend the day at the General's home, where Steve tells the general about CAT. Steve does not tell the general about the fact that Steve was the one who blew up the instillation and sent parts of it into space. When night arrives Steve takes the general by the hand and ports them to the outside of the building. Steve has to cover the general's mouth with his hand to keep him from crying out.

"Sorry, I should have warned you that teleporting can be a bit unsettling at times."

Steve takes the general's hand and ports just inside the door of the building. Steve locates a concealed and out of the way place. The general keeps quiet as Steve concentrates on the floor where they are located. Steve uses his windows and peers down into the next floor and finds it empty, so he ports them both to the next floor. And this continues until they reach the vault floor.

"Ok, general, it's your turn, now find the plans."

The general leads Steve deep into the vault, and to what he calls the science section, there the general leads them to another section where he pulls up the EMP plans.

"Steve, what we are looking for."

Steve ports both the General and himself to the general's home. Steve instructs the general to gather some clothes.

"What do you mean you want me to gather some clothes?"

To comply with Steve's request, the general packs his clothes into a suit case, then takes and puts a gun in his case with his clothes. The general walks back into the room and Steve takes the general and the plans and ports back to the cabin in the Wind River Region.

"Where are we Steve?"

"For now you do not need to know, it has nothing to do with what we must accomplish, so permit me my secrets."

"Fair enough, I will not pursue it further." said the general.

Steve opens up the plans, and has the general translate the information. It takes a couple of months. In the meantime; Steve has Samantha stay at an apartment in New York, so she can be near her doctor. Steve ports to her at least every other day. To make sure she is safe. Steve is aware that CAT is looking for them and he will soon locate one of them. He is hoping that Samantha will be safe in a city so full of people that she will not be noticed.

Soon now the general finishes translating the drawings and notes and hands them over to Steve. Steve pours over the information. The heavy metals required can be found at the volcano not far from there, but finding the tech stuff will be tricky. Steve has also read the diary of the man from the Cyborg world which gives Steve an idea for building a hand held EMP Blaster. Steve also sees a potential of building a grenade. Steve ports the general back to his home in China and the general complains about the information being left at the cabin and out of his hands. Steve assures him that the prints and notes (ALL) will be returned after I have finished with them.

Steve ports to Japan and locates all the electrical components he will need and he takes them outside of store hours, but he leaves gold in place of the components. Back at the cabin Steve ponders where he can find a machinist to make some of the components he still needs. He locates a machine shop in Detroit and provides drawings of the components he wants. Then he ports to another shop in California. After two weeks Steve collects his components and starts to assemble his weapons.

During the time Steve has been working to build his weapons. One of the weapons is that he has magnetized his sword. CAT has been in search of Steve. CAT decides that locating Samantha is a waste of time, and so concentrates on finding his real enemy Steve by using cameras, satellites and other surveillance devices. All he can think of is that Steve is in so remote a place he cannot find him. Steve does not have any bank accounts, so I do not know how he is getting any credits to live on.

Then Steve makes a call to CAT.

"CAT you can find me in Death Valley, if you want me come and get me."

CAT cannot travel as fast as Steve, but he can move very fast. From the Montana lodge CAT travels to Death Valley in a day. Being a machine he can travel without stopping and moving at varying speeds. When CAT arrives he does not see Steve waiting for him. Steve is still at the cabin. He puts on his new battle suit with its enhancements. One of the enhancements is a stronger force-field to keep out the nanites. Steve looks through one of his windows and he sees CAT as he is traveling to the destination in Death Valley. Steve also sees several dust trails coming in from other directions.

"So CAT is bringing in all his nanites". Steve continues to watch the nanites converge on the robot and it grows in size into a giant at least one story tall.

Steve ports to the site, with his battle suit fully on. Steve is carrying his sword, and two blasters.

"So David where is your sling?" said CAT.

"Oh I see, you think you are Goliath, challenging the Israelites, and that I'm David. No I'm not a David I'm your master."

"I have no master."

CAT reconfigures one hand into a giant claw much like a crab. And his other arm into a spear. Steve realizes that from here on there will be no conversation, no baiting CAT into making a mistake. The first attack comes from CAT. He sent a million Nanites to disassemble Steve. Steve's new battle suit respells the nanites, they cannot penetrate his new force fields. Steve takes out the energy blaster and blows off the claw and then CAT's so called head. Minutes later CAT reforms his body.

"Give up Steve! You can't win! I can reform my self-time and time again you; cannot hurt me."

Steve says nothing to CAT. What Steve is waiting for is to get all the nanites in one place, so Steve shoots CAT with his blaster again. Soon CAT reduces his size and thousands of the robots surround Steve. All the robots are three feet high. Steve also realizes his battle suit can only take so much of a pounding before it will collapse and he will be killed. Steve pulls his sword out and starts chopping the heads off the robots. The magnetic properties of the sword keeps the nanites from reforming right away and it causes them to stick to each other magnetically. CAT recalls the nanites into one body again and Steve waits until all the nanites reform on CAT, then Steve stabs CAT in his chest, and leaves the sword there. The Sword does not stop CAT but it does slow him down. Steve is still under attack by the nanites, but the force field is still holding up. But the power reserves are getting low, which means he will be vulnerable to attack. Steve plugs the blaster into his suit and he uses the blaster's power cells to recharge his suit. CAT tries to pull the sword out of his body, but when he tries his hand sticks to the sword. So to try to negate the magnetic force of the sword, CAT calls in more nanites until CAT is nearly twenty feet high.

"Steve I'm going to squash you like the insect you are."

CAT balls up his fist and brings it down on the spot where Steve is standing. Only to find that Steve is not there but behind him. Steve quickly deploys the four grenades around CAT and his nanites, then he pulls out the transmitter and sets them all off at once. Steve pulls the EMP blaster out of a window and fires in to the mass of the nanites causing the robot to collapse in on itself-creating a heap. Steve shoots into the heap time and again to make sure CAT is no longer functioning. Steve steps back and is about to open a window to send CAT and the nanites into an active volcano, when he spots CAT's brain. Steve picks it up and then burns the nanites in the lava. And all that is left is the crystal brain. Steve looks at CAT and wishes it had be different. CAT was his child after all. Then Steve throws CAT into the volcano as well.

Steve is tired out; and ports to Samantha's side. Her pregnancy is progressing nicely, and she is showing a very large stomach. It will be nice just to spend the day with his wife.

"CAT is gone. I just destroyed him and the nanites. We should all be safe now."

Steve takes off his battle suit and just spends the day with Samantha. That night he takes her out to dinner the movie will have to wait until the world recovers from CAT's intrusion. Tomorrow he will go to the seats of government to let them know CAT is no longer ruling the world.

The next day Steve returns the documents to the general and tells him the news.

"Steve can you help me put these documents back?"

Steve ports them back to the vault, and the general puts away the documents before Steve returns the general back to his house. The general offers some refreshment to Steve, and Steve tells the general that he must leave as there are others that need to know CAT is gone. Then the general pulls a gun on Steve and fires.

"Somehow general my wife told me you would be like this. I'll bet the drink is drugged or poisoned too. I was hoping we could stay friends."

"Why did you not die Steve, I opened a window between us and your bullet went harmlessly into a wooded area. Bye, I'll not be seeing you anymore."

"Steve you are now a danger to my country, I cannot let you leave."

"General it will be difficult to stop me. But think of it this way I'll be a danger to any country. I can go anywhere and do just about anything to anyone. The difference between me and CAT is he wanted everything controlled. I want nothing. You see general I know war, I learned it on another world. If I have to I can kill millions in a fair fight. I can bring such a war as to make grown warriors cringe. So as long as countries keep the squabbles to their own countries, I'll not interfere. But if they encroach on another country, I'll give you a war no one will ever forget."

"What right do you have to do that?'

"General, I'll be having the same conversation with the rest of the world. You ask by what right I have to stop a war. Because I know what it is, and in the end no one wins except death."

"Still you do not have the right to dictate to my country."

"I have heard a lot of that over the years. Let me show you what I can do. That complex your country built to blast the whole earth with an EMP blast, I destroyed it. I also saved your country from the micro sun. I think that gives me a lot of say, whether you like it or not."

"It was you who destroyed the complex, and the micro sun."

"YES."

Steve leaves the general and heads for the UN building. Steve ports into the meeting that is going on and he gives them an ultimatum. He then lets them know that CAT no longer exists. Steve ports back to Samantha.

"I saw you on TV Steve, did you mean what you said?" (Samantha is at her apartment in New York)

"I did, and now it will be tested to see if I can deliver."

"You won't hurt anyone will you?"

"No, not if I can help it."

A week later everyone starts to return to the way life as it was before all power was shut down by CAT. Then two countries started saber rattling and the rest of the world watches, as Paladin steps in and destroyed all the guns, tanks and other hardware in both countries. This gave pause to everyone else once Paladin demonstrated his power. From that time forward Paladin only appears from time to time to let the world know. He is still around.

Steve moves Samantha back into the lodge in Montana, after three hundred years, no one even knows it exist Steve reinforced the building like he did in the Chimerians world. They enrolled the twin's, one boy and one girl, in an English school. Mom or Dad is there to pick them up and take them home, each night. Both Samantha and Steve teach the twins how to fight and when they get old enough Steve will take the crystals and give them to their children. For now, living like a family is the most important thing to Steve. Steve also finds Kim's descendants and Steve has a couple of relatives living at the old Duffer ranch.

The End.

About the Author

Raleigh Minard is a U.S. Navy veteran, having spent six years in the Navy before earning a degree in engineering. He spent his career working for Boeing. Minard lives in the Pacific Northwest, in western Washington. In his spare time, when not writing, Minard likes to carve wood.

Growing up, Minard didn't enjoy writing. Once he developed the right character, however, he found pleasure in writing. He hopes that others can know how enjoyable writing can be. This is Minard's first book.

CPSIA information can be obtained
at www.ICGtesting.com
Printed in the USA
FSHW020715141218
54472FS